Carrie Elks

By Virtue

Fall

Leabharlanna Poiblí Chathair Baile Átha Cliath

Dublin City Public Libraries

piatkus

PIATKUS

First published in Great Britain in 2018 by Piatkus

1 3 5 7 9 10 8 6 4 2

A CIP catalogue record for this book
is available from the British Library.

ISBN 978-0-349-41553-6

Typeset in Caslon by M Rules
Printed and bound in Great Britain by
Clays Ltd, Elcograf S.p.A.

Papers used by Piatkus are from well-managed forests
and other responsible sources.

Piatkus
An imprint of
Little, Brown Book Group
Carmelite House
50 Victoria Embankment
London EC4Y 0DZ

An Hachette UK Company
www.hachette.co.uk

www.littlebrown.co.uk

To Diane. Because you are strong.

1

What's in a name? That which we call a rose
By any other name would smell as sweet

– Romeo and Juliet

'But I've always dreamed of yellow roses,' the bride said, leaning forward. 'Yellow roses mixed with white lilies, hand tied with string.'

'Yellow is very vulgar, Melanie,' Mrs Carlton, the older woman replied, waving her hand as if to dismiss her future daughter-in-law. 'At the Smithson wedding they had peach flowers. They were very elegant and tasteful.' She gave a nod at the end, as if that was her final word.

Juliet chewed the top of her pen lid, watching the two women debating their wedding flower preferences. Since she'd started her florist business a year before, it had become a familiar scene. Sometimes she felt more like a therapist than anything else.

Pulling the blue pen lid from her mouth, Juliet scribbled on the pad in front of her. 'You know, yellow and peach roses can look fantastic together,' she suggested, quickly sketching out a picture of a bouquet. 'We did something similar at the Hatherly wedding in the summer, and it looked divine.' She leaned in towards Mrs Carlton, as if they were bosom buddies. 'And you know how discerning Eleanor Hatherly is.'

She was name-dropping but she didn't care. Though she was an outsider, she'd lived in Maryland long enough to know that in these circles snobbery was still a thing. Hell, she'd been married to one of the biggest snobs in Shaw Haven, after all.

Was still married to him, she corrected herself. For now, at least. Thanks to Maryland divorce laws, she and Thomas had to live separately for a year before their divorce could be finalised. Six months in, and she was already counting the days.

Melanie looked up at Juliet, a flash of hope in her eyes. 'I'd love a peach and yellow bouquet.'

Patting her on the hand, Mrs Carlton smiled. 'I knew we'd be able to agree on this. It's the small details that are so important. You'll learn that when you're a Carlton, too.'

Grabbing her tablet, Juliet scrolled through her catalogue to show them the different arrangements, helping them narrow down the choices until they found the perfect one.

Welcome to married life. A world where you'll run yourself ragged pleasing your husband, your in-laws and even your friends, while putting all your hopes and dreams on the backburner.

Juliet found her thoughts drifting back to her own wedding. She'd met Thomas when she was studying Fine Arts at Oxford Brookes University, and he'd been a Rhodes Scholar, an American studying at the more prestigious Oxford University. It had been a meeting of pure chance – she'd been working in a local florist at the weekends to try and eke out her student loan, in charge of deliveries in the local area. As she was walking up the path to Christ Church College, dodging the students and tourists who were admiring the fountain in the middle of the green, she'd been practically run over by the suave American post-grad who was running late for dinner.

He'd swept her off her feet both literally and figuratively that day. She'd been as besotted with his intelligence and sophistication as he'd been with her beauty and artistic flair. Their relationship had felt something like a holiday romance – from the moment they met they'd spent every day together – eating picnics in the park, or wandering aimlessly through the arboretum. He'd wanted to know everything about her, from her childhood dreams to her plans for the future.

And then she'd fallen pregnant.

That's not when the cracks started to show, though. They were still desperately in love, and the differences in their backgrounds and experience meant nothing compared to the all-encompassing passion they felt for each other. So when – being the perfect gentleman he was – Thomas had asked her to marry him, she'd said yes without hesitation. After all, they were made for each other, weren't they?

They were married in London. His family didn't attend – she wasn't even sure if he'd invited them. Instead she was supported by her three sisters. Lucy – her eldest sister – had always been the organiser. Within a few days of Thomas's proposal she'd secured the town hall location for the ceremony, and arranged for a venue for their wedding party. Even Kitty and Cesca – still young at seventeen and eighteen – had helped, decorating the tables and making the invitations. Heck, they even agreed to wear the bridesmaid dresses that Juliet had made.

It *had* been a fairy-tale wedding, in spite of their haste. Twenty-year-old Juliet had never felt more beautiful as she walked up the small aisle on her father's arm, her baby bump barely visible beneath the layers of white lace she wore. And when Thomas had turned to look at her, his eyes warm with what looked like love, she'd felt as though it was the beginning of a wonderful life together.

Better not to think about that. Not now.

'Where did you two meet?' Juliet asked the bride-to-be.

'At Harvard,' Melanie replied.

She was about to say more when the older woman spoke over her. 'David was at law school there. Imagine our surprise when he came back with more than a qualification.'

Melanie blushed but said nothing.

Juliet swallowed hard, trying not to remember her own mother-in-law's reaction when Thomas introduced his new wife. They'd been married for two weeks by that point, moving back to his home town here in Maryland, where he planned to work in the family business. He'd assured her his family would feel the same way he did about her.

But from the start she'd felt like a disappointment. The differences he'd loved about her back in Oxford somehow morphed into embarrassments that made him shake his head. She didn't dress in the right way, she was too artistic, she hadn't even finished her first degree for goodness sake.

But that was all water under the bridge, wasn't it? Or it would be, once the divorce was finalised. At least then she'd be able to move forward with her life, even if she would always be tied to Thomas by their six-year-old daughter, Poppy.

'We'll definitely go with that one,' Mrs Carlton said, pointing at the photograph on Juliet's iPad. 'Now let's choose the table décor.'

Juliet looked at Melanie, who nodded again. 'You'll look beautiful,' Juliet told her, and the woman's smile widened.

Part of her wanted to warn Melanie that it wouldn't get any better. Once the wedding was over, that's when the real power play would begin.

Stop it.

Maybe the groom wasn't as much of an ass as Thomas turned out to be. Or maybe Juliet was too jaded. She'd stayed for seven years, after all, it wasn't all doom, was it? Anyway, she needed to be positive. Weddings were the most reliable form of income for *Shakespeare Flowers*. She was still trying to build up the business and her reputation. Her projections showed she should start making a profit some time the following year, but right now, cash flow was king.

Her phone buzzed in her pocket, vibrating against her hip. She pulled it out, taking care not to be caught, knowing how bad it would look to this woman who put appearances over everything else. Her heart dropped when she checked the display.

Surrey Academy.

The most prestigious educational establishment in Shaw Haven, the five-thousand-dollar a term school ranged from Pre-Kindergarten to High School seniors. Poppy had been attending for a year now, and seemed happy there in spite of the turmoil at home.

'I'm so sorry, it's my daughter's school. I need to take this.' She flashed an apologetic smile at the women in front of her. 'I'll be right back.'

Swallowing hard, she walked out into the hallway of the expensive, colonial house. Sliding the screen to accept the call, she braced herself for a telling off. Not that it had been her fault Poppy was late to school that morning. It was her neighbours – the new ones moving into the house next to hers.

Their removal truck had blocked her driveway, and by the time the driver had moved it Poppy had been twenty minutes late for school.

'Mrs Marshall? This is Marion Davies.' The clipped tones of the principal reminded Juliet of her mother-in-law. 'I've been trying to get hold of you for the past half-hour. We really need our parents to be responsive when we try to contact them.'

'I'm so sorry, I was in a meeting. I didn't hear the phone.' She felt like a naughty school child. 'Is everything okay? Nothing's happened to Poppy has it?'

'Nothing at all. Unfortunately she's been involved in an . . . incident. I need you to come into the school now so we can discuss it face to face.'

Juliet's mouth turned dry. 'Now? Is it serious? Are you sure she's not hurt?'

'No, she isn't hurt. She is, however, in a lot of trouble. It's not something I wish to discuss over the telephone. If you come to my office I'll tell you all about it.'

Juliet glanced at her watch, grimacing. 'Could I come in at the end of school instead?' She had ten deliveries to make before then. Fitting them in before class finished at three was already going to be a close-run thing.

Lowering her voice, Principal Davies played her trump card. 'Of course, I'd be happy to call Mr Marshall if you prefer.'

'Oh no, that won't be necessary. I'll get there as soon as I can.' She really didn't want Thomas getting involved in this. The more distance she could keep between them the better.

'Very well. I'll see you imminently.' With that, Principal Davies rang off, leaving Juliet still holding the phone to her ear.

Ugh, she was going to have to call Lily and ask her to stay late at the shop, and beg her to do the deliveries. And she hated doing that, even though Lily never complained. Like Juliet, she just gritted her teeth and got on with things.

And right now it looked like both their days were about to get a heck of a lot worse.

'Mrs Marshall? Please go in.' The school administrator pointed towards the principal's office. Juliet stood, her legs feeling suddenly shaky. She smoothed the denim down her thighs, tucking her shirt in to try and regain a semblance of smartness. Being called 'Mrs Marshall' sounded alien to her now. Strange how quickly she'd shrugged off that name, in her head at least. Nowadays she thought of herself as Juliet Shakespeare again, the girl who grew up in London. In the years since her shotgun marriage, she'd somehow lost the very joie de vivre Thomas had fallen in love with. A victim of trying to squeeze her square peg self into a perfectly round hole.

As soon as she walked into the principal's office, all heads turned to look at her. She sought Poppy out first, seeing her six-year-old girl sitting in the corner, her eyes wide as she stared imploringly at Juliet.

She flashed her daughter a reassuring smile. Poppy was lively and headstrong, but she was a good kid who'd been through so much.

'Please sit down,' Principal Davies said, pointing to the only vacant chair.

Juliet sat next to Poppy. That's when she noticed the other child – a small blond-haired boy, looking tiny as he sat on the adult-sized chair, his hands clutched around a blue toy train.

There was a fresh bruise on his cheek.

As if he'd been slapped.

Oh no.

7

'Mrs Marshall, this is Mr Sutherland. His son, Charlie, started here with us at Surrey Academy today.'

'Mrs Marshall?' a deep, husky voice asked. 'One of the Shaw Haven Marshalls?'

Juliet's heart immediately started to pound. She slowly turned her head to look at the man. Everything about him was breathtaking. From his height – visible in spite of his seated position – to his broad shoulders and chest. But it was his face that made her words stick to her tongue – the sculpted bones of his cheeks and chiselled square jaw making him one of the most beautiful men she'd ever seen.

'Um ... yes. My husband is Thomas Marshall.'

The man raised his eyebrows, but said nothing.

'Mrs Marshall, let me explain what happened between Poppy and Charlie,' the principal interjected. 'During recess, they were playing with the train set.' The hushed tones of the principal's voice forced Juliet to lean forward. 'They had an argument about the blue train, and Poppy slapped Charlie. I'm afraid the force made him fall against the wall and caused a nosebleed.'

Juliet opened her mouth to say something, then closed it again, failing to find the right words. Blood rushed through her ears, drowning all other sound out. Principal Davies and Mr Sutherland were staring at her as if she was the worst parent in the world.

Maybe they were right.

'Poppy,' she finally said, the anxiety making her words wobble. 'You shouldn't hit anybody, you know it's wrong.'

'You hit Daddy's friend when you found them at the house together,' Poppy said. 'You said that people shouldn't take things that belong to other people.'

Juliet covered her mouth with her hand. How the hell did

8

Poppy know that? For a moment she was back there, finding Thomas and his PA in the most compromising of positions. The image made her want to throw up. Her face flamed as she glanced at Principal Davies to see her reaction. The older woman's face was as impassive as always.

Mr Sutherland, on the other hand, was trying to bite down a smile. He was looking at her with new interest.

'It's still wrong to hit people, sweetheart,' Juliet said again. Her mouth felt drier than the desert. How could she even explain to her six-year-old child the rage she'd felt when she realised she'd been betrayed? That it was the first time she'd ever thrown a punch in her life. 'I shouldn't have done it and neither should you.'

'It was *my* train.' Poppy's voice was full of that familiar stubbornness. 'I told him it was mine and he still tried to take it. It's always been mine. He can't just come here and steal it from me.'

Juliet glanced at the man from the corner of her eye again. For some reason she found it hard not to keep looking at him. His cheeks were high, his jaw firm, but it was the dark shadow of beard growth on his face that surprised her. He had a rough edge to him she rarely saw around here.

Oops. He was staring straight back at her.

'It's not your train,' Juliet pointed out. 'It belongs to the school, and everybody's allowed to play with it. You need to apologise to Charlie.'

'No way.'

The small boy looked up at her, his eyes wider than ever. Juliet realised he hadn't spoken at all. His sandy hair was falling over his brow, and his clothes were a little too tight for his body.

'It's Charlie's first day. You should have been welcoming, shown him around. You can't just treat people like that. Now say sorry.' This time she was sharper. Even Poppy looked surprised at her tone.

'I'm sorry.'

'Now say it and mean it.'

Poppy's bottom lip stuck out, and she started to chew it. For a moment she stared at Charlie, her eyes narrowed as if she was weighing up her options. 'Okay, I'm really sorry. It's a stupid train anyway. Half the wheels are missing. Next time you should play with the green one, it goes the fastest.'

Charlie nodded silently, as if she was the fount of all school-based knowledge.

'Well, that's a start I suppose,' Principal Davies said. 'But I'm sure you'll agree that we can't just let this go. Poppy hit another child, we need to punish her for it. We have standards we expect all our students to live up to.'

'Hey, there's no need to punish the kid,' Mr Sutherland said. He really did have a sugar-coated voice. 'She said sorry, right? Can't we just leave it there?' He flashed a dimpled smile at the principal.

'No, I'm afraid we can't just leave it there.' Principal Davies shook her head, turning to Juliet. 'We have a zero tolerance policy for violence here at Surrey Academy. I'll have to ask you to take Poppy home with you today, and to keep her off school for the rest of the week.'

'You're excluding her?' Juliet asked, alarmed. How the hell was she going to explain this to Thomas?

'Hey, come on,' Mr Sutherland said. 'Charlie's fine, Poppy's sorry. No need to make a big deal out of this. Everybody makes mistakes, right?'

'I don't know . . . ' Principal Davies looked first at him, then at Juliet. 'Poppy's always been a lively girl, I don't want her to think we condone this kind of violence.'

Juliet licked her dry lips. 'She won't do it again, I can promise you that.'

Principal Davies formed her fingers into a steeple, resting her chin on the intertwined tips. She turned her eyes to Poppy, who was still sitting silently. 'Poppy, do you understand what you did was wrong?'

Poppy nodded fervently.

'And are you very sorry for what you've done?'

Another barrage of nods.

'Hmm,' Principal Davies said. 'All right then, I won't exclude you this time. But if you ever hurt another child again, I'll be down on you like a ton of bricks. Do you understand?'

This time, Poppy's voice sounded as small as she was. 'Yes, Principal Davies.'

'Very well then, go back to class.'

If Poppy was half as frightened as Juliet was, then she understood all right. But Juliet's anxiety was tempered by the relief of not having to tell Thomas what had happened.

It was a small consolation, but she'd take it.

'Can we stop at the ice cream parlour on our way home?' Poppy asked, swinging her legs so her tiny feet hit her car seat.

Juliet glanced in the rear-view mirror, noticing the car behind her – a huge battered truck. 'Not after you hit that poor boy. You'll be going straight to your room when we get home.'

'That's no fair.' Poppy grimaced. 'We always go to get ice cream after the first day. It's a trad . . . trad . . . a thingy. You promised.'

'It's not a tradition, because we've only done it once before.' Juliet was trying to keep her patience.

'But you promised.' Poppy's voice took on a tremble. Her bottom lip was wobbling.

'That was before you hit Charlie,' Juliet pointed out. She had to bite down on her own lip to try to stem the emotions. If there was one thing she hated, it was seeing Poppy cry, and the poor kid had cried enough for them both over the past six months.

'I said I was sorry. I played with him in recess this afternoon. I even gave him the green train as well as the blue one. He said we're friends.'

'I'm glad you made it up with him. That's good.'

'So can we get ice cream?' Poppy leaned forward until the seat belt stopped her. 'Please Mommy?'

There was a line of cars ahead, all waiting at the four-way-stop. Juliet put her foot on the brake, slowly coasting to a standstill. Staring out of the window at the cars ahead, she wondered how things had gotten this hard. Parenting was tricky enough when there were two of you, though at least then you had somebody to shoot ideas off and to commiserate with.

When there was just one of you it seemed almost impossible. It was one of the few times she missed Thomas.

'Please Mommy?' Poppy said again. The cars in front began to move slowly, and Juliet glanced in the mirror. The black truck was right behind her now, and when her eyes flicked up, she could make out the driver behind her, sitting beside his son with a mop of blond hair.

One look was enough to send her pulse soaring. Why the hell did that man have such an effect on her?

It had to be another stage of separation. Maybe even a sign

she was getting over Thomas. It could have been anybody, Mr Sutherland just happened to be there at the right – or wrong – time. Blame it on the hormones. She'd barely looked at a man since she'd split from Thomas six months earlier, and they'd not been intimate for a good few months before that. It was her body's reaction to enforced celibacy, nothing more, nothing less.

Damn it, maybe something cold would do them both good.

'Okay, we'll go for ice cream,' Juliet conceded. 'But if you hit anybody again, you'll be banned from that place for a year.'

Poppy nodded, a serious expression on her face. 'And so will you, Mommy, if you hit anybody again.'

Touché. Juliet tried – and failed – to bite down her smile.

2

Two households, both alike in dignity

– Romeo and Juliet

'Hey bud, d'you want an ice cream?' Ryan eased the truck forward, crossing the four-way intersection. 'There's a really cool place over there, we used to go there when I was a kid.'

Charlie looked suddenly interested, the way he always did whenever Ryan mentioned his childhood. 'What was your favourite ice cream?' he asked.

'Pecan and maple syrup,' Ryan said smiling. 'It was sickly as hell but tasted so good. I wonder if they still serve it?'

'That's what I want to order.' Charlie looked resolute. 'I love pecans.'

The fact was, Charlie loved nearly every food he tried. He'd grown up learning about different tastes and cuisines, joining Ryan regularly on his travels from the time he was a baby.

'Pecan and maple it is, then.'

Ryan still couldn't get over how strange it was to be back in Shaw Haven after all these years. There were a few changes – a micro brewery on main street, a new art gallery on the waterfront – but at its heart it remained a sleepy harbour town. Full of painted houses and salty air, Shaw Haven had been here for centuries, ever since the first Shaw had stepped off his boat and laid claim to this land on the edge of Chesapeake Bay.

Being here felt like stepping back in time.

Ryan pulled the truck into the parking lot beside the parlour. There were only a couple of spaces left. Everybody must have had the same idea.

When they were inside, Ryan looked around at the plastic checked tablecloths and the mismatched chairs. They looked old, familiar. He was shocked by the way it made him feel like a kid again. It was almost fourteen years since he'd last set foot in Shaw Haven – and he thought he'd left the town and the way he'd felt about it behind for good.

And he had. At least until now.

'Can I help you?'

Ryan blinked, focusing on the woman in front of him. She was smiling broadly at him, holding an ice cream scoop in her hand.

'Do you have pecan and maple syrup?' he asked.

'Sure, you want a cone or a bowl?'

He turned to Charlie, who was staring at the huge glass freezer full of plastic tubs, the colourful ice cream flavours looking enticing. 'What do you say, bud?'

'Can I have a bowl?' Charlie asked quietly. He'd never been a brash kid, in spite of his father's outgoing nature. His face usually held a serious expression, as if his brain was full of thoughts he couldn't quite work out how to express. Before he'd started at Surrey Academy they'd insisted on testing him – and it hadn't come as a huge surprise that he was already scoring well into third grade school levels, even though he'd never been in formal education before.

'Make that three scoops,' Ryan said, giving the woman

an easy smile. 'And two spoons, the kid might need a little bit of help.'

The woman laughed as if Ryan had told her the funniest joke ever, fluttering her eyelashes rapidly at him. His cheeks flushed.

The after-school rush meant the only free seats were in the far corner, and they headed over there, Charlie gripping tightly to the round colourful tub of ice cream, while Ryan carried their spoons. They'd almost made it to the empty table when a woman and her child got there first, pulling two of the four chairs out.

He recognised her right away. Only had to glance at the cloud of red hair to know it was Poppy Marshall's mom.

Ryan looked around, hoping to spot somebody who'd almost finished, planning on hovering until the table was vacated. But everybody seemed to have arrived at the same time – it was natural really, since they'd all come from school – but unless they sat down soon Charlie's ice cream was going to melt.

Ah, what the hell.

'Can we sit with you?' he asked, looking at the two empty chairs next to Poppy and her mom.

She turned around to look at him. Christ, she was pretty. Not that he was surprised, Thomas Marshall always did like the best in life. Why would his wife be any different?

'Um, yeah, sure, please sit down.' She gestured at the two seats. Charlie immediately chose the one next to Poppy, leaving Ryan to sit next to her mom.

'Thanks. I'm Ryan, by the way. Ryan Sutherland. I don't think we were properly introduced.'

Like the Marshalls, the Sutherlands were well known in Shaw Haven. Where one family owned half the land, the other owned the rest. When he was a kid he'd spent a lot of time with the Marshalls and their mutual friends. By the time he and Thomas were in high school, there was no love lost between them. Even in his teens, Thomas had reminded Ryan of his father. He'd had the kind of careless confidence that left people drowning in his wake.

He blinked that thought away. He really didn't want to think of Marshall – or his own father – right now.

'I'm Juliet.' She offered him her hand, giving him a surprisingly strong handshake. Her fingers were long and elegant, but no sign of a manicure. In fact her nails were cut short. They looked like working hands, not the kind you'd see on a trophy wife.

'It's a pleasure to meet you, Juliet.' He glanced over at Poppy and Charlie who were digging into their ice creams. 'Those two seem to have made up.'

'Yeah, kids have short memories,' she agreed, looking more at ease. 'But I'm so sorry she hurt him, and on his first day at school, too. I hope he isn't too upset.'

Her embarrassment made him want to smile. 'He's fine. Apparently they're practically best friends now. And he's used to meeting new people. I'm a photographer, we've travelled a lot.'

'Please make sure you apologise to your wife for me, too.'

He frowned. 'I'm not married.'

'Oh, sorry. Your girlfriend then?' Juliet glanced down at his left hand. Of course that made him immediately glance at hers. No wedding ring either – just an almost imperceptible indentation where one must have been. With his photographer's eye, Ryan often noticed details that others didn't.

Ryan shook his head. 'Sheridan – Charlie's mom – and I

are just friends. Charlie was a happy surprise for both of us.' He ate a spoonful of Charlie's ice cream, his eyes not leaving hers. 'She catches up with us when she can, but I have primary custody of him.'

'You do?' She looked at him with interest. 'Is she okay with that?'

He shrugged. He wasn't embarrassed about explaining his situation, he was used to it by now. 'It's what we both wanted. She loves him, but her job isn't exactly compatible with bringing up a child. When she's not touring she spends as much time as she can with Charlie. She wants the best for him. We both do.'

'I'm sorry, I'm being rude. I shouldn't ask all these questions.'

He couldn't help but grin at her. 'You're English, right? You're doing that whole Brit thing.'

'What Brit thing?'

'The one where you make small talk then get all worked up over it.'

'Do we all do that?'

He couldn't help but laugh at her perplexed expression. 'I guess I've met a lot of Brits on my travels, and yeah, a lot of them did that. Like you really want to know something but don't like to ask.' He tipped his head to the side, enjoying the way she was frowning at him. 'Where in England are you from anyway?'

'I grew up in London,' she told him. 'But I've lived here for almost seven years.'

'With the Marshalls?' He glanced at her empty ring finger again.

'Yes.' She looked down at the table. 'Well no, not now. It's complicated, if you know what I mean.'

He knew exactly what she meant. 'You want me to talk about something else?'

For the first time, she smiled. It was tentative, but it lit up her whole face. 'That would be lovely,' she said, tipping her head to the side. 'Maybe you can tell me about you. When did you guys get into town?'

Unlike Juliet, Ryan didn't mind talking about himself at all. Not in a brash, 'look at me' kind of way, but he was comfortable enough in his skin to be open and honest. 'We moved in at the weekend. We were meant to be here last week, but I got delayed on an assignment, so everything was a bit hurried. The removal trucks only got here this morning, it's gonna be a mess. A good reason to stay here and eat ice cream, I guess.'

'Removal trucks?' she asked.

'Yeah, we haven't got that much stuff, but I've had to buy a lot of furniture. It's our first permanent home.' He shrugged. 'Well, semi-permanent anyway.'

'Semi-permanent?' she echoed.

'We're here until next June. Then we're moving to New York. We're just here for Kindergarten year while Charlie gets used to going to school.'

'Did he not go to pre-K or preschool?' Juliet asked. Her brows were pulled down, as though she was trying to understand.

'No. We used to travel a lot for my work. Now he's getting older we're gonna put down some roots. I've been offered some work in New York starting next June. So we'll be moving up there after the end of the school year.'

'What made you choose Surrey Academy?'

It was a good question. 'I went there as a kid so there was kind of a connection already. It's all new to me, this school stuff. I thought I'd start us off gently, with somewhere I know.

19

I'll worry about the New York education system once he's settled in.'

'Dad, can Poppy come over to play today?' Charlie interrupted their conversation.

'I don't know ...' Ryan glanced at Juliet. Her face was impassive. He wanted Charlie to make friends, to fit in, but her kid had just hit him. Plus the house was full of boxes waiting to be unpacked.

'Not today, I'm afraid,' Juliet said. 'I have to go back to the shop for a couple of hours, and Poppy's coming with me.'

'I'd rather go play with Charlie. Please Mommy?'

'Not today.' Juliet shook her head.

'What about tonight? Can we play then?'

She gave a half-laugh. 'You'll be in bed tonight.'

'After tea?'

'No honey, you can play in the garden after tea, but then you'll need your bath and go to bed. It's been a long day.' She met Ryan's eyes, shrugging her shoulders.

'Let's meet in the garden, then,' Poppy said, turning to Charlie. 'I've got a cool rope swing.'

'Poppy, Charlie can't just come around after tea.' She looked at Ryan. 'I'm so sorry, one minute she's hitting him, the next minute she's practically inviting him to live with us.'

'Well he does almost live with us,' Poppy protested. 'Or next door, anyway.'

'What?' Juliet glanced at Poppy and Charlie before turning to look at Ryan. He didn't bother to bite down his own smile. 'Don't tell me you've just moved into the Langdon house. On Letterman Circle?' She gave a half-smile. 'I should have known when you said about the removal trucks.'

Now he was grinning. 'Yeah, that's the one.'

20

'I didn't know it was you. I was planning to pop over this evening with a plant or something to say welcome. I'm so sorry.'

Ryan had no idea whatsoever why Juliet was apologising to him, though he'd noticed before that English people had a habit of doing that. She was still blushing like crazy.

'You're at number forty-eight?' he asked.

She shook her head. 'No, forty-four.'

'The bungalow?'

'Yeah, that's the one. We only moved in a few months ago.'

'In that case, it's a pleasure to meet you, neighbour.' He offered her his hand again. When she took it, he curled his fingers around hers, feeling her soft smooth flesh.

There was something about Juliet Marshall that intrigued him. Made him want to know more. She was soft, yet brittle, an intriguing combination.

It was also a dangerous combination, he reminded himself. And he was only here for a while. He needed complications like Juliet Marshall like he needed a hole in the head.

They were neighbours. That's all they were, and as far as Ryan was concerned he should be perfectly happy to keep things like that. Friendly, neighbourly, but definitely minding his own business.

Even if part of him wanted to get all up in hers.

It was just after eight that evening when Ryan heard a rap on the front door. Charlie was sitting on the floor, playing with LEGO, while Ryan was drinking from his half-empty bottle of beer. He felt more American than he had in a long time, his stomach full of food he'd cooked on the grill. Tuna steaks rather than meat ones, and a local brew clutched in his hand. Strange how fast he was becoming reacclimatised.

Charlie looked up from his half-built fort. 'Who's that?'

'I don't know, kiddo. Forgot to put my x-ray specs on this morning.' He shot him a grin. 'I guess I'll have to do it the old-fashioned way and actually answer the door.'

'Maybe it's Poppy,' Charlie said hopefully. 'Can I go out and play?'

'I'm pretty sure Poppy's getting ready for bed by now.' He'd heard Juliet calling her from across the yard earlier. Ryan was more relaxed about bedtimes – as long as Charlie got enough sleep, everything was good.

'Dammit.' Charlie pursed his lips. 'That's no fun.'

Ryan was still chuckling at Charlie's response when he opened the door. The smile slid off his lips as soon as he saw who was standing there.

'What do you want?' he asked. He glanced back to check that Charlie wasn't in earshot.

The man in front of him seemed smaller than he remembered. Frailer, too. And yet looking at him made Ryan feel like he was ten years old again, watching his father's face turn puce as he yelled at Ryan's mother.

'Someone told me they'd seen you in town. I wanted to check for myself,' his father said.

'Got back yesterday.' Ryan kept his face impassive.

'But why?' the old man asked. 'Why are you here after all these years?' His eyes narrowed. 'Your mother's been crying all day.'

'I'm sorry to hear that.' If he'd been younger, more impulsive, Ryan might have pointed out that it was his father who usually made her cry. But he wasn't that child any more. He was a man. And he had his own child to protect.

'It's none of your business why I'm here,' Ryan said.

Charlie popped his head around Ryan, his hand full of brightly coloured bricks. 'Dad, can you help me with this?'

For a moment his father said nothing. Just stared down at Charlie. He looked back at the car, but Ryan's father still hadn't moved. 'Is that your son?'

He sounded surprised. Ryan liked the fact he hadn't found out everything. He'd assumed they'd discovered Charlie's existence – it was just like his father to keep tabs on him wherever he was in the world. But at least he'd managed to keep this element of surprise.

'Yes he is.' Ryan hooked his arm around Charlie, pulling him close. It was impossible to ignore the need to protect him.

Charlie blinked at Ryan's tone, staring up at him with guarded interest. But he said nothing, just watched and observed.

'How long are you in town for?' his father asked.

'I don't think that's any of your business either.'

For the first time his father reacted. He narrowed his eyes, his thin lips disappearing into nothing. 'It is my business. It's family business. I want to know whether you're planning on interfering with the company.'

Ryan stifled the urge to laugh. It wasn't humour that made him want to let it out, more the realisation that some things hadn't changed in all the years he'd been gone. The company came first, as always.

He might have held a third of the shares in the company – thanks to the inheritance he'd got from his grandfather – but Ryan had never wanted to be involved in the business. He gave all the dividends he earned away to charity – helping out the small town in Namibia where Charlie had been born. But he knew it killed his father to know that Ryan had any control.

Charlie shifted next to him, taking in every word. The need to get this man off his doorstep outweighed Ryan's need to goad him. 'I wasn't planning on it. Unless you need my help.'

'I don't need anything from you. I just want to make sure you don't interfere where you're not wanted.'

'Is that it?' Ryan asked, pushing Charlie gently behind him as he stepped back into the hallway. 'Because I have things to do. Perhaps next time you want to talk to me, you can make an appointment.'

'You shouldn't have come back. You know that.' His father took one final look at him, then turned his back on Ryan and Charlie, heading back to the black sedan parked next to the sidewalk. Ryan closed the door, leaning back on it for a moment, trying to catch his breath.

It had been a heck of a day. From the moment he'd woken up he hadn't had a chance to take a breath. The removal trucks, Charlie getting beaten up at school, meeting the pretty woman with the dark clouds in her eyes. Seeing his father for the first time in years was the icing on the cake.

Coming back to Shaw Haven had seemed like such a good idea a few weeks ago. What the hell had he been thinking?

'Mommy, do you think Daddy's lonely?' Poppy was lying in her bed, face up to the ceiling, while Juliet was curled up next to her. She was still holding the copy of *The Cat in the Hat* which they'd been reading together, Poppy spelling out the words as Juliet pointed to them.

This was Juliet's favourite time of the evening – lying next to a sleepy Poppy, the two of them discussing how their day had gone.

'I don't know, honey,' Juliet said. 'But I think he's okay.

He's busy at work, and when he comes home he has Grandma and Grandpa to talk to.' They lived on the same land, after all. Two properties built next to each other, overlooking Chesapeake Bay.

'And Nicole. She looks after him too.'

'Yes she does.' Juliet licked her lips, so dry in spite of the early fall humidity. 'So I think your daddy is just fine.'

'He was grumpy last weekend when I stayed with them. I heard him arguing with Nicole. Something about a party she wanted to go to.'

Juliet kept herself still, not wanting to show any reaction. But if she was being really honest she couldn't help but feel a bit of satisfaction at the thought of Thomas and Nicole having a row. She just wished they didn't have to do it in front of Poppy.

Sometimes she wished a lot of things. It didn't mean they came true though.

'Well, lots of people have arguments,' Juliet said, trying not to remember all the ones she'd had with Thomas. 'But then they make up again. Look at you and the new boy at school. You seem like you're friends now.'

'I like Charlie. He's cool. He's been to eleventy-hundred different countries, and he knows how to say no in ten different languages.'

Juliet smiled. 'He sounds like a clever boy.'

'But not as clever as me. I'm the cleverest in the class.' Poppy smiled. 'I got all our spellings right today. The teacher gave me a star.'

'You did?' Juliet turned her head to smile at her daughter. 'You are a clever girl.'

'I'm going to tell Daddy when I see him this weekend.'

Juliet kept the smile firmly on her face. 'He'll be so proud.

But you know you could have called on the phone to tell him. He always likes to hear from you.'

'I like to hear from him, too.' Poppy stared up at the ceiling, where Juliet had fixed fluorescent stars to the plaster. When they'd first moved in, they'd decorated every room in the bungalow. It had felt cathartic, marking it out as hers. Freeing, even, as she'd stood in front of the paint chart in Home Depot, and realised that nobody was going to criticise her choice, or tell her it wasn't in keeping with the rest of the house. She could have painted the whole place vermillion, and nobody would have blinked an eyelid.

'Can we get a cat?' Poppy asked.

Juliet laughed at her complete change of subject. 'What makes you ask that?'

'I just like them. Noah has a cat and a dog. But dogs are big and they bark too much. Cats are much nicer.'

'I don't think we can have a pet right now, sweetheart. I'm out at work all day and you're at school. It wouldn't be fair to leave it on its own all that time.'

'Can't you stay home like you used to? I liked that.'

Juliet's heart clenched. That felt like a lifetime ago – she was a different person then. She'd had enough time not only to take care of her daughter, but to take care of herself, too. It had been expected of her. Regular trips to the beautician, her own personal shopper, dinner out at least four times a week, supporting Thomas as he wined and dined clients.

As much as she loved having her own business – and being her own boss – she'd be lying if she said she didn't miss having more time on her hands, especially for her daughter. It felt as if the only time she got to sit still was when she was reading Poppy a story. Maybe that's why they both enjoyed it so much.

'I can't stay at home,' she said, her voice thick with emotion. 'I need to be at the shop. I have a lot of customers to look after, they'd miss me if I wasn't there.'

'I love flowers,' Poppy said, the cat already forgotten. 'I like it when you bring them home.'

She was sounding sleepy, her voice low and dragged out, like a record being played at the wrong speed. Turning onto her side, she nestled into Juliet, curling her legs up beneath her.

Juliet stroked Poppy's hair, her heart full of love for her daughter. This was the silver lining to her separation from Thomas. No more missing bedtime because she had to accompany him to a dinner. Instead she got to read to her daughter every night.

Leaning down, she pressed her lips to Poppy's cheek, feeling the warmth of her skin. 'Good night, honey,' she whispered, though Poppy's steady breaths told her she was already asleep. 'Dream sweet dreams. I love you so much.'

Sometimes that was the only thing Juliet was certain of.

3

Women may fall when there's no strength in men

– Romeo and Juliet

'We've set a date,' Juliet's younger sister, Cesca, said, her beaming smile lighting up Juliet's laptop. She was Skypeing with her sisters – Cesca, of course, plus Kitty and Lucy. The four of them tried to talk once a week, no matter where in the world they were. And right now Kitty was in LA, Lucy in Edinburgh and from the looks of it Cesca was in Paris.

Maybe one day they'd all be on the same continent, at least.

'You have?' Juliet asked, grinning. 'When's the big day?' Cesca's engagement to her movie-star boyfriend, Sam, had been one of the few light moments in Juliet's darkness this year. 'And where are you going to do it?'

There was no mistaking the glow on Cesca's face. 'Next July in the Scottish Highlands. We want to get married at Lucy's castle.'

Lucy, the eldest of the four, rolled her eyes. 'It's not a castle and it's not mine,' she pointed out, but she still couldn't hide her smile. None of them could – it was just such good news.

'Okay, at Lachlan's lodge then,' Cesca said. Lachlan was Lucy's boyfriend, and the previous year he'd inherited an estate in the highlands of Scotland. According to Lucy, Cesca and Kitty it had one of the most beautiful landscapes they'd ever seen. No wonder Cesca wanted to be married up there. It also had the added advantage of privacy – something Cesca and Sam had very little of during their everyday lives. The paparazzi loved them too much.

Juliet was the only one of them who hadn't seen the castle.

'And of course I want you all to be my bridesmaids,' Cesca said. 'And for Poppy to be my flower girl.'

Juliet watched as Lucy and Kitty agreed noisily, already asking about colours and dress styles. She tried to smile, tried to ignore that sick feeling in her stomach that was tugging at her. But her efforts were futile.

'What about you, Jules, what colour do you think she should have?' Lucy asked, finally noticing Juliet's silence. 'You've got the best eye out of all of us.'

Juliet stared at her three sisters, taking in their happiness, their expectation. Her chest tightened like a snake was squeezing her.

'I don't know if I'll be able to come.'

'What?' Lucy asked, frowning.

'Thomas won't let me take Poppy out of the country until we have a separation agreement. And we don't, not yet.' Juliet licked her dry lips. She hated bringing her sisters down, especially when Cesca had such good news.

'What?' Cesca asked, looking appalled. 'Can he do that?' She shook her head. 'Lucy, surely we can do something?'

'Not until they have a legal agreement,' Lucy said. Of the four of them, she was the only one who knew exactly how bad things were for Juliet. As the two eldest, they'd been the ones to keep things going after their mother's death when they were both teenagers. They'd always been each other's confidantes, and Lucy had proved to be Juliet's rock over the past few months.

'When will that be?' Cesca asked. 'It must be soon, right? You two have been separated for months, he can't make you wait that much longer.'

Juliet shrugged, but she felt anything but nonchalant. 'I don't know. There's a lot to sort out. Not just custody but our assets, alimony and child support.' And Thomas was playing hardball. It was as if he was deliberately dragging everything out.

'But I don't want to get married if you aren't there,' Cesca said, her face crumpling. Juliet bit her lip to stifle the tears that were threatening to rise to the surface. The thought of her sister getting married and Juliet not seeing it was awful. She felt like an exile, separated from the ones she loved. She wasn't sure how much longer she could take it.

She took a deep breath, then forced a smile back onto her face. 'I'll ask Thomas,' she said, as much to calm Cesca down as anything else. 'Maybe he'll be flexible if I explain what it's all about.'

'That's a good idea.' Lucy smiled at her warmly. 'Maybe he'll be reasonable for once.'

'Maybe,' Juliet agreed, her cheeks starting to ache. But she wouldn't bet on it. Sometimes she wondered what had happened to that charming, handsome man she'd met in a park in Oxford all those years ago.

Life. That's what had happened. The same things he'd loved about her had become annoyances. In the last year of their marriage she'd heard him sigh more than she'd seen him smile. And if she was honest, she'd been exactly the same.

Nowadays the only thing they had in common was Poppy – and thankfully they both loved her very much. Everything else seemed like a fight that was impossible to win. But that didn't mean she wasn't going to try.

'Are you nearly ready, honey?' Juliet called out. Poppy came running into the bedroom, still in her pyjamas, clutching a picture she'd drawn in school on Friday. It was of the three of them – Juliet, Thomas and Poppy – though Juliet and Thomas were on opposite sides of the page, and Poppy had strangely long arms as she was holding each of their hands. Juliet watched as her daughter laid the paper on top of her folded clothes, then helped her close up the case.

She wasn't sad to see the back of that drawing. It was a scene that happened the world over – two people divided, their child pulled between them like Stretch Armstrong. But it hurt like hell to look at it.

'You need to get dressed,' Juliet reminded her. 'Daddy will be here in a minute.'

It was barely nine in the morning – a few minutes before Thomas was due to arrive. The weekend stretched out in front of Juliet like an unwelcome visitor.

Thomas's car pulled up outside the house five minutes later. He climbed out of the black sedan, his face screwed up as he looked at the house. Seeing him was enough to make her chest constrict. He looked like the man she knew, he still sounded like the man she knew, but everything else felt so alien.

'Daddy's here,' Poppy called out.

She came running down the hallway, skidding to a stop beside Juliet. With wide eyes Juliet took in her daughter's clothes. She was wearing a blue and white stripy top, red

31

leggings and a pink fluffy tutu. On her feet were her very favourite silver sandals, glittering in the sunlight.

'That's a pretty outfit,' Juliet said.

Poppy beamed. 'I chose it all myself.'

'I know.' Juliet tried to smile. 'All your favourite things at once. Are you sure you're going to be okay in those sandals? It's getting cold outside.'

Poppy nodded her head vigorously. 'I've got socks on, see?' She wiggled her toes. 'I'll be nice and cosy.'

Thomas knocking on the front door dashed any hopes of persuading her to put on something more suitable. Grabbing Poppy's bags, Juliet stepped outside onto the porch.

'Hello, sweetheart.' Thomas leaned down to kiss his daughter's head. Then he looked her up and down, and the familiar frown returned. 'Are you going to get dressed before we go?'

An almost hysterical laugh bubbled up in Juliet's throat. It took everything she had to swallow it down. 'She is dressed.'

'Do you like them?' Poppy beamed at her father. 'Aren't I pretty?' She took the edges of her tutu in her hands, dipping her legs to give him a curtsey.

'You're beautiful.' He blinked as though something was caught in his eye. 'But maybe you can put something a little smarter on. We're going to breakfast with some of my business associates. One of your dresses would be perfect.'

Poppy's lip trembled. 'Don't you like my clothes?'

'Of course I do.' He looked up at Juliet, as if expecting her to say something. He wasn't used to talking to Poppy about clothes – they'd always been Juliet's domain. He was a wide-eyed fish out of water.

'Mommy liked them.' Poppy looked up at Juliet. Her eyes were shining with tears. 'You did, didn't you, Mommy?'

Juliet took a deep breath, trying to find the right words. She didn't want to dent her daughter's confidence. She knew all too well how easily that was done. 'I do, sweetheart. You look beautiful,' Juliet said, stroking her daughter's dark glossy hair. 'But we didn't know Daddy had planned to take you out, did we? Maybe you can go and change into a pretty dress, and wear these clothes tomorrow instead?'

Poppy opened her mouth to protest, but seeing the look on her father's face she closed it again. 'Okay. But I'm definitely wearing my sandals.' She ran back to her room, leaving Juliet and Thomas alone at the front door.

'Are you doing this on purpose?' Thomas asked her. 'You know what time I was picking her up, the least you can do is have her ready.' He shook his head. 'You're making everything as difficult as you can.'

'I didn't know you were going out for breakfast,' Juliet said, trying to keep her voice steady. Every conversation with Thomas seemed to be like walking a tightrope – one stumble and they were at each other's throats.

Poppy appeared back by Juliet's side, wearing a red jersey dress and a white cardigan. 'I'm ready now.' She smiled widely at her parents, unaware of the atmosphere bubbling between them.

'You look beautiful,' Juliet said, giving her daughter a big squeeze. She hated this bit, the saying goodbye for two days. Hated knowing she wouldn't be tucking her daughter up in bed that night.

'Yes you do. That dress is perfect. Now go get in the car, sweetheart,' Thomas said, clicking the back door open with his keys. Juliet watched as her daughter skipped down the front path, then handed Thomas her small suitcase.

'While you're here, there was something I wanted to ask you,' she said, as Thomas turned to leave. 'Cesca's getting married next year, and she wants Poppy to be her flower girl. Would that be okay with you?'

'Where's she getting married?'

'In Scotland.'

Thomas tipped his head to the side, scrutinising her with unkind eyes. 'We're not allowed to take her out of the country until we agree the separatation terms, remember? And even after that we both have to consent to it.'

'But it's my sister's wedding,' Juliet said, trying not to sound panicked. 'We'd only go for a few days. I promise I'll bring her back.'

'It's what we agreed,' Thomas said again, his tone measured. 'Unless you want to start breaking your promises.' He raised his eyebrows, as though he'd had a great idea. 'If you're that desperate, you could always go alone. Poppy can stay with us.'

The thought of leaving her daughter here while she travelled thousands of miles felt like an ice-cold spear poking at her spine. 'I can't do that.'

Thomas shrugged, the way he always did when it wasn't his problem. 'I have to go now. I'll see you on Sunday. Try to be ready for us.' With that, he walked down the pathway towards his car, tugging the driver's door open and climbing in. Juliet watched them pull away, her whole body tense.

She wasn't sure what made her look to her left, but when she did, her eyes met with *his*. Bright blue, piercing, half-obscured by sandy hair. Ryan Sutherland was staring at her, the strangest expression on his face.

How long had he been there? Probably enough to see her exchange with Thomas. The thought made her skin flush up.

Ryan smiled at her, his eyes crinkling, and her cheeks got even warmer. There was something about him that made her feel more nervous than she'd ever felt.

More alive, too.

It was uncomfortable, it was invigorating, but more than anything it was dangerous. She'd followed that feeling before, and look where it had landed her.

In a tangled web with no possible way of escape.

There weren't many things in life that ruffled Ryan's calm exterior, but seeing a man treating a woman badly was one of them. Growing up, it had been his maternal grandfather who'd taught him what a man should be; loyal, protective, and always a gentleman. Such a stark difference to Ryan's father, who regularly criticised his mom when he was a kid. Seeing Thomas Marshall stirred up all those memories.

Ryan had been on the deck when Thomas arrived, replacing a plank that had split in the sun. Looking up, he'd seen that familiar strut, the one he'd seen when they were both in high school. It reminded Ryan of a stalking animal, one that pushed everything out of its way to get to its prey. Ryan had stilled his movements, balancing his hammer in his hand, as he strained to hear the conversation between Thomas and his soon-to-be ex-wife.

But it wasn't Thomas's words that had reminded Ryan of his father, it was the way he'd stood in front of her, his shoulders back, his chest puffed out. As though he was trying to show his dominance through body language alone.

Juliet had turned around from where she was talking to her husband, catching Ryan's eye. He'd smiled at her, trying to show her some support if nothing else. Her eyes widened, but the next moment she'd looked away.

Ryan had looked down to see his own knuckles bleached white, where he was still holding tightly to the hammer. He really didn't want to watch them over there on the porch any more.

'Charlie,' he called out.

His son looked up from the swing chair where he'd been sitting and watching Ryan. 'Yes?'

'Get your shoes on. We're going down to the wharf.' The need to get away from this place nagged at him.

'Where?' Charlie hopped off the bench, leaving it swinging behind him. 'What's a wharf?'

'It's like a boatyard. On the riverbank.' Ryan ruffled his son's hair as he ran past him and into the house, heading for the closet to grab his sneakers.

Fifteen minutes later, Ryan parked his black truck in the gravelled lot next to the wharf. As soon as he stepped out onto the worn wooden boardwalk, it felt as though he was finally home. The autumn sun was beating down, its rays reflected in the water lapping against the wooden poles. The familiar aroma of freshly caught flounder and crabs wafted up from the boats moored up on the edge. In the middle of the boardwalk – as weathered as the wooden deck that surrounded it – was an old hut. *Stan's Shed* was painted in thick brushstrokes across the front, the white letters peeling away from the wood.

'What do you think of this place?' Ryan asked Charlie. His son was looking around, his brows pulled down low as he took everything in. He'd visited fishing villages all over the world, but this was Charlie's first view of the one Ryan had grown up in. For some reason, he found himself hoping his son would love it as much as he had.

'Can we go out on a boat?' Charlie asked, his face bright with hope.

Ryan was about to answer him when a familiar figure shuffled out of the shed.

'Who's that?' Stan was frowning. 'Do ya know this is private property?'

Ryan felt the corner of his mouth twitch. Stan was as brash as ever, and for some reason he found that reassuring. 'I heard there was some good fishing in these parts,' he replied, smiling.

'Yeah, well, that may be true, but these are private boats. We don't hire none of them out.' Stan shuffled a little closer. 'You'll need to drive over to Hyattsville if you want a tourist ride.'

'What about that boat?' Ryan asked, inclining his head toward a forty-footer in the corner. It was an old one, but beautifully maintained. The exterior was painted white, with *Miss Maisie* printed across it in blue script. At the front of the boat was a small covered cabin, with windows looking out from three sides.

'No, sir, that one's definitely not for rent. The owner wouldn't like that, not at all.'

Beside him, Charlie started to shuffle, as if he was getting nervous. Ryan reached out and placed his hand on his shoulder. Charlie immediately relaxed. 'Who's the owner, maybe I know him?'

'He doesn't live around these parts.'

'What kind of guy owns a boat like that and doesn't live near it?' Ryan asked. 'Sounds like an asshole if you ask me.'

Stan started to frown. 'I don't like the way you—' He stopped suddenly, finally looking Ryan dead in the eye. 'Ryan Sutherland? Is that you, boy?'

'Last time I looked.'

'Jesus, you're a sight for sore eyes. I should have known it was you, the moment I walked out of the hut I thought you looked just like your grandfather.'

A rush of warmth suffused Ryan's skin. Being compared to Cutler Shaw was the biggest compliment he could think of. 'You haven't changed at all.'

'Ah, shaddup. I can't hardly walk without a stick any more. Plus I can't see much without my glasses. That's why I didn't believe my eyes.'

'You never could see much,' Ryan teased. 'We used to get away with hell whenever you forgot to wear them.'

'Oh, I knew what you boys were up to, I just chose to ignore it. Now come over here, and introduce me to this little fella.' Stan pointed at Charlie.

Ryan walked forward, grabbing Stan's hand in his own. Charlie shuffled shyly next to him. 'This is my son, Charlie.'

'Well it's mighty good to meet you, Charlie. I can tell just by looking at you that you're a good kid. Not like your wayward dad, here.' Stan's voice was teasing, enough that even Charlie got the joke. The small smile that curled at the corner of his lips made Ryan want to grin.

'Hey, less of the wayward. And it's good to see you, too.'

'How long're you back for?'

A ray of sun bounced off the windows of one of the yachts, causing Ryan to blink. 'We're here for Kindergarten year, aren't we, Charlie?' Ryan said. 'Thought we'd settle down enough for the boy to see how he likes school.'

'He won't like it that much if he's anything like his pa.'

Ryan shrugged. 'Luckily he takes after his mother, too.'

'She's a singer,' Charlie added, still so close to Ryan he could feel his warmth. 'She's on a tour.'

'Is that right?' Stan asked, shooting a quizzical look at Ryan. 'So it's just you and your dad?'

Charlie nodded, becoming braver by the minute. 'I want to sail a boat like he used to.'

'You know that little beauty is his, right?' Stan asked, inclining his head at *Miss Maisie*. 'Used to belong to his grandpa, your great-grandpa, and he left her to your pa after he died. I've been looking after it while he's been away.' Stan glanced at Ryan. 'If you want to take her out, I just need a couple of days to get her ready.'

'Yeah, I'd like that a lot,' Ryan agreed. 'You think she could be ready by next weekend?' He could feel Charlie's body stiffen with excitement next to him.

'Yup, no problem at all. Just need to give her another wax and fix the sails. Things are quiet around here now the summer's over, I've not got a whole lot of work on.'

Though the wharf was still a working one – the fishing boats leaving first thing in the morning, coming back later in the day with decks full of catches – it was the rich yacht owners that kept it going financially. Being within driving distance of both New York and DC, Shaw Haven had its fair share of second-homers, who increased the wealth of the already well-to-do town.

'In that case, we'll be back next Saturday,' Ryan said, grasping the old man's hand again. 'It's good to see you again, Stan.'

'Yes it is, boy, yes it is.'

4

It is the east, and Juliet is the sun

– Romeo and Juliet

One of the reasons Ryan had chosen this house was the fact it already had a dark room in the basement. A legacy from the previous tenant, who'd dabbled in photography for a while.

Not that Ryan *dabbled*. For him it was more of a compulsion. He'd grown up seeing life through a 24mm lens. Now that he earned a wage from it – and a damn good wage at that – it didn't lessen his excitement every time he captured the perfect scene.

Nowadays most of his photographs were digital, developed on the shiny screen of his laptop rather than in a dank, dark basement. But like a man who preferred to chop his own wood, just to feel the heaviness of the axe in his hand, there was something reassuring at being able to develop the photographs he took with his grandfather's 1950s Kodak. He worked under the red glow of the safelight as he moved the print from the developing bath to the stop bath, then through the fixer until he could hang it up to dry. It felt good to be doing things this way – using the same processes he had as a kid. Using the same camera he had, too – the one his grandfather had gifted him for his fourteenth birthday.

Back then he'd lost more than a few prints due to overexposure, or not getting the paper into the stop bath fast enough. It took years of practice to develop the perfect print, and yet still there was always the possibility that something could go wrong. For some reason he enjoyed it so much more than messing around on his MacBook.

Ryan finished the final print – of Charlie, clambering over *Miss Maisie* – then left the room, careful not to expose it to light. Climbing up the stairs to the ground floor, he checked on Charlie, smiling as he saw his sleeping son curled up on top of his covers, his fist jammed against his mouth as he sucked at his thumb. Charlie was used to sleeping anywhere he could – a by-product of his upbringing – but he'd still found it hard to settle down during his first week here in Shaw Haven.

Grabbing a beer from the refrigerator, Ryan ignored the lure of his laptop, instead heading for the deck. He grabbed his camera, intending to unscrew and clean up the lens as he watched the sun go down. But as he stepped outside he realised he wasn't the only one planning to spend some time out in the evening sun.

Juliet was kneeling on the grass in front of her bungalow, a small spade in one hand as she dug earth from the flowerbeds surrounding the house. He watched as she carefully planted the red and pink flowers, refilling the soil before sprinkling them with water from her blue-painted metal can.

Her hair was pulled back into a French braid that hung down her back, the colour still as striking as ever. He sat there, his camera on his lap, his fingers softly touching the black plastic lens, and watched as she tended the small garden. She was oblivious to the world, her neck long and slender as she leaned

41

over the soil, her hips swaying as she moved from side to side picking up plants and moving them to the right spot. She was a portrait waiting to be taken, a study in perfect beauty.

Pulling his gaze away, Ryan picked up the soft cloth he used for his camera, and gently cleaned the lens. When he glanced up a few minutes later, Juliet had finished her planting. She was standing, her arms crossed as she surveyed her handiwork. She brushed a stray lock of red hair from her face – the strands dancing in the soft evening breeze.

She was completely oblivious to his presence, so wrapped up in the exact placement of the plants that nothing else existed around her. She was classically beautiful – like those seventeenth-century women you saw on the walls at art galleries.

His thoughts turned to Sheridan, Charlie's mother. They'd never really been an item. More friends than anything, with a few benefits thrown in for good measure. When she'd discovered she was pregnant, they'd both taken it in their stride, and when Charlie was born in Namibia Ryan had fallen in love with his tiny scrap of a son right away. It had made sense that Ryan be the primary carer – taking a baby with you on a photographic shoot was a lot easier than taking him on tour with a band. They met up with Sheridan as often as they could – in places as exotic as Tijuana and Beijing – but for the most part it was just the two of them, and they were as close as a father and son could be.

Witnessing Poppy's handover this morning first hand made him thankful for everything he had. The disdain for his ex that seemed to seep from every inch of Thomas Marshall's body, had felt alien to him. Thomas Marshall had been a bully at school. It looked like he still was.

From across the yard, Juliet glanced over her shoulder, her brow dipping as she realised she wasn't alone. Ryan lifted a hand to wave at her.

'Hey, London, how you doing?' he called out.

Her brows rose up as she shouted back. 'My name's Juliet.' The smallest smile flittered across her face before she added, '*Mr Sutherland*.'

He couldn't tell if she was teasing or not. The not knowing made him want to stare closely at her, try to work out what was going on in her head.

'If you call me Mr Sutherland, I'll think you're talking to my dad.'

'I think I've met your dad,' she told him.

More and more intriguing. 'You've met him? When?'

She moved a little closer. Still on her side of the yard, but close enough that he could see the hazel of her eyes without having to look through a lens. 'At dinner with Thomas's parents. One of those interminable ones where the women get sent off after dessert so the men can talk business.' She sighed. 'I don't miss those at all.'

Interesting. 'You don't?' he asked her, putting his camera down and standing up. 'Why not?'

He walked across the deck and leaned on the rail, smiling at her. She looked up at him, running the tip of her tongue across her lips. 'They bored me to death. Just because I'm a woman doesn't mean I don't want to talk business.' She flashed him a smile. 'And I definitely didn't enjoy talking about Mary Stanford's latest grandbaby.'

His stomach contracted. He remembered those kinds of dinners too. He didn't miss them either. He pushed himself up off the handrail and walked down the steps towards her.

She looked up at him, and he could see a smudge of earth on the tip of her nose. He wanted to reach out to rub it away. 'You want a beer?' he asked her, tipping his head at his deck. 'Come and watch the sun go down with me.'

She shook her head. 'I can't, I've got some . . . some things to do inside. Poppy will be back tomorrow, I want to get all my work done before then.'

He ignored the pulse of disappointment shooting through him. 'Maybe another time then?'

Her nod was slight. He took that as a good sign. 'I don't drink beer. But maybe a lemonade . . . or something.'

For now, he'd take it.

'Or perhaps a shandy,' he said, grinning. 'We will get you over to the dark side, whatever it takes.'

From the way her mouth fell open, he suspected it would take quite a lot.

Juliet's hands were shaking as she pulled the gardening gloves from them, laying them down on the counter before washing her hands beneath the running faucet. Her cheeks flamed at the memory of him catching her looking at him. It wasn't the first time she'd been looking, either. When she'd been kneeling at the flowerbed she'd snuck more than a few glances over her shoulder, intrigued by how carefully he'd been cleaning his camera. The concentration on his face had called to her like a siren. She knew how easy it was to get caught up in something that you loved doing. It happened to her every day in the shop.

And of course she hadn't noticed just how handsome he looked in the orange light of the setting sun. She was way too busy for that.

Looking up from the sink, she caught sight of herself in the window, the darkening skies outside turning the glass into a mirror. It was impossible not to wince at the way she looked. Her hair was a mess, her face – unadorned by any make-up – was smudged with earth, and beneath her eyes were those ever-present shadows.

What would Thomas think of her if he could see her like this? During their marriage she'd always taken such good care of her appearance. Monthly trips to the hair salon, weekly trips to the beautician's. Not to mention the personal shopper at Garvey's, the local department store, who always called her whenever they had new additions to their designer range.

To the unpractised ear it sounded like a fairy tale, and maybe it was at first. But in recent years those cinched-in tailored dresses had felt more like a prison uniform. No, maybe they were more like a costume – clothes she put on to pretend to be somebody she wasn't. She'd tried so hard to be perfect, and it still wasn't enough. Not for Thomas or for her.

Sighing, she tucked the hair that had fallen out from her braid behind her ear. It was one thing to dress down, but quite another to look like this while your hot neighbour happened to be watching you from his deck. Her face flushed with embarrassment at the thought of him seeing her like that.

Growing up, she'd always been labelled the most beautiful of her sisters. But right now she'd never felt less beautiful, less confident of her appearance. Seeing your husband in bed with someone else did that to a woman.

She dried her hands on the old towel she'd grabbed from the dresser. Her nail varnish was chipped again. An occupational hazard for somebody who spent most of her time working with her hands, but also another reminder of how much things had changed. Thank goodness none of the Marshalls could see her now. It would only confirm their opinion that Juliet could never be the kind of wife they'd envisaged for Thomas.

She shook her head, flipping on the kettle to boil some water. That was the problem with her weekends off – the ones Poppy spent with her father. Too much time for introspection. She'd spent most of the day in the shop, doing her accounts, and sending out quotes, anything to take her mind off the empty house. Then this evening she'd worked on the backyard, determined to make this house look a little less ramshackle and a little more lived in. But now the sun was dipping beneath the tree line behind the house, she'd run out of distractions.

That had to be the reason her mind kept drifting towards the imposing house next door, and its intriguing owner. Because try as she might, she couldn't stop thinking about the way Ryan had offered her a beer, suggesting they watch the sun go down together. He'd said it so easily, so naturally, and she'd been desperate to sip an ice-cold drink on his deck. Desperate and afraid in equal measure.

She flicked the kettle off before it had even come to a boil, and reached into the refrigerator, pulling out a bottle of chilled white wine.

She might not have been a beer drinker, but right now the thought of mellowing out with a glass or two of wine was more temptation than she had the willpower to resist.

And maybe, just maybe, it would be enough to get Ryan Sutherland out of her thoughts.

5

Come not between the dragon and his wrath

– King Lear

'Okay, that's the last one. We just need to get them into the van and drive them over to the hotel now.' Juliet tucked her hair behind her ear. It must have fallen out of her hairband when they were head down tying the flowers together. 'Thank you for all your help.'

Lily smiled. 'It's a pleasure. And I can drive them over if you like. Save you the journey.'

'No, it's already half an hour past your finish time. I feel guilty enough. And anyway, I wouldn't subject you to the manager's wrath. I swear he always finds fault in the arrangements, no matter how carefully we do them.'

'He can't find that much fault. He offered you the contract after all.'

'That's true. And thank goodness he did.' Thanks to the Shaw Haven Hotel's contract to supply them with their weekly displays, Juliet had enough regular income to hire an assistant for the shop. Lily was a floristry student at the local community college, and she'd jumped at the job offer.

It was a match made in heaven. Their mutual love of flowers

might have brought them together, but in the past weeks that Lily had been working here, a friendship had budded between them, too. They'd found themselves talking non-stop as they worked alongside each other, creating floral displays and serving customers.

Lily had filled a void in Juliet's life she hadn't even known was there. A space left empty by the fact her sisters were so far away, and the friends she'd thought she had in her previous life had stuck firmly to Thomas's side.

It was nice to have a grown-up to talk to, sometimes.

There's always the man next door, a little voice inside her head whispered. Juliet shook it off and picked up the first floral display, heading towards the back door. She didn't need to think about Ryan Sutherland right now. She'd thought about him enough on Saturday night, after they'd talked across the yard.

Lily pushed on the back door and kicked the wedge beneath it to hold it open. The van was parked just outside. She unlocked it and unlatched the back door, taking the first display from Juliet and sliding it into the trunk.

'I really love what you've done with the trailing vines,' Lily said, standing back to admire the displays she and Juliet had created. 'It's so pretty.'

They worked methodically, Juliet carrying out the boxed displays, and Lily carefully arranging them in the van. By the time they'd finished, it was five-thirty p.m., half an hour past closing time, and more than an hour since Lily was supposed to be home.

'I'll pay you for the overtime,' Juliet reassured her, shooing her back into the shop to get her coat and purse. 'Now get out of here, your mom must be wondering where you are.'

'You don't need to pay me, I'm learning so much. I feel like I should be paying you.'

'Yeah, well that's the highway to becoming bankrupt.' Juliet shot her a smile. 'I won't be taking you up on that offer.'

'You should get out of here, too.' Lily threw Juliet the van keys, and then pulled on her jacket. 'I know you like to see Poppy before bedtime. If you hurry you should make it.'

'Thank heavens for good babysitters.' Juliet smiled. 'At least I know she's well taken care of.' She leaned forward to give Lily a quick hug. 'Now shoo, get out of here. I'll see you tomorrow.'

'Good luck with the delivery.' Lily walked over to her car.

'Thanks, I think I'll need it.'

An hour later, Juliet was pulling her car into the driveway, the tyres crunching against the gravel as she pressed her foot on the brake.

'Mommy!' Poppy's voice carried across the yard. Juliet was only halfway out of the car, one leg on the gravel, the other still in the foot well. She grabbed her purse and bucket of flowers she'd rescued from the shop, too old to use at work, but too pretty to throw away. A smile worked its way across her mouth as soon as she set eyes on her little girl.

'Hey honey. How was school?' She dropped her things on the porch, reaching out just in time for Poppy to throw herself into her arms. 'Where's Melanie?'

She looked around for Melanie Drewer – the babysitter who picked Poppy up and watched her at home every Thursday. It was strange that she was nowhere to be seen.

'She started being sick after teatime. It was yucky. The smell made me want to throw up too.'

'She's sick?' Juliet looked around. 'Where is she, in the house?'

'Nah, ah. She went home.'

'And left you on your own?' She felt her voice rise up an octave, like some kind of panicked soprano. 'She can't do that.'

'It's okay. Ryan told her to go. He said I could play with Charlie until you came home.' Poppy shrugged as if it was the most natural thing in the world, going to play with a practical stranger and his son.

Her mouth turned dry at the thought of what Thomas would say if he ever found out.

'Poppy, come look at this,' Charlie called out. Poppy turned and ran down the porch and back to the house next door, her hair flying out behind her. She came to a skidding halt next to Charlie, the two of them kneeling down at the corner of the house, both of them staring at something.

Her gaze rose from the two of them to the deck above. That's when she saw Ryan, sitting on the comfy two-seat sofa, a laptop propped up on his denim-clad legs. He was frowning at something, using a mouse to click at the screen.

He wasn't even keeping an eye on the children. Anything could have happened to them.

Turning on her heel, she walked back down the pathway and over to the Sutherland house. He looked up when he heard her footsteps, his blue eyes meeting hers.

'Hey. How was your day?'

His question stole the breath from her lungs, the same way his smile stole her good sense. How long had it been since anybody had asked her that? Even Melanie was usually too busy trying to get supper on the table on the nights she worked to even acknowledge much more than Juliet's arrival. As for

Thomas, well, he'd never really been interested in how things were going.

'Um, fine.' She blinked a couple of times. 'I was a bit surprised to hear Melanie was sick. She should have called me, I would have come home right away.' She felt all kinds of awkward, looming over him as he looked up at her. Why the heck was she getting so flustered at the way his eyes crinkled as he smiled?

'She was going to call you, but I told her I'd take care of things. She looked as green as a dragon, I thought the best thing to do was send her home before she spread her germs all over the neighbourhood.'

'You should have called me,' Juliet said. 'I can't have Poppy being looked after by strangers. It's not right.'

'I haven't got your number.'

'Well, Melanie should have given it to you. What if something had happened? What if Poppy had hurt herself when you were looking after her, and needed me? You can't just ... I don't know ... make decisions about other people's children like this.' Not even if the way he filled those jeans was making it hard to find the right words.

Ryan was looking at her as though he couldn't understand a word she was saying. Three furrows lined his otherwise smooth face, half-obscured by his sandy hair. 'If something had happened we would've tracked you down. But nothing did happen, and it wasn't likely to, either. Unless you count those two getting covered in mud.' He gestured at Poppy and Charlie, who were currently on their knees, digging in the earth. Charlie pulled a worm from the soil, holding it in the air and wiggling it toward Poppy. 'We're neighbours, we're hardly strangers. And I know you'd do the same for me if I needed help.'

The common sense of his answer took the wind out of her sails.

'I'm sorry,' she finally said, her voice quiet. 'I'm not used to getting any help.'

Ryan was silent as he stared at her. She felt scrutinised, but not in a bad way. Still, she could feel herself flushing under his inspection, her chest and cheeks pinking up as the blood rushed to her skin.

'You know, that's one of the reasons it took me so long to come back here,' he said, closing up the laptop and putting it on the table beside him. 'This whole notion that nobody else is responsible for your kids except you. It only happens in places like America. In the rest of the world, the less *civilised* places, raising a child is seen as a village project. If one parent isn't around to watch them, the others take charge. If a kid misbehaves, they get chastised, doesn't matter who by. If they're crying they get comforted. It's seen as everybody's responsibility to make sure the village raises strong, well-rounded kids. Because all of us benefit in the end.'

The timbre of his voice – all low and mellow – was hypnotising, but it was his words that took her breath away. She reached out, steadying herself on the balustrade that ran around the outside of his deck.

'That sounds almost beautiful,' she said. 'But nothing like we experience over here.'

Ryan frowned. 'But you had your husband didn't you?'

'Thomas wasn't great when Poppy was a baby.' That was the understatement of the year. She didn't need a whole hand to count the number of times he'd changed a nappy. When Poppy was tiny, he'd moved into a bedroom in the other wing to get some sleep. 'He had this big contract at work, and was there all the hours he could be. I guess his mom helped as best she could.' And the truth was, they all adored Poppy. They just weren't used to babies. How many times had they urged Juliet to get a nanny, to make all of their lives easier? 'Things are better now though.'

'I'm glad to hear it.'

She tried to ignore the way her breath shortened when he grinned at her. Did he realise how attractive he was? Whenever she looked at him it was like staring into the sun – there was a brightness to him that was almost dazzling.

And like the sun, she needed to stop herself from getting too close. She was married, she was a mother, and most of all she needed to learn from her mistakes, to stop making rash decisions she'd only live to regret later.

Otherwise, she was certain to burn.

6

These violent delights have violent ends

– Romeo and Juliet

Like his son, Ryan Sutherland had learned to sleep anywhere and everywhere. From the earthen floors of nomadic tents in Pakistan, to the luggage compartment of a battered old bus in Cambodia, if there was enough space for him to curl up there, then drifting off was almost a given. Strange, then, that in this luxury king-sized bed in the air-conditioned atmosphere of his Shaw Haven home, he found himself lying awake for hours, staring wide-eyed at the ceiling.

Tonight he found himself abandoning the quest altogether, choosing instead to creep down the polished stairs and grab his MacBook, sorting through photographs from his last assignment. He'd deliberately not taken any more assignments this fall. Between settling Charlie into Kindergarten, and thinking about their move to New York, he'd decided to take a break. He missed his work, though. Photography was his passion, and sorting through each shot, seeing the infinitesimal differences between them, had a calming effect like no other.

Still, he was feeling cranky when morning arrived, having finally drifted off just before dawn. Charlie, on the other hand, was chirpier than usual, talking with his mouth full as he shovelled spoonfuls of Cheerios between his lips.

'Can Poppy come over to play again after school?' Charlie asked. 'We're going to look for some more worms, and make a worm farm. She says we should be able to train them to do tricks.'

Immediately, Ryan's thoughts turned to Juliet. The way she'd looked so angry as she'd stomped across his yard. But as her fury fizzled out, replaced by a vulnerability that touched him to the core, he'd seen her anger for what it truly was.

Fear.

But fear of what? That's what he couldn't understand. He shook his head at himself – here he went again, thinking about things that weren't his concern. Didn't he have anything better to do? Getting his kid ready for school would be a start.

'I don't know. We'd have to ask her mom.' Ryan grabbed Charlie's empty bowl, half-throwing it into the dishwasher. 'If not we can ask somebody else to come over. Don't you have any other friends at school?'

Charlie shook his head. 'I want to play with Poppy. The other kids suck.'

Ryan pushed the dishwasher door closed and turned to look at his son. 'They do? Why?'

His son blinked twice, then looked down at his sneakered feet, frowning. 'They're nasty. They told her she couldn't play with them because she didn't have a dad any more.' Looking up at Ryan, he was still frowning. 'But she does have a dad, doesn't she?'

'Yeah, she does.' Ryan licked his lips. 'Just because you don't live with somebody, doesn't mean they don't love you. Look at your mom, she's crazy about you.'

'That's what I said. But nobody believed me that my mom didn't live with us. They said moms have to live with you.'

A glance at the clock told Ryan that they were going to be late if they didn't leave soon. Yet this seemed too important to gloss over. 'And what do you think?'

Charlie pursed his lips together, deep in thought. 'I think it doesn't matter whether you live with your mom or your dad. As long as they love you, everything is okay.'

Ryan hunkered down in front of his son, placing his hands on Charlie's shoulders. His chest ached with love for his boy. 'Nobody could be more loved than you,' he said, his voice thick with emotion. 'And you'll always be okay. I'll make sure of it.'

Charlie nodded, the serious expression still on his face. 'And Poppy will be okay, too, won't she?'

Ryan pictured the little girl the way she'd been the first day he'd seen her. Her jaw set, her eyes flashing. 'Poppy will be more than okay. She's got guts, just like you.' Pulling Charlie towards him, he gave him a hug. 'Come on, let's get in the car. You're going to be late for school.'

Charlie pulled on his shoes, pressing the Velcro straps carefully together. Then he grabbed his bag, slipping it over his arms until it rested snugly on his back. It was too big for him. He looked like a turtle that hadn't grown into its shell.

When he pulled the front door open, Ryan came to a halt in front of a huge bunch of colourful flowers. Arranged in a simple glass vase, the white tulips and purple hyacinths were tied together with twine, with green foliage adding a luxurious touch. In the middle of the bouquet was a white envelope. He picked it up and slid his finger through to open it, pulling out a small handwritten card.

White tulips and purple hyacinths mean I'm sorry.
Thank you for helping me with Poppy yesterday, I
appreciate it.
  Juliet

He stared at the vase for a moment, trying to recall if anybody had ever given him flowers before. It felt personal, almost too personal, and yet there was a warmth inside him that wasn't there before.

The woman next door was almost impossible to figure out. Maybe that's why he found her so intriguing.

After dropping Charlie off at school, Ryan turned his truck in the direction of the business district, right at the heart of Shaw Haven. Though the meeting he was due to attend was an official one he hadn't bothered dressing appropriately for the occasion. He didn't own a suit, hadn't needed one on his travels.

And now? It was a matter of pride more than anything, to wear the same clothes he wore every day. As he stepped into the shiny office block that housed Shaw & Sutherland, his jeans and dark T-shirt made him look more out of place than ever. When he was a child he would have felt uncomfortable at being different, but right now he liked that feeling.

'Can I help you?' One of the well-groomed associates looked up from the reception desk. Her eyes showed no recognition at all. Why would they? The last time he'd walked into this building he'd been little more than a kid.

'I'm here to see Matthew Sutherland.' Or rather, he'd been summoned. And as much as he disliked his father, his curiosity outweighed his antipathy. Plus he didn't want him turning up at his home again.

The mention of his father's name was enough to make the receptionist sit up straight. Anybody invited to see his father was obviously *somebody*. 'What's your name, please?'

'I'm Ryan.'

She waited for a moment, as if expecting him to give a surname, but Ryan kept quiet. He still didn't like the way a simple word changed the way people treated him in this town. For good or bad.

'Please take a seat.' She pointed at the bank of leather chairs in the corner of the marbled entrance. 'I'll let his assistant know you're here.'

'No need, I'll find my own way up.' Ryan wasn't about to wait around at his father's beck and call.

'Do you have an appointment?' the receptionist called out at his retreating back. He was already halfway towards the elevators. 'Mr um … Ryan, you can't just go up there. Nobody's allowed to roam the building without an escort.'

He ignored her increasingly frantic calls, stepping into the first elevator that arrived. The inside felt familiar, and as he pressed the button for floor eleven, it felt as though he was stepping back in time, back to that young kid who would come visit his father on very special occasions, his sweaty hand clutching at his tightly knotted tie, feeling out of place the way he always did.

The air in the elevator tasted stale, as if it had been trapped inside for too long. Ryan took a big lungful of it anyhow, watching the display tick past each level, until it finally came to a stop on floor eleven. He stepped out, ignoring the assistant whose desk was angled to welcome whoever exited the elevator, instead turning left, his brown shoes barely making a sound on the carpeted floor.

Strange how easily things came back to him. The conference room had been behind the door at the end of the corridor in his grandfather's day. And there it still was, though the name had been elevated to 'boardroom' according to the gold letters affixed to the thick, oak door. The atmosphere felt the same, too, the air pressing down on him oppressively. Reminding him exactly why he could never work in an office building like this.

He didn't bother to knock, just pushed the door open, the hinges creaking as the light from the boardroom flooded the corridor beyond. Six faces looked up from the piles of paper on the table.

His father was the first to speak. 'Ryan.' There wasn't a hint of reconciliation on his face. Not that Ryan would have welcomed it after all these years. But he was a father himself now, he couldn't imagine not having laid eyes on Charlie for all this time, then barely acknowledging him. It went against every impulse he had. 'Shall we wait for your lawyer to join us?' his father asked.

'He's not coming.' Ryan folded his arms across his chest.

His father was taking him in, those watery blue eyes not missing a thing. It took everything he had not to squirm in his chair, just like he was a child again, being measured, and found wanting.

Why had he come here again? To show them he wasn't afraid? Or maybe to show them they should be the ones who were scared.

'That's a shame. I was hoping you'd have some wise counsel.' As always his father's voice was mild. He lifted his water glass to his thin lips, taking a mouthful of liquid.

The lawyer sitting to his father's left shifted in his seat, frowning, but saying nothing.

'Why did you come back, Ryan?'

Ryan tried to ignore the way his father's question made him feel. It wasn't as if he hadn't asked himself the same thing a dozen times anyway. Still, something about the way his father was looking at him compelled Ryan to answer. He wasn't going to be the kid that ran away again.

'Because I wanted to show my son where he was from. Because I wanted to show him the town his great-grandfather helped to build. Because you may think you own this place, but the last time I looked it was a free country. I can live anywhere I like.'

'Yet you chose to live here. Out of three million square miles in this country, you chose little old Shaw Haven to send your boy to Kindergarten. Is that what you expect us to believe?' His father shook his head slowly, still maintaining eye contact.

There was silence for a moment. His father's stare didn't waver, but still, Ryan could see a vulnerability that he hadn't noticed before. Not quite fear, but definitely not a man in total control of the situation. For the first time, it dawned on him that his father was afraid of his reasons for coming back. Afraid of what he could do to the business – and his life.

'Why do you think I'm back?'

His father took another sip of water. 'I think you have unfinished business. Or at least that's what you believe. But I'm here to tell you to stop it before it starts. I may be older, but I'm not afraid to defend what's mine.' He gave a half-smile.

'You don't need to defend anything. Not everything's about you. I told you why I'm back and that's it.'

'So you're not here for the business?' There was still disbelief in his father's voice.

For a moment Ryan considered playing with him, the same

way his father had played with his mother for years. But really, what would that have gained him? As far as he was concerned he was just another shareholder. Nothing more than that. 'I'm not interested in the business at all.'

'In that case I have an offer for you. A very generous one. I'll email your lawyer the details after our meeting, but I'm certain he'll advise you to accept.'

'What offer?' For the first time, Ryan wanted to sigh. Swallowing down the impulse, he rolled his shoulders, trying to loosen the tension there. His father gestured at one of his lawyers.

The man pushed his glasses up his nose, then lifted a pile of thick white paper. 'Ry ... Mr Sutherland, we've prepared a very generous offer for your shares. We'd like you to sell them back to the company.'

'You want to buy me out?' His voice was low. Clipped. But none of them took the warning.

'We want to get rid of our liabilities,' his father said. 'And you're the biggest one.'

'Grandfather left me those shares for a reason,' Ryan said. 'He didn't want the company to be in your hands, otherwise he'd have left them to you.'

'I think we both know the old man had lost it by the end,' his father said. 'He didn't know what he was doing. If you weren't family I would have contested the will, but you'd put your mother through more than enough by then. You should look at the offer; it's a good one. We'll keep it open for a week. Pass it by your lawyer, and get back to us with any questions.'

The lawyer slid the documents into a large buff envelope, then pushed it across the table to Ryan. He ignored it, refusing to pick it up.

'I don't need to read it. The answer's no.' Without looking at the envelope, he used the tips of his fingers to push it back across the polished wooden surface. Though his stomach was churning, he kept his expression implacable. He knew from past experience that to show weakness to his father was tantamount to surrender. 'I promised my grandfather I would never sell the shares,' Ryan said. 'Not to an outside buyer, and not to you.' He flicked his eyes up, meeting his father's gaze.

'We'll send the offer to your lawyer,' his father said. 'He'll tell you it's a good one. You have five days to accept it.'

'Send it where you want.' Ryan shrugged. 'I won't be accepting it anyway. You're wasting your time and mine.'

'Then I'd say this meeting is over.'

'That's the first sensible thing I've heard all morning.' Leaving the envelope on the table, Ryan left the room, not bothering to say goodbye, not wanting to look back at his father. It was taking all of his effort just to keep himself from exploding. He was angry, but also really hurt. He should be used to it, he really should, but it didn't stop him from wanting to break something on his way out of the building.

Almost fifteen years ago, he'd walked away from his parents and swore to himself he'd never let them hurt him again.

So why did it feel as if he'd just been stabbed in the back?

7

Wisely and slow. They stumble that run fast

– Romeo and Juliet

'Are you sure everything's okay there?' Juliet spoke into her phone.

'It's all good. I've opened up, sold a couple of bouquets. And the driver called to confirm the deliveries for later. Now stop talking to me and enjoy your day, okay?' Lily reassured her. 'I promise I've got it all covered.'

'I really appreciate your help. Thanks for stepping in.' Juliet still couldn't help but worry. 'I'll call you tonight to make sure it all went well.'

'You do that.' Lily sounded amused. 'But for now you're a mom not an entrepreneur. So hang up and get on with it.'

Planning a day off from her own business had been hard work. She'd spent the whole weekend trying to get everything ready, so that Lily could run the shop alone. It had meant paying a courier service to deliver the flowers, pretty much wiping out any profit she had hoped to make, but really, what choice did she have? Poppy was desperate for Juliet to be one of the parent-helpers on the school trip, and the thought of disappointing her was too much.

Yet another joy of being a single, working parent; every choice left a casualty somewhere. All too often, the main casualty was Juliet's sanity.

She glanced at her phone as she walked with Poppy into her classroom. No messages yet. Hopefully that was a good sign.

The classroom was buzzing with the children's excitement. Though it was early October, they were all dressed in their Halloween clothes; as princesses and witches, ghosts and football players.

Poppy was dressed as Merida – her favourite Disney princess – complete with a wig full of tumbling red curls. The colour wasn't too far off Juliet's and she found it amusing that for once the two of them looked as though they were related.

'Mrs Marshall? Thanks for coming to help today.' Brenda Mason, Poppy's Kindergarten teacher, shot Juliet a harassed smile. 'We're just waiting on two more parents then we'll get onto the bus. Bathroom break first though!'

Juliet bit down a grin. Miss Mason had been a Kindergarten teacher for more than twenty years. Everything in her classroom was ruled by bathroom breaks.

She drifted over to where the other helpers were waiting. Like Poppy, their children had been at the expensive private school since preschool, graduating first to Pre-K, and then on to Kindergarten. They'd known her back when she'd been Mrs Marshall, trophy wife and mother, before her world had fallen apart. Since she'd separated from Thomas the invitations for coffee or supervised play dates had dried up. If she hadn't been so busy trying to set up her business, it probably would have bothered her more.

'Hi Susan. Hi Emily.' She shot them a smile and they nodded back at her. 'Who else are we waiting for?'

'Marsha, of course,' Susan said, rolling her eyes. 'Oh, and Charlie Sutherland's dad. You know, the good-looking one.'

'He's smoking hot,' Emily agreed. 'That blond hair makes him look like a young Robert Redford, well before he got all wrinkly, anyway. And he's such a good dad, too. Poor guy is all on his own, I don't know how he does it.'

'Oh, he's amazing. Have you seen how good he is with Charlie? We asked him over for a play date this weekend, try to give his poor dad a break. God knows, it's impossible to be a parent twenty-four-seven. I was saying to Rich, I've no idea how I'd cope if I didn't have him coming home every evening. I'm so lucky I'll never have to be a single mom.'

Juliet felt all the muscles surrounding her chest tighten. She should be used to talk like this. It wasn't so long ago that she was one of *them*, married with money and help and everything else she could ask for. Not that she'd ever been as smug as Susan was.

But still, she'd taken it for granted. Until everything changed.

'I'm so sorry, Juliet, how are things going for you?' Susan finally asked. 'It can't be easy, living on your own. But at least you have Thomas's money. That's something, right?' Her laugh was tinkling. 'Plus every other weekend you're child-free. I dream of that sometimes. There's nothing worse than getting woken up on a Saturday morning. You must love sleeping in.'

'I don't sleep in. I have to work at the weekends,' Juliet pointed out. 'I can't remember the last time I stayed in bed past six.'

'How's the little shop going?' Susan asked. 'I keep meaning

65

to drop in. I think it's wonderful that you've got somewhere like that to keep you busy, now you're not a career wife.'

Juliet was trying – and failing – to keep the frown from her face. A career wife – was that what she'd been? She'd thought she was just a wife, plain and simple. Not always a perfect wife, no matter how hard she'd tried, and she had tried really hard. *Career wife* made it sound as if she'd failed to meet standards she'd never known even existed.

'Come by any time,' she said. Her throat felt scratchy. 'I'll show you around.'

'Sure. I'm sure it won't take long anyway will it? It's only a tiny little shop ...' Susan trailed off, staring over Juliet's shoulder, a dreamy expression softening her face. 'Oh my, he really is something.'

Juliet didn't have to turn around to know exactly who Susan was talking about, the tingles shooting down her spine did the job for her. The blood rushed to her face, warming her cheeks, sped up by the rapid beats of her heart.

She almost didn't want to look at him. Didn't want him to see how flustered she became whenever he was around. Since she'd left those flowers on his doorstep a couple of weeks ago, she'd only seen glimpses of him as she was leaving for work.

Maybe it was better that way.

'Mr Sutherland, thank you so much for coming. And look at you, Charlie, what are you dressed up as? Is that a Mexican costume?' Miss Mason asked.

'I'm a Peruvian,' Charlie corrected. 'It's from Cuzco.'

'Of course you are, dear. What lovely colours they are, too.' Miss Mason took a deep breath before shouting for attention. 'Okay, children, please get in line. We're going to take you to the bathroom five at a time, and then you'll get on the bus. Make sure you have your bagged lunches and raincoats please.'

All the kids rushed to be at the front, shouting and laughing as they pushed each other out of the way. Juliet watched as Miss Mason and her classroom helper tried to get them to form a line, listening patiently as the children complained it was 'no fair' that they weren't at the front.

'Hey.' Ryan's voice was so close to her ear she could feel the warmth of his breath as he spoke. It sent another shiver down her spine.

Ignoring her own stupid reactions, she forced a smile onto her face. 'Hello, Mr Sutherland.'

'I'll take a simple Ryan, if it's all the same to you, London. Or if you really want to annoy me you can call me "Ry".'

'That annoys you? Why?'

He didn't get a chance to answer before Susan slid smoothly between the two of them.

'Oh, hi, Ryan, it's so good to see you again. Franklin is so looking forward to Charlie coming to stay at the weekend. He's such a lovely boy, a real credit to you.' Susan turned her back on Juliet, giving Ryan no choice but to look at her. 'Maybe you can join us for lunch on Sunday? If the weather stays like this we'll probably light up the barbecue. My sister will be visiting and I know she'd love to meet you.'

'Um, yeah, sure. Sounds good.'

'Let's say one o'clock?'

Juliet tried to drown out the noise as Susan started asking him about what sort of food Charlie liked. Ryan was keeping his voice polite, unteasing, not at all the way he'd spoken to her. She looked over at the children, now standing in a perfect line, all of them staring up with interest at Miss Mason as she described their plans for the day. Then each set of children were assigned to a parent or helper, sent off to the bathroom and then to the school bus. Within seconds Juliet was surrounded by Poppy and four of her school mates.

It was barely nine-thirty in the morning, yet it already seemed like it had been one hell of a long morning. God only knew how she was going to survive the rest of the day.

'Climb on board, kids. Mind the step, now, you don't wanna be falling off. We've got a hay ride to enjoy.' The tractor driver helped the group of kids climb onto the trailer, watching as they clambered over the bales of hay laid out as seats on the flat bed. Silently Juliet counted them on, something she'd been doing all day. Though she was only in charge of five children, there was no way she was going to lose any of them. After her last encounter with Principal Davies, she wasn't exactly jumping at the chance of being hauled in front of her again.

'Mind if we tag along?'

She turned to see Ryan standing there, his own group of kids clinging onto his arms. She'd seen him earlier at the pumpkins – had watched with amusement as he'd managed to smash twelve of them while the kids had cheered him on. The farm was big enough that she'd only bumped into him once before now. He'd been the only helper – apart from Juliet herself – who'd joined in the fun on the climbing castle, clambering over bales and through holes in the wall, laughing along with the children as he swung on the rope swing.

'I think there's space.' Juliet looked at the driver.

'Yup, there sure is. Welcome aboard, kids.' When all the children were safely on, Juliet turned to grab hold of the ladder.

Ryan reached out for her hand, closing his own palm around it, helping her up onto the trailer.

There was a small space left at the back of the trailer, and Juliet crawled over to it, thankful she'd worn jeans today. She'd spent most of lunchtime picking hay out of her hair, and was certain that when she undressed that night she'd find more inside her shirt. Ryan sat down next to her, his warm body pressed against her side. She couldn't have moved if she'd tried – the trailer was small, and the children took up the rest of the space. She was cornered.

'Give them ten minutes, and they'll be fast asleep,' Ryan said, nodding his head at the kids in front of them. 'It's impressive what fresh air and activity can do.'

Juliet smiled. She was feeling sleepy herself. As the tractor began to pull away, the wheels rolling rhythmically on the grass, she could see exactly what Ryan meant.

'I'd forgotten about places like this,' Ryan told her. 'I haven't been to a Pumpkin Patch in years. It's funny that the more I'm away from the States, the less I remember about the culture.'

'I'd never heard of them before I moved over here,' Juliet admitted. 'We don't have things like this in England.'

'You don't celebrate Halloween?'

'We do, but nowhere near the way you do over here. A few kids might go trick or treating, but that's about it. There's not a whole industry built around it. And if you dress up in a costume over there it has to be scary. No Disney princesses or Nemos.'

'How boring.'

She laughed. 'We have other ways of celebrating. Like Guy Fawkes Night.'

'Is that the one where you burn human-sized dolls in big bonfires?'

69

She looked at him with an eyebrow raised. 'It might be. Do you have a problem with that?' She was teasing. And she liked the way he grinned when he realised.

'Just sayin'. You guys have some messed up traditions over there, London.'

Why was it, that every time he used that nickname on her, she felt her whole body light up?

'At least we have some history. We don't have to just invent stuff for the fun of it.' She almost stuck her tongue out at him. Crazy how easy it was to tease him. Even crazier how it made her pulse speed up.

'Do you miss it?'

She frowned. 'Miss what?'

'Living in England?'

The tractor hit a hole, jostling them around. The kids giggled as she was almost thrown into Ryan's arms. He reached out, steadying her with his strong hands. Juliet's breath caught in her throat.

When he smiled, the corners of his eyes crinkled up. For the first time she noticed the scar running through one of his eyebrows. She wanted to reach out, trace the white line. Wanted to ask where he'd gotten it from.

Damn it, no she didn't. It was just those hormones sparking up again.

'You okay?' he asked softly.

She tried to pull away from him, but his hands stayed firm on her upper arms. She could feel goosebumps breaking out all over, her body shivering in spite of his warmth. It had been so long since she'd been this close to a man. But that wasn't what made her heart beat wildly. It was *this* man. The blond-haired, easy-going Romeo next door.

Stop it Juliet. *Stop it*.

'I'm fine.'

He brushed his thumbs along her biceps, the sensation only making her shiver more. He really needed to let go of her now, before she made a fool of herself. She was a grown woman, a mother, and they were surrounded by children. There was no way she should be feeling like this.

'I'm fine,' she said again, this time managing to pull herself from his grasp. She looked around at the kids. They were all safely seated. As he'd predicted, more than one of them had fallen asleep. 'Thank you.'

'You're welcome.'

She pulled her knees up to her chest, circling her arms around them, turning herself into a ball. The ground ahead looked more uneven than ever. There was no way she was going to fall into him again.

Even if it felt too good. Or especially because it did.

'I do miss London, yes,' she said, trying to get back on track. 'I miss my family, of course, and I miss my friends. But more than anything I miss that feeling of belonging, of having grown up somewhere and knowing it inside out. I might have been living here for more than six years, but I still feel like a visitor.'

He wrinkled his nose up. 'I can't imagine living in one place for my whole life. There's a big world out there.'

'I'd be too afraid to travel the way you have,' she told him. 'I need to know where I'm going. I can't imagine turning up in a new country and having no idea where I'm going to sleep that night.'

'That's the fun part. It's only scary the first time. After that you know that no matter what happens, you're going to be okay.

So you might have to sleep in a few bus stations, or on a dusty road, but you'll still wake up in the morning and be fine. The sun will come up, the world will keep turning.'

'But you decided to settle down anyway,' she said, trying to ignore the drumbeat of her pulse in her ear. 'You're here after all.'

'Until June. Then we move to New York.'

'Oh. I'd forgotten . . .' She trailed off. Picking up a piece of straw, she rolled it between her fingers. It was the colour of the sun, golden and light. 'I remember you saying that at the ice cream parlour now.' She licked her lips. 'What's in New York?'

'I've been offered a long-term contract as a principal photographer for a magazine. Plus I'll be doing some freelancing too – there's a lot of work up there.' He raised his eyebrows. 'It's a change for us both, settling down in one place, but Charlie needs some stability now he's in full-time education.'

'Aren't you worried about him having to start all over again at a new school?' she asked.

'Should I be?' Ryan frowned.

She regretted her words immediately. They came from her own anxieties, not his. 'No, you shouldn't. Children are adaptable.' After all, look at how quickly Poppy had adjusted to their new home. 'I'm just a helicopter parent sometimes. Always worrying about something.' She winced. 'And now I'm worrying about worrying, which is so crazy I should shut up.'

'Maybe I should worry a bit more,' Ryan said, smiling at her. 'I know I can come off as too laid back sometimes.'

The ride was coming to an end. The tractor pulled up to the steps, moving forward slightly until they were aligned with the trailer. Nearly every kid had fallen asleep on the hay.

'I'll tell you what,' Ryan said. 'Maybe you can teach me to worry a bit more, and I can teach you to be more laid back. Between us we might just make it work.'

Between *us*. 'That sounds good.' It really did. And if she could just stop her body from reacting to him, and put him firmly in the friend zone, it might even work out.

He reached for her hand, shaking it firmly, his lips still quirked up in that sexy smile. 'In that case, London, it's a deal.'

8

There is a tide in the affairs of men,
Which taken at the flood, leads on to fortune

– Julius Caesar

'Your first lesson is how to take your kid out on a boat without panicking.'

Juliet blinked, trying to focus on Ryan as he stood at her front door. He was wearing long, navy shorts and a white shirt, his sleeves rolled up at the elbows. Dark glasses covered his eyes, shielding them from the October sun. Though the leaves were changing colour, the temperature remained unseasonably warm. Yesterday they'd hit the high seventies.

'What?'

'I'm teaching you to be laid back, right? What's more laid back than taking your kid out onto the water? You have to be chilled out to do that.'

'Or have the best life jacket ever.'

He laughed. 'Life jackets I have. Now are you up for the challenge?'

She glanced at her watch. It was seven-thirty on a Saturday morning. 'You mean *now*?' she asked. 'I have to be at work later this afternoon.'

'I'll have you both back on dry land by then,' he said, sliding his glasses over his head. 'Probably.' That last word was accompanied by a wink.

'You'd better,' she told him. 'Otherwise I'll have to teach you my first lesson. Which is if you have responsibilities, you meet them. Otherwise you can lose your only source of income.'

His face took on a serious expression. 'I hear you, and I promise you'll be back in time for work. I'd never get in the way of a lady and her source of income.'

Half an hour later, they were all dressed and scrambling into Ryan's car. Juliet strapped Poppy into her seat, testing the straps to make sure they were secure.

'How big is your boat, Ryan?' Poppy asked, leaning as far forward as her car seat would let her. She frowned when the straps stopped her in her tracks.

'She's a forty-footer. Bigger than a row boat, smaller than a ship.'

'How do you know she's a she?' Poppy asked. Juliet couldn't help but smile. Her daughter was always full of questions, but at least somebody else was bearing the brunt today. She glanced at Ryan from the corner of her eye. His hands were firmly on the wheel, his eyes trained on the road ahead, but it was impossible to ignore the grin on his face.

'Because she's beautiful,' he told her.

'Boys can be beautiful too,' Poppy protested. 'So it can't be that.'

'She's called Miss Maisie,' Charlie interjected. 'So she can't be a boy. I wish she was though, boys are cool.'

'Girls are cooler.'

Juliet tuned the two of them out, this time turning to look at Ryan. Though he was concentrating, he was still relaxed, his expression light and easy. She took advantage of the fact he was looking away to take him in. Square jaw, straight nose, eyes that matched the ocean.

He was way too attractive for his own good. Or her good for that matter. They were just friends, she reminded herself, nothing more.

'Are you sure this is okay?' she asked him, glancing back at Charlie and Poppy. 'I hope they don't bicker all day. She can be a bit of a handful.'

Ryan pulled out onto the harbour road. 'She's nothing like you, is she?'

'She's fearless. So yeah, nothing like me at all.'

'You don't think you're fearless?'

She shook her head. 'I'm the complete opposite. Nearly everything scares me.'

'You moved to a strange country when you were twenty. That sounds pretty fearless.'

'I was blinded by love.' She said it deadpan, making him laugh.

'What about being a single mom? That takes guts.'

'It takes having no other choice.'

They were at a stoplight. He glanced at her, and she saw herself reflected in the mirrors of his sunglasses.

'There's always a choice. You could have stayed with him. You could have gone home to London and left Poppy behind. You could have done so many things, but you chose to stay and fight for your kid. That takes guts.'

There was the strangest feeling in her chest, as though a hundred butterflies had come to life, fluttering their wings inside her ribcage. Behind her, Poppy and Charlie were still chatting, this time about their worm farm.

'Keep telling me that, and I might just start to believe you.'

'You *should* believe me. I grew up with parents who did nothing but think of themselves. That's the coward's way out.'

It was as though he was revealing little parts of himself, piece by piece, and she was doing the same. Every time they were together the armour was coming off, revealing vulnerable skin that could so easily be pierced. She'd never felt so comfortable and so exposed at the same time.

He steered the car through the gates to the parking lot, pulling into a space facing the harbour. The water was lapping against the side of the boardwalk, the moored boats gently rising and falling with its movement. As soon as they stepped out of the car there was tranquillity to the air that surprised Juliet. The only times she'd been here before was for dinner cruises – when the whole boardwalk was full of chatter and expensive voices.

Not now, though. It was as though somebody had put a little spell on the river, holding back the flow of years and progress. It was timeless in its beauty.

'Is that your boat?' Poppy asked, pointing at a tiny fishing vessel. 'Can we even fit on there?'

'That's not our boat.' Charlie looked almost offended. Then his face softened as he pointed over to a large sailing boat moored up by the pier. 'That's *Miss Maisie*. Our boat.'

For a moment he looked so much like his father, he took Juliet's breath away. The same piercing eyes, the same expression of wonderment. It wasn't difficult to imagine Ryan as a child, playing on these planks, climbing over the boats and getting up to all kinds of mischief.

The man himself had climbed out and was unloading the back of his car, pulling out two bags and slinging them over his shoulder. Then he led the way to the jetty, reaching out to slow Poppy down as she sped along the gangplank.

An old man was waiting for them by the side of *Miss Maisie*, a blue cap pulled down on his head where a few wispy grey curls escaped from beneath. He looked at Juliet with interest, as if he was trying to place her.

'Hey Stan,' Ryan said, reaching for the old man's hand. 'She looks perfect. Thanks for getting her ready at such short notice.'

'You always were the impulsive one,' Stan told him. 'And I see you each brought a lady along. Remember to keep the language clean on there, young Charlie.'

Charlie giggled, making Poppy laugh too. The two of them stood stock still as Ryan slid their life jackets on, fastening them firmly as he gave them instructions on how to behave on the boat. Then he passed a larger life jacket to Juliet, smiling as she struggled to tighten the straps across her body. He reached out, putting his hands over hers, gently guiding her as the jacket became firm against her body.

'You ready?' he murmured, dragging his own lifejacket on.

'I'm ready,' she told him. And she was. Ready to get on the deck, to feel the air lifting her hair. To put the distance between them she needed, because right here, right now, she was a hair's breadth from wanting to run her palms all over those tight biceps of his.

'So what are we waiting for?' Poppy asked impatiently. 'Christmas?'

A few minutes later, Stan was throwing the rope to Juliet as Ryan steered the boat out from the jetty. She coiled it around her hand and arm, the way he'd shown her, before hooking it onto the side in a large loop. Ryan called out instructions to her as they reached the open water, smiling at her as she tried to follow them as best she could. Even when she stumbled on the deck, all he did was give her the once-over with his eyes, satisfied she was okay.

It didn't take long for the boat to work its magic on her. Feeling the air rushing over the deck, and the almost magical sensation of floating on the water, was enough to make her heart pound in the best kind of way. She could see the same response in Poppy and Charlie, as they sat on the deck the way Ryan had shown them, their eyes tightly closed as the wind blasted their faces.

'You okay?' Ryan mouthed at her. She nodded, a smile curving her lips. It was impossible to feel anything else right then. She felt exposed in the best kind of way. Free of everything she'd left behind on the wharf. It was just the four of them and the water, and right then nothing else mattered.

No wonder he loved the sense of freedom he got from being on the open bay. It was as if anything was possible. She felt the sudden desire for them to keep sailing until they reached the horizon line, and to disappear from sight. To reach the ocean and keep on going, until they sailed into some foreign land.

'How old were you when you learned to sail?' she shouted, her words half-swallowed by the hissing wind.

'I can't remember. My grandpa started to take me out pretty much as soon as I could walk. I kind of grew up knowing how to sail just by watching him, the way other kids grow up knowing how to sing or dance. Of all the things I left behind when I moved away, I think I missed this old gal the most.' He tapped his hand against the wheel.

'You look like a man in love,' she teased.

'You can't help but fall in love with Maisie,' he said. 'She

79

has this irresistible lure. You watch out, you'll be falling at her feet before too long.'

He'd pulled his sunglasses over his head, trying to keep his hair from blowing in his face. Even with the distance between them, she could see the sun sparkling in his eyes.

'She's very seductive,' Juliet agreed. 'It's like she's making all these promises. Whispering that she can take you on adventures and journeys you'll never believe. It's hypnotic.'

Ryan laughed. 'She's a siren all right. She entranced my grandpa and then turned her magic on me.' He inclined his head at Charlie and Poppy, who were talking excitedly, their hands gripping the rail the way Ryan had shown them. 'I think he might be falling for her, too.'

'It would be hard not to,' Juliet said. 'Hard not to fall for the beauty of this bay, either. Do you know I've lived here for six years, and the only time I've been out on a boat has been in the evening.'

'What kind of boat?'

'The kind of boat that you have to dress up for. Full of tuxedos and shiny dresses. Where deals are done below decks, and the surroundings are only secondary.'

'That's no way to experience this bay.'

She caught his eye. He was staring at her with a mixture of interest and pity.

'I can see that now.'

She was starting to see a lot of things differently since she'd left Thomas.

It was beginning to look breathtakingly beautiful.

'You can hop down.' Ryan climbed out of the dingy and into the shallow water, pulling the small boat to the shore. He held his hands out for Poppy, and Juliet helped her climb to standing in the still-rocky boat, lifting her daughter up and passing her to Ryan. The two of them swished their way through the water, their trousers rolled up, laughing as the spray splashed up at them.

When both Poppy and Charlie were safely on shore, Ryan turned back to Juliet. She was wearing a pair of jeans – rolled up to reveal her slim ankles and bare feet, her shoes tied together and looped over her shoulder. The light shirt she was wearing was unbuttoned, blowing in the breeze, revealing the thin T-shirt beneath. Every curve of her body was visible, slim and lithe. She was breathtaking.

'You need some help, London?' he asked, trying – and failing – to keep his voice light. Instead it came out rough, as though it was being dragged out of his throat. He didn't wait for her to answer, stepping forward and wrapping his hands around her tiny waist. The feel of her warmth against his palms made his whole body tingle in a way he hadn't felt in years.

He watched her swallow, the tight skin of her throat bobbing up and down. Then she rested her hands on his shoulders, bracing herself against him as he lifted her up. She felt light as air. For a moment he wanted to pull her against him, feel her legs wrapping around his waist. The urge was almost too overwhelming, making him forget where he was, what he was doing, who he was with.

'There you go,' he said softly, gently releasing her into the water. Her hands still stayed on his shoulders for a moment, soft and warm. They were an arm's length from each other, and it seemed too far. 'Let's go join the kids,' he suggested. 'It's cold in here. I packed a blanket as well as the food.'

They spent the morning exploring the tiny island, helping

81

the children sort through the pebbles, looking for the perfect stone. Ryan told them the stories his grandfather had told him, about the pirates who had hidden their loot in the caves here, stealing from the English ships and selling the black market goods to the desperate colonials who'd made their home on this wild coast. He kept an eye on Juliet as he spoke, claiming London had it coming after all the taxes they'd put on the food they'd exported.

She'd stuck out her tongue in response, making him laugh out loud.

Later, when their stomachs began to rumble after an hour of playing in the sand and pebbles, he pulled out the food; thick sandwiches full of ham and cheese, with bags of chopped fruit and trail mix for dessert. Ryan trained his camera on the ragtag group, watching the three of them laughing and talking through the glass of his lens. He'd taken photographs of the kids, of their pebbles, of the way they laughed so abandoned and free. And then he'd turned his viewfinder onto Juliet herself, catching her completely unawares as he took close-ups of the freckles that trailed across the bridge of her nose. He was fascinated by the way the soft skin behind her knee folded together as she crouched in front of the picnic blanket.

He wasn't going to develop them – not these intimate shots – but there was so much beauty in her form that he couldn't help wanting to frame it.

As if she could feel the heat of the lens as he trained it on her, she slowly turned, a small smile playing on her lips. Though the breeze was light, it still managed to lift the tendrils that framed her face, until the strands were dancing against her skin in a rhythm of their own.

'Are you taking pictures of me?' she asked.

'No.'

'Liar. Let me see.' She stood up and cleared the space between them, reaching for the camera he had slung around his neck.

'It's an SLR, there's nothing to see.'

'You don't take digital photographs?' she questioned.

'I do when I'm working,' he said, still holding tightly to the hard plastic case of his camera, even though she wasn't reaching for it any more. 'But when I'm taking photos for pleasure, I still like to use this old thing. I like being able to develop the film, to watch it come to life. There's something amazing about the way the image slowly shows itself on the paper.'

'That sounds fascinating. I'd love to see how it works.'

She was smiling again, and he decided he liked that more than he could say. In the weeks since he'd met her – on that embarrassing day at the school – she hadn't smiled a whole lot. Maybe that's why earning a curve of her lips felt like he'd hit the jackpot.

Maybe that's why he'd felt the need to capture it on camera, too.

'I'll show you some time,' he said, making a mental note to get rid of the more embarrassing frames. 'But in the meantime, I need to get you back to the wharf. I made a promise I wouldn't interfere with your job, and I plan to keep it.'

'Is it that time already?' She looked almost disappointed. 'I didn't realise it was getting so late.'

He could hear regret in her tone, and he liked it very much. Liked the thought that she was having a good time with him. She was like a flower slowly unfurling from a closed-up bud, and it was going to be beautiful when she finally bloomed.

And if he was being really honest, he wanted to be there when she did.

9

For my part, I may speak it to my shame,
I have a truant been to chivalry;
And so I hear he doth account me too

– Henry IV Part 1

'I hear you took Poppy out on a boat last Saturday. I don't remember you asking me about it first,' Thomas said. He was standing at the door, his arms folded across his chest. His tailored jacket was tight across his shoulders. Had he put a little weight on? Strange how she still noticed things like that.

'We just went out for a couple of hours. She had a lovely time.'

'With Ryan Sutherland, or so they say.'

There was an edge to his voice she didn't quite understand. She looked up at him, taking in his face. His cheeks were flushed, his eyes narrow.

Was he jealous? Surely he couldn't be. He had Nicole, after all. If anybody was entitled to be jealous it was Juliet.

And yet she didn't feel jealous. Not at all.

'That's right,' she said, trying to keep her voice light. She really didn't want every meeting to end in an argument. 'He's moved in next door.'

A look of surprise. Aha! So maybe he didn't know everything.

Thomas glanced back over his shoulder, frowning as he took in the house to the left of her bungalow. 'He lives there?' he asked abruptly. 'Why didn't you tell me?'

'I didn't think anything of it,' she said. Though her voice was calm, her heart was starting to pound. 'What does it matter anyway?'

'Anything to do with our daughter is a concern to me. And I don't like the thought of her being around Ryan Sutherland, not one little bit. The man's little more than a drifter. Did you know he left his family behind without a word to go travelling, yet still expected them to keep the business going? They even pay him dividends every year though he does nothing to deserve them.'

'Isn't that how business works? Shareholders receive dividends. It happens the world over.'

'He's always been unreliable. Even at school he let people down.' His eyes narrowed, as though his thoughts were drifting back twenty years. 'I don't like you spending time with him.'

'But you don't get to decide who I spend time with any more. We're separated, remember?'

Thomas winced. 'But not divorced. We're still married.'

She felt her chest tighten. She could remember the day she and Poppy had left to move into the bungalow. Thomas had asked her to stay, to try again. But the pain of his betrayal had been too much to bear.

'Maybe you should move back onto the estate,' Thomas said, catching her eye. 'We could renovate one of the old cottages for you and Poppy.'

'I don't think—'

He reached out, touching her arm with the tip of his fingers. 'Just hear me out. I know what I did was terrible. And I know I broke your heart. But if you came back – even if we didn't live together – it would be so much better for all of us.'

He looked so earnest, it took her by surprise. 'Not for me. We're happy here,' she told him. 'And anyway, what would Nicole say if we moved back?'

'I don't know. I haven't asked her.'

She took a step back, folding her arms across her chest. 'Well before you make an offer like that, maybe you should. I remember what it's like having your life turned upside down without being consulted.' And yes, Nicole had been involved too, but that didn't mean that it was her fault. It was Thomas who'd been the married one.

Thomas raked his hand through his hair. 'I messed up, I know I did. And I'm paying for it, too. You think I like this? Only seeing my daughter at the weekends? Finding out that you've been spending time with other men from gossips at the club?'

What the hell did he think was going to happen when he started his affair with Nicole? This conversation was going nowhere, the way all their conversations seemed to go. 'I need to go,' she said, stepping back inside the house. 'I have to cook dinner.'

'I just wanted to ask you something.' Thomas lingered on the porch.

'What?'

'Can you have Poppy ready on Friday? We're going away for the weekend.'

'You are?'

'It's Nicole's birthday. We're going to the beach house for

the weekend. The Fratellis are going, and so are the Simons, in fact most of our friends will be there. Poppy will enjoy it, I'm sure.'

Of course she would. Poppy loved the beach, and she loved the huge, wooden house that had been in the Marshalls' hands for generations. They'd spent most of their summers there before ... before ...

Before their whole world had been shaken inside out.

Every time a memory hit, Juliet's heart broke a little more for her child. It was her daughter who was paying the price. She'd had so much stolen from her already, and she didn't even know it. Juliet was damned if she was going to let her child lose any more. Which was why she was going to keep things civil, even if it killed her.

'I'll have her ready,' she said quietly. 'What time will you be picking her up?'

'I'll pick her up from school. Can you send her suitcase in with her?'

'Of course.' Thomas had been an awful husband, but he was a good father, and she was grateful for that. Poppy was surrounded by love on all sides. She'd never feel lost or alone, the way Juliet had after her mother died. She'd never have to be the one singled out because her father was perpetually late.

Thomas nodded, and walked back to his car. She watched him from the doorway, and felt a sense of bewilderment at how fast her life had changed. Once upon a time she'd been so in love with Thomas Marshall it made her heart hurt. But with every day that passed the pain was dissipating, right along with the love.

One day he'd just be somebody she used to know.

*

An hour later, she was walking down through her back yard and to the woods beyond, clutching a bag full of soda cans and home-made cookies. Poppy was spending the day with Charlie and Ryan as they worked on a tree house, and Juliet was thankful she'd not seen the discussion between her and Thomas back at the house.

She heard them before she could see them. Loud shouts and giggles echoing through the forest, accompanied by the banging of a hammer, pushing nails into thick planks of wood. When she rounded the corner, the two children were standing at the bottom of the huge oak, watching as Ryan was half-suspended about ten feet up, his muscles flexing as he pulled the hammer back then launched it forward.

She'd never met a man who lived so much in the moment. He made decisions and went with them, never worrying about where he was going or where he came from. Look at the tree house – only a week ago Charlie was telling Poppy about the place they'd lived in when they stayed in the rainforest of Costa Rica, and the next minute Ryan was downloading plans for a tree house of their own.

He was so different from Thomas, even though they were from similar families, and brought up in the same town. She found it stupidly attractive.

'I brought some snacks,' she called out as she walked into the clearing. Poppy and Charlie looked up. Their eyes widened when they saw her bag of goodies, and the two of them ran over, their tiny hands already searching through the bag for their favourites.

It took Ryan a moment longer to realise she was there, but when he did, a big grin formed across his face. His obvious pleasure in seeing her warmed her from the inside. She was getting used to the way her body responded whenever she was around him, feeling like the giggly teenager she'd never been.

'You brought me food, London?' he called down. 'Where have you been all my life? You're a godsend.'

'Always with the compliments,' she said, grinning. 'You need to stop doing that. I'll get a big head.' She grabbed a can of Coke, still ice cold from the refrigerator, and threw it across to him. He caught it easily, pulling the key, then lifted it to his lips. He closed his eyes, taking a long mouthful of drink. As soon as he swallowed it down, he sighed.

'Man that's good. Thanks for bringing the snacks.'

She shrugged. 'Think of it as payment for looking after those two.'

They both turned to look at the children. They were arguing furiously over a packet of chips, neither of them willing to give in.

'They've been bickering all afternoon,' he told her. 'They're like an old married couple. I keep having to stop working on the tree house so I can silently laugh at them.'

'What have they been doing?' She was intrigued. Charlie and Poppy's relationship seemed more like siblings than friends. They'd grown close so very quickly. Though they were fiercely protective of each other, they never seemed to agree on anything.

'Poppy was talking about the kinds of flowers we should pick to put in the house.'

'She was?' Why did that surprise her? Poppy was constantly around flowers in the shop, after all.

'Yeah, and Charlie wasn't having any of it.'

'That's because it's *my* tree house,' Charlie piped up. 'And I don't want flowers in it.'

90

'But flowers will make it pretty,' Poppy said, frowning. Juliet sensed this was simply a rehash of their earlier row.

'I don't want it pretty. I want it manly. Flowers are for girls.'

'They're so not.'

'Yes they are. Boys don't do flowers.'

'Some boys do,' Ryan said, catching Juliet's eye. 'Some boys like flowers very much.' He leaned down to pick up a purple aster, from the cluster growing around the tree. Winking at Juliet, he slid it behind his ear. 'See?'

Even with that flower in his ear he looked ridiculously attractive. Poppy laughed and picked another flower. 'You want one, Charlie?' she asked him.

Torn, Charlie looked from Poppy to his father. 'I ... I don't know.'

'Did you know that in the old days people thought asters could ward off evil snakes?' Juliet asked him.

Charlie turned to her, leaning his head to the side. 'Really?'

'Yep. And the purple ones are symbols for wisdom. So they're pretty cool if you think about it.'

Licking his lips, Charlie turned to Poppy. 'I guess you can put it in my hair ... if you have to.' He stood still as Poppy slid the aster behind his ear. When it was firmly in place, she tugged hard at his earlobe and stuck out her tongue, before running away from him. Charlie chased her, the two of them weaving in and out of the tree as they giggled loudly.

Juliet looked at Ryan. He was staring right back at her. For a moment she held his gaze, the heat of his stare searing at the air surrounding them. This was getting crazy. It seemed as though every time she looked at him her breath got caught in her throat.

She needed to get over herself fast. If Thomas was already

getting angry about her being seen around the wharf with Ryan, God only knew what he'd think if he could read her mind.

Poppy and Charlie were still dodging in and out of trees, paying their parents no attention as they shouted and laughed at each other, Poppy's attempts at stealing Charlie's flower failing each time she got close. They were about a hundred yards away – audible, but not visible – when he looked at Juliet, and caught her staring right back at him.

She was beautiful. Her features were delicate and yet defined, her blue eyes wide and sparkling. And her smile – oh, her smile – it was like the sun bursting out through a thick layer of cloud.

She took a step towards him, that smile still illuminating her face. 'That flower really does suit you,' she said, reaching to touch it. 'Purple is definitely your colour.'

There was a teasing tone in her voice that made his heart race. Letting his mouth curl up into a lazy grin, he reached up and grabbed her hand where it was touching the flower, sliding his fingers between hers.

'I'm not afraid of showing my feminine side,' he told her, even though every thought rushing through his brain felt masculine as hell. He brought her hand to his face, breathing her in, then brushed his lips lightly against her wrist.

Her breath hitched. She was still staring up at him, her eyes framed by thick lashes that swept down every time she blinked. He kissed her wrist again, sliding his lips along her delicate skin, and the sensation made every cell in his body explode with desire.

For a second he could see his desire reflected in her own expression. Then without warning she pulled her hand away, taking a step back from him. She shook her head and frowned, before turning to call for her daughter.

'Poppy, we need to go.' Her voice was tight. The teasing from only a few moments ago had disappeared completely.

'I'm sorry.' Ryan looked at her, seeking her eyes, but her gaze was still firmly stuck on her daughter. 'I was out of line. I shouldn't have—'

'It's fine,' Juliet said quickly. 'I just need to get back to the house. There's a lot to do.'

He wanted to reach out and take her hand. To ask her what she was thinking, because all he could see was a blank expression. He wanted to kick himself, too. He wasn't the kind of guy who kissed a woman against her wishes. Wasn't the kind of guy who did anything that wasn't mutually desired.

'Do we have to go, Mommy?' Poppy said when she ran up to them, her voice breathless from chasing Charlie around. 'Can't I stay here? We're having fun. And Charlie said I can go to his for tea.'

'No.' Juliet's reply was vehement. 'We need to go home now.'

When she finally looked at Ryan, her expression was calm, yet somehow as closed as it could be. 'Thank you for taking care of her today.'

'You're welcome.'

Putting her arm around Poppy, she turned and they started to walk through the trees up to the clearing beyond, which led to the backyard of their houses. Ryan looked down to see Charlie beside him, frowning as he stared at their retreating backs.

He looked as stunned as Ryan at their abrupt departure. And he couldn't blame him one little bit.

*

As they trudged through the trees, their feet squelching against the freshly fallen leaves, Poppy kept up a constant stream of chatter about the tree house, and her plans for it.

'Do you think we can sleep in the tree house?' Poppy said. 'We could take our sleeping bags up there and have a campfire.'

'Maybe. But it's probably going to be too cold at night now.'

'Oh poop. We'll have to wait until summer. Maybe we can do it then.'

Juliet opened her mouth to tell her daughter that Ryan and Charlie would be gone by next summer, but then she shut it again. It wasn't her story to tell. She didn't even know if Charlie was aware of Ryan's plans to move to New York, and she certainly didn't want to be the one to spill the beans.

When they emerged from the woods and into the clearing, her heart was still pounding in her chest, the same way it had been since Ryan had kissed her arm. Her mind was a mess, too, full of thoughts and questions that were almost impossible to answer.

From the look on his face as she left, Ryan must have thought she didn't like the way he'd touched her. The truth was, she'd liked it too much. Just a simple brush of his lips against her skin had been enough to set her on fire, making her body feel sensations she hadn't experienced in a long time.

Maybe she'd never experienced them. Not like that.

She took a deep breath in as they came in sight of the bungalow, but her lungs refused to play ball. Poppy ran ahead, leaving Juliet walking alone, and the thoughts came crashing down on her again.

It would be so easy to fall for somebody like Ryan Sutherland. He was funny, strong, and as handsome as they came. But there was something else, too – a vulnerability that touched her, a softness inside that contrasted greatly against his hard exterior.

Yes, it would be easy to fall for him. But there was no way she could let herself. Not after everything she'd been through. If her marriage to Thomas had taught her anything, it was that she threw herself into love too quickly, and paid the price later. This time, she needed to guard her heart.

'Can we go to the shop tomorrow?' Poppy said, dancing on the step next to the back door. 'I want to pick out some flowers for the tree house. Cool ones. Like the purple asters that scare snakes away.'

Juliet smiled. 'Of course we can.' Catching up with her daughter, she reached out and ruffled Poppy's hair. This was what it was all about. She was a mother and a business owner, not a teenager who couldn't control her emotions.

Ryan would be here for a few months, and then he'd be gone. They were short-term neighbours and nothing more. She could cope with that, couldn't she?

10

He capers, he dances, he has eyes of youth

– The Merry Wives of Windsor

'Lily, can you pass me the asters?' Juliet put her hand out to Lily, the other keeping the bouquet together.

'The asters?' Lily sounded confused. 'We're not using asters.'

'I meant the alliums.' Juliet frowned. 'Did I say asters? This damn wedding is driving me crazy.'

She had asters on the brain, thank you, Ryan. Or rather, she had Ryan on the brain. She hadn't been able to think about much else, after the way he'd kissed her wrist last weekend. Every time the memory took over her mind she found herself blushing. Feeling his soft lips on her skin had been such a shock, and yet every time she thought about it she could remember the way it had sent a shot of pleasure through her.

It was so damn confusing.

'Weddings really don't bring out the best in people, do they?' Lily mused, passing the bucket of alliums across the counter to where Juliet was standing. 'If it's not the bride having a meltdown, it's her mom being overly demanding. And then there's the mothers-in-law . . . ' She trailed off, grimacing. 'Why is it the guys have it so easy? They just have to turn up and pin a flower to their lapel. They let the women do all the work.'

Juliet grinned, her eyes meeting Lily's. 'That's marriage for you.'

'Ugh. Don't say that. You're such a cynic.'

'I just got burned a little, that's all.' Juliet wrapped twine around the stiff stems of the bouquet, cutting them off with her craft knife. 'Anyway, would you want the guy to choose the flowers? It's the best part, isn't it?'

'Yeah, guys and flowers, I guess they don't match.' Lily took the bouquet from Juliet and carefully slid it into a box.

Sometimes they did. Sometimes guys and flowers went together really well. Juliet couldn't help but think of Ryan with that purple aster behind his ear. The way he'd smiled at her, the skin around his eyes crinkling up. The thought of it made her chest ache.

Confusing didn't begin to cover it. Her feelings were all over the place. Thank God for this wedding – it had given her the perfect excuse to work late all week, and ask Melanie Drewer to help her with Poppy. It also helped her to avoid seeing the guy next door.

It was better that way. She didn't need to open herself up to any more hurt, not after everything she and Poppy had been through. Best to keep away for a while, until things had settled down.

And she'd forgotten just how good his mouth had felt on her wrist.

'Okay, that's the last one, right? Let me just check we have everything before we head over to the venue.' They had two hours to get everything ready before the bride was due to arrive. Between her and Lily they had to decorate the seats for the ceremony, and then make sure all the table displays were set up for the wedding dinner. It was so important to make sure everything was perfect.

The bride was depending on her. And so was the shop's reputation.

'Everything's here. I've checked it twice.' Lily looked up from the clipboard, running her finger down the printed order. 'And Natalie's arrived to cover the shop while we're gone.'

'All right then, let's do this thing.' Juliet grabbed the van keys from the hook beneath the counter. 'Time to make somebody's special day a perfect one.'

Juliet had been avoiding him all week, or at least that was how it felt. Ryan had found himself missing her at the strangest moments. He told himself it was because he didn't have many friends. Or maybe it was the fact that Charlie was at yet another sleepover, leaving Ryan with way too much headspace to fill.

And now it was Saturday, and there was still no sign of her. He lifted his coffee cup to his lips, looking over at her bungalow as he swallowed a mouthful. The few times he'd seen her from a distance, she'd been in a rush, too busy to wave, and too busy for him to disturb her.

Yeah, she was definitely avoiding him. Who could blame her?

He still wanted to kick himself for kissing her wrist in the woods. What had he been thinking? Maybe the problem was he hadn't been thinking at all. He might've lost the only friend he'd made since he returned to Shaw Haven, and it hurt. Putting his coffee mug back on the low table in front of him, he leaned his head back and took a deep breath of fresh air. How could he make this better? He couldn't live next door to her and not talk to her. The thought of it made his chest contract.

That's when he remembered the photo – a candid he'd taken of Charlie and Poppy a few days earlier. In it, the two of them were staring at a picture book they were reading together, their faces crumpled in concentration. Walking into the house, he grabbed it from his dark room, turning it over and uncapping a pen.

London,
   I'm not talented enough to make you a bouquet of flowers. But we both made two beautiful children, and I was lucky enough to capture them on camera.
   I'm sorry for overstepping the line. It won't happen again.
   Your friend,
   Ryan

She wasn't home – her car was gone from the driveway. And as he'd seen Thomas picking up Poppy yesterday from school, the only place he could imagine she could be on an overcast Saturday morning was at the flower shop. So he propped the photograph against her door and wandered back to the house, prepared to wait as long as it took until she made it home from work.

After lunch he grabbed his laptop and made his way back onto the deck. Placing his steaming mug of coffee on the table beside him, he decided to do a little paperwork. There were contracts to sign, banks to deal with. A few emails from his financial adviser about setting up the new business. And then there were the messages from his lawyer, asking him if he really wanted to reject his father's offer for his shares in the family business. He sorted through them quickly, letting them distract him from the envelope across the yard.

Just before four he heard the crunch of rubber against gravel, as Juliet pulled her car onto the makeshift driveway beside her bungalow. He watched as she climbed out, carrying her usual array of flowers she hadn't managed to sell in the shop. Her boots clipped her stone steps as she wearily made her way up to her front door. He wondered if it was the empty house that made her sad, or something else entirely.

She paused when she saw the photograph, a small smile forming on her lips as she read the words he'd written on the reverse. Then she turned the photo back again, admiring the picture he'd developed for her, rolling her bottom lip between her teeth as she took it in.

She glanced over her shoulder, seeing him staring straight at her, and he was struck yet again by how beautiful she was.

'Ryan?' She propped her flowers against the door. Still holding onto the photograph, she walked down the steps, and made her way across the yard towards him. 'This is a beautiful picture.'

'I hoped you'd like it.' He was still sitting down. After last week's fiasco, he was determined not to crowd her.

She'd reached the bottom of his porch. Her hand curled around the rail, but she came no further up. 'I like it very much.' She offered him a tentative smile, and he felt as if he could breathe again. 'Thank you for thinking of me.'

'It was the only way I could think of for saying sorry,' he admitted. 'I shouldn't have touched you like that.'

She looked up at him. The expression on her face told him

she knew exactly what he was talking about. 'It's okay.' Her chest lifted as she took a deep breath in.

'No, it wasn't. I hate that I touched you when you didn't want me to. I'm not the kind of man who crosses boundaries. I shouldn't have done it.'

Her eyes softened. She was still standing on the bottom step of his deck, her face inclined towards his. 'I know you're not that man. I honestly never thought you were. I was just surprised, that was all. And my life's such a mess at the moment. With the divorce from Thomas, and trying to get my business running, everything's so up in the air. I wasn't expecting any more complications.'

Ouch. 'I don't want to make your life any tougher than it already is.'

Without him asking, she walked up the steps and sat down next to him on the old couch. He felt the warmth of her arm against his.

'I don't think you could make it any worse,' she said, leaning back on the cushions. 'I keep telling myself that this time next year, everything will be better. I'll be divorced, the business will be established. And I'll be used to not seeing my daughter every other weekend. This is all just a transition, right?'

Her hand was resting lightly on her leg, only inches away from his. He resisted the urge to slide his fingers between hers, even if it was only a sign of friendship.

'Is Poppy with Thomas this weekend?' He hadn't seen the little girl since school the previous day.

She nodded. 'Yeah. They've gone to the family beach house. We used to spend a lot of time there when Poppy was smaller.'

'That must be tough.'

Slowly, she nodded her head. 'The house feels empty every time she leaves, and it's all a reminder of what I can't give her any more. A family, security. The peace of knowing where she's from.'

Ryan shifted again. 'You think you can't give her those things? Don't you know what a good mother you are?'

'I try my best,' she said. 'But I can't give her the thing I always wanted for her. My family was torn apart when I was still a kid. We were left with only one parent who never really showed any of us he loved us. And though I had my sisters, all I really longed for was the perfect family. When we had Poppy I thought I had my chance to do things right this time.'

'There's no such thing as perfect, London.' He kept his body still, determined to maintain the space between them. 'I was brought up in a nuclear family. I watched my father belittle my mother every day, or so it seemed. I watched her slowly disappear in front of me. And I couldn't wait to leave that family behind, because no matter how perfect it might have looked from the outside, it was killing me. So don't go around looking at all those married couples with two point four kids, or whatever the hell it is, and think everything's amazing behind closed doors. Because it's usually anything but.'

Juliet opened her mouth to ask him more, but the clouds behind his eyes stole the words from her mouth.

'It can't all be a lie can it?' she questioned. 'There must still be some good people out there somewhere.'

'Of course there are. I'm looking at one of them.' The clouds cleared a little, but there was still a tinge of sadness to his expression.

'I think you'd find a lot of people around here who disagree.'

'Ignore them. I don't care what your ex thinks, or what anybody else has to say. I know you're a good person, and so do Poppy and Charlie. You should, too. Nobody else is important.'

'You're such a good liar.' She gave him a conspiratorial smile. The easiness between them had returned, and it felt as if a weight had lifted from her shoulders. She'd missed seeing him in the past week, even if she'd been deliberately avoiding him. She'd missed his friendly banter and his eye-crinkling smiles. And now she was sitting next to him again, it felt as though she could breathe without it hurting.

'You're so typically English. You can't take a compliment to save your life.'

'And you're so all-American I bet you dreamed of being the quarterback at school.'

His eyes narrowed. 'I was running back, for your information. And my parents would argue I'm very un-American. I've spent most of the last fourteen years out of the country. I can imagine what they'd say if they knew I'd danced the tango until dawn in a square in Buenos Aires.' He laughed. 'Or put a flower behind my ear for that matter.'

'You danced until dawn?' She lifted an eyebrow. She couldn't imagine him throwing himself into a tango. 'Really?'

'Do you find that hard to believe?'

She shrugged, trying to hide her incredulity. 'I don't know. You just don't seem like the dancing type.'

'Don't be fooled by the jock exterior, babe, when I'm on a dance floor these hips don't lie.'

'A jock who quotes Shakira?'

'I dance like her as well.'

She burst out laughing. 'Oh stop it. You forget, I've been married to a jock. He couldn't throw any moves to save his life.'

Ryan leaned forward, until his face was inches from hers. 'Just because I like sports doesn't mean I don't like dancing. I can like more than one thing, London.' His voice softened when he said her name.

'Seeing is believing,' she said, pointing at the open deck in front of them. 'Dance for me now.'

'What am I, a dancing poodle? No way.'

She ran the tip of her thumb along her chin, unable to hide her grin. 'Oh come on. I thought we were supposed to be friends. You can't go bragging about your prowess and then not prove it. What am I supposed to think?'

'I don't have any music. Plus I can't dance alone. Haven't you heard it takes two to tango?' He tipped his head to the side, grinning right back at her.

'Well there goes my Saturday entertainment. I guess I'll just go back to my accounts.' She sighed. 'It's a hard life.'

His eyebrows dipped as he looked at her, as though he was thinking deeply. His frown deepened.

'Are you okay?' she asked him.

'Yeah. I just had an idea. But it's probably stupid.'

'You can't say something like that and then go silent. Now I'm all intrigued.'

He laughed, and the frown disappeared. 'It isn't that exciting.'

'You know how to tease don't you? Now you know I'm not going to leave without hearing your idea, no matter how stupid it is.' She shook her head. 'Come on, out with it.'

'Okay, but feel free to say no if you want to.'

She didn't say anything. Just looked at him expectantly.

'I heard about this place in town,' he said, lifting his shoulders in what looked like an easy shrug. 'It's called the Iguana

Lounge, or something terrible like that. One of those Latin clubs where you can dance until dawn.' His smile was tentative, as if he was afraid she was going to run away again. 'Poppy's away, and Charlie's at a sleepover. We could go dancing. As friends, of course.'

'You want to go dancing?' she echoed. 'With me?' A ripple of excitement went through her. When was the last time she danced? A long time ago, unless you counted those stilted waltzes with Thomas when they went out for expensive dinners. He'd never really liked dancing – he preferred sitting and talking.

'It was just a thought. We don't have to.'

'No, I want to.' She nodded, catching his eye. She wasn't going to listen to those voices in her head telling her what a bad idea it was. They were friends, she could handle it. 'It sounds like fun.'

This time his grin was broad, and it matched her own. 'Okay then, Ginger Rogers, dancing it is. The Iguana Lounge won't know what's hit it.'

11

When you do dance, I wish you a wave o' the sea,
That you might ever do nothing but that

– The Winter's Tale

'We're here.' Ryan turned off the ignition and climbed out of his truck, walking around to the passenger side to help Juliet down. It was one of those perfect autumn evenings. The sun had disappeared beneath the horizon, leaving only the faintest of red staining the deepening blue sky. And though the temperature had dropped, the evening still held a hint of the summer's warmth, wrapping around them as they made their way across the parking lot.

'It's not what I expected,' Juliet said, looking across the lot to the low building that housed the Iguana Lounge. From the outside it could have been anywhere. It was just grey concrete blocks and a slate roof. She didn't sound disappointed, though. More curious than anything. She walked slightly ahead of him, her long red hair tumbling down past her shoulders.

Her dress was perfect for dancing, tight on the bodice, flowing from the waist, with a halter neck that bared her toned upper back.

'What were you expecting?'

'I don't know.' She shrugged, still smiling. 'My sister went to a salsa club in Miami once. She said it was full of palm trees and coloured lights, and people sitting outside.'

'I guess Maryland's a bit different to Miami.'

'You can say that again. I can't believe how diverse all the states are. When I talk to my sister Kitty – she's in LA – it feels as though we live in two different countries.'

'What does your sister do?' he asked her. He hadn't heard her speak about her family before. He'd assumed they were all living in London.

'Kitty? She's a film producer. She's not my only sister, though. I have two more.'

'There are four of you? Do you have any brothers?'

She shook her head. 'No. Unfortunately for my dad. He was always surrounded by women.'

'What a hardship.' He winked at her, and she laughed. He liked that a lot.

'And you're an only child, right?' she asked him.

'Yep. Just me.' But he really didn't want to talk about that. 'What do your other sisters do?'

They'd reached the entrance. There was a glass booth inside the door. Ryan slid the entrance fee across, and the man passed him two wristbands. 'First drink is free. After that you have to pay. If you want tuition, speak to Louisa behind the bar. The professionals are on now. Public dancing starts at nine.'

Ryan took the wristbands, fastening his around his right arm. He went to pass the second one to Juliet, but she held her arm out, instead. He circled the yellow plastic around her wrist, trying not to think about the way her skin had felt that day he'd kissed it.

They were friends. He could do this.

'Lucy's my eldest sister,' Juliet said, carrying on their conversation from outside the club. 'She's a lawyer. And then Cesca is the next one. She writes plays, but she's also writing a screenplay at the moment. She's just got engaged to her movie-star boyfriend.'

'A movie star?' Ryan tried not to look amused. 'Have I heard of him?'

'You might have. His name's Sam Carlton, he's in this franchise called *Summer Breeze*. I don't think it's really aimed at your demographic, though, unless you're into screaming whenever he comes on screen.'

'I'm guessing it's not a horror franchise.' He raised his eyebrows up.

Juliet grinned. 'Not unless you've got a phobia about surfing. Or seeing your future brother-in-law half-naked in every scene, which, by the way, I think I'm developing. Anyway, you can see for yourself soon. Sam has some meetings in Washington, so they're going to come over for a visit while they're this side of the country.'

At the end of the hallway, there were black lacquered double doors that led into the club itself. Ryan reached out, placing his hand on the handle, feeling the rhythm of the bass vibrate against the metal.

'You ready, London?' he asked, looking over at her.

She smiled, waiting for him to push it open. 'As ready as I'll ever be.'

'Then let's go dance.'

The club might have looked nondescript from the outside, but as soon as they walked in through the black lacquer doors, the atmosphere was palpable. The music was loud, the bass pumping through speakers on the wall, and there was already a crowd of people inside. Some were leaning on the long bar that ran the length of the room, sipping multi-coloured cocktails stuffed with fruits. Others had already hit the dance floor. She watched as they shimmied and spun around the room, moving apart and then back together in synchronised moves.

It was fast, fun and dynamic.

'Can you dance like that?' she asked Ryan.

'Kind of. That's the salsa. It's full of energy. It's a little bit more extroverted than the tango. All about showing off and looking the best.' He gestured towards the bar. 'Shall we get our free drinks? I've got a feeling we might need them.'

She nodded, still interested in his description. She could waltz with the best of them, but she'd never danced Latin. 'So what's the tango about?'

'It's more intimate. You hold your partner close, you feel the music. It's a dance of seduction.'

'Oh.' She felt herself heat up. 'Will we dance the tango tonight?'

He laughed. 'No need to look so alarmed. It's all salsa until midnight. They play the tango music after that. But we don't have to stay if you don't want to.'

'What can I get you?' the barman asked. 'First drink is on the house.'

'What would you like?' Ryan turned to ask her.

She opened her mouth to ask for a glass of wine, but then hesitated. 'Um, what are those?' she asked, pointing over at the fruit-filled cocktails.

'Mango mojitos. They're good.'

'I'll have one of those then.'

'And I'll have a water.' Ryan raised his eyebrows at her. 'The perks of driving.'

'At least you'll dance with a clear head,' Juliet said.

They took their drinks over to a table in the corner, both sliding into the booth on the same side so they could look out at the dance floor. She sipped at her cocktail – sweet, yet remarkably delicious – and watched the professionals as they moved across the boards.

'I'm not sure it's a good idea to put the best dancers on first,' Juliet said, taking another sip of her drink. 'Nobody can follow that without making themselves look like an idiot.'

Ryan laughed. 'The aim is to show us all how to do it. Don't worry, once they leave the dance floor, we'll all be stumbling around.'

'Not you,' she teased. 'You're almost a professional too, right? Mr "Dance in Buenos Aires until Dawn".'

He shook his head. 'You're never going to let me live that down are you?'

'Those hips don't lie.' She winked at him. She felt so light in here, so at ease with herself. She wasn't sure if it was the club or Ryan having that effect on her.

He really was attractive. Wearing a pair of dark blue trousers and a white shirt, open at the collar, he was getting a lot of looks from women both on the dance floor and off. It was all she could do not to put a proprietary hand on his arm and warn them all off.

At nine, the professionals cleared the dance floor, and it was empty for a moment, as people hesitated to step on board. Juliet finished the last of her cocktail – the alcohol already making her feel mellow – and watched as the first tentative dancers started to move to the beat. In the corner, one of the professionals was coaching a couple – a paid lesson, Juliet guessed, remembering what the man at the ticket booth had said.

'Do you want a lesson?' Ryan asked. He must have followed her stare.

'No. I reckon I can pick it up myself. With you teaching me.'

'Okay then.' He stood up. 'Shall we dance?' He offered her his hand. Sliding out of the booth, she took it, and let him lead her to the dance floor. When they reached it, he took her other hand too, and took a step back, leaving a gap between them.

'So what do I do?' she asked him, feeling the warmth of his hands against hers. She had to shout for him to hear her over the beat.

'Let's start with an easy step,' he replied, his voice as loud as hers. 'If you can do the waltz, you can do this.' He looked down at their feet. 'Think of it as walking. Except when I walk forward, you go back and vice versa. On the first beat I'll step forward, on the second I'll rock back, on the third I'll bring my feet together and on the fourth I'll pause. Then we'll do it all over again but in the opposite direction.'

'Okay.' Juliet nodded, frowning with concentration. 'Forward, together, back. I can do that.'

'Let's go.' He slid one hand around her back, and stepped towards her, as she stepped back. Then they were back together and she was the one stepping forwards, rocking towards him as he rocked back.

A few more tries and she'd got the hang of it, able to move her feet in some kind of rhythm, matching the beat that echoed through the room. Ryan led her gently, his hips swaying as he stepped back and forth. Compared to him she was as stiff as a board.

'Okay, now let's try a turn.' He pulled his hand from her back, keeping his other clasped around hers, and lifted it up and over her head. Juliet tried to turn, stumbling over her shoe, almost falling to the floor before he caught her and brought her up.

'Oh my God, I'm an idiot.' She laughed, shaking her hair back behind her shoulders. 'I must be the only one here tripping over my own feet.'

'You're doing great. You're an easy teach. You pick it up fast.' He took her hand back in his. 'Let's try it again.' This time she managed to turn without falling over, ending back in position, facing him, before they moved forward and back again. Within ten minutes she'd mastered the turn, the cross-body lead and the chaîné. And Ryan was leading her around the dance floor, his hand firm against her shoulder as he moved her right and then left, his feet fast and rhythmic as he kept to the beat.

And they were dancing, really dancing, not just swaying this way and that. Instead she was being led forward and backwards, around and back again, her hair flowing out behind her and her skirt fanning out as she spun. With each song that came on she gained more confidence, grinning at Ryan as their bodies moved together.

She couldn't remember the last time she had this much fun. Or the last time she'd laughed so much. Every time she looked at Ryan he was smiling at her – enjoying at much as she was – letting the music take over and wash all their worries away.

They only stopped once – to grab a glass of water each – and then were back on the dance floor again. The time passed in a blink of an eye. Before they knew it, it was midnight and the salsa was over, and the dance floor was clearing once again.

'You ready to go home?' he asked her. He didn't sound that

enthusiastic about it. She wasn't either. In spite of the fact her muscles were aching and her body was glowing with sweat, she could have danced all night.

'Can we sit down for a minute?' she asked him. 'Just to catch my breath?'

'Sure. You want another drink?'

'Sounds good.'

'Water or mojito?'

She smiled wickedly at him, feeling like a rebel. 'A mojito, please.'

By the time he came back with the drinks the tango had started. The midnight changeover had seen a lot of people leave and there were a lot less couples on the dance floor. Juliet marvelled at how different this dance was to the salsa. The music was slower, the beat more deliberate, and the dancing was much more seductive. She watched the couple closest to them, swallowing as the man led his partner around, his hands firm yet sensual on her body, his chest touching hers.

She looked up at Ryan. 'Can you dance like that?' she asked him. She tried to imagine him holding a woman that way and moving her across the floor. A flame of jealousy licked at her.

'Yeah. I can dance the Argentine tango.' He took a mouthful of water. He sat down next to her, being careful to leave an inch between them. And yet she had the strangest urge to close the gap, to feel the warmth of his thigh against hers.

'Is it hard to learn?'

He shook his head. 'It's a bit harder than the salsa. Though they say that if you can walk you can tango. It all depends on who's leading I guess.'

She took another sip of her mojito. 'I don't know if I've got it in me to learn another dance. But it looks amazing.'

'You could try it once,' he suggested. 'The Argentine tango is based on improvisation, so you don't have to learn the footwork. You just follow where I lead.'

Pulling her lip between her teeth, she looked at him for a moment, then nodded, not taking her eyes off his. The sensible part of her told her to go home, to go to bed, to sleep off the alcohol. To end the night now, when everything was just fine and dandy.

But she didn't want to. It was as if another Juliet had woken up from a long slumber, and was stretching her arms and getting ready to play. She didn't want the night to end – not yet. She wanted one last dance. And she wanted to dance the tango with Ryan.

'Okay. Let's do it,' she said, her gaze still locked with his. 'Let's dance the tango.'

Dancing with Juliet felt like some kind of exquisite torture. It had been bad enough when they were dancing the salsa, but at least the gap between them had given him some breathing space. Now, as the slow, sensual beat of the music enveloped them, it felt like a labour of Hercules.

He took a deep breath in. How many times had he danced the tango? He could pretend he was back in Buenos Aires, dancing with one of the locals, enjoying themselves without worrying about anything else.

'Okay. We're gonna need to get a bit closer for this one,' he told her, wrapping his hand around hers. Instead of placing his hand beneath her shoulder blade, he slid it down to the small of her back, stepping towards her until their chests were touching.

She looked up at him through those vibrant eyes as he slowly began to move his hips to the beat. Then she moved hers too, her body still pressed against his, her lips falling open as she took a breath in.

He'd heard people call tango 'a vertical expression of horizontal desire', and right now nothing seemed more apt. He could feel her breasts pressing into him, could smell the sweet fruit on her breath, could hear the pounding of his heart as it tried to match the music.

Gritting his teeth together, he stepped forward, pushing with his hand until she mirrored his move. Then he was sliding her across the dance floor, his palm still pressed against the small of her back, the fingers of his other hand entwined with hers.

As they reached the centre of the dance floor he dipped her back, watching as her spine arched, and her hair cascaded down, exposing the delicate curve of her throat. When he lifted her up her eyes were wide, her flushed face matching his own excitement.

Christ, he wanted her. Wanted to kiss her like she'd never been kissed before. It was taking every sliver of self-control he had to stop himself from doing it.

As soon as the song finished, he let her go and took a step back, trying to regain his composure.

'Is everything okay?' she asked him. He couldn't tell from her expression if she was feeling the same way as he was.

It didn't matter anyway. They were just friends.

'Yeah. We should probably go now. It's late.' His voice was thick with grit.

She smiled at him, as if unaware of the effect she was having. 'But the night is young. And the children are away. We can dance until dawn, remember?'

He wanted to laugh at how easy she made it sound. Right

now he wasn't sure he could make it another ten minutes. His whole body ached for her. 'I'm beat,' he said, even though he'd never felt so wide awake. 'My bed is calling me.'

She slid her hand back into his. The sudden contact shocked him. They'd somehow changed places; she'd become the laid back relaxed one, and he was on high alert. 'Okay, party pooper. I'd hate to steal away your beauty sleep. Goodness knows you need it.' She raised her eyebrows at him, her lips still curved up in that sweet, sexy smile.

Even when they were sitting in the cab of his truck, he could still feel the atmosphere vibrating between them. He could smell her perfume, enticing its way into his senses, tempting him like he'd never been tempted before.

Frowning, he switched the ignition on and held firmly onto the wheel, sliding the truck into reverse. As he pulled out of the parking lot and onto the main road, he glanced at the clock on the dashboard. Ten minutes, that was all it would take to get them home.

He could make it couldn't he?

'So, photography, sailing, dancing … is there anything you're not good at?' Juliet asked. The smile in her voice hit him like a sledgehammer.

He kept his eyes firmly on the road. 'I only show you the stuff I'm good at. Who wants to admit they're bad at something?'

'Come on. You don't strike me as the type to brag. There must be something you're bad at.' She was teasing him again.

He gave a humourless laugh. 'Of course there is, but I'm not going to tell you that, am I?'

'You're being very modest.'

He tapped his fingers on the steering wheel. Only nine minutes now. 'Okay, I'm not a great cook.'

'What a let down. I don't think I've met many men who are great cooks, unless you count those chef guys on TV. Is that your only failing, the only skeleton in your closet?'

They pulled up at a stoplight. He willed it to turn green. Instead it hung around, the red glow illuminating the truck. Against his resolve he turned to look at her, and she was staring straight at him. Everything about her was soft and sweet. He wanted to bury himself in her. 'There are plenty of skeletons in my closet,' he finally said, his voice thick. He pulled his gaze from hers and stared back out of the windshield. At last the lights turned green, and he pulled away, almost speeding in his need to get home.

She tilted her head to the side, that devastating smile pulling at her lips. Her skin looked so soft and supple in the lamplight it was all he could do to keep his hands on the wheel.

'Now I'm intrigued,' she said.

'You shouldn't be.' Four minutes. What was that, two hundred and forty seconds? He could count them down if he needed to, anything to take his mind off the woman sitting next to him.

'You know, I'm really good at finding out secrets.'

'I bet you are.'

If he didn't know better he'd have thought she was flirting with him. Everything in him wanted to flirt right back. It would be easy, so much easier than this. He'd park up in the driveway, reach across and cup his palm around her smooth neck. He could lean in, feel that perfect moment of hesitation before his lips brushed against hers.

But that wasn't going to happen, because this was London. She'd made it clear exactly where the boundaries lay. And he was going to keep firmly behind them no matter what it took, because he respected her too much to do anything else.

Two minutes.

One minute.

Then they were home. Thank God.

When was the last time she came home this late? Juliet couldn't remember. It must have been before she left Thomas, but even then she couldn't recall the night feeling this magical. Couldn't recall the last time she felt this alive, either. She hadn't wanted to stop dancing, hadn't wanted to leave the club at all.

She didn't want tonight to end.

Ryan pulled her door open, and offered her his hand. She took it, and climbed out of the truck, lingering next to him as he locked it up. Shoving his keys into his pocket, he glanced over at her, and she couldn't quite read the expression on his face.

She wanted to make him smile again. 'I feel like Audrey Hepburn in *My Fair Lady*. I could have danced all night.'

'You would have regretted it tomorrow. You still might. We probably used muscles we've never used before.'

'No regrets here.' Her voice was firm.

Something flashed behind his eyes, but she couldn't quite name it. 'I'll walk you home,' he said, his voice gruff.

She waited for him to take her hand, or put his palm on her back the way he had in the dance club. But instead he just walked alongside her, keeping a steady distance between their arms. She couldn't help but miss his touch.

When they reached the bottom step, she turned to look at him. There was still a gap between them – of two feet or more. But when their eyes met she could feel her heart start to drum inside her chest, a steady, fast beat that made her feel breathless.

If this was a date he'd step forward and kiss her now. For a second she wondered if he would anyway.

'Thank you for a lovely evening,' she said, keeping her voice low in the quiet of the night. 'I can't remember the last time I had so much fun.' She was still looking at him, still holding his gaze. Still questioning if he might try to kiss her.

'You're welcome. I'll just make sure you get inside before I go.'

'Okay.'

Without even thinking about it, her lips parted. It felt as though every inch of her skin was tingling with anticipation. Her breath was shallow, her muscles felt achy, and it all led to a startling conclusion.

She wanted Ryan Sutherland to kiss her. Really wanted it. Was aching to feel his body press against hers one more time.

'Good night, Juliet.'

There was a look of determination on his face. Was he feeling the same way as she did? Was he going to do it now? But instead of walking forward, he stepped back, squaring his shoulders as he gave her a nod.

It felt as though she was being dismissed. He wasn't going to kiss her at all. He was going to go home and go to bed. A sense of disappointment overwhelmed her.

'Good night, Ryan.' Swallowing down the taste of regret, she walked up the steps, half an eye still on him. He hadn't moved an inch. He was still watching, still waiting for her to get in. His scrutiny was making her feel self-conscious.

The first time she tried to fit the key into the lock it slipped. Her hand was shaking too much. When it finally slid in, and turned to open the door, she could see him turn and walk away in her peripheral vision.

She stepped inside the hallway, catching a glimpse of herself in the mirror. Her face was flushed. She wasn't sure whether it was from all that dancing, or the crazy way she'd felt attracted to him. Either way, she needed to cool off, and fast.

In the morning she'd be grateful nothing happened. The last thing she needed was any more complications. They were friends, and it worked – she didn't want anything to compromise that.

Yes, tomorrow she'd be glad they didn't kiss. And tonight? She'd just wallow in the disappointment.

12

Come, sit down, every mother's son,
and rehearse your parts

– A Midsummer Night's Dream

'Mommy, do I look stupid?' Poppy frowned, pulling at the straw sticking out of her sleeves. 'Ruby said I look like an idiot.'

'You don't look stupid,' Juliet said, placing a battered old hat on her daughter's head. 'But even if you did, then that would be good. Because the Scarecrow had no brains, remember? So if Ruby says anything else, tell her it's because you're a great actress and play the Scarecrow really well.'

'Ruby won't care. She says Dorothy's the best role ever, anyway. Especially because she gets to take a dog everywhere with her. It's not fair.'

'It's a stuffed dog. Not that exciting.' Juliet tried to hide her smile. 'And Dorothy's boring. All that talking about home. She doesn't even like Oz, and that's crazy. It's full of yellow brick roads and lollipops.'

Poppy looked slightly mollified. 'At least Charlie looks stupid, too,' she said, looking out of the window to the house across the way. Charlie was standing on the deck outside the front door, scowling as Ryan tried to put his tin helmet on. 'And I have a heart still, don't I? Unlike Charlie.'

Juliet was too busy looking over at Ryan. Thank goodness they hadn't kissed after the dance club, the way she'd wanted to. In the few days since they'd gone dancing, he'd gone back to being the perfect friend. Smiling, easy-going, waving at her when he saw her. It was as if any heated moments between them last Saturday had never happened.

And that was a good thing, wasn't it? She had enough to deal with in her life, she didn't need any more complications.

Not even ones as perfectly packaged as Ryan Sutherland.

'Mommy, at least I have a heart, right?' Poppy repeated. Juliet tore her eyes away from her hot neighbour.

'Charlie has a heart, it's his character that doesn't.'

'And I have a brain.'

'That's right.'

'So can he come over and sleep here tonight still?'

Juliet never ceased to be amazed by the way Poppy's mind worked. She'd segue from one conversation to another with very little logic to the change. It made Juliet wonder just how jumbled her kid's mind must be.

'Of course he can.' Ryan had brought his sleeping bag and pyjamas over earlier. The plan was to come straight back home from the play, and then make some popcorn and put a movie on.

'And when he invites me over to his, we can sleep in his tree house, can't we? Because that would be fair.'

'What?' Juliet was hardly listening. She was too busy watching Ryan as he ran a hand through his hair. Was he looking over at the house? She couldn't tell.

Poppy sighed dramatically. 'Nothing. Can we go now?'

The play was due to start at seven, but Miss Mason had asked all the children to arrive an hour before. They'd have a final run through in the classroom before walking to the stage. Juliet made her way to the auditorium, which was already half-full of parents and families. Looking around, she spotted a spare row of chairs in the middle, and made her way over.

'There's a seat here if you want it.' Ryan's low voice made her whip her head around. He was sitting two rows back, all on his own.

'Oh, hi.' She shot him a tight smile. 'Thanks, but I probably shouldn't.'

He tipped his head to the side, frowning. 'Why not?'

A thousand reasons almost slipped from her tongue. *Because every time I see you it makes you harder to resist? Because I still wonder what it would be like to kiss you?*

'Thomas and his parents are coming. I don't want to cause any more trouble.' She walked to the far side of the row, not wanting to sit in front of him. Shrugging off her jacket, she looped it behind her, then pushed her bag under the seat with her feet. Her muscles were already feeling stiff with anxiety, and she circled her neck a couple of times to try and loosen it up.

That's when she saw him.

Sitting behind her.

Again.

'Ryan?'

'Yes, London?'

'Why are you sitting behind me?'

'There's a better view from here.'

She turned to look at the stage, half-obscured by the curtain on the left-hand side. 'It's a terrible view.'

123

'Not from where I'm sitting.'

When she turned to look at him again, his face was softer, somehow. 'Ryan, I really don't want to cause any trouble. Thomas was mad about the sailing. We've still not agreed on divorce terms yet, please don't make more problems for me here.'

'I won't cause any trouble. I promise.'

There was a noise from the stage, as the chorus started to file in, sitting on the benches at the back. Juliet turned to look at them, her eyes wide, as she licked her lips to try and get rid of the dryness.

'Are these the best seats you could get?' Thomas huffed, pushing through the people who had seated themselves around her. 'I thought you'd get here early, and save us seats at the front. You can hardly see the stage from here.'

'You could have come early yourself.'

'Some of us have a business to run. I had to leave an important meeting to get here in time. You could have been more helpful.'

'I have a business to run, too,' she pointed out.

He ignored her words, ushering his parents along. 'There are only three seats. We need four.'

Four? She frowned, looking over to Thomas and his parents. Behind them, looking as immaculate as ever, was his girlfriend. Or was she still his assistant?

Whatever. It didn't matter.

'I didn't realise you were bringing Nicole.'

'Poppy told her all about the play, and asked her to come.' He said it matter-of-factly.

'Okay.' She waited for them to leave, but Thomas lingered there, with his parents and Nicole standing behind him. He was staring at her expectantly, and she wondered if she should say something else. It was only when he cleared his throat that she realised he was waiting for her to offer to move.

Yeah, that wasn't going to happen.

'There are still some seats at the back,' she said. 'You could all sit together there.'

Thomas looked over her shoulder, and frowned. Then he brought his eyes back onto her, letting out a deep sigh. 'You always have to be obstructive.' He said it beneath his breath, a passive aggressive attempt to make her rise to his bait. But she ignored it, turning her head to the front, refusing to give him the satisfaction of seeing her riled. Within moments the four of them had left the row and made their way to the back.

Her mouth was dry, her heart was speeding, but the sense of elation she felt for staying calm and holding her own more than made up for the agitation.

She'd almost certainly pay for it later, but right there, right then, she was proud of herself.

'Can we sleep in here?' Poppy asked. She was kneeling inside the fort they'd made up using an old sheet and a stack of cushions. Charlie was beside her, shining his torch around, watching as the light pierced the thin fabric, making shapes on the ceiling above.

'Sure you can. Once you've finished your snacks I'll bring some sleeping bags in here.' Juliet had set up her laptop with a movie, ready for them to lay out and watch it as they stuffed their faces with kernels. 'And then it will be time to sleep, okay?'

Poppy looked at Charlie, trying her best not to smile. 'Okay.'

Leaving the room, Juliet shook her head. The two of them

had clearly been scheming, but she didn't really mind at all. It was the weekend, after all, and they deserved a treat after all the work they'd done on the play. Her eyes watered as she remembered how proud she'd been earlier that evening, as the children took a bow after acting their hearts out. She'd practically worn out her palms applauding them, with tears streaming down her face.

Even Thomas had been touched. He and his family had descended on Poppy with hugs and congratulations as soon as the play had finished. Luckily he hadn't mentioned the seat issue again. She was sure he would, though, at some point.

She wouldn't worry about that right now. Pushing Thomas to the back of her mind, she cleared up the kitchen, sliding dirty plastic beakers and plates into the dishwasher, before wiping down the sides with a clean, white cloth. She was rinsing it when she heard a rap at the door, three consecutive knocks that made her heart jump out of her chest.

Thomas.

Was he never going to leave her be?

Wringing the wet cloth in her hands, she placed it on the drainer. She put her hands on the counter, trying not to sigh.

Another knock made her stand up straight. She was so sick and tired of the way Thomas thought she was always at his beck and call. His lack of empathy, combined with his complete sense of entitlement was almost unbearable.

She'd had enough.

Juliet stomped her way down the hallway and wrenched the front door open. She narrowed her eyes, waiting for the barrage of insults. Her mouth was set in a tight line.

Until it dropped open with surprise.

'Ryan?'

'You look pissed. What have I done this time?' He leaned casually against the door frame, a stuffed toy in his hand. 'Did I laugh too loud at the play?'

She was still trying to compose herself. She'd been all ready for a fight, and her body hadn't yet relaxed. 'I could live with the laughing. It was the crying that really annoyed me,' she told him. 'Who knew you were such a softy?'

'I reckon you knew.' He gave her a lazy smile. 'So anyway, why were you looking so angry?'

'I thought you were Thomas.' She moved back from the door, letting him step inside. He followed her to the kitchen, propping the soft toy against the tiles.

'That's not the best compliment I've ever had.' He leaned against the counter. 'Why would he be coming around at this time of night anyway?'

'Because I made him sit at the back,' she told him. 'He'll want to have the last word at some point.'

'Well, you stood up for yourself like a badass. You should be proud of yourself.'

'Thank you kindly.' She gave him a mock curtsey. Looking up at him, his gaze immediately caught hers. The expression on his face took her breath away. A slow smile curled at his lips, and his eyes were soft, yet somehow heated. It was the same way he'd looked at her in the dance club, and it made her heart race.

Against her will, her own lips lifted in a smile. She could hear the rapid beat of her pulse in her ears, feel the pounding in the ribcage, all reminding her of one inimitable fact.

She still wanted to kiss him.

Taking a ragged breath in, she tried to ignore her body's response to him. Tried to remind herself why this was such a bad idea. But his closeness was overwhelming her, making her want to reach out and touch him.

'Ryan ...'

He looked as conflicted as she did. 'Yeah. I should go.'

But she didn't want him to. She couldn't stop thinking about the way he'd felt in the dance club, holding his body tight against hers. His muscles hard against the softness of her curves, the two of them fitting together as though it was meant to be.

'Stay.' She reached out to touch his arm. *Bad idea, Juliet, bad idea*. Pushing that thought down, she circled her fingers around his wrist.

'London, I can't.' He looked as if he was in pain.

'Why not?'

'Because every time I look at you, I want you.' He closed his eyes, pinching the skin at the top of his nose between his thumb and forefinger. 'You've made it clear you just want to be friends. I'm trying to respect that.'

'Oh.' She let go of his wrist. A mixture of emotions washed over her. Sadness that her friend was upset, elation that he wanted her. But more than anything she felt fear. Not of him, but of herself. Of her own desire.

'I'm gonna go.' He went to turn and make for the hallway. An impulse overtook her, made her reach out for his arm again. He looked at her with a quizzical expression, and without letting herself think about it, she stepped forward, rolling onto the balls of her feet, and pressed her lips against his.

His mouth was soft and warm, and for a moment he was a statue, as though the shock had frozen him still. But then she moved her lips against his, lifting her hand to cup his jaw, and he leaned into her. Still kissing, he threaded his fingers through her hair, deepening their embrace until his tongue slid softly against hers.

She couldn't believe she was doing this, and yet it felt so good, so right. She looped her arms around his neck, pressing her body against his, squeezing her eyes shut tight as they gave in to their desire. Her skin was flushed all over, tingling with need. He overwhelmed her senses – the feel of him, the taste of him, the sound of his rapid breaths as he tried to take in some air.

'London,' he murmured against her lips. She opened her eyes, and he was staring straight at her. She kissed him again, leaving him in no doubt how much she wanted this. She needed it, like she needed air.

'Mommy, can we have some more popcorn?' Poppy's voice carried through the thick atmosphere between them. Alarmed, Juliet stepped out of Ryan's embrace. They exchanged an anxious glance.

'What, honey?' she called out, her voice sounding unnaturally high. Her eyes were still wide as she glanced over Ryan's shoulder, seeing Poppy running down the stairs, holding a bowl.

Juliet ducked under Ryan's arms, trying to put some space between them. She could feel the blood pooling in her cheeks, making them flame as she tried to calm her body down.

'We've run out of popcorn,' Poppy said impatiently. 'Oh, hi, Ryan.' She sounded normal, unalarmed. Had she seen anything? Juliet wasn't sure, but either way she wanted the ground to open up and swallow her whole.

Kind of the way she'd wanted Ryan to do the same thing only seconds earlier.

'You've eaten it already? You guys are going to explode.' Ryan grinned, taking the plastic bowl from her daughter.

How could he be so calm when she felt moments away from combusting? 'Maybe you should take a break before you have any more.'

Still trying to control her breathing, Juliet took the bowl from Ryan, being careful not to touch his fingers with hers. She didn't trust herself not to do something embarrassing if she did.

'Oh, is that Fluffy? Charlie was wondering where he was,' Poppy said, still oblivious to the atmosphere in the room. 'Charlie, Fluffy's here!' she shouted. Moments later, Ryan's son came running down the stairs, his face lighting up when he saw his dad, and his favourite stuffed toy on the kitchen counter, where Ryan had left him.

Suddenly, they were back to being mom and dad. Juliet wasn't sure whether she was disappointed or relieved.

Either way, it felt as if there was unfinished business between them.

And she wasn't sure if she wanted it finished or not.

Ryan closed his front door behind him, and leaned against the wall, rubbing the heel of his palms against his eyes in an attempt to calm himself. What the hell just happened? One minute he was leaving, the next they were kissing like teenagers. He touched his lips, remembering the sensation of her mouth against his, the sweetness of her tongue as she opened up to him.

He'd wanted to ask her what was happening. But Charlie and Poppy had hung around, asking for more drinks and demanding Juliet watch the movie with them. In the end he'd left the house with nothing more than a meaningful look, and questions that wouldn't stop ping-ponging around his brain. What was she thinking? Did she make a mistake? Or did she want him as much as he wanted her?

He didn't know the answer to any of those questions, and he wouldn't without talking to her. Yet he'd made himself a promise, not to push her. That he'd respect her wish to be just friends. If she wanted something more than that, he wasn't going to be the one to push it. He respected her way too much for any of that macho bullshit. As much as it killed him, he was going to have to wait for her to make any moves.

Whatever happened next – if anything happened at all – it was up to her. And the wait was going to be the death of him.

13

No sooner met but they looked,
no sooner looked but they loved

– As You Like It

'So, your neighbour's kind of hot,' Cesca said, as the two of them were walking through the woods at the back of the house.

Juliet rolled her eyes. She'd deliberately steered her sister clear of the tree house that Ryan had almost finished, though the growl of his electric saw still echoed through the trees.

'So says the girl with the movie star fiancé. And you shouldn't be looking.' It came out sharper than Juliet intended. Cesca raised her eyebrows, looking at her suspiciously.

'You're not jealous are you?'

'No.' Juliet's reply was almost instantaneous. 'He's just a neighbour. And I'd prefer it if you didn't ogle him.' Her mouth was dry, as she remembered their kiss the other night. She hadn't had a chance to speak with him since – she'd been dealing with a big order at the florist. Maybe it was better that way, she still had no idea how she was supposed to deal with her feelings.

'Hey a girl can still appreciate the view.' They clambered

over a moss-covered log. 'And so should you. It's not often you get a next-door neighbour that looks like that. Especially one that's so good with kids.'

'You've only been engaged for a few months. Has Sam's lustre already worn off?' Juliet tried to turn the conversation back to Cesca. She wasn't enjoying being grilled.

Cesca's smile lit up her face. 'Not at all. He's still lovely, and to be honest he makes your neighbour look like a troll. But beggars can't be choosers.' She winked at Juliet to show she was teasing. 'But seriously, what gives between you two? When we dropped Poppy at school this morning he couldn't take his eyes off you.'

Cesca had arrived in Maryland the night before, having flown in the previous day. She'd left Sam in Washington DC, where he was due to meet with reporters. He would join them that evening, and the four of them would squeeze into Juliet's tiny bungalow. She couldn't help but think how unglamorous they'd find it, after living the movie-star life.

'Are you sure you wouldn't be happier staying in a hotel in town?' Juliet asked again. 'Sam might be more comfortable there.'

Cesca stopped, leaning against an old oak tree. 'Are you trying to change the subject?' she asked.

'Yes.' Juliet didn't want to talk about Ryan. Didn't want to think about him. Every time she remembered that kiss, she felt like she was blushing all over, like a sixteen-year-old girl with her first crush.

'Well to answer your question, we came to see you and Poppy, not to spend the night in some swanky hotel. And if we need to sleep on the floor in your basement, then we'll be happy to do that.' Cesca shot Juliet a smile. 'And as to changing the subject, that's not going to happen. I saw the way you were looking at him, too.'

'There's nothing going on between us.'

'But you want there to be?'

They'd reached the brook at the bottom of the tree-lined slope. The water bubbled and danced as it made its way through the trees, heading for the Chesapeake River on the other side of town. They walked along the bank, their boots sinking into the soft mud. 'I don't know what I want. I'm in the middle of a painful divorce and I'm trying to protect Poppy from the fallout. Ryan may be the best looking man I've ever laid eyes on, but the timing's totally wrong.'

'But apart from that?' Cesca started laughing. 'Come on, we both know that when love strikes, there's nothing you can do to stop it. I'm living, breathing evidence of that.'

Juliet couldn't help but smile. Cesca and Sam's love story had touched all their hearts. The two of them had been enemies for years, before they'd been thrown together in an Italian villa for the summer. It was there, in the Mediterranean heat, that they'd thawed out, and somehow fallen in love.

'Well, if there's anything I know, it's that this isn't love. Lust, maybe, but definitely not love.' She stepped on a dried-out branch, feeling it crack beneath her feet. The sound reverberated in the air. 'And anyway, it doesn't matter, because as I said before, I'm still married. If Thomas found out—'

'He'd have to put up with it,' Cesca interrupted. 'Because he isn't acting married. He's got a girlfriend, after all. And you're in the middle of negotiating your divorce. You can't use that as a reason not to move forward, Jules, not unless you want to be alone for the rest of your life.' She leaned down to pick up a pebble, then threw it into the water with a satisfying splash.

'And I should know, I stopped moving forward a long time ago. It took me years to realise the only person holding me back was me. I don't want that for you, too.'

'But you didn't have a daughter to think of,' Juliet said, coming to a halt beside her sister. 'And Thomas has already made his dislike of Ryan clear. There's bad blood between them, and this is a small town. It wouldn't be difficult for him to use it against me in court.'

'Jules, this will always be a small town. What are you going to do, live like a nun for the rest of your life? Let yourself be a sacrifice to the feud between the Montagues and the Capulets? You're not the kind of girl who gives up like that. Thomas doesn't have the right to dictate who you see any more, just like you don't have the right to dictate to him. He's trying to control you, even though you're apart now. Don't let him do that to you.'

Juliet rolled her lip between her teeth, staring out through the trees to the rolling fields beyond. Her family had always thought Thomas too controlling. It turned out they were right. She was just too blinded by love to see it at the time.

'He's not controlling me, not any more. But I'm not going to jump into anything, or onto anybody, without thinking things through first.'

Cesca was smiling. *'Jump onto anybody?* Is that what you want to do to him?' She waggled her eyebrows, Groucho Marx-style. 'Is there something you want to tell me?'

'No.' Her answer was too short, and too fast. She knew it would only pique her sister's interest more. That was the problem with having a writer as a sibling, they were practised people-watchers, and Cesca could read Juliet like the words on her page. Growing up, they'd all naturally fallen into roles. As the eldest, Lucy was the strong one, the organiser. Juliet had been the dreamy perfectionist, pursuing a degree in fine arts that was cut short by her romance with Thomas. Cesca had been the observant writer, always listening, watching, typing away. Like their poor dead mother she'd dreamed of a career in the theatre, though unlike Milly Shakespeare, her heart belonged backstage, not right at the front, taking a bow. Their youngest sister, Katherine – or Kitty for short – was quieter than the rest of them, but no less affected by their family tragedy. She was in LA now, working as an assistant producer on a major production.

Sighing, Juliet met her sister's gaze. She knew better than to try to hide things from Cesca. 'Something happened between us the other day. But it's not going to happen again.'

'What?' Cesca was all wide eyes and open mouth. 'You can't just leave it at that. What happened?'

'I kissed him.'

A smug smile crossed Cesca's lips. 'I knew it. I knew as soon as I looked at the two of you that you weren't just friends. When he was staring at you it felt like the room warmed up ten degrees. So what was it like, was it a good kiss?'

The memory of his warm lips pressing against hers sent a shiver down her spine. 'Yeah, it was good.' That was the understatement of the year.

'So why are you frowning?'

'Because it wouldn't work.'

'Why not?' Cesca asked.

'We're too different. He's all laid back and sunshine. Nothing fazes him. Plus he's moving to New York next June. There's no future in it.'

'Why's he moving?' Cesca asked, her interest piqued.

'He's got some kind of contract there, I think. From what I can tell he's not interested in staying around here.'

'What about Charlie's mom? Where's she? Are they divorced?'

'They were never really together. She's on tour with her band at the moment. But from what I can gather she's as laid back as Ryan. The two of them were only casual, I think. Maybe friends with benefits.'

'Those are some hot benefits. I can see why she'd go for that.'

Juliet felt her face warm up. 'Well, yeah, but I don't think she gets them any more.'

'That's because he's saving them for you.'

'Stop it.' She laughed, and Cesca joined in. 'Seriously, the last thing I need is a friend with benefits.'

'Bullshit, more than anybody I know, you need to get laid.'

'You can hardly talk, you're the one who swore off guys for six years.'

'Ah yeah.' Cesca grinned. 'But I'm making up for lost time now. And so should you. Look, whatever's going on between you and Mr Hot Stuff next door, you should just enjoy the moment. He doesn't have to be your star-crossed lover or even your next boyfriend. Just do what feels right. Don't overthink it.'

They'd reached the end of the woods. Turning back, they retraced their steps beside the brook, as the earth squelched beneath their feet. 'You mean have an affair?' Juliet clarified.

'No, because you're not married any more.' Cesca sounded exasperated. 'Just have a fling. This guy isn't going to be around forever, and let's face it, you aren't ready to settle down with anybody until everything's done and dusted with Thomas. But

I can't think of anybody I know who would benefit more from a bit of fun than you.'

Juliet couldn't help but stare at her little sister. Though she'd known her all her life, this was a side to Cesca she hadn't seen before. Gone was the wallowing, the loneliness, the settling for a life that wasn't fulfilling her. Instead she seemed vibrant and alive.

'You've changed,' Juliet said. 'Not in a bad way, though. I mean you've grown, you've got this confidence, this strength.'

Cesca nodded. 'I feel strong. And the reason I do is because I left the past behind. I stopped letting my past regrets shape my present. It's so freeing I can't even explain it.' She grabbed Juliet's hand, sandwiching it between her own. 'And I want that for you, too. You're only young, after all. Most women your age are still playing the field, settling into their careers and enjoying life. It's as though you've tried to squeeze everything into the last seven years, and not been able to enjoy any of it. So if this gorgeous guy who lives next door is offering you a bit of fun, why shouldn't you take it?'

Juliet thought about her sister's words as they made their way back to the house. They walked in companionable silence, their feet crunching over the freshly fallen leaves. The fall colours had arrived, turning the trees burnished orange and blood red, and now the leaves were slowly making their way to the ground. The first year she'd lived in Maryland they'd waited for the colours with bated breath, rushing out to the National Park along with the rest of the state as soon as the leaves had started to turn. Back then, her stomach had been swollen, her heart had been full, and she'd thought she'd married the man she would spend the rest of her life with.

What a difference a few years made. This year, for the first time, she hadn't been to the park at all. She'd been too busy making bouquets and floral decorations. A pang tweaked at her heart as she realised how much she had already missed this year, being so deep in the misery of losing her marriage. It was as though her pain was a gauze curtain in front of her eyes, obscuring life until she was isolated from it.

Maybe it was time to lift up the veil.

They'd reached the part of the woods that fell at the boundary line of the houses. She looked over at the tree house behind Ryan's yard. Her heart stuttered when she saw the man himself, leaning back to survey the structure. It looked almost complete. The windows were fixed in, the roof was nailed on, with a waterproof sealant applied. All he had left to do was put up the ladder – and after that it would be good to go.

But it wasn't the wooden house that drew her interest. It was the man himself, clad in jeans that skimmed his thigh muscles, and a T-shirt whose cotton seemed to kiss his pectorals. She was ogling him, even though she knew she shouldn't.

'Like I said, he's hot,' Cesca whispered, her gaze following Juliet's. 'He's gorgeous, he's available and he's into you. What's not to like about that?'

At that moment, Juliet couldn't think of a single thing.

Ryan was staring into a half-empty kitchen cupboard, trying to decide what to cook for dinner, when the sound of the doorbell echoed through the hallway. He slammed the cupboard shut and walked to the front door.

As soon as he opened it, she took his breath away.

'London.' He smiled at her. 'You okay?'

She was wearing a pair of skinny jeans that looked almost sprayed on, the denim accentuating her soft curves. She'd matched it with a cream cashmere sweater. With her red curls tumbling over her shoulders, she looked almost too good to be true. He remembered how that hair had felt as he tangled his fingers in the strands, how her body had fitted perfectly against his that night she kissed him. It was hard to think about anything else.

'I'm fine. I just wondered if you and Charlie would like to join us for dinner. My sister's visiting – she's the one you saw me with this morning – and her fiancé is here too. I thought he could do with a bit of male company. Being surrounded by Shakespeare women is too much for most guys.'

Ryan felt his mouth turn dry. The only woman he wanted to be surrounded by was standing right in front of him.

'Dinner?' he repeated. 'Tonight?'

'It's just a takeout. Does Charlie like Chinese food?' Though there was colour on her cheeks, she was displaying none of the discomfort Ryan was feeling. The sexual attraction that was pulling him in seemed almost one-sided. He didn't like that at all.

'Yeah, he likes Chinese food,' Ryan murmured. He dragged a hand through his hair, pulling it out of his eyes. 'Though he's been eating ever since he got home, so I doubt he has much of an appetite.'

She shrugged, a half-smile still tugging at her lips. He frowned, trying to work out what looked different about her. 'It's okay. We'll grab them some egg rolls and put on a movie for them. If the Chinese doesn't work, then I'm sure popcorn will.'

Did her smile turn into a smirk? Ryan wasn't sure, but whatever it was about her was making her more attractive than ever. Which definitely wasn't a good thing. Not at all.

'Popcorn?' he repeated faintly.

'Yeah, we both know how much they like popcorn.'

He frowned, his eyes fixed on her face. Something about her was nagging at him. It was like one of those wispy dandelion clocks dancing just above his reach. He licked his lips, as she continued to smile at him. It was taking all his self-restraint not to run his finger across her jaw.

Then it hit him. 'It's a school night,' he said, almost shaking his head to get some sense in.

'So?'

'And it's almost seven o'clock. Haven't you fed Poppy already? Isn't it nearly her bath time?' He knew their routine like clockwork.

Juliet shrugged. 'My sister's visiting, I figured we could throw the routine out this once.'

'Just like that?' he questioned.

She threw her head back and started to laugh. If he thought she was beautiful before, it was nothing compared to seeing her caught in a moment of carefree abandon. 'Am I really that bad? You make me sound like a cross between a sergeant major and Mary Poppins. I can be flexible when I want to be.'

'You can?' Damn. As if he needed *that* image in his brain.

She nodded slowly. 'So are you coming over to join us or what?'

A slow smile lifted the corners of his mouth. 'I wouldn't miss it for the world.'

Leaning back in his chair, Ryan lifted the wine glass to his lips as he drained the last of his Chianti. It was warm and mellow, adding to the sense of relaxation he already felt, thanks to the easy ambience of the evening. The four of them had talked and laughed all night, and he'd found himself liking Sam Carlton.

They'd visited so many of the same cities, it made for easy conversation.

As for Juliet, he'd never seen her look so comfortable. It was as though she'd shrugged her worries off for the first time since he'd met her, and contentment seemed to radiate off her in waves.

They'd exchanged so many heated glances it was almost embarrassing. Whenever she spoke or laughed he found his eyes seeking hers, a jolt of pleasure washing through him each time their stares collided. He couldn't help but smile as the wine worked its magic on her, making her both giggly and open. Like the girl he imagined she once was.

But she was all woman now.

'I guess we should clear this lot up,' she said, wrinkling her nose as she surveyed the devastation of cardboard cartons on the kitchen table. 'At least most of it can go in the bin for once.'

His mouth twitched at her English words. Another effect of the fine wine Sam had brought with him. His nickname for her was more than apt tonight.

'We call it a trash can, London,' he teased.

She stuck her tongue out at him. 'Tomayto-tomahto.'

'Nope. Definitely a trash can.' He winked, then stood to pick up a few of the empty cartons. 'I guess I'll have to make a move soon. Get my boy to bed.'

'You need to live a little,' Juliet said, her eyes sparkling at the tables she was turning. 'Relax, Charlie's fine. The last time I popped my head around the door he and Poppy had fallen asleep. I even made them clean their teeth earlier, so at least we don't have to worry about cavities.'

'Yeah, cavities, we definitely don't want them to get those.' He winked at her.

'Why do you call her London?' Sam asked, walking over to open another bottle of wine.

'Why do you think?' Cesca answered him before Ryan could. 'Because she's from London, stupid.'

'And because I hate it,' Juliet said. 'He'll do anything he can to aggravate me.'

'Tell me about it,' Cesca agreed. 'Sam will do anything to wind me up. It's like some kind of weird mating ritual.'

'It works doesn't it?' Sam grabbed Cesca around the waist with one arm, the other hand still grasping the wine bottle. He nuzzled his face into her neck. 'You hated me from the minute I walked into the villa two years ago. Why fix something if it ain't broken?'

'Oh, get a room.' Juliet shook her head, still smiling. Then she looked at Ryan again. This time she didn't look away. Instead her eyes widened as he caught her gaze.

Christ, he wanted to kiss her again.

'We've already got a room, and luckily for you, it's next to yours,' Cesca said, laughing as Sam squeezed her tight.

Juliet looked at Ryan in mock-horror. 'Can I stay at yours tonight?'

The thought of her in his bedroom was alarming and enticing in equal measure. He had to take a deep breath to even himself out. It wasn't wrong to flirt back when she was the one who started it, was it?

'What's mine is yours.' He smiled at her. No, it wasn't wrong at all.

'And they think *we* should get a room,' Cesca said. 'Is it me or is getting hot in here?' She started to fan herself, making Juliet roll her eyes.

'Shut up.'

'Make me.'

'Oh, I'll make you if I need to,' Juliet warned her sister. 'Remember what I used to do when we were kids?'

Cesca made a disgusted face. 'Oh no, not the infamous Chinese wrist burn? Anything but that.' She glanced at Sam. 'She's a demon with her hands. She brings grown men to their knees, tears in their eyes.'

Ryan coughed out a laugh. 'I bet she does.'

'*Et tu*, Ryan?' Juliet said, poking him with her finger. 'What is this, let's gang up on Juliet day?'

He couldn't help but grin. Having her sister around was relaxing her in a way he'd never seen before.

He really wanted to see her that way again.

'Are all your sisters like this?' he asked her.

'Yep,' Sam said, handing him a full glass of wine. It looked as though Ryan wasn't going home any time soon. 'They're a nightmare when they all get together. You can't hear yourself think. The only time they all quieten down is when their dad has something to say, which isn't often, poor guy.'

Juliet looked down, and he saw the sadness flashing in her eyes.

'You okay?' Ryan asked her quietly.

When she looked up, her eyes were watery. 'Yeah, I'm being stupid. It's just that I miss my family. I hadn't realised how much until Cesca mentioned it. I couldn't even go to the premiere of her play in London, because Thomas wasn't happy about it. And now he's banned me from taking Poppy back at all, even for a visit. And I want her to see my dad while she can.'

'But you're doing something about that, right?' Cesca asked. 'Lucy told me she's been looking at everything, and has given you some things to talk to your lawyer about?'

Ryan remembered that Lucy was the eldest, their sister who was a lawyer herself.

'Yeah, but it's taking so much longer than I thought. And in the meantime, Dad's not getting any better, is he?'

'Why's it taking so long?'

Juliet shrugged. 'Part of it is the system. You have to be separated for a year in Maryland before you can divorce. But Thomas doesn't seem to be in a hurry to agree any terms in advance. It's as if he doesn't really want to get divorced.'

Ryan said nothing. Even though the mention of Juliet's soon to be ex-husband made him want to grind his teeth together.

'Maybe you should get a better lawyer,' Cesca suggested.

'I've already paid mine a hefty retainer. I don't want to spend more money if I don't have to.'

'If you're worried about the money, we could help. I'm pretty sure Lucy and Kitty would want to, as well.'

'Thank you, honey, but I can handle it myself,' Juliet said. 'This is my mess, and I'll clean it up. Don't think I don't appreciate the offer, though, because I do.' She slapped her hands together, signalling the end of that conversation. 'Okay, let's change the subject. Can you believe it's Thanksgiving this week?'

'Do you celebrate?' Ryan asked her. 'Being from London and all.'

'I don't, but Poppy does. She'll be with Thomas this year. I'm planning to spend the day cleaning the shop. It's long over-due.' She smiled at him, and he grinned back. 'How about you? Will you be cooking a turkey?'

'I was planning to. I'll save you some if you like.'

Their eyes met again. It was happening so often, he could almost count down the seconds until they did.

She propped her chin on the palm of her hand, her gaze never leaving his. He wanted to know what she was thinking – whether she was remembering that kiss the same way he was. His attraction for her hadn't dissipated at all in the days since their lips had connected, but he was doing his very best to keep it reined in.

'You know what, Ryan?' she said, leaning her head to the side. 'I'd like that very much.'

14

I can no other answer make but thanks,
And thanks, and ever thanks

– Twelfth Night

Ryan steered his car into a free space next to the gate. Though the rain had let up a little, the storm had kept most people away from the cemetery. He was thankful for the silence – it had been a long time since he'd visited this place. Too long. The last time he'd stepped through these wrought-iron gates was when he was carrying his grandfather's coffin to its final resting place.

All these years later, he was back, but this time with his son. His flesh and blood. Somebody who didn't judge him for his money, for his choices. The one person in the world who took him for what he was, never asking or demanding more.

The one person he'd give his life for without blinking.

'You ready?' he asked Charlie, grabbing the umbrella from the backseat, and walking around to help his son out of the car.

Charlie nodded. He was carrying a small potted plant he'd decorated at home. 'Is this where Grandpa Cutler's buried?'

'That's right. And Grandma Maisie.'

'But they're your grandpa and grandma, right? Not mine?

My grandma is Samantha isn't she?' He was talking about Sheridan's mom. Charlie still hadn't quite grasped how family relationships worked, and Ryan knew that some of that was his fault. He rarely spoke of his family to Charlie – apart from his grandfather – no wonder the kid was confused.

'Cutler and Maisie were your great-grandparents.'

Charlie nodded seriously, wrapping his small hands around the metal handle of the umbrella, and pulling it close to his head. 'Okay then.'

Inside the gate, the paths that wound around the graves were as empty as the parking lot. Ryan wiped the rainwater from his face, then put his arm on Charlie's back, leading his son deeper into the graveyard. Occasionally they passed a family – heads down, black umbrellas up – paying respects to their loved ones on this Thanksgiving afternoon.

Finally they passed the bank of trees he knew led the way to his family's plot. It was a private part of the cemetery, marked by marble busts and intricate stones, and everything about the graves reflected the wealth of his ancestors. Shaws had lived in this town since the seventeen hundreds, though it was only in 1835 that this cemetery had been constructed.

The two of them took a left, past the familiar names of Ryan's ancestors; Marthas and Williams, Johns and Eleanors, all of them long buried, though their blood still ran through him today. With his hand still on his son's back, he steered him to the far right-hand side, where two simple, white stones marked his grandparents' final resting place.

That's when he realised he wasn't alone. Standing there, in a thick, red coat, with a pale grey umbrella sheltering her body, was his mother. She was staring at the gravestones, her red lips pursed, her eyes narrow. She looked smaller than he remembered – smaller and thinner – and her hair, once big and healthy, was sparse around her head. As he and Charlie approached the gravestone, she glanced up, blinking as she tried to focus on the figures in front of her.

'Ryan?' Like the rest of her, Nancy Sutherland's voice seemed almost weightless. 'Is that you?'

His heart was racing. He cleared his throat, trying to dislodge the lump that had made its home there. The last time he'd seen this woman – half a lifetime ago – she'd been crying, her face red with sadness, her eyes wet with tears. She'd begged him not to leave, but she never understood. Watching his father belittle her every day was killing him.

'Mother.' He nodded. He felt Charlie shift his feet beside him, but his son said nothing.

'I heard you were back in town. And this must be your son.'

Ryan nodded. 'Yes, this is Charlie.'

Her face softened. 'Hello Charlie, I'm your grandmother.' She licked her thin, red lips and took a step towards them. Charlie shrank against Ryan as if seeking protection.

'My grandmother lives in San Diego. Her name's Samantha.'

His mother's lips trembled. 'But I'm your other grandmother.'

Charlie frowned, and looked up at Ryan. 'Is that true?'

Ryan placed his hand on his son's shoulder. 'Remember I told you about my mom and dad? That they lived in this town?' Charlie nodded, his eyes still wide. 'Well, this lady is my mom. Her name's Nancy, and she's your grandmother, too.'

She'd cleared the distance between them, coming to a stop in front of Charlie. Her eyes were watering, her mouth still quaking, and she bit down on it as if to still the shakes. 'Charlie, I've been hoping to meet you. I'm so happy to finally be able to say hello.' When she glanced at Ryan, he could see his reflection in the mirrors of her eyes. 'He looks just like you did at his age. A Shaw through and through.'

'My name's Charlie Shaw Sutherland.'

A single tear rolled down her papery cheek. 'That's a very nice name. And a very significant one, too. Has your father told you that the Shaws built this town from nothing? And that our family – your family – are very important?'

Charlie looked up at Ryan, his face full of questions.

'I haven't told him that, no,' Ryan said. 'Because I've brought him up to realise that everybody's important. And that we're no different to anybody else he meets – rich or poor.'

His mother flinched, and Ryan immediately regretted his harsh tone. 'I'm sorry, I—'

She waved her hand. 'Don't apologise. I understand what you're trying to say. But he is your son, half of his blood comes from this land. He is as much the product of the Shaws and Sutherlands as he is of his upbringing. And he should at least know something about his history, even if you turned your back on it.'

'He'll know when he's ready,' Ryan said, keeping his voice free of emotion. 'And he'll know why I found it so suffocating, too. I want him to grow up knowing he's more than a name, more than a small town where everybody knows everyone's business. And more than anything I want him to know that no man should ever treat a woman the way Dad treated you.'

'He's not so bad any more,' she told him, though the quiver in her voice didn't back up her words. 'He's getting old, we both are, he's mellowed.'

'He's still a bully. I saw that when he called me into his office.'

'You saw him?' Her mouth fell open. Ryan guessed there

were still secrets between them, the way there always was. Growing up, his father had ruled their house with an iron will. What he said always went. If anybody dared to stand up to him, they'd feel the force of his wrath.

Maybe that's why Nancy Sutherland had stopped standing up for herself. And when Ryan had tried to stand up for her, she'd told him to stop, to respect his father. That she would never leave him.

In the end it was Ryan who'd left. From the moment he'd stepped on the airplane he'd felt free.

'Yeah I saw him. It was as pleasant as always.'

'Why did you come back if you hate him so much? What made you choose this town?'

That was the million-dollar question. And the simple fact was, he'd chosen it for a reason. Or maybe it had chosen him. Whichever way you looked at it, he'd spent half his life avoiding the place that held all his bad memories, and yet it held everything else too. His family, his history, a town built by his forefathers that had made him the man he was today. When he and Sheridan had discussed where Charlie should spend his Kindergarten year, the first words that slipped from Ryan's tongue was the name of his home town. Shaw Haven, the place of his birth. He'd left under a cloud with nothing more than his tarnished name to cling on to, and he'd come back as a man, one who had succeeded in spite of everything, who'd made his own life, his own luck, and yet still had something left to prove. He'd come back because there was still part of his story left to write.

And when it was written, he'd leave and they'd start their new life together. Far away from this place.

Ryan wiped the rain from his brow and looked at his mom.

'I came back because I wanted to.' Pulling his attention away from her, he looked at Charlie. 'Do you want to put your plant on Grandma Maisie's grave?' he asked him.

Charlie nodded, walking forward, Ryan following close behind to shelter him with the umbrella. His son squatted down, placing the plant pot gently next to the headstone. Ryan squeezed his eyes shut, trying to block out the maelstrom of emotions seeing his mother had unleashed. Trying to ignore the painful memories she'd stirred up.

Almost immediately his thoughts went to Juliet. And suddenly the need to see her overwhelmed him. He was surprised by the intensity of his feeling. It was like a magnet, dragging him in.

'There,' Charlie said, wiping his hands together. 'Is that okay?'

'It's perfect.' Ryan smiled at his son. From the corner of his eye he saw his mother still watching him. 'Let's go, buddy,' he said, putting his arm around Charlie's shoulders. 'I promised Juliet some turkey.'

Juliet rolled her shoulders, moving her head from side to side to relax the stiff muscles in her neck. She was wearing yellow rubber gloves, the sleeves of her checked shirt rolled up to her elbows, her hair twisted on her head to keep it out of the cleaning fluid.

'Today I'm thankful for this shop,' she murmured. It was her haven, the place she felt surrounded by nature at its most beautiful. That's why she'd decided to spend Thanksgiving Day in here, washing the floors and the counters, sorting through old stock, making enough space for the holiday designs she had planned. A clean, fresh start, and a way to keep herself occupied while Poppy was spending the next two days with her father and her grandparents. It beat sitting around moping, which was what she would be doing if she weren't here.

By early afternoon everything had been polished to a shine. She'd sorted through the shelves of vases and boxes of florist wire, making notes of the things she'd need to reorder. Every now and then she'd pick up her phone, only to find there were no messages from Thomas, or from anybody else. The few friends she had in Shaw Haven were celebrating with their own families, and her friends in the UK probably didn't even know it was a national holiday over here. For them, it was just another dreary Thursday in the November rain.

But that was okay. It gave her enough time to get the shop ready before the holiday season really set in. And by trading off Thanksgiving, she'd have Poppy on Christmas Day. At least that was something to look forward to.

She was standing on the wooden stepladder, reaching up to replace a light bulb when there was a loud bang on the glass door. She looked over, trying to see who it was through the rain-obscured glass, but she couldn't make anything out.

Almost immediately her thoughts turned to Poppy. As she quickly climbed down the rungs, she touched her pocket. Her phone was still there. Surely Thomas would have called if there was something wrong.

Still, by the time she made it to the door she was breathless, and not from the exertion of running across the tiled floor. She squinted as she flipped each lock in turn, still trying to see if it was Thomas on the other side, but the water-splattered window was impossible to look through.

Pulling the door open, she felt her mouth drop when she realised it was Ryan standing there, his hair plastered to his head, rivulets of rain making their way down his skin. He was wearing a lightweight jacket – way too thin for this time of year. It was soaked through, sticking to his body in a very distracting way.

'Oh my, look at you, you'd better come in.' She took a step back, to let him come inside.

'I can't, Charlie's in the car. I just came to bring you some turkey.' He lifted a plastic bag and passing it to her. It was heavy – with two large plastic boxes inside. 'Like I promised, remember?'

She allowed herself to smile. There was something about this man – standing in the entrance of her shop, offering her food because she was alone on Thanksgiving Day – that made her feel she wasn't alone. As wet as he was, his mere presence felt like the sun coming out.

'Thanks, I could use a break from cleaning.' She pulled the yellow plastic gloves she'd been wearing off. 'Did you cook it yourself?'

'With a little help from Boston Market. But it's good. Even Charlie said so.' He looked behind her, at the shop. His eyes widened when he saw how out of place everything was. 'You're not running a Black Friday sale?'

She shook her head. 'Not a lot of point. Nobody's after a bargain bouquet on Black Friday. Plus the holiday season should be my most lucrative time of year, so I thought I'd get the shop Christmas ready.'

'Are you working tomorrow?'

Over his shoulder she could see his old truck, raindrops splashing off the metallic roof. Charlie was sitting in the passenger seat, his face pressed against the window. She waved at him, and he smiled, waving tentatively back at her.

'I'm not planning to. Hopefully I'll finish everything here by tonight, so tomorrow I'll get to chill. Poppy's not coming home until Saturday.' She could already picture it. A warm bath to take the cold from her bones, plus a nice big glass of red wine. She was beginning to discover there were some advantages to shared custody, after all.

'Come sailing with me tomorrow.' The smile on his face sent a shiver down her spine. 'Charlie's got another sleepover – he's going to the movies to see that dragon thing. So I'm on my own, too.'

'Sailing in this weather?' she questioned. 'Is that a good idea?'

'The forecast's better for tomorrow. It'll still be cold, but we can wrap up warm and bring some hot chocolate with us. As long as there's no storm, then we can set sail. The Chesapeake is beautiful in the summer, but in the fall it's in another league, like God's own country. I want to show it to you.'

'What if it starts raining while we're out there?'

'Then we'll hunker down in the galley and I'll show you what a poker fiend I can be. Come on, London, take a chance and come sailing with me.'

Her immediate response was to refuse. Yet she found herself questioning that response, analysing it. Was it fear of Thomas that was stopping her from agreeing, or fear of herself?

What was it Cesca had said when she visited? *If somebody is offering you a bit of fun, why don't you take it?*

She already knew that a day out with Ryan would be fun. She hadn't laughed as much in years as she had with him. He was attractive, kind and full of humour – and more importantly he'd be gone in a few months. Like her, he wasn't looking for something permanent.

Just a bit of fun. She could do that.

'Okay,' she said, her mouth widening into a smile. 'I'll go sailing with you. And if I end up falling overboard after a squall hits, I expect you to come in and save me.'

His grin was as big as hers. 'Sweetheart, you can count on it.'

15

O, then, dear saint, let lips do what hands do

– Romeo and Juliet

Cleaning the shop on Thanksgiving Day had worn her out, until every muscle in her body ached. After walking back through the door in the late evening, her hair covered in cobwebs, the skin on her hands raw from scrubbing, Juliet had called Poppy and talked to her for a while, satisfying herself that her daughter was happy and well looked after, before collapsing into her much-anticipated bath. But rather than drink from the glass of Malbec she'd poured for herself, she'd fallen asleep until the water had turned chill against her skin. And of course, by the time she dried herself, and crawled into bed, she somehow found a second wind.

She lay there, listening to the creaking of the house, of the whistling of the wind as the storm slowly steamed its way out, and tried to order the thoughts as they rushed through her head.

'That man's got a thing for you.' That's what Cesca had said to her, as Ryan had carried a sleeping Charlie back home, his muscles flexing beneath his son's weight. *'He's been making love to you with his eyes for half the night. And the way he kept staring at*

you, Jesus, Juliet, it made me realise your eyes weren't the only thing he wanted to make love to.'

It was a good thing neither Ryan nor Sam had heard her. It was bad enough having to put up with Sam calling her *London* for the rest of his stay, his huge grin making her want to stab him in the eye with a pen. As for Cesca, when she wasn't trying to support Juliet through her issues with Thomas, she was singing Ryan's praises, telling her the best way to get over one man was by getting under the next.

As soon as they'd left to fly back to LA she'd missed them. And now, the house was quieter than ever. Just Juliet and her thoughts – and they weren't proving to be the best company right now.

Dawn arrived, heralding a change in weather. Though the sky remained overcast, any hint of yesterday's storm was gone, leaving yellow-tipped clouds that seemed desperately trying to dissolve. Juliet pulled at the corner of her curtain, looking out at the yard where broken branches and twigs lay on top of mushy brown leaves, puddles of water still covering them from yesterday's rain. It was sweater weather, for sure.

She carried her coffee cup out onto the porch. The old bench creaked as she sat down, curling her denim-clad legs beneath her. Wispy clouds rose up from her mug, mingling with the vapour that escaped every time she exhaled. It reminded her of her daughter, and the way Poppy called it 'dragon breath'.

She was swallowing the final mouthful when she saw the front door open in the next house over. Ryan emerged, wearing a dark grey sweater and jeans. The denim clung to him like it couldn't bear to let go.

Wow. He was breathtaking.

158

'Hey.' A smile curled at his lips as he walked down the steps, and across to her bungalow. His old sneakers squelched across the wet grass. 'You ready to go?'

'As soon as I've finished my coffee.' She lifted her mug up. 'There's still some left in the pot. Would you like one?'

Every time he was near, her body reacted to him. He only had to stand close for her to become hyper-aware of his height, his muscles, the way his face looked like sculpted perfection. He smelled of fresh water and sandalwood, a combination that fired something in her synapses, her mind a whirl as adrenaline shot through her body.

'Coffee sounds good.' His voice still held the thickness of sleep. 'Do you have a travel mug? We can take some with us.'

He followed her into the kitchen, and she could feel his body heat as he stood behind her. The room seemed small, more closed in than she remembered. As if by walking inside it he'd somehow made everything less significant.

'I made us some sandwiches, too. I wasn't sure how long we'd be out for, so I thought I should bring something just in case.' She was talking just to fill the silence, afraid of what would happen if she let it overwhelm her. 'It's ham salad – do you like ham? Maybe I should have asked you first.'

'Ham sounds great, thanks for making them. And we can be out as long as you like since we're child-free. The day is ours.'

Oh. She felt an excited nervousness pricking at her skin.

The drive to the wharf passed in the blink of an eye. He turned the radio to a rock station, and hummed along as he drove through the town and towards the water's edge. His foot tapped to the beat, his muscled thigh rising and falling, and she couldn't tear her eyes away. When they reached a stoplight he looked over at her, a small smile playing at his lips. Their eyes locked, as if they shared a secret nobody else could know. Her skin started to tingle all over again.

'You doing all right, London?'

'Yeah, I'm good.'

'You're being very quiet.' He tipped his head to the side, still staring at her. 'Is there something wrong?'

'I'm just a bit tired, that's all. It's been a busy few days.'

'That sounds like the perfect reason to get on the boat and relax. I'll need your help to get out in the water, but after that you can sit down and enjoy the view. I'll try not to wear you out too much.' He grinned after that last sentence, and a bolt of delight rushed through her.

'I like to pull my own weight.'

Still with the grin, though it was more smirk than anything. 'You don't have a whole lot of weight to pull.' He glanced at her body – at her striped blue and white sweater, and tight jeans. His eyes softened as he took her in.

The atmosphere between them felt electric, the way it had that night at the dance club. She could feel it fizzing on her skin, making the tiny hairs on her arms stand up.

'That sounds like a compliment,' she noted, keeping her voice light. 'But I guess it could be an insult too.'

'It's all compliment.' His voice was gravelled. 'You should definitely take it that way.'

When they pulled into the parking lot, the wharf was busy – full of leisure sailors taking advantage of the holiday. The two of them made their way up the jetty towards *Miss Maisie*, the forty-footer standing tall and unaffected by yesterday's storm.

Like the last time she was here, the boat was ready for

them, no doubt polished to a shine by Ryan's friend Stan. But unlike last time, it was just the two of them, and being without Poppy and Charlie made her feel exposed and yet excited.

Ryan climbed on board first, reaching his hand down to help her up. His fingers folded around hers, warm and strong, pulling her up easily until her feet landed on the deck. He was standing close, his body towering above hers. The breeze lifted her hair, a stray piece escaping from her ponytail, and he reached out to tuck it back behind her ear.

He dragged his finger back over her neck, leaving a trail of ice behind him. A shiver slid its way down her spine, making her inner thighs shake with need. She had never been as affected by a man before. He was strong and warm and beautiful, and he scared the hell out of her.

Love hurt. She'd learned that more than once. It had destroyed her when her mother died, and then turned around and did the same thing again when Thomas left her. It was a knife wrapped in velvet, soft to the touch yet deadly.

But this wasn't love, it was lust. And she could deal with that, couldn't she? She could let herself surrender to the desire, to the sensations of Ryan's fingers. They were both adults, they were both single, and they both knew where they stood.

A fling. No more no less. A few months of fun, while she sorted out her life and Ryan waited to move away, and then they could both move on without regret. Nobody needed to know, it could stay their little secret. It could be that simple, if only she could stop herself from overanalysing it.

'Are you ready?' he murmured, his hand cupping her neck, his fingers brushing softly against her skin.

Was she? Yes, she really was. Ready for whatever happened next, and determined to face it head on.

'Yes, I'm ready.' She nodded. 'Let's go.'

The wind picked up out in the bay, making the sails flap against the mast as the boat sped its way through the water. Juliet was standing at the front of the boat, her hair blowing out behind her, as she held on to the rail to keep herself standing. She was staring out into the bay, her back towards Ryan, and for a moment she reminded him of the carved wooden figureheads on ancient ships.

Britannia ruling the sea.

When she turned around to look at him, her face was flushed from the breeze. Her lips were swollen and red, her eyes sparkling. Her vitality was intoxicating, a live wire he couldn't help but want to touch. He wasn't surprised any more by the intensity of his reaction to her, but that didn't diminish its impact one iota. Every time he looked at her, he couldn't help but remember their passionate kiss. The warmth of her mouth, the softness of her breasts as they pressed against him.

They'd been sailing for just under an hour, leaving Shaw Haven behind them as they made their way down the bay. And for sixty minutes he hadn't been able to take his eyes off her. It was driving him crazy not to touch her. And yet he couldn't help but remember the promise he'd made himself that night when he'd returned to his home. *Whatever happened next was up to her.* He wasn't the kind of guy to force the issue – not after seeing his father dominate his mother during his childhood. If she wanted something, she was going to have to make the first move.

'I'm going to anchor us up over there,' he shouted, trying

to be heard above the wind. He steered the boats towards the grassy bank on the left that opened up into a small inlet. Far from any town, it was deserted save for the birds that swooped and hovered above the marshland.

Juliet nodded, clambering over the foredeck to grab the anchor while he steered them into shore. He loved the way she was a natural, anticipating his instructions before he'd even had a chance to shout them. She was an easy crewmate, at one with the water, and it was sexy as hell to watch her take control.

He brought the boat to a stop twenty feet from the land, not wanting to risk the shallow waters that might bring them aground.

'How deep is it?' she called out.

'About fourteen feet.'

Without another word she measured out the anchor line, tying a cleat knot to make it the right depth, before lowering the anchor into the water. He straightened the boat up as the anchor slowly made it's way to the bottom, and Juliet knotted the remaining rope around the bow cleat.

'Does that look okay?' She frowned, pulling at the knot to make sure it was tight. 'I did it the way you showed me, but that was a while ago.'

He released the wheel and walked over to her. A glance at the knot was enough to tell him it was sturdy. The boat bobbed gently in the water, rising up and down with the rhythm of the tide.

'It's perfect,' he told her, not looking at the knot any more. He was too busy staring at her face, her lips, her deep hazel eyes.

He felt the warmth of her stare as her eyes held his. She looked different out here on the river. Stronger somehow. Even though she was wearing flat sneakers, she seemed to have grown a few inches.

The boat bobbed up and down in the water as he stood and stared, neither of them breaking the connection between them. The gentle ebb and flow of the water against the bank accompanied the sound of the blood rushing through his ears. A Canada Goose flew down onto the riverbank. Nestling among the tall grass he let out a deep honk.

'Shall we go explore?' he asked her, pointing at the bank. 'We have enough time.'

Without taking her eyes from his, she shook her head. 'No. I don't want to explore.'

He frowned. 'You don't?'

'No.'

'If you're cold I have a sweater in the galley. You want me to bring it up?'

The hint of a smile curled at her lips. 'I'm not cold. I don't need a sweater.' She took a step forward, until the gap between them almost disappeared. He could smell the sweet fragrance of her shampoo, mixing in with the crisp, cool aroma of the river. He had to curl his hands into fists to stop himself from reaching out and touching her.

'London . . . '

'Sshh. It's okay.' There was a determined look on her face – one he hadn't seen before. 'You don't need to look so worried, Ryan.'

'I'm not worried.'

She reached up to trace the lines in his brow. 'You're frowning,' she murmured, running her finger along the skin to his temple.

He closed his eyes for a moment. Even the briefest touch

from her was enough to fire up the need he'd tried to keep buried. His fists were so tight his nails were digging into his palms.

When he opened his eyes, she'd closed the gap between them completely. She was on her tiptoes, staring at him, her eyes soft and yet deep.

'Ryan,' she whispered.

'Yeah?'

'What are you thinking?'

What was he thinking? Was she crazy? With her so close he could barely conjure up a lucid thought at all. 'I'm thinking you're awfully close.'

'You want me to move away?'

'No.'

'You want to know what I'm thinking?' she asked him. He could feel the warmth of her breath when she spoke.

'There's nothing I want to know more.'

His answer elicited another smile. 'I'm thinking about that kiss. The one in my kitchen. And I'm thinking about what might have happened if the children hadn't been there.'

'Like now you mean?'

'Yeah. Exactly like now.' Her finger traced down from his temple to his jawline. 'Because I can't get it out of my head. Haven't been able to since that night. I keep remembering how warm your lips were, how hard your body was. How I wanted more.'

'More?' His voice cracked.

'So much more.' She ran her finger along his bottom lip. He was standing as still as was possible on a moored-up boat. He was too entranced by this version of Juliet to do anything but stand and admire her. 'Ryan?'

'Yes?'

'Do you want to kiss me again?'

In that moment, he couldn't think of anything else. Yet still he waited, keeping his desire curled up tightly inside him, his eyes staring right into hers. 'Yeah, I want to kiss you.'

'So why don't you?' She was flirting with him. He could tell by the look in her eyes and the sound of her voice. Damn if he didn't love it, didn't love the way she could be so vulnerable and yet so strong. It was touching him in places he didn't know he had.

'Because I want you to kiss me first.'

The smile that had been playing hide and seek on her face broke out into a full grin. Her shoulders relaxed, her cheeks plumped up, and she looked more desirable than ever.

'Why didn't you say so?'

16

*Why then, can one desire too
much of a good thing?*

– As You Like It

It was just a kiss, right? A simple press of one mouth against
another. It wasn't even a first kiss – that honour went to
the kitchen clinch, that delicious embrace against the hard
wood worktop. But that had been a spur of the moment
impulse, a kiss without agenda. Free of prior planning or
deep meaning.

But not this kiss. She'd been thinking about this one all
morning. Been wondering when – not if – it would happen.
Wondering if it would feel as good as it did that night in
her bungalow.

The fact was it already felt better and she hadn't even done
it yet. Even the hesitation was delicious, thick with need and
meaning, and it pulsed through her body until her skin felt
raw with desire.

It meant something, because it was her choice. Her decision. She wasn't just letting things happen any more, she was
making them happen. She was laying claim to her own desires,
unafraid where they might take her. For the first time in

forever she was living for the moment, knowing that might be all they had.

And she was loving it.

She tightened her hold on his neck, placing the flat of her other palm against his chest to stop herself from falling forward. She could feel the planes of his muscles beneath his thin sweater, hard and unyielding.

She was still smiling when she kissed him, the elation of their connection making her want to laugh out loud. But then her lips softened, melted into his, moved against him with a demand she didn't need to speak. It was as if she had flicked a switch, and the lights had come flooding on. Ryan kissed her back, his hands sliding around her back and pressing against the curve of her spine.

This wasn't a fight for domination. They were two people – different yet equal – with needs and desires that matched each other's. She wasn't sure who opened their lips first, or whose tongue slid against whose, because they were both aching for the same thing.

When they pulled apart to grab a breath of air, she let her head fall back, exposing her neck. She didn't have to ask for him to kiss her throat – he just knew.

When did she last feel like this? He'd only touched her with his lips and yet she was on fire. She moved the hand resting on his chest, tracing his pectoral muscles down to his abdomen, letting her fingers rise and fall over the taut ridges.

'You're beautiful,' he whispered against her ear, the sensation of his breath making her shiver. 'So beautiful.'

He wasn't the first man to say it, and yet it felt so new. As though he was seeing something deeper inside her, not just the attractiveness of her face.

'So are you.' She moved her head to the side, capturing his lips again. Letting out a moan, he kissed her back, lifting a hand to run it through her hair. Above them, another goose swooped down to the riverbank, letting out a loud call as he made it to the grass.

'Ryan,' she said against his lips, unwilling to break the kiss.

'Mmmhmm?'

'I think you better take me to bed.'

'London?'

She rolled over, feeling the warm blankets enveloping her. Her mind was teetering on the edge of consciousness, still half-cloaked in dreams. There was a rocking sensation she couldn't quite place. For a moment she almost plunged back into sleep, not wanting to let go of its soft embrace.

'London? You need to wake up.'

Her eyes flew open. Ryan was sitting on the edge of the bed, his legs encased in denim, his torso bare. His hair was wet, slicked back from his head, and his skin glowed as though freshly scrubbed clean.

'What's going on?' She sat up, rubbing her eyes in an attempt to focus them. Looking around, she took everything in. Where was she?

The cabin.

Of his boat.

Naked.

Oh holy hell.

Without thinking, she pulled the blankets up to cover her bare chest. Ryan watched her, a smirk playing at his lips, as though everything about her amused him.

'What time is it?' she asked, glancing around for her phone.

'Just after four.'

'Four? What the heck?' She scrambled to her knees, still trying to cover her modesty. Her frantic movements were making him laugh, as he watched her, his eyes soft.

'We should head back to the wharf soon, before it starts to get dark. It gets pretty cold on the water when the sun goes down, and I haven't brought enough blankets.'

She rolled her lip between her teeth. 'I didn't realise it was so late. I must have slept for hours.'

'About five. But who's counting?'

Her spine straightened. 'I'm counting. I can't believe I was out for so long. You must have been bored out of your mind.'

'On the contrary, I had a lot of fun. You're interesting when you sleep.' Ryan grinned. 'Did you know you talk a lot when you're dreaming?'

'I do not.'

'Oh, yeah you do. I'd tell you what you said but most of it was X-rated. Let's just say that my name was one of the most used words.'

'Stop it.' Forgetting about her naked body, she scooted across the bed and hit him on the side of his arm. 'You're making it up.'

He caught her wrist, pulling her towards him. The covers fell from her body, revealing her flushed breasts and pale abdomen. The smile slid from his face, replaced by a longing that moulded his lips and narrowed his eyes. Reflecting the need she felt for him.

'Damn, London,' he said, still holding to her tight. 'My control's about as strong as your punches right now, and we need to get back to the mooring. You want to hit me, save it for when we're home.'

She opened her mouth to point out that they didn't share a home. That when they got back to Shaw Haven, he'd be back in his house and she'd be back in hers. But as soon as she saw the warning in his eyes, she closed it again, her lips smacking together like a fish blowing bubbles.

Ryan kissed her softly on her brow. She could barely feel the pressure. Releasing her wrist, he ran his hands down her hair, twisting the strands through his fingers. 'You should probably get dressed before I lose it altogether,' he said, moving back and pulling a T-shirt over his wet hair.

'What if I want you to lose it?' She smiled at him.

He raised an eyebrow. 'You want to see me out of control?'

She licked her dry lips. 'Maybe.'

'Then get dressed, London, and get your sweet little behind back on deck. We'll sail back to the wharf and drive home. As soon as we walk through my front door I'll show you exactly what I'm like when I lose it.'

She wasn't sure whether it was a threat or a promise. Either way his words made her skin tingle and her heart race. The thought of Ryan Sutherland losing control in front of her was more tantalising than she could say. She couldn't wait to see it.

The sun was almost setting by the time they'd tied the boat up on the jetty, casting a fiery glow over Chesapeake Bay as it slowly slid beneath the horizon. Ryan helped Juliet climb down from the deck, the rubber of her soles squeaking against the wooden planks of the boardwalk, her muscles complaining about the sudden jolt.

She was aching all over, from the delicious combination of sailing and sex. Unlike Ryan, she hadn't had a chance to stand under the tiny showerhead in the cabin bathroom, and she still felt sweaty and slick from all their afternoon exertions.

She watched as he made his final checks on the deck, coiling up the rope and lowering the sail. He locked the door to the cabin, sliding the key and its cork key ring into his pocket, then climbed down to join her on the jetty.

'You ready?'

They were almost at the car when he stopped short, frowning as he read a sign that had been fixed to the fence.

For Sale, all enquiries to Within and Cross Realtors.

Nine words that made anger flash in his eyes.

'What the hell?' His frown deepened as he looked across to the wooden hut, where they'd seen Stan only that morning. It was locked up now, wooden shutters firmly closed across the windows. For some reason that made Ryan even angrier.

'What is it?'

He reached out to touch the sign, then pulled his hand back, fingers curled into a fist. 'They should've told me this was for sale.'

'Maybe Stan didn't know.' Juliet kept her voice quiet. Something about the fire in Ryan's eyes made her feel edgy.

'I don't mean Stan. I meant my parents. My mom at least should have let me know about this.'

'Your family own the wharf?' She didn't know why she was so surprised. It was no secret that the Sutherlands owned half of Shaw Haven, and the Marshalls owned the rest. Two families with such power – and both she and Ryan seemed to be the black sheep.

'They do. And so do I.'

Her mouth dropped open. 'You do?'

'I'm a shareholder.'

'I didn't realise. I thought . . . ' She trailed off. What did she think? Of course he had shares and money – the kind of money only a Sutherland or Marshall would have around here. Thomas had told her as much, after all.

He was one of *them*, even if he pretended not to be.

'What are you going to do?' she asked him.

He looked around at the deserted wharf. 'Nothing right now, I guess.' He rolled his shoulders, as if to relieve the tension. 'Come on, let's go home.' He grabbed her hand, and they walked over to his car, feet crunching as they made their way across the gravelled lot. His muscles were stiff, his body unbending, and she knew that the *For Sale* sign they'd seen had affected him. More than once on the journey home she opened her mouth to ask him about it, but the thin line of his lips and furrowed brow had frozen the question on her tongue. It was as though he'd drawn an invisible boundary around himself. She had no idea how to breach it.

By the time he pulled up on his driveway, she was unsure what to do. Maybe he wanted to be alone to think about the wharf. And though she definitely didn't want to be alone, she could give him that at least.

'I'll head on home,' she said, climbing out of the passenger seat, as he held the door open. 'Thank you for a lovely day.'

He put a hand on her shoulder. 'I thought I was taking you home?'

'I am home. That's where I'm going.'

'To *my* home. That's where I meant. I don't want you to leave.' His face softened, some of the tension leaving his jaw. 'I was distant on the way home, I know. I was shocked by the sign, I wasn't expecting it. I'm trying to take it all in.'

She let out a lungful of air, her muscles relaxing at his words. 'Don't you want to be alone, make some phone calls or something? I guess that place means a lot to you, huh?'

'You could say that. But no, I don't want to be alone. I want to take you home, and have you all over again, but this time on dry land. And when you go to sleep, I want it to be in my arms, not over there on your own.' He put his hand out, offering it to her, his fingers outstretched.

It didn't take longer than a second to decide. She took Ryan's hand, her warm palm resting against his, and let him fold his fingers around hers. A ghost of a smile played on his lips, then he led her up his front steps and across his wooden deck, to the front door. He slid his key into the lock, and as he turned it, she felt as though something was turning inside her, too. Unlocking her emotions, laying her bare, opening her up in a way she hadn't been for the longest time. Her chest felt full with the knowledge of it.

'Come inside, please,' he said softly. Still holding his hand, she followed him in. She'd never been in his hallway before. She usually came into his kitchen by the back door.

The walls were covered in framed prints. Images of people, of destinations, of Charlie posing on beaches and in cities. As well as the photographs there were mementos from all over the world. Old masks and brightly covered dream catchers were hung next to tribal artwork and framed silken fabrics. It was like stepping into a living museum.

'Wow,' she breathed, looking around, trying to take it all in.

'What?' A perplexed smile pulled at the corner of his lips as he stared at her. 'Is there something wrong?'

'It's just this.' She gestured at his walls. 'I wasn't expecting it. I don't know why, I mean you've been to so many places, it's natural you'd want to remember them. But I always took you as the kind of guy who travelled light.'

'I am.'

'Then how did you bring all these things back with you? There are enough souvenirs to fill a trailer.'

'I don't carry all this stuff around with me. I just find things I love and send them to my storage unit. When we came here, I decided the walls looked a little bare, needed some decoration.'

She stepped towards the wooden mask, its face painted in greens, reds and blues. 'Can I touch it?' she asked.

'Sure.'

She slid her finger across the surface, feeling the oily paint, the rough wood, her path rising and falling with the undulations of the face. 'Where's this from?'

'Bonsaaso, in Ghana. It's a small village in the rainforest.' His voice was louder than she expected. He was standing right behind her. 'We spent a few weeks there taking photographs for a magazine.'

'What about this?' She pointed at a wooden shield.

'That's from the Philippines. It's called a *kalasag*. They were traditionally used in battles by Filipino warriors.'

Juliet felt his breath on her neck, sending a shiver down her spine. He was so close she only had to turn for their bodies to be touching. She breathed in, smelling the mixture of fresh water and soap that was becoming familiar. Everything about him was enticing.

'They're all so beautiful,' she breathed, unable to take her eyes away. 'No wonder you had to have them here.'

She turned to face him, and he was staring at her. This time it was Ryan who reached out and feathered his fingers along her jawline, gently tipping her chin up as he leaned down to kiss

175

her. 'I've got something else to show you, too,' he murmured, his lips curling up against hers as he spoke.

'I bet you have.' Her smile matched his. When he took her hand and led her to the stairs, she wasn't sure who was more eager to get to his bedroom.

In the end it was a dead heat. But really, they both won.

17

Parting is such sweet sorrow,
That I shall say good night till it be morrow

– Romeo and Juliet

Juliet lay curled up on his bed, her body illuminated by a shaft of moonlight. He stared at her face, following the curves of her profile with his eyes, imagining capturing them in a photograph, one that was only meant for him. They were both naked. He'd cranked the heating up enough for neither of them to feel the chill they'd had on the boat.

She mumbled in her sleep, turning over, and he glanced at the clock beside his bed. The illuminated numbers told him it was almost one in the morning. If only he could stop his mind from racing and join her in sleep. Instead thoughts were rushing through him like a river down a waterfall, crashing against his skull until he acknowledged their existence.

Good thoughts – ones about Juliet, the way she'd kissed him on the boat, and the lightness in her smile when she'd teased him. He'd seen a different side of her today, and he'd been so damn pleased that she'd finally made a move.

But there were darker thoughts, too. He blinked, trying to take the memory of that For Sale sign out of his mind, but it stubbornly remained. His stomach dropped at the thought of it. Of what the money men would do to that piece of real estate once they got their hands on it.

Trying not to wake Juliet up, he rolled to the edge of the mattress, and climbed out of the bed, pulling his shorts on. He padded down the wooden hallway in his bare feet, then down the stairs and into the kitchen, where he poured himself a glass of water.

The cold liquid soothed his parched lips as he emptied the tumbler, then refilled it, carrying it into the living room. Opening his MacBook, he clicked on the Internet, quickly searching for *Within and Cross*, the realtors who were trying to sell the wharf. He found them almost right away. The listing for the wharf was on their front page, and he clicked on the 'more information' link to see what they had to say.

Development Opportunity.

This old-fashioned wharf has been part of Shaw Haven since the 1760s. Originally a merchant port, this has now become the playground of the rich, and is ripe for redevelopment. With permission for a hotel and leisure complex, plus easy access to all major routes and to Baltimore Airport, we don't expect this to be available for long. All enquiries to Within and Cross, by telephone, email or in person to our Baltimore offices.

He took another mouthful of water, trying to stem the anger he could feel rising up from his gut. Of all the things his father could sell, he must have known the wharf would be the one to rile Ryan up into a fury. Had he planned it that way?

Ryan grew up on that wharf, following his grandfather around, learning how to sail and fish. And when his grandfather had been dying from cancer in a sterile hospital room, Ryan had promised him to protect the wharf, to ensure Stan always had a job there, and to make sure the *Miss Maisie* never went anywhere else. Ryan closed his eyes as he remembered his teenaged self, gently holding his grandfather's papery hand as he listened to his hoarse, old man voice. He'd agreed to protect it, to make sure it never passed into the wrong hands. Stupidly, he'd thought it was an easily kept promise. His mother had loved the wharf as much as he did – surely she wouldn't let his father sell it.

He shook his head at himself. That was exactly what his father would do. When did he ever listen to his wife?

'Are you okay?' Juliet walked into the room. She was wearing his white T-shirt and nothing else. Just the sight of her was enough to stir him, filling his mind with the promise of her body. 'I woke up and you were gone. I didn't know where you were.'

He pushed the screen of the MacBook back down. 'I couldn't sleep, I came down to grab a glass of water.' He pointed at the half-empty tumbler on the table in front of him.

She leaned on the back of the sofa. 'What were you looking at on your laptop?'

She felt too far away. He needed her closer. Ryan reached for her, grabbing her hands and guiding her around the arm of the sofa, then pulled her onto his lap. She was facing him, her bare legs on either side of his. He felt the softness of her skin, the warmth of her inner thighs, and the need stirred inside him again.

'I looked up the wharf listing.' He ran his hands down her

gorgeous hair, his eyes roaming her body as if it were a feast. 'They're offering it for redevelopment.'

'What kind of redevelopment?'

'The expensive kind, I guess. It's prime real estate, close to the big cities, close to the interstate. The perfect place to build hotels or condos, for rich people looking to spend the weekend here. Add in the views and the river access, and it's ripe for the picking.'

She frowned. 'Why are they selling it? Hasn't it been in your family for years?'

'Generations.' He nodded. 'Pretty much as long as there's been a Shaw in Shaw Haven, we've owned the wharf and the area around it. That's how the Shaws built up their wealth, controlling what came in and out of the area. We all grew up with half a foot in the Chesapeake. That river is part of us.'

She ran her hands over his chest, tracing circles with her fingers. Just the sensation of her touch was enough to calm him.

'Could you afford to buy it?' she asked. 'That way you could prevent it from being redeveloped.'

'Not the amount of money they're asking for it. I'd need to raise the capital, and I could only do that if I had a business plan. Which would mean redeveloping it, or thinking of something else we can do.' He looked up at her. 'Plus I'll be leaving in a few months, I don't need any more ties here.'

She licked her lips, trying to compose her features. 'So why are they selling it now? Is the company in trouble?'

'No, the last set of accounts I saw were healthy as hell. Plus I know they can raise money if they want to. They offered me enough to walk away from the company.'

'They tried to buy you out?' Her eyes widened with shock. 'Why?'

'Because they think I'm a liability. My father hates the fact that I'm a shareholder. There's no love lost between us – there hasn't been for years – and he just wants me gone.' He pressed his face into her neck. She smelled of fresh apples. He was distracted by the sweetness of her skin.

She trailed her finger up his torso, her eyes following their progress. He could see her trying to work through his words, make sense of what he was saying. 'But why wouldn't you just take the money and go? You've already said you don't want to stay here, that you'll be leaving soon. So why have the hassle of being dragged into this when you don't need it? You could sell up, let them do what they want with the wharf and never look back.'

He wrapped his hands around her lower back, pulling her closer until their chests were pressed together. He could feel her breasts beneath the fabric of his T-shirt, and the warmth of her against his skin.

'I made a promise to make sure the wharf stayed in the family,' he said. 'And it's not just about me, it's about Charlie, too. He's a Shaw and a Sutherland and I owe it to him to protect his heritage.'

Her lips brushed against his neck, her hair trailing over his shoulder. 'That makes sense,' she said. 'It's amazing the things we'll do for our kids.'

'Like stay in a town where we don't feel as though we belong.'

He could feel her smile against his skin. 'And the way we'll put up with shit from other people just to protect them,' she agreed.

She caught his earlobe between her teeth, gently flicking it with her tongue. The sensation made him gasp, tipping his head back, as he inclined his hips to press his hardness against her. She was driving him crazy, with soft touches and warm lips, and he was loving every minute of it.

'Maybe that's why this thing between us is so important,' she whispered, her fingers trailing down his arms. 'Having a little haven for the both of us. Somewhere we can escape from the assholes and the family and everything that brings us down.'

Is that what this was? An escape from reality? He closed his eyes as she moved her lips to his jaw, kissing and licking at his skin until he ached to kiss her back. She was soothing and arousing and finding every emotion in between.

Her legs were warm and soft as she straddled him, lifting herself up, and using her hand to guide him until he was exactly where he wanted to be. Pressing against her, feeling her desire, her need, countering it with his own.

He'd be her haven if she'd be his. He couldn't think of anywhere he'd rather escape to.

They were sitting on the porch swing at the rear of his house, hidden from the road and the neighbours. Juliet was on Ryan's lap, a blanket wrapped around them both, his arms encircling her beneath the wool. She curled into him as he used his feet to rock them back and forth, his movements slow and gentle, as though he was as exhausted as she was. She closed her eyes, breathing him in as she pressed her cheek to his sweater-covered chest, not wanting the moment to end.

'What time is Thomas bringing Poppy back?' Ryan asked. His voice held a tone that felt as wistful as her heart. It felt as though summer was coming to an end even though they were reaching the end of November. It was that aching last-day-of-holiday feeling, and it made her want to stamp her feet and cry.

'In about an hour. The same time you have to pick Charlie up,' she murmured, her voice half-muffled by his chest. 'I'm hoping she's feeling as tired as I am, I'm going to need an early night.'

She felt his laugh, as his chest rose and fell against her. 'So I did wear you out.'

'We wore each other out. You don't seem full of beans either, my friend.'

'Yeah, well sex every other hour will do that to you. And maybe you're right, I must be getting old.'

'You'll never be old.'

'Tell that to my muscles. Right now they're saying I'm beat, and that even if I wanted more sex – which I do, by the way – they're not going to play ball.'

Her smile deepened. 'I like playing with balls.' When she looked up he was grinning at her. He was devastatingly attractive. Her golden man with the sexy smile.

'I know you do, London.'

Funny how she'd bristled at that nickname when he'd first used it. Now she loved it. It was like a little secret only the two of them knew. She wanted to cover it in bubble wrap and keep it safe, protect it from the harsh winds of the outside world. Because right then everything felt fragile. Like a wisp of smoke blowing on the wind.

'What are you going to tell Charlie if he asks what you've been doing?'

'Ah, I'll probably say something like "sailing, eating … spending some time in London".'

She sat up on his lap, slapping him on the arm. 'Stop it!'

He shrugged. 'Charlie's not going to care what I've been doing. He'll be too full of his sleepover and the movie to ask

183

me how I've been. And that's how it should be, he's a kid. He doesn't need to worry about his old man.'

He was staring at her, making her body react in that old, familiar way. Her chest tightened, her thigh muscles ached. She couldn't get enough of him. 'Poppy will definitely want to know. That girl can smell a lie from a mile away.'

Ryan brushed her hair from her face, his hands gentle as he trailed them against her cheeks. 'So what are you going to tell her?'

'Well, nothing about this, of course.' Her eyes widened at the thought. 'I guess I'll tell her about clearing the shop out, and making plans for the holiday displays, hopefully that will get her excited enough to stop her asking any more.'

'What if Charlie tells her we went sailing? He was in the car when I asked you, remember? I told him we were going out on the boat.'

'You did? Damn.' She pulled her lip between her teeth, biting hard enough for it to hurt. 'Ugh, I'm such a terrible liar. She can read me like a book.'

He was laughing again, pulling her into him, wrapping the blanket around them snugly. 'Hey, calm down, it's not that bad. And so what if Poppy finds out? Is that the end of the world?'

She stiffened in his arms. 'Only if she tells Thomas . . .' She trailed off, not even wanting to think about it.

He tightened his hold on her. 'Poppy won't think to tell him, and neither will we. So we'll be fine.' His voice was reassuring.

She looked up at him, blinking rapidly, his face obscured by her lashes. 'We will?' She wanted to ask him what he meant by 'we', but the question died on her tongue. She wasn't supposed to be thinking about the future.

'Sure. Look, it's not long until Christmas, the kids will be going crazy for the holidays, the school's going to send them crazier still. And it's not as if I'm going to be marching into your kitchen at tea time while the two of you are eating and kiss the hell out of you against the stove, is it?'

Her breath caught at the image. Why did that turn her on so much? 'Um, no?'

'Well, at least not when the kids are around. But if I catch you on your own, or bending down planting some flowers on a day Poppy's not here, then I can't be held responsible for my actions, okay?' He grabbed her hair, pulling it into a thick pony-tail in his palm, then slowly tugged, until her face was inclined to his. 'Because if I catch you alone, London, I'm going to have to kiss you.' His mouth brushed against hers. 'And if I kiss you, I'm going to have to take your clothes off,' he whispered into her lips. 'And if I take your clothes off, I'm going to have to have sex with you.'

'I don't know if that's a threat or a promise,' she replied, her words mumbled against his mouth.

'It's both, beautiful. It's both.'

18

Sin from thy lips? O trespass sweetly urged!
Give me my sin again

– Romeo and Juliet

'Momma, did the Native Americans really cook turkey for the Pilgrims?' Poppy frowned, colouring the page with her brown pen. 'And where did they buy it from? Was there a Whole Foods at Plymouth Rock?'

Juliet was staring out of the window at the house on the other side of the yard. Was it only five hours since she'd been there? 'I don't know, honey,' she said, not actually hearing Poppy's question. 'Maybe we should Google it.'

'Nicole doesn't like turkey. She says eating meat is cruel. She's a vegetable.'

Juliet stifled a laugh. 'You mean a vegetarian.'

Poppy frowned. 'That's what I said. Anyway, she thinks Daddy should be one too. He said maybe he'd try it out some time.'

'He did?'

'Yeah, and then when Grandpa cooked burgers on Friday night, Nicole and Daddy had vegetable ones.'

Juliet pulled her gaze from Ryan's house, staring at her daughter. She waited for the pain to set in. Hearing about

Thomas and his girlfriend was usually like a fist to her gut, but instead of feeling sick she felt . . . nothing.

It was disconcerting.

'What about you, what did you eat?' Juliet closed up the dishwasher and pressed the buttons. The machine began to whirr as it took in water.

'Oh I had a burger, and a hot dog, too. Grandpa burnt the sausages, but it was still okay.'

'Sounds delicious.'

Ryan's back door opened, and he walked out onto the deck. He had his camera in his hands, and leaned on the railing while he aimed it at the trees behind the house. He was oblivious to her stare, concentrating hard on whatever it was he'd seen in the leafless branches. She watched as he took his photographs, his face serious, his arms flexing, his hair falling over his brow. There was something undeniably sexy about his absorption, and the way his camera seemed like an extension of him. Poppy continued to chatter at the table, her attention taken by her colouring book, and Juliet answered her without thinking, her eyes still trained on the beautiful man from the house next door.

In an agonisingly slow movement, he turned the lens from the tree, until it was pointing straight at her window. He reached out to adjust it, as if zooming in, and she felt herself freeze as she stared at him through the glass.

Her breath caught in her throat as she saw him smile, a soft curve of his lips that made her ache inside.

Ryan turned from his spot on his deck, and walked back through his back door and into his kitchen. She stood for a minute, hoping he'd come out again, and somehow they'd be able to communicate from a distance.

The next moment her phone buzzed in her pocket. She pulled it out, staring at the screen absentmindedly.

You look beautiful in that dress, London.

Oh. Her hand fluttered to her chest. She could feel her heart hammering beneath her ribcage in response to his words. Black letters on a screen were no substitute for the real thing, but he was thinking about her, and that knowledge filled her with joy.

Still smiling, she quickly tapped out a reply.

What were you photographing?

It only took a moment for him to send a message back.

A red cardinal. It was hiding in the bare branches.

She thought again about his absorption, and how attractive it had been. For a moment she imagined herself travelling with him, watching him catalogue the beautiful scenery, the animals, the people. She bet it was something to see.

Can you send me the picture?

I took it with my SLR. I'll develop an extra print for you.

Another thing that enticed her. His love of the whole process of photography. Though he'd told her he mostly used his digital camera when he was on a job, she knew from his description that it was his old-fashioned camera he loved best.

Thank you. BTW I miss you.

I miss you, too. I keep fantasising about
climbing up through your bedroom window.

She smiled at his suggestion, picturing him calling up to her
like Romeo wooing Juliet on her balcony.

What are we, high schoolers?

I feel like a high schooler when you're around.
Fancy hitting some bases with me?

You want to play baseball?
Won't that wake the kids up?

You have a lot to learn, London.

Then teach me.

Oh, I plan to.

Another promise veiled as a threat. She was getting used
to those.

'I've been expecting you.' Ryan's father sat back in his tall
leather chair, his hands steepled in front of him. The sleeves
of his expensive wool suit showed just a hint of his white
cufflinked sleeves. His office was spotless and paper-free.
Everything was carefully in place, the way his father liked it.
Even as a young child, Ryan had known how much his father

hated mess. Every night, half an hour before his dad was due home, his mother would run around the house picking up toys and books, then drag Ryan into the bathroom and make him scrub his face and clean his teeth. Anything less than perfection wasn't allowed.

He stared at his father for a moment, trying and failing to fathom him out. 'Then you'll know what this is about.' Ryan hadn't been able to get it out of his mind since Thanksgiving. He'd been stewing on it for days.

'I was hoping you'd reconsidered my offer for your shares.'

Ryan sat down on the corner of his dad's desk, purposely avoiding the low chair Matthew Sutherland had pointed to.

His father winced. 'That's a three thousand dollar desk,' he pointed out. 'Made from Carpathian elm. I'd prefer if you didn't scratch or dent it.'

'I'd prefer if you didn't sell the wharf to some developer.'

'Well it looks as though neither of us will be getting what we want today, doesn't it?' His father folded his arms across his chest.

'Why didn't you tell me you were planning to sell?'

'It's business. You may be a shareholder, but we don't have to pass every executive decision through you. As long as we keep our end of the bargain and keep delivering dividends, you've got nothing to complain about.'

'Does Mom know?'

His father's eyes narrowed. 'She doesn't need to. As I pointed out the last time we met, you're merely a shareholder, and so's she. You've never worked in this business, and you have no say over how it's run.'

'That's not true, I could call an extraordinary meeting.'

'And say what? That you're upset because we're selling

some piece of shit land that's been haemorrhaging money for years? That as a business we've been shoring that place up, without any hope of ever turning it into profit? It's prime real estate, Ryan, selling it for development is part of what we do.'

'But it's not just a piece of land, is it? It's part of our history. Part of the Shaw family. It's where my grandparents met, where I grew up. This isn't just a business transaction, some company is going to buy that land, overdevelop it and take away the one thing that makes this town beautiful.'

'Try telling that to the rest of the shareholders. There's no place for sentiment in business. We're here to make money and nothing else.'

'Grandpa made me promise to take care of that place. You know how much it meant to him. I can't believe you're just going to throw all that away for a few bucks.'

'If you're so worried about the place, buy it yourself.'

Ryan scowled. 'I don't have that kind of money.'

His father leaned forward, resting his chin on his fingertips. 'I know a way you can get some. Maybe think about selling your shares.'

An ice-cold shiver snaked down Ryan's spine. 'Is that what this is about?'

'What do you mean?' His father widened his eyes in mock innocence.

Ryan leaned forward, keeping his eyes narrow, his voice low. 'You know exactly what I mean. Are you doing this to make me sell my shares to you?'

'I'm just trying to offer you a solution. If you want to save the wharf, what better way to do it than sell your shares? We can even make it part of the deal.'

Ryan leaned back from his father, flexing his bicep muscles in an attempt to keep his fisted hands by his side. His nose flared as he breathed in, feeling the anger swirling up in the pit of his stomach, then rising through his abdomen. It was as though every muscle in his body was tensed, waiting, waiting, until he unleashed the fury building inside.

'You're an asshole, you know that?' Ryan hissed. 'This is going to break Mom's heart.' He couldn't believe she'd let go of her heritage so easily, not when she'd been so effusive about it to Charlie.

'Your mother leaves the decisions to me.'

Yeah, she did. Ryan knew that much from experience. His father had him over a barrel with no way to turn. Either he sold his share of the business or he lost the one place that felt like home. It was a lose-lose situation.

'So that's it?' Ryan asked, his throat dry. 'You're gonna let them build a whole load of condos on our history and not give a damn.' He shook his head. 'Where's your family loyalty?'

His father's laugh was harsh and low. 'Where's yours?' he replied. 'At least I've stayed here and kept the business going. You left town and never looked back, so don't come here wailing about your heritage when it hasn't meant anything to you for years.' He stood, gesturing at the door. 'I'll let you see yourself out. Unless you'd like me to call security to escort you.'

'Call whoever the hell you want,' Ryan said, wrenching the door open. 'I'm sure they'll kiss your ass and tell you how wonderful you are. But the fact is we both know what kind of man you turned out to be. One who bullies his wife to get what he wants. You're a coward through and through.'

'Don't bother coming back unless you plan to sell me your shares.'

'Oh, I'll be back. I own a bit of this place, and I own a bit of you, and I know how crazy that makes you. So I'll be back, Dad, and I'll be sure to make your life hell.' Ryan stalked out, not bothering to look back, even though he could picture his father's sneer. He knew how to get to him, and enjoyed winding him up. Ryan could feel the fury taking over his body.

It remained his constant companion as he drove back home.

'Is Poppy asleep?' Ryan's jaw was rigid, the bone at the corner twitching, as he stood at her back door. He had a hand on the doorjamb, but his body was as straight as a rod. The tension was radiating from him in waves.

Juliet licked her lips, trying to moisten the dry skin. 'Yeah, she went off about an hour ago.' She frowned. 'Is there something wrong? Is Charlie okay?'

He nodded. 'Yeah, he's asleep, too. They must have worn him out at soccer practice.' Even his words sounded stiff. Juliet wanted to reach out, to touch him, to soothe, but her hands remained by her side. What on earth was going on? She licked her lips, looking at him with soft eyes. She'd never seen him so uptight before.

'Would you like a drink?' she asked.

'No. I just wanted to see you. Just wanted to hear your voice.' He swallowed, his Adam's apple bobbing up and down. 'It's been a shitty day.'

'Is it something to do with the wharf?' she asked, remembering how angry he'd been the previous weekend.

'Yeah. Turns out my father wants to use it as leverage against me. He's offered it in return for my shares in the family business.'

She wanted to reach out and smooth the lines on his forehead. Even though they were a foot apart, she could feel the tenseness radiating from him. 'What are you going to do?'

'I have no goddamn idea.' He closed his eyes and took in a mouthful of air. 'I promised my grandfather . . .'

'Promised him what?'

'I promised him I'd never sell the shares.' He winced. 'But I also promised him the wharf would never be developed. And I've got no idea how to keep them both.'

'Which would be more important to him?' she asked.

'I don't know.' Ryan shook his head, and the confused expression on his face deepened. 'The business was his life. But the wharf was his love. Jesus, I've no idea how to make this better.'

She looked up at him, taking in those deep eyes, and the clouds just behind them. 'Doesn't love matter above anything?' she asked. 'Wouldn't you save the thing you loved over the thing you'd worked for? If your house was on fire you'd go in and get Charlie, not your camera or your photographs.'

Ryan leaned against the door frame, his strong shoulder pushing onto the wood. 'You're right,' he said, his voice soft. 'Strange how you're always right.'

'You should tell that to Poppy,' she said, a half-smile on her face. 'She wouldn't agree with you.'

As if he couldn't stop himself, he reached out and traced his finger along her bottom lip. 'You don't know how much I need to be with you right now, London. How much I want to bury

194

myself in you until we've both forgotten everything except the way our bodies fit together.'

Her breath caught in her throat. Because she needed it too. Ever since last weekend her thoughts had been full of him. There was barely any room for anything else. 'I want you, too.'

'When's Thomas having Poppy next?' he asked her.

'Not for a couple of weeks.' She grimaced. 'He's got a lot on at work, he asked if he could swap some weekends around.'

'Shit.' Ryan shook his head. 'It's a good thing you're worth waiting for.'

His words were like a touch paper, lighting her up. She tried to dampen her excitement. She was technically still married, they were sneaking around, and he'd already told her he was leaving next year. She needed to learn how to guard her heart.

'Mommy.' Poppy's voice cut through the heated atmosphere between them. 'Can I have a glass of water?'

Ryan pushed himself off the doorjamb, an almost-smile flitting across his lips. 'Ah, the old water trick. Some things never get old.'

'They don't.' She returned his smile.

'Hey, Ryan.' Poppy ducked underneath Juliet's arm, and grinned up at their neighbour. 'Is Charlie with you?'

'No he's not. And I'd better get back to him.' Ryan reached out and ruffled her hair, his fingers sliding against Juliet's arm as he pulled his hand back. 'Good night, Poppy, I hope you're not too thirsty. Be good for your mom, okay?' His voice softened. 'And good night, London. Thanks for talking with me.'

'Any time.' She watched as he turned and walked across

the backyard, covering the distance to his boundary line, his shoulders square, his gait long and strong.

'I like Ryan,' Poppy announced, clearly watching him as well.

'I do, too,' Juliet murmured. And wasn't that the truth?

19

Love is like a child,
That longs for every thing that he can come by

– The Two Gentlemen of Verona

'So there's no way I can block it?' Ryan frowned, resting his elbows on the boardroom table. Frank Daniels, his lawyer, was sitting opposite him, papers spread out across the surface, his reading glasses halfway down his nose.

'You don't have a veto. Even if you call an extraordinary meeting, your parents' shares combined would be enough to vote you down.'

Ryan took a deep breath in, the air rushing through his lips. They'd combed through everything, looking for loopholes or clauses that might just let him have his own way.

But nothing was going to stick.

'Shit.'

'I've put some feelers out about the wharf. There's currently a preferred buyer. The North Atlantic Corporation.'

Ryan looked up. 'I've heard of them. Didn't they buy up half of Virginia Beach?'

'That's the one. I called in a couple of favours with their lawyers. They already have plans drawn up for a casino resort.

And if they grease enough palms they shouldn't have any problems with the zoning committee. According to my source it's pretty much a done deal.'

Ryan lowered his face into his hands. Any hope he'd had of staving off the redevelopment and saving the wharf had pretty much disappeared. And with it any possibility of keeping his promise to his grandfather.

'And Stan?'

Frank shrugged. 'Your guess is as good as mine. He'll get a severance package I imagine, but as he lives in a cottage on the land, he'll have to look for somewhere to live.'

'That's a crock of shit.'

'But a legal one. I'm sorry, Ryan, but these are the facts. Selling the wharf is perfectly legal, as is terminating Stan Dawson's employment and evicting him from his home. If your father's feeling charitable, they may find him somewhere else to live, but they're under no obligation.'

'Then what can I do? Surely there has to be something.'

'Honestly? I don't think you can do anything apart from accept that sometimes the bad guys win. And there are some positives, the resort should bring in some employment and wealth to this town.'

'Yep, it'll help the rich get richer.'

'That's business. And life.'

Ryan stood up, pacing the floor between the window and the door. 'But it doesn't make sense. My parents love Shaw Haven, they love the small town feel. This development is going to change the town completely, why the hell would they want that?'

'They're your parents. You tell me.'

He came to a stop in front of the window, overlooking the

town. The familiar roofs of the central business district greeted him – old-fashioned churches and shops mingled with modern glass office blocks. On the far right-hand side he could see his father's building.

'I don't think they would. Not Mom, anyway. I guess Dad's another matter. Money's always been more important than sentiment to him.'

'There's always the option of selling your shares,' his lawyer reminded him. Ryan went to speak. 'Hear me out. I know you don't want them to win, but really it's not about them is it? It's about what you want, and you want to save the wharf.'

'But not at the expense of what's right.'

'There are no easy decisions here, I know that. I wish I could give you some other options. But the way I see it you either take their offer of the wharf for your shares, or you do nothing and walk away from the whole thing.'

The second option was sounding pretty appealing right then. He'd never imagined that coming back home would have unleashed a whole new set of problems. He couldn't help but feel it was his fault that the wharf was being sold and Stan was losing his job.

'What about if I sold my shares to a third party? Would I get the same amount for them?' It would still mean breaking a promise, but somehow it felt more palatable.

Frank leaned back, staring at him. 'I don't understand.'

'I need to get the money, but there's no way I want to give in to my father's demands. So what if I sell those shares to somebody else, then buy the wharf with the proceeds? That way I get to save the place without him winning.' Ryan started to pace again, shoving his hands into his jeans pockets. 'That could work, couldn't it? If we quietly looked for a buyer?'

'I can certainly put some feelers out. But then you'd need to work out how to buy the wharf, because presumably they won't be seeing you as their preferred option. You'd need to set up an umbrella company. And all this takes time, Ryan. Who's to say they won't have completed the deal before you even get someone to take the shares off your hands?'

'It's a risk, granted, but one I'm willing to take.'

'And if you buy the wharf, what the hell are you going to do with it? You told me you're not planning on staying around in Shaw Haven after the school year is over. Owning a property is completely different to holding shares, it takes time and decisions and needing to be contactable.'

'I don't plan on changing anything. I'll get a manager in.'

'And who's going to check on the manager? How do you know you'll be able to trust him? I'm not trying to stop you from doing this, but it's my job to point out all the pitfalls. As the owner of the wharf you'd be liable for the safety, for any problems, hell you could be sent to jail if something goes wrong. It's a liability, and one that could end up being a millstone around your neck. You need to really think about whether this is what you want.'

None of this was what he wanted. The wharf had been part of the Shaw family for centuries. It was inconceivable that it would ever be sold off. His mother had always loved the wharf, and his father had always kept a boat there. He'd thought they'd loved the place as much as he did.

His phone buzzed in his pocket. He pulled it out, checking the screen.

London.

'I gotta take this okay? Don't go anywhere.'

Frank pointed at the door at the far end of the boardroom. 'You can use that office. It's private.'

He strode across the room, swiping his finger on the screen to accept the call. 'Hey, you all right?'

'Not really. The wedding we're doing this evening has grown by about twenty floral displays. Lily and I have been working all day, and we still aren't ready yet. There's no way I can get to school in time to pick up Poppy. I've called everybody I know. Melanie is out of town, and all her other friends have after-school activities. I wouldn't ask you if I didn't need to, Ryan—'

'Of course I'll get her for you.' He interrupted her frantic flow. 'I can't work out why you didn't call me first. I live next door to you after all.'

'I don't want you to think I'm using you.'

His chuckle was low. 'You mean exchanging sex for child-care? Well that would be a new one on me.'

'No!' She sounded appalled. 'I mean that I don't expect anything other than ... whatever it is that's going on here.'

'Whatever it is that's going on here?' he repeated her words, frowning. 'What do you mean?'

'I didn't mean anything.' Her voice was strained. He could almost see the blush on her pale cheeks. 'All I was trying to say was, just because we've been messing around a bit, that doesn't mean you owe me anything. And you shouldn't, because we said we'd keep the kids out of this ... thing. Which makes me an idiot for calling you and even asking for help.' She sighed. 'I should probably ask Thomas to help.'

Well that about made up his mind.

'I'll pick Poppy up. I'll even give her a plate full of whatever Charlie wants for dinner tonight. And it won't mean anything more than one neighbour doing the other a favour. I won't expect you to drop down on your knees and offer your undying thanks, even if the thought of you on your knees is doing very dirty things to me right now. So chill, stop worrying, and let me go pick up our kids, okay?'

'Okay . . . ' Her voice was tentative.

He laughed softly. 'Go and do what you gotta do. I've got this covered.'

She sighed. 'Thank you.'

'You're welcome.'

Juliet almost fell out of her car, tripping over the mat as she stumbled onto her driveway. Reaching out, she steadied herself on the fence, only just stopping herself from falling over. A broken leg would be the perfect end to the perfect day. Exactly what she needed.

To top it all off, she'd had a message from Thomas waiting on her phone.

We need to talk about Christmas. I'd like to have Poppy
from the 24th to the 27th.

It was getting so that his name flashing up on her screen was making her roll her eyes. There was no tenderness to his messages. She felt like just another business transaction.

So far he'd had Poppy for July 4th and Thanksgiving – two days Juliet had been happy to give up. After all, they were American holidays, and in her heart she felt her daughter should spend them with her American family. He'd promised her Christmas, and now he was trying to take that, too? What the heck did he think Juliet was going to do all alone?

She squeezed her eyes shut for a moment, trying to calm the nerves that had taken hold of her. Inhaling a lungful of cool, Maryland air, she felt her heart start to slow, her muscles relaxing with the fresh intake of oxygen.

It was going to be okay.

A moment later she was rapping at Ryan's door. She could hear music coming from inside, along with children's laughter, and for the first time that evening she felt a smile crossing her face.

'Hey, welcome home.' Ryan's smile reflected her own as he pulled the door open. 'How was your day?' He was wearing his usual jeans and a shirt, sleeves rolled up, his feet bare as he stood on the wooden floor. His casual ease felt like a balm to her soul.

'It was terrible.'

'Then come inside and let me make it better.' He moved to the left, to let her in.

'I should get Poppy and take her home, we've infringed on your hospitality for long enough. I can't tell you how grateful I am for your help today. You saved my life.'

Ryan tipped his head to the side, scrutinising her. 'Babe, you look beat. Come in and eat some pizza with us. Kick your shoes off, sit down, I'll pour you a glass of wine, and you can stuff your mouth with pepperoni. How 'bout it?'

Another shout of laughter echoed from the kitchen. Just hearing how happy Poppy and Charlie were made her want to go in and see their faces. 'I guess I could come in for a little while, as long as you're sure?'

He grabbed her hand, pulling her into the hallway. The rough movement made her almost slam into his hard, muscled torso, and the sudden closeness to him made her gasp.

'London, I'm certain. You've had a crappy day, so let me take care of you for once. You deserve to be looked after sometimes.' He ran his palm down her back.

The combination of his words, her terrible day, and the way he was touching her brought hot tears to her eyes. She couldn't quite pinpoint the emotion she felt, but whatever it was it was consuming. 'I'm not used to being looked after,' she whispered.

'I know that, but sometimes you just have to let go. You're a strong woman, but even the strongest need someone to lean on sometimes. So lean on me, just for tonight.'

'We can't let the kids know about us.'

He smiled. 'I know that. I promise not to do anything untoward with you in front of our kids. I'll keep my hands to myself.'

She raised an eyebrow at him. 'What a disappointment.'

He grinned. 'I can't guarantee I won't be thinking dirty thoughts, though.'

Leaning in, she pressed her lips against his ear. 'I guarantee they're not as dirty as mine.' She let her breath linger on his skin, causing him to gasp.

'Every time I think I've got you pegged, you surprise me,' he told her. His expression was warm.

'Is that a bad thing?' she asked him.

Slowly, Ryan shook his head. 'No, London, it isn't. It's a very good thing indeed.'

'Momma, you're cheating.' Poppy frowned, craning her head to try to get a look at Juliet's cards. Juliet pulled her hands close to her chest, obscuring her daughter's view.

'I am not.' She felt her mouth twitch. After dinner, she and Ryan had cleared up while the kids played in the den. Then they'd all come together around the kitchen table for a game of *Go Fish*. So far Juliet had won all but one hand, with Ryan losing miserably.

'Oh she's definitely cheating,' Ryan agreed, his eyes twinkling as they met hers. 'Nobody's that good at cards.'

'I'll have you know I spent my whole childhood playing cards. There wasn't much else to do growing up. Don't ever suggest a game of Rummy whenever my sisters are around, it always ends up in war.'

'I'll remember that.' He was still smiling at her. How was it possible that each time he did, her heart missed a beat? Even in his kitchen, playing a stupid game of cards with their children, he still had this overwhelming effect on her.

'Have you got any tens?' Charlie asked Poppy.

'Go Fish.' Poppy narrowed her eyes, her knuckles white as she gripped her cards.

'You're lying, I can see you've got a ten in your hands.' Charlie pointed at her hand.

'Yeah, well you shouldn't be looking. That's cheating, isn't it, Mom?'

Juliet shook her head. 'Don't ask me. I'm the queen of cheating, remember?'

'Even if I've got a ten, I want it. I'm collecting them. So go and pick up another card.' Poppy slammed her cards on the table, face down. The furious expression on her face made Juliet want to laugh.

'I see she gets her feistiness from you,' Ryan whispered, his breath tickling her ear.

Juliet looked at her daughter. 'Poppy, the whole point of the game is that if the person next to you asks for a card, you have to give it to them. Otherwise it's not a game.'

'But he knew I had a ten. If he didn't know he wouldn't have asked for it,' Poppy protested.

'I did not know. And even if I did, you still need to give

me the card. That's the rules. You need to obey them.' Charlie narrowed his eyes at her.

'I see he gets his sense of wrong and right from you.' Juliet raised her brows at Ryan.

'I guess they're both chips off the old blocks.'

'Less of the old,' she said, kicking him in the shin. He grabbed her leg, stopping her from doing it again, caressing her calf with his fingers. He drew small circles on her skin, sending a shiver straight through her.

'That's cheating, too,' she whispered.

He winked at her, running his hand beneath her skirt, his hands warm against her upper thigh. Just as she thought she was going to have to hit him, he let go, leaving her skin cold where his touch had just been.

Damn, he knew exactly how to drive her crazy.

'Shall we just call this a draw, do you think?' Ryan asked. 'Before we end up in a war, Shakespeare Sister style. I feel as though there's going to be a plague on both our houses.'

'That sounds like a perfect idea. It's getting late, and Poppy needs to hop in the bath before bedtime anyway.'

'Mommy! I'm not tired. And I want to stay here.' Poppy folded her arms over her chest. 'Can't we stay here?'

'No we can't. We live next door, remember?' Juliet was trying to ignore the seductive voice in her brain, telling her a sleepover with the Sutherland boys was the perfect idea. 'Plus Daddy is picking you up tomorrow, so you need to make sure you get some sleep.'

'I can sleep here. In fact I'll sleep better here because there's no horrible noises coming from the boiler.'

'Yeah, she can sleep on my bed,' Charlie joined in, all bad blood between them forgotten. 'We can build a fort and eat popcorn like we did at your house.'

Juliet slid her eyes to Ryan's. Popcorn. The word reminded her of his kisses.

'Please, Ryan, please can we have a sleepover?' Poppy pleaded.

'It's up to your mom. She's had a long day at work, and we don't need to give her any more hassle. If she wants you to go home, then we'll plan to have a sleepover another day.'

Her throat went dry. The way he was deferring to her was so different to anything she'd known. Every decision she'd made in the last six years had felt as though she was in battle, trying to stand her ground while being hit on all sides.

She looked at Poppy and Charlie, their eyes big and their mouths open as they waited expectantly for her answer. Her heart clenched with love for their children. 'I guess a sleepover will be fine,' she said softly. 'As long as you promise to get up super early so you're home when Daddy comes to pick you up.'

'Of course I will.' Poppy smiled, allowing the excitement to take over. 'Thank you, Mommy, thank you! Can I use my Princess Merida sleeping bag? Can I wear my new pyjamas? Oh this is going to be so much fun.' She started to clap her hands together. 'I can't wait to sleep here with you, Charlie.'

'Like mother like daughter, just as I said,' Ryan whispered.

'Shut up, or I'll kick you again.'

'Feel free, as I recall I kinda liked it when you did it earlier.' He grinned.

'Another thing I've noticed about you Sutherland boys, none of you fight fair.' She widened her eyes at him.

'Right, Mommy?' Poppy nodded rapidly, having caught Juliet's words. 'They cheat don't they? All the time.' She sighed. 'We're going to have to keep an eye on them. They're tricky.'

'Yes they are,' Juliet agreed. 'Very tricky indeed.'

20

Small cheer and great welcome
makes a merry feast

– The Comedy of Errors

'What's this?' Juliet frowned at the paper Thomas handed her. It was a printout of a spread sheet, different blocks coloured in pink and blue. It looked like something she'd see in a corporate office, not on the front step of her house.

'It's a custody plan for next year. Your times are coloured pink, mine are coloured blue. I think you'll see I've been very fair. I've given you Easter and Spring Break, plus six out of the ten weeks in the summer.'

She glanced behind her, making sure Poppy wasn't within hearing. The sound of running water came from the bathroom – they were running late and she'd just gotten around to cleaning her teeth. 'But it's only just December. We haven't even agreed how to split Christmas yet. Shouldn't we talk about this in mediation?'

'Of course we've agreed Christmas. I sent you a text, remember?'

'One I didn't reply to.' She could feel her teeth clenching. This wasn't a conversation she wanted to have on the doorstep, particularly when Poppy was so close to them. 'And I didn't agree to.'

'Well you should have told me you weren't happy. I've already made plans.'

She could feel her blood starting to heat up. 'Thomas, you sent the text yesterday. I decided to hold off replying until I'd had a chance to check my work schedule and suggest an alternative. But I wasn't going to agree to not seeing my daughter from the 23rd December until way after Christmas.'

'I'll have her home by the 27th, surely you can do something together then?'

She curled her hands up, digging her nails into her palms to stop herself from screaming. 'I'd kind of like to see my daughter on Christmas Day. She's six years old, and I'd like to watch her open her presents and see her face light up. I know you want to see her, too, but we need to come to some compromise here.'

'I knew you'd be like this.' Thomas shook his head. 'It's pointless even trying to discuss anything with you. I expect you'd be happy if I just disappeared out of your life, just as long as I keep sending you those cheques.'

'I'm not being like anything. I'm simply trying to point out that I'd like to spend some time with my daughter at Christmastime. And I know you would too. I don't want you out of her life, I want her to know her father, and I want her to spend lots of time with you. But I can't be the one to always give. You had Thanksgiving and other holidays, why can't we share this one?'

'Because I want to take her away. We've booked to go skiing in Colorado. I'd have preferred to go for a week, but I knew you wouldn't agree to that, so a few days will have to do.'

Oh this was perfect. 'You booked a holiday for her without asking me?'

Thomas threw his hands up in the air. 'Oh Jesus, what do you think yesterday's text was about? I just want to take my daughter away for a few days, teach her to ski and spend some time with our family. That's not unreasonable is it?'

'It's unreasonable when you take her away for the whole of Christmas. We agreed I'd have her for Christmas and you'd have her for Thanksgiving. You're being unfair.'

He sighed, shaking his head at her. 'You're making this very difficult. What is it you have planned for her? Won't you be working in the shop up until Christmas Eve? If you think about it I'm doing you a favour.'

'You haven't done me a favour in your life.'

'I married you didn't I?'

Her mouth dropped open. She tried to think of a smart retort, but her brain turned to mush. All she could manage was, 'Go to hell, Thomas.'

'Mommy?' Poppy's quiet voice came from behind. 'Is there something wrong?'

Her stomach dropped. Poppy took her hand, and cuddled into her side, the way she used to when she was a kid. Her toddler-like reaction made Juliet want to cry. In the months since their split, not once had Juliet been acrimonious towards her ex in front of their child. She'd made it her mission not to be. Okay, so Poppy knew things weren't right, and knew the story of Juliet hitting her father's PA, but she'd never heard her mother swear at her father before.

'There's nothing wrong, darling.' Juliet deliberately tried to keep her voice light. 'We're just having a disagreement. You know, like you do with your friends at school sometimes.'

'But you're still friends with Daddy, right?'

'Of course we are.' Thomas leaned forward to ruffle Poppy's

hair, painting a smile on his thin lips. 'We were just having a conversation, that's all.'

'It's fine, Poppy. Now let's get your bag, did you put your toothbrush in there?' Juliet turned around, glad Thomas couldn't see her face. A band of guilt around her chest replaced all the anger she'd felt at him.

She'd promised herself she wouldn't be that sort of single mother. A bitter, angry one, throwing out accusations whenever she saw her ex. And yet here she was, arguing with him on the doorstep.

'There you go,' she said, false cheeriness still lightening her voice, as she passed Poppy's case to Thomas. 'Okay then, darling, I'll see you tomorrow, have a lovely time.' She kissed the top of Poppy's head, inhaling the flowery fragrance of her shampoo. Her eyes squeezed tight, as she tried to commit that smell to memory. Saying goodbye didn't get any easier, even when it was just for one night.

'We'll talk about that thing in the week,' Thomas said, turning to walk down the steps. His words left her in no doubt he was still planning to get his own way.

Yeah, well, they'd see about that.

'What are you doing right now?' Ryan asked. Juliet smiled as she held her phone to her ear. Simply hearing his voice felt like fresh rain following a drought.

'Not much,' she admitted. Unless you counted rearranging the shop for the second time in a few weeks as *much*. Anything to take her mind off Thomas's demands, and the anxiety that was nestling in her stomach. 'I spent the afternoon at the shop, and now I'm beat. How about you?'

'I had a day trip with Charlie on the boat planned out, but

then he got a better offer. Apparently swimming and fast food plus a sleepover trump sailing with your old man.' Though Ryan's words sounded petulant, his tone was anything but. Juliet knew he worried that Charlie didn't have enough friends his own age. It sounded as though things were changing for the better.

'Poor you,' she teased. 'Jilted for McDonald's. At least you know where you stand.'

'Pretty much at the bottom of the list,' he agreed. 'Which was why I'm calling.'

'Oh yes?'

'I wondered if you'd like to join me for dinner.'

'At your place?' She sat down on the kitchen stool, leaning her head against the painted wall, trying to ignore the way his simple request sent her heart racing.

'No, I want to take you out. I'm sick of sneaking around between your place and mine. Plus I've got a hankering for crab cakes and steak.'

'You can take the boy out of Maryland,' she teased, as much to give herself time to regain her breath as anything else. 'But seriously, it's not a good idea is it?'

'To eat crab cakes?'

'To go out for dinner together. It's a small town, people will talk.'

'Then we'll go to another town. I know a great place in Annapolis. They serve the best fillet steak you'll ever taste. And if anybody sees us, then we're friends and neighbours who've been abandoned by our kids. What's to talk about?'

She couldn't deny that the thought of it was enticing. And it wasn't just the offer of dinner that was making her stomach growl. It was the thought of him, of talking to him, laughing with him, of seeing his face across the table from her. Of actually being out together like a normal couple.

But they weren't a couple. Were they?

Blowing out a mouthful of air, she looked around the kitchen, imagining what an alternative Saturday night would look like. She'd probably take a bath, pour a glass of wine, put some terrible reality show on the television while she fell asleep on the sofa halfway through. How did she end up like this?

'Steak does sound good,' she said. 'But if Thomas found out, he'd make my life a misery.'

'That's why he's not going to find out. We'll head over to Gilbert's, eat our dinner, and come straight home.'

'To bed?'

'To my bed,' Ryan told her. 'In case there was any misunderstanding.'

No, definitely no misunderstanding. Her stomach rumbled again, and she realised just how hungry she was, and not just for steak.

'In that case, it's a date.'

'What can I get you?' the server asked, standing next to their table with a pen in his hand. Though he was dressed in black pants and a crisp white shirt, his stance somehow echoed the ambience of the restaurant. Relaxed, laid back, but definitely expensive.

'Juliet?' Ryan asked, offering her to go first.

'I'm still deciding. You go.'

'I'll take the Maryland crab cakes, followed by the ten-ounce steak with extra fries.' He handed the black leather menu back to the server. As always she was entranced by how easy he found everything.

'I'll just take the burger. No starter.' She offered the server a quick smile then handed back her own menu.

Ryan frowned. 'You're not having steak?'

She shrugged, trying to feign nonchalance. 'I'm not hungry.'

'Hungry enough for a burger,' he pointed out. He didn't look angry as much as worried. 'You should really try the steak. It's amazing.'

'It's the best,' the server agreed. 'Though of course our burgers are good too.'

A year ago she wouldn't have blinked twice at the cost of the steaks. But then a year ago she was Mrs Thomas Marshall, and money was no object. But right now she had a bit of a cash flow problem, thanks to lawyers' bills and Poppy's Christmas presents. 'The burger is fine.'

'Can you give us a minute?' Ryan asked, looking up at the server.

'Yes, sure, I'll be back in five.' The man didn't look perturbed at all, even though Juliet felt more embarrassed than ever. He walked away and over to another table, topping their wine glasses up with an expensive red.

'London, are you ordering a burger because you want it, or because you've got some messed-up idea that you're paying for dinner?'

It took a lot of effort to make herself meet his gaze, but when she did, all she saw there was kindness. 'Why do you ask?'

'Because the burger's the cheapest thing on the menu.'

'But I'm really not that hungry.'

'Babe, somebody who's not hungry doesn't order a burger.'

She stared into his deep blue eyes, taking in the way the skin crinkled at the corners, from a lifetime of smiles. His skin was still tan in spite of the cold North East weather, his mop of blond hair framing it perfectly. 'I'm saving money,' she finally admitted, her voice low from embarrassment. 'The divorce is taking much longer than I'd thought. I just had to send my lawyer a few thousand dollars.' She licked her lips. 'Thomas is being difficult.'

'Sounds about right.'

'We're due to meet at the courthouse for mediation next week. Things should be better after we agree on the separation terms.'

'If he agrees to anything.'

'Of course he will.' She didn't sound convinced. 'We both want what's best for Poppy.'

Ryan opened his mouth to say something, then closed it again, rubbing his temples with his fingers as if to calm himself down. 'So I guess we have two choices. Either you let me buy you a steak, or we leave and grab some takeout together. It's up to you.'

'Don't be silly. I'm happy to have a burger, and you've been dying for a steak. We can stay here and eat.'

'I'm not going to sit here and eat a steak while you eat a burger because that's all you can afford. This is supposed to be a date, and I'd like to treat you. So what's it to be, shall we just leave and get a takeout?'

'But you've been jonesing after a steak all day, you said so yourself.'

'London, I've been jonesing for you. I'd eat a sandwich if it meant I could sit with you. Steak or takeout, I don't care. I just want to make you happy.'

There went her heart again, galloping like an out of control racehorse. She could tell by the way he was staring at her – hot and heavy – that he meant every word. The strength of his desire took her breath away.

It was on the tip of her tongue to say they'd get a takeout, then drag him home to bed. But he'd brought her out to eat steak, hadn't he? It felt as though she'd be letting him down if they didn't stay for dinner.

'I guess I could eat a small steak,' she said.

'And a crab cake?'

A smile broke out across her face. 'And that too.'

After ordering their food, Ryan reached out and took her hand in his, grinning widely. 'You'll need the energy for what I've got planned later.'

'And what's that?' she asked, looking up at him through her eyelashes. 'Are we running a marathon or something?'

'No, London, I'm going to take you to bed and make love to you seven ways to Sunday.' Reaching across the table, he took her hand in his, lifting it to his lips. But then he frowned, his smile dissolving into the air, as he stared over her shoulder.

A ripple of unease slithered down Juliet's spine, making her sit up straight. She turned around to see the couple from two tables down staring at her and Ryan with narrowed eyes.

'Oh shit, that's Susan Stanhope.' She swallowed, even though her mouth was dry. 'And her husband Richard. He's a golfing buddy of Thomas's.'

'I know. I've met them, remember?'

Of course. Susan's son was in the same class as Charlie and Poppy. It didn't make Juliet feel any better, though.

'Do you think they saw you kiss my hand?' she asked him, alarm making her freeze. 'Do you think they'll tell Thomas?' She pulled her fingers from his grasp, and put her hands beneath the table, clasping them together tightly.

'I don't know,' he answered honestly.

'Two Maryland crab cakes,' the waiter announced, sliding their plates in front of them. 'Enjoy your appetisers.'

Taking a deep breath, she picked up her silverware, using her fork to prod at the crab cake. It crumbled at her touch. And though it looked – and smelled delicious – she didn't think she could eat a thing.

Her appetite had completely gone.

They drove home in silence, passing houses lit up with early-December decorations, waving Santas and nodding reindeer nestled among lit-up evergreens. Juliet stared out of the partially misted windshield, trying to calm the torrent of thoughts that kept rushing through her mind.

'You okay?' Ryan asked her, finally breaking the quiet. He pulled up at a stoplight, about twenty minutes from home.

'I don't know if I'm okay,' she admitted. The lights turned to green and he pressed his foot to the gas, slowly turning left towards Shaw Haven. 'I wasn't expecting to see anybody I knew there.'

'It was just a mom from school,' he said, his voice reassuring. 'So there might be a bit of gossip, we can live with it can't we?'

'You make it sound so easy.'

'That's because it is.'

Her stomach rumbled, reminding her she'd hardly eaten a thing. 'It isn't,' she said, her voice tight. 'It isn't easy at all. They've only just stopped talking about me splitting from Thomas, now they have something new to talk about. Susan's probably texting all the other moms right now.'

'So what? Let them gossip.'

She sighed. 'You don't understand. Thomas is just looking

for ammunition to use against me. We have mediation next week, and if he finds out about us ...' She trailed off, squeezing her eyes shut. She didn't even want to think about that. 'It looks bad. Really bad.'

'He can only hurt you if you let him,' Ryan said, his voice low.

'What?' Juliet frowned. 'Are you saying this is my fault?'

'I'm not saying it's anybody's fault.' It was Ryan's turn to sigh. 'I'm just pointing out that you can't control what he does to you, but you can control your response.'

'And how do you think I should control my response when he's making everything so difficult? Do you think I wanted to be a single mom? None of this was my choice, Ryan.' She bit her lip, trying to stop the tears from forming in her eyes. Not that she felt sad, oh no. She was furious.

'No, it wasn't your choice. But what would you rather happen? Do you want to get back with him? Is that why you're worried about him finding out?' There was an edge to his voice she hadn't heard before.

'Of course I don't want to get back with him.'

'So why does it matter if you chose this or not?' Ryan was drumming his hands on the wheel. 'When you're where you want to be?'

There was a tic in his jaw that seemed to be in rhythm with her speeding pulse. His eyes were narrow, his brow furrowed. His reaction to her words seemed over the top. As if he was ...

Jealous?

Her mouth felt dry, her lips cracked. Was it really possible he was jealous of Thomas? Neither of them had spoken much about their relationship, they'd been too busy keeping things on the down low for that. They weren't dating, they weren't exclusive, they weren't anything.

And yet, the thought of him being jealous sent a jolt of excitement through her, dissolving her anger into thin air.

'It doesn't matter, I guess,' she said, calming down. 'And I am where I want to be. I just hate the uncertainty of it all. Knowing that Thomas can use Poppy to hurt me.'

'I wouldn't let him hurt you. You should know that by now.'

'I don't need a knight in shining armour,' she reminded him.

Ryan nodded, his expression serious. 'Yeah, well there are different ways to be a knight. Maybe I can be the sort that stands behind you and supports you, telling you that I'll be here for you.'

Her breath caught in her throat. 'Maybe you could.'

He steered the car to the right, pulling into his driveway, the headlamps flashing against the white stone of his house. When they came to a stop, he slid the stick into park, but instead of turning the engine off, he turned to look at her instead. 'You are so much stronger than you think, London. And on top of that you're a good, kind person. I believe in karma, and that your asshole of a husband will get everything that's coming to him. But sometimes you have to help karma along a little bit.'

'So what should I do?'

'Believe in yourself the way that I do.'

There he went with his sweet tongue, letting the words trip out and tangle their way around her heart. What was it about this man? He seemed to know exactly what to say to make her swoon.

And it was working.

21

Is this the generation of love?
Hot blood, hot thoughts and hot deeds?

– Troilus and Cressida

There was something satisfying about the way she fitted into the crook of his arm, her head nestled between his biceps and his shoulder. Her long, red hair was fanned out across his skin, the tendrils tickling his chest when she moved. They'd spent the rest of the evening talking, until neither of them had the energy to talk any more. In bed they'd made sweet love – so different from the sex he'd envisaged them having, yet so much more satisfying, too.

A shaft of moonlight had found its way through a gap in the curtains, lending a pale glow to the grey painted wall opposite the bed. It bounced off the glass covering the photo frames he'd fixed with nails there, and for a moment he stared at the black and white scenes beneath them, remembering where he'd been when he'd taken those shots.

Manila had been the first place he'd visited after leaving home, catching a connecting flight from DC to Seoul, and then on to the bustling city in the Philippines. They called it the Pearl of the Orient, and with good reason. It had been the duality of Manila that had struck him as soon as he'd arrived. Extreme poverty mixed in with ostentatious wealth in a way that he'd never encountered in the US before. And yet there hadn't been the envy towards him he'd expected, nor the kind of animosity such a divide would spark in the west. Instead he encountered a set of people who loved life, who partied hard, and welcomed him with open arms. He'd spent his days taking photographs, wandering around Intramuros, the ancient walled city, setting up his tripod and waiting until the light was exactly right. And at night he'd meet with friends, go to local restaurants, dance with pretty girls who seemed all too willing to spend time with a handsome young man.

It was there, too, that he sold his first photographs, before landing a commission from *National Geographic*. He'd become friends with a local reporter who had connections, and for the first time Ryan had realised he could get paid for doing something he loved.

Pulling his gaze away from the photographs, he looked at the woman lying in his arms, taking in her pearlescent skin, and the way her soft pink lips formed an 'o' as she slept. She looked peaceful, unworried, so much more relaxed than when they'd walked in that evening. They'd agreed not to talk or think about what had happened at the steak house. After all, there was nothing they could do about it. Instead they'd closed the door and curtains, blocking the world out until it was just the two of them as he'd led her up to his room.

He'd cradled her as he slid inside her, keeping his eyes open in spite of the way her warm wetness overwhelmed him. And she'd stared right back, her eyes wide, her moans soft, her legs circling around his hips as she pulled him closer into her until he couldn't work out where she ended and he began.

Their lovemaking made him feel raw, almost painful in his vulnerability, and it had left him shaken in a way he'd not felt for a long time.

The closest thing he could compare it to was the moment Charlie had come into the world, all red and screwed up and screaming, heralding his arrival to the world in the loudest way possible.

It felt like a beginning, but also an ending. If he was a romantic, he'd say it felt like love.

The shaft of moonlight had moved, slowly sliding its way, inch by inch, across the wooden floorboards. In less than an hour it would probably hit the bed, waking her up. He gently removed his arm from beneath her, laying her head back down on the pillow while she continued to sleep, then swung his feet to the floor, standing up to grab the shorts he'd discarded earlier that night.

Swiftly tugging the curtain back to cover the final sliver of inky night, he turned around, seeing her lying there in the gloom. Her naked body was curled up on the white sheets. Compared to the huge bed she looked tiny. And yet she had a strength, too. One she wasn't even aware of. A steel core beneath that soft, supple skin, that would fight to the death to protect her daughter.

It was mesmerising.

Strange to think that when he first met her, he'd made so many wrong assumptions. He'd been taken in by her beauty, by her name, and in his mind he'd pegged her as a society wife.

But she was so much more than that. And as he watched her on the bed, he felt the urge to protect her, the way she protected her daughter. To ride in on his charger, sword aloft, and fight Thomas Marshall for her.

He climbed back into bed, and she stirred for a moment, before turning onto her other side. She didn't need his protection, she didn't need his support. She could take care of herself the way his mother never had. And though he was glad about that, a part of him – the same part that had slunk out of town all those years ago – was whispering in his ear, telling him he wasn't needed. That everything between them was as fragile as the old Egyptian scroll hanging over his bed.

He lay back down next to her, pulling her warm body against his. Maybe she didn't need his protection, but he could still hold her. At least for tonight.

Even if it didn't feel like nearly enough.

'Somebody's looking happy.' Ryan blinked the dryness from his eyes, waiting for the scene before him to come into focus. Juliet was standing there, wearing just his white shirt and nothing else, her long, lean legs uncovered from her thighs. She was holding a tray with coffee, orange juice and pastries on it, a big smile plastered across her face.

'Well, maybe I got some last night,' she teased. 'There was this guy who took me out for steak, promised to love me seven ways 'til Sunday, and then held me all night while I was sleeping. So yeah, I'm not doing too bad.'

He tipped his head to the side, trying to detect any bravado underlying her words. But they seemed too simple and honest for that.

'I think you'll find I only loved you two ways. We still have five more to go yet.'

She raised an eyebrow. 'But it's already Sunday.'

'Correction, it's already *a* Sunday. Plenty more where they come from.' Sitting up, he took the tray from her, sliding it onto the table beside the bed. Then he lunged for her, grabbing her around the waist and pulling her onto the mattress, until she was straddled across his hips. She'd only buttoned his shirt up halfway, and from this vantage point he could see her breasts beneath the thin cotton. Her nipples were tight, pointing upwards, rosy and ready for his lips.

'You look good in my shirt.'

She grinned. 'Why thank you. I thought about bringing you breakfast naked, but it was too damn cold to try.'

'Always best to keep covered when pouring out coffee, too,' Ryan pointed out.

'Health and safety before sex,' Juliet agreed, nodding seriously. 'After all, we're responsible adults.'

He slid his hand along her bare thigh, letting his fingers trace the soft skin inside. 'Less of the responsible, babe.'

'You're right, you're not responsible. You're reprehensible.'

'I'm what?'

'Reprehensible. Like a rake.'

He started laughing, his thumb still brushing her silken flesh. 'Just when I think you're normal, you go all London on me. What the hell's a reprehensible rake?'

'You know, a cad. A bad man. Somebody who's only after one thing.'

He raised an eyebrow. 'What kind of thing?'

She leaned forward, giving him the perfect view of her chest. 'The kind of thing that seems to be on your mind right now. The dirty kind.'

He could feel the amusement rising up. Sometimes, when she wasn't thinking, she came out with the funniest things. All English and proper. It was as sexy as hell. 'Say dirty again.'

She rolled her eyes. 'Seriously?'

He nodded. 'Yes, seriously. Talk dirty to me. Let me hear your worst.'

'You do it first.'

Ryan laughed. 'You know I can talk dirty. I do it every time we have sex. But I haven't heard it from you. Come on, let me have it.' His eyes twinkled. 'Or are you too prim and proper for that?'

She narrowed her eyes, tipping her head to the side while she stared at him. 'Are you setting me up, Mr Sutherland?'

'No way. I just want to hear how bad you can be.'

She leaned closer still, until her hair was trailing along his chest, and her breath was fanning his face. A small smile quirked at her lips, as she whispered in a sexy voice against his mouth. 'Mud.' She pulled back, her smile wider. 'That's dirty, right?'

'Yeah, really dirty.' He grinned.

'Absolutely filthy,' she agreed, giving him a wink. 'I shock myself sometimes.'

Laughing, he pulled her towards him, kissing her softly as he circled his hands around her waist. 'I never knew you had such a foul mouth.'

'Well there's probably a lot you don't know about me,' she pointed out.

'I'd like to find it all out.' He wasn't kidding. There was something fascinating about her. He wanted to ask her all the questions.

'I eat steak, I talk dirty, and I can throw an anchor like a pro. I'm pretty much the female version of you.' She grinned. 'What else is there to know?'

He slid both hands beneath her shirt, letting his palms come to rest on her hips. Her skin was warm and soft, her body slender. His own body ached with desire for her. 'I'd like to know what's going on beneath this shirt.'

'Pretty much what you'd expect.' She wiggled her eyebrows. 'The usual.'

'The usual,' he repeated, brushing the pad of his thumbs against her stomach. 'I like the usual.'

'You do?'

'I do with you.' And wasn't that the kicker? He'd spent most of his adult life in search of new experiences, but now he wanted to have the same one, over and over again.

As long as it was with her.

22

Oh, beware, my lord, of jealousy!
It is the green-eyed monster which doth mock
The meat it feeds on

– Othello

'So what do you think?' Cesca did a twirl, the white gown fanning out behind her. She was in a bridal shop with Kitty, who was holding her camera and letting Lucy and Juliet watch as she tried on dress after dress. 'Is it too big do you think?'

'I liked the last one more,' Lucy said, 'but you still look beautiful. You could wear a sack and you'd still bowl everybody over.'

'It needs to be right though,' Cesca said as the assistant unzipped the back. 'Elegant but eye-catching. Demure but sexy.'

'You don't ask for a lot do you?' Kitty said from behind the camera. Juliet bit down a laugh. It was bittersweet watching her younger sister trying on wedding dresses on her laptop screen. She couldn't help but wish she was with Cesca and Kitty – and Lucy too – with champagne glasses in their hands, gossiping about men and weddings and whatever else they always found to talk about.

She missed them like crazy. The thought of missing Cesca's wedding was like a knife to her heart.

The assistant carried out another gown. 'I've saved this one for last,' she said. 'It only came in last week.' She lifted it over Cesca's head, being careful to avoid her hair. 'It's a little different from the others.' She stepped around the back as Cesca slid her hands out of the sleeves, and then fastened the zipper. Kitty's hold on the camera wobbled as she took in the sight before her. Juliet had to lean in to try and see the dress.

'That's the one,' Kitty said firmly. 'Without a doubt.'

'I can't see it,' Lucy said. 'Can you hold the phone up, Kitty?'

When she did, the vision took Juliet's breath away. The assistant was right, this dress was different to the others, but in a perfect way. The dress itself was simple – a sheer layer of tulle over a nude underdress, the sleeves long and the bodice tight, forming a low v on Cesca's chest. The tulle was embellished with white silk flowers, cascading down the bodice and over Cesca's hips. On some people it might have looked too much, but it was perfect for Juliet's sister. It was whimsical yet fashionable, and clung to her curves without looking too sexy.

'She's right,' Lucy said. 'That's definitely the one.'

Juliet's throat was tight. She felt tears stinging at her eyes. She was so happy to be able to share this with her sisters, delighted to see Cesca looking so beautiful. And yet there was that nagging thought again, the one she couldn't quite banish.

What if she couldn't go to the wedding itself?

Cesca walked over to the long mirror on the wall of the bridal shop, staring at herself as she moved this way and that. Even from behind you could tell how special she felt, the dress making her hold her shoulders higher and her spine straighter.

'It is perfect,' she said softly. Then turning to look at

Kitty – and the camera – she smiled. 'Thank you so much for doing this with me, I wouldn't want to be here without my sisters.'

'There are some amazing bridesmaid dresses to go with this,' the assistant said, smiling like the rest of them. 'I'll bring them out for you to take a look.'

'Do you have flower girl dresses too?' Cesca asked. 'My niece is six.'

Juliet felt herself stiffen. She really could do with that glass of champagne, even though it was barely the afternoon. She listened as her sisters chatted about the wedding plans, about Sam's wedding suit, and where they were planning to honeymoon. Juliet stayed silent, not wanting to spoil her sister's excitement. But that bitter taste was still in her mouth, no matter how many times she tried to swallow it down.

'You okay, Jules?' Lucy asked. 'You've gone a bit quiet.'

'I'm fine.' She nodded tightly.

'You don't sound fine,' Kitty said, turning the camera to herself. She was frowning. 'What's the matter?'

Juliet rolled her lip between her teeth. 'I still don't know if Poppy and I will be able to come,' she admitted, hating the way her voice sounded. 'Thomas is still being stubborn.'

On the screen she could see Lucy lean forward. 'But the mediation is happening, isn't it?' she asked. 'Then you'll be able to agree the terms of your divorce.'

Juliet nodded. 'That's right.' Her sisters were as frustrated with the Maryland divorce laws as she was. Having to live separately from Thomas for a year before her divorce could be finalised felt like a special kind of purgatory. She'd hoped they would have agreed the terms of their separation long ago, but Thomas had other ideas. He'd cancelled their final mediation session three times. It was as if he didn't want to get things settled between them.

'We have the final mediation on Wednesday. I'm hoping we'll be able to agree on custody and maintenance. But none of it will be implemented until next year, once we can prove we've been apart for twelve months.'

'And after that you'll be able to travel?' Cesca asked, looking hopeful.

'I will.' Juliet nodded. 'But I'll only be able to take Poppy out of the country with Thomas's agreement.' She curled her hands with frustration. 'And you know Thomas, with him there's no such thing as a free lunch.'

Lucy gave her a sympathetic smile. 'Is everything else going okay with the mediation?' she asked. 'How about custody and maintenance?'

'My lawyer thinks they'll agree to 70/30 custody,' Juliet said. 'That's really all I want. Everything else is negotiable. Most of Thomas's assets he had before we got married, and my business should make a profit next quarter. I'm hoping that we won't be dependent on him for anything other than school fees and extras for Poppy by the end of next year.' She opened her mouth to tell them about Ryan, and being spotted out with him for dinner, before shutting it firmly again. She'd promised herself she wouldn't think about that, not until their negotiations on Wednesday.

'The business is going well?' Kitty asked. 'Oh, I'm so happy for you. Cesca sent me some pictures, your flower arrangements are gorgeous.'

'They really are,' Cesca agreed. 'I want her to do my wedding flowers. We'll get you and Poppy to England somehow.'

'Cesca's right, you're doing so well. You're a single mum,

you've started up a business, and you're standing up to your asshole ex. One day he's going to wake up and realise what he's thrown away, and I wish I could be there to witness it.' Lucy grinned. 'Because by that point, you won't give a damn.'

'Because she'll be in the arms of a good man,' Kitty added, always the romantic. 'One who knows exactly how to take care of a woman.'

'She's already been in the arms of one,' Cesca pointed out, then covered her mouth in horror. 'Oh bugger. Sorry, Jules.'

'What?' Kitty asked loudly. 'What man?'

'Is there something you're not telling us about?' Lucy asked, leaning forward with interest. 'Or someone?'

'It's nothing.' Juliet shook her head. 'Cesca's exaggerating.'

'Cesca doesn't exaggerate.' Lucy's eyes were narrow. 'So who is he?'

That question struck closer to home than Lucy realised. Because, really, who was Ryan? A neighbour? A friend? A man who could make her laugh and scream and swoon with lust.

A man she'd fallen for, without even knowing it?

The problem was, he was all those things, and yet none of them really mattered. He'd be leaving next year when the school year ended, and she'd be left here in Shaw Haven, dealing with everything the way she always had.

'Nobody.'

'Oh come on, he didn't look much like a nobody to me,' Cesca said. 'Unless nobody means tall, hot, and with a massive crush on you.'

'He's just a friend.' Juliet shrugged. 'He lives next door.'

Kitty grinned. 'The boy next door? Oh, I'm intrigued now. What's his name?'

'He's definitely not a boy,' Cesca said. 'He was all man

231

when I met him. I thought Sam was tall and muscled, but Ryan kinda dwarfed him. Is it wrong to say I wanted to lick his biceps?'

'I don't know who to be more annoyed with for keeping this a secret,' Lucy said. 'Jules, why haven't you said anything? And Cesca, you are too guarded for your own good. I'm the eldest, you're supposed to tell me everything.'

'There isn't anything to tell,' Juliet said quietly. 'Honestly, he's a lovely guy, but he's going to be leaving next summer. We're friends, there can't really be any more than that.' She didn't sound very convincing. And why should she? It was obvious there was no long-term future in it, but that didn't mean she was okay with it.

'What if he doesn't leave?' Lucy asked. 'What if he decides to stay? How will you feel about that?'

Juliet rubbed her eyes with the heels of her hands, the pressure causing stars to explode against the black backdrop of her lids. When she opened them again, the stars remained in her vision for a moment, a shimmering veil that obscured the faces of her sisters.

'I don't know,' she replied, her focus finally becoming sharp. 'Because it won't happen. He'll leave town to move to New York, and I'll be here sharing custody with Thomas.' She took a breath in, trying to ignore the tightness inside her that always seemed to come when she thought of Ryan leaving. 'It's just a fling, that's all.' She didn't sound convincing.

All three of her sisters were smiling sympathetically at her. They'd grown older since those days when the four of them roamed the house while their father hid himself away in his office, mumbling about writing a paper or doing some research, but they were still a gang of four. They were spread far and wide, but they were a family and it counted for a lot.

'Would you be willing to agree to a 70/30 split in custody?' Mary Reynolds, the divorce mediator turned from Juliet to look at Thomas. He was sat at the end of the table, his arms folded against his chest.

'As long as the financial agreement is based on a 50/50 split, then yes,' his lawyer interjected. Thomas's face betrayed no emotion. 'I don't see why he should be penalised for being gracious.' Thomas was wearing a new suit – or at least it had been bought since Juliet had moved out – another reminder of how their lives were moving on. 'And we'd like any personal property that existed before the marriage to remain outside the agreement.'

In the months since Juliet had moved out of the Marshall Estate, they'd each met with the mediator four times. This final meeting was the first time all of them had been in the room together, with the aim of agreeing the terms of their separation. Once those terms formed part of their divorce, they would be legally binding.

'Would you like some time to think about that?' the mediator addressed Juliet.

Juliet glanced sideways at her own lawyer. They'd discussed this earlier, and her lawyer had been vehement in telling her to pursue more. But the settlement would still be generous – enough to not worry about paying the rent, or feeding her child, and that was all she needed. 'I don't need time,' Juliet said. 'I can agree to it now.'

She wasn't sure who looked more shocked; Thomas, his lawyer or the mediator. The three of them were staring at her, frowning.

'Okay then,' the mediator finally said, scribbling on the pad in front of her. 'So I think that's all the points agreed.'

'I wanted to add a final discussion point in,' Thomas said. It was the tone of his voice that alerted her, she recognised it all too well. The same tone he used when he thought he was getting one over on her.

The mediator had no choice but to let him speak. That was the problem with mediation, it was only binding if both parties agreed. Either of them could stand up right now and leave, and all these months of negotiation would be for nothing.

She'd been anxious through the whole meeting, her body on high alert for any Thomas-style curve balls he might think of. Every time he'd opened his mouth she'd expected him to mention seeing Richard Stanhope at the golf club on Sunday, and ask her about Ryan and what he meant to her. The fact he'd gotten through an hour of mediation without talking about any of it had given her a false sense of comfort. Maybe the Stanhopes had kept her business quiet after all.

His next words told her it wasn't over yet.

'I want to have a veto over any partners she may have until the divorce is absolute.'

'What?' The word escaped her mouth before she could stop it.

'Well that's very unusual,' the mediator said. 'I'm not sure we should do that.'

Juliet took a sharp breath in. Had he been saving this all along, waiting to spring it on her when she least expected it? That was something he'd do, wasn't it?

'If we're going to discuss that, which we're not agreeing to at all,' Gloria Erkhart, Juliet's lawyer, said, 'then we'd want it to cover both parties. Mrs Marshall should also have a veto.'

Thomas caught Juliet's eye. 'I'm in a committed relation-ship, and my daughter has already met my partner. I'm comfortable that her spending time around Nicole isn't disruptive. However, my wife's situation is more . . . ' He paused for effect. 'Unstable. And if she's going to have Poppy for seventy per cent of the time, I think it's only fair I have the right to say who she brings into the home.'

'That's bullshit,' Juliet spat out. 'You know I'd never do anything to hurt Poppy.'

Thomas kept hold of her gaze, his own unwavering. 'I don't know what you'd do, Juliet. I never thought you'd hit anybody, either, but you did. After we separated I realised how troubled you were. Maybe another condition should be getting some therapy for your anger problems.'

It was on the tip of her tongue to tell him to go screw himself. Maybe if she didn't love her daughter as much as she did, it would be an option. But as everybody had told her – as long as Poppy was a minor Juliet had to deal with this asshole sitting across the table from her, and as delicious as it would be to flounce out, it wouldn't achieve anything.

Apart from giving him some satisfaction.

'I can't agree to that.' She kept her reply terse.

'Why not?'

'Because it's unreasonable. I let you make decisions for me for the past seven years. I refuse to do it any more.'

'So you'd rather put our daughter in danger?'

She hated the way he kept his voice so reasonable. He had this way of making himself look like the good guy even when he was completely in the wrong. The trouble was, she'd let him, and he'd grown stronger, and now he thought he was invincible.

Even though he'd been the one to cheat, and the one to introduce his daughter to the other woman, without so much as consulting Juliet, he was still trying to turn it back on her.

Well, he could try as hard as he wanted. She wasn't going to let him get away with it this time.

'I've never put our daughter in danger,' she told him. 'Everything I do has her best interests at heart. I'm not the one who ended this marriage, and I'm not the one who brought another woman home and had sex with her in our bed. If you want to talk about instability, let's talk about morals, too. And whether you or Nicole actually have any.'

'I really don't think this is helping . . .'

Thomas waved the mediator off. 'You want to talk about morals, sweetheart? Why don't we talk about how you *accidentally* fell pregnant and forced me to marry you? Or how you physically assaulted my new partner. Don't come the high horse with me, because you're going to lose.' He leaned across the table, his face twisted with fury. 'If I don't trust you with our daughter, that's because you haven't earned any trust. I ask you for reasonable things and you do everything you can to put up roadblocks.'

'Is that what this is about?' she asked him. 'Are you punishing me because I didn't agree to you having Poppy for Christmas?'

Thomas laughed. 'You're making it all about you again. I just want what's in my daughter's best interest.'

'She's *our* daughter, and I want what's best for her too. But that doesn't include you having any say in my personal life. I won't agree to anything that gives you control over me.' She felt empowered, as though a weight was falling from her shoulders and smashing to smithereens on the ground. Thomas stared

236

at her, as though surprised at her vehemence. He wasn't used to not getting his own way.

'Then let's agree to you not having any men into your home,' he said. 'And not introducing them to our daughter. That includes the asshole who lives next door to you.'

Juliet froze in her seat. She'd been waiting for him to mention Ryan. Her mouth went dry as she looked over at him, trying to work out what he knew.

But then, what did it matter whether he knew about her and Ryan or not? There would always be something he could hold over her if he wanted to, some way of controlling her and any reaction she might have. As long as she was afraid of him, he would keep winning.

The only way Thomas could have power over her was if she let him. It was her choice and hers alone. She could spend the next twelve years cowering in fear of him, or she could stand up for herself, be proud, show him she wasn't about to take any more.

'Ryan Sutherland's a good man, and a good influence on Poppy.' She sat up a little straighter. 'He's also a very close friend of mine. He's always welcome in my home.'

For the first time Thomas looked flustered. His eyes narrowed into slits. 'Are you fucking him?'

The mediator gasped. Juliet turned to look at her horrified face. Even both their lawyers – normally so poker-faced – looked shocked.

For a moment, nobody said a word. The silence settled its way into the room, lying heavy in the air like an over-filled cloud. Juliet could hear her own breath – a little rapid, but still steady – as she tried to take in his words.

'Your question doesn't deserve a reply,' she told him, her

heart pounding in her chest. 'But I'll answer it anyway. No, I'm not fucking him, because unlike you I don't fuck anybody. When Ryan and I are together, we make love.'

She stood up, slinging her purse over her shoulder as she caught her lawyer's eye. 'I think this mediation is over, don't you?'

23

We should be woo'd, and were not made to woo

– A Midsummer Night's Dream

Juliet's elation at finally standing up to Thomas lasted for all of her drive home. She pulled her car onto the gravelled driveway and put it into park, letting her head fall back onto the chair rest, closing her eyes as she took a breath in. Had she really just done that?

Yes, it seemed that she had. She'd stood up for herself, taking control from Thomas. She'd refused to stay silent any longer. Opening her eyes, she caught a glimpse of herself in the reflection of the glass, and she couldn't help but smile. Staring back at her was a kick-ass woman who wouldn't take crap any longer.

She was stronger than that.

She'd grown sick of being told what to do. Somewhere in the past weeks she'd stopped being afraid of Thomas and what he might decide next. She'd realised something important – he could only hurt her if she let him. And on that point she had all the power.

She glanced over at Ryan's house, and her smile widened. He might not know it, but her newfound strength had a lot to do with him. Would she have stood up to Thomas without him? Maybe, but she wouldn't have felt so good about it.

The lightest dusting of snow had fallen in the night, making the ground outside sparkle like a carpet of diamonds. It would be gone before school was out, leaving only a few damp puddles behind, but for now it made everything look magical.

But she couldn't just stay in here all day. She had things to do – a quick change of clothes and then off to the shop, where poor Lily had been holding the fort. A few hours of fixing up orders lay ahead before she'd need to pick Poppy up from school. There wasn't time to think about this now. Maybe she'd buy a bottle of something sparkling on her way home and invite Ryan over to celebrate later. They could toast her newfound freedom, and enjoy each other's company.

Sliding the keys from the ignition, she turned to pull open the door when a glint of winter sun flashed across her eyes. It bounced from the car behind her. The one that was pulling up on her driveway to block her in.

Thomas's car.

He pulled the black sedan up until his fender was touching the rear of her small Ford.

Was he trying to intimidate her? Her heart immediately started to race. Opening the door with a shaking hand, she swung her feet onto the path, the thin heel of her court shoes sliding against the slippery surface.

Almost immediately Thomas opened his door too, his feet crunching on the gravel as he covered the distance between them. He looked as furious as he had in the lawyer's office.

'We need to talk.' He grabbed her arm. His fingers easily closed around her slender wrist.

'There's nothing to talk about.' She yanked her arm back.

'If you want anything from me, you can go through my lawyer.' She walked carefully towards the house, trying to keep herself upright in her best shoes. What had she been thinking, wearing them in today's conditions? Another way to show him that she was doing just fine without him. She could dress up, look good, and it wasn't for him any more.

It was for her.

'There's everything to talk about.' He was right behind her, his steps mirroring hers. 'When you were going to tell me you were sleeping with that asshole?'

'How about never?' she replied. 'We're almost divorced, Thomas. Who I spend time with has nothing to do with you. The sooner you get that through your head the better.'

'It has everything to do with me.'

She whipped her head around to face him. Though her heels had added a couple of inches, he was still taller than her. Intimidating as hell. But damned if she was going to let him know it.

'As long as Poppy is healthy and safe, it doesn't. And if you hadn't noticed, she's happy. She's doing brilliantly. So if I choose to spend time with another guy, you don't get a say, okay?'

He shook his head, frowning. 'No, it's not okay. It's not okay at all.' He reached for her again, and she stepped back, flinching. When she looked at him, he had the strangest expression on his face. A mixture of confusion and something else. Was it panic?

She sighed. 'Look, I know things are changing. It took me a long time to come to terms with the thought of you and somebody else. But you will, too. I don't expect you to like the guys I date, I don't even expect you to tolerate them.

But I do expect you to respect my right to spend time with whoever I choose.'

He shook his head again. 'No, I can't do that.'

Her muscles tensed up in her stomach. 'Why not?'

'Because you're my wife.'

'I'm your soon-to-be-ex wife,' she corrected. 'And don't forget, this was what you wanted. You chose Nicole, you want to be with her. We're not puppets dangling on a string. You can't keep changing your mind.'

There was a war going on behind his eyes. He reached up to rub the back of his neck, his suit jacket lifting with the movement. 'I didn't think . . . ' He trailed off, frowning. 'I didn't think that you would move on. Not this quickly. I don't like it.'

Her skin felt cold, and it had nothing to do with the air surrounding them. 'I don't understand.'

He stopped rubbing his neck, and reached for her face, cupping her jaw with his soft hand. 'This isn't what I want. I don't want you seeing other guys. I don't want you spending time with them. You're mine, Juliet. You're *my* wife.'

'No.' She shook her head. 'No, you can't do this. You can't.' He was playing mind games. Just when she'd gathered the strength to release herself from him, he was trying to drag her back in. 'You don't get to say those things any more. I'm not yours, and I won't be your wife for much longer.'

'But you can be, don't you see? We can try again.' His face lit up as if he'd had an epiphany. 'You and Poppy can move back home, and we can be a family. Isn't that what you want? For her to grow up with both parents?' His voice softened. 'We were happy once, weren't we? I miss you both. I want you home with me.'

For a moment her thoughts went to that big mansion by the

river. Happy memories sprung up – the ones she'd forgotten in the darkness of the last year – of Poppy as a toddler, running into Thomas's arms as he got home from work each night.

'*I* was happy,' Juliet said. 'But it wasn't enough for you.' The image of Thomas holding Poppy disappeared, followed by the memory of Nicole standing in their bedroom, wearing nothing but a draped sheet. 'When were you planning to tell Nicole about this?' she asked drily. 'Or did you want us both in your bed?'

'Nicole doesn't mean anything.'

'She meant enough to throw your marriage away.' Juliet didn't even know why she was engaging with him. Maybe there was some satisfaction from hearing him throw Nicole under the bus, but in reality it changed nothing.

'It's not too late. We can try again,' Thomas was repeating himself. 'Let me talk to Nicole. You could move back in next week.'

She could picture it all. They'd go back to the way it was, Juliet taking care of Poppy and the house, sitting on charities and making small talk with his parents. He'd go to work, come home, and expect to be taken care of. And all the time she'd be waiting for another Nicole to show up.

'I don't want to try again.' Her voice was strong, even if she felt like a child inside. 'I'm not the same woman you married. And you know what, Thomas? I'm so glad I'm not. Because I don't want to be your wife, I don't want to live in your house, and I don't want to wake up and wonder if you're going to be faithful to me today. I want so much more than that, and I've got it. Without you.'

His expression hardened. He leaned closer, his eyes narrowing as he stared at her. Goosebumps broke out on her skin.

'You won't get a better offer,' he told her. 'The older you get, the harder you'll find it. You're getting past your prime.' He shrugged his shoulders. 'Single woman with a kid – what guy's going to stick around you with that baggage? And in the meantime, I'll be battling off the women throwing themselves at me.'

'Really, Thomas?' She rolled her eyes. 'Last time I looked, it takes two to make a baby, and from what I remember you were a more than willing participant. You're a single father with a kid, too.'

He opened his mouth to reply when the rumble of an engine echoed from the road. They both turned to see Ryan pulling up on his driveway. His black truck came to a stop, and the door opened. He climbed out of his car, running his hand through his hair, unaware that he was being scrutinised.

'Sutherland?' Thomas said quietly. For a moment she'd forgotten he was even there. 'That asshole.'

'You need to leave now, Thomas.' A sense of urgency washed over her. The two men being in one place was a really bad idea. Especially since Ryan had no idea she'd blabbed all about them to Thomas. 'We'll talk later, when we're both a bit calmer.'

He shook his head. 'I'm not going anywhere.'

Ryan turned and stared at them. She willed him to turn away, to walk up the steps to his house, to ignore them. If she could keep the two men separate, they all had a chance of walking away from this unscathed.

'You doing okay, London?' Ryan called out to her.

Damn it.

'She's fine. Now get the hell out of here, this is none of your business.' Thomas's reply came before she had a chance

244

to answer. The viciousness of it made her spine tingle. Ryan froze to the spot, frowning as he took in the words.

Then he turned and walked towards them.

Damn.

'Go, now, Thomas,' she hissed through gritted teeth. He ignored her, his eyes firmly trained on Ryan's approach. As he came closer, she could almost taste the testosterone in the air. It sizzled around them, hot and mean, making her as uncomfortable as hell.

'You need any help?' Though Ryan's face was tight, his eyes were gentle when they caught hers. Even standing next to her soon-to-be ex-husband, she could feel the pull of this man, unable to resist his magnetic energy. There was something about the two of them together that slotted into place.

'Thomas was just leaving,' she said. 'We finished mediation today.'

With his six foot two stature, Ryan dwarfed Thomas. He was more muscular, too. But height and weight counted for nothing next to intent, and she could feel the antipathy in Thomas's stare.

'I'll leave when I'm ready.' Thomas's dismissal felt all too familiar. 'In the meantime I think you and I have something to discuss, Sutherland.'

'Thomas, don't.' She reached for his arm, but he shrugged her away. Ryan took a step towards them, his eyes darting from Juliet to her ex, as if he was trying to weigh up the situation.

'I have nothing to discuss with you,' Ryan said.

'Apart from the fact you've been fucking my wife,' Thomas spat out.

She wanted to scream. Torn between throwing herself between them, and running away and hiding, she found herself rooted to the spot. Frozen in that moment just before a crash,

245

she could see everything that was going to happen, but was powerless to stop it.

'She's right, you should leave. Before you say something I might regret.' Ryan's stare didn't waver.

'Oh, is that a threat?' Thomas raised his eyebrows. 'I'm not scared of you, Sutherland. I despise you.'

'The feeling's mutual. So why don't you slide your scrawny ass into your car and get the hell out of here?'

'Oh, am I interrupting something?' Thomas laughed. 'Did the two of you have something planned? Maybe I should go, leave you to have sex with my wife the same way you've been doing for who knows how long?' He shook his head, that mean smile still painted on his lips. 'Is she a whore in bed for you, the same way she was for me?'

Ryan's jaw was tight. 'If you call her a whore again you'll regret it.'

'Will I?' Another laugh. This time shorter and harsher. 'You couldn't hurt a damn fly.' Thomas turned to Juliet. 'Is this what you want? He left his family behind without a word, you know he's not gonna stick around for you. He'll just wander off into the sunset leaving you all on your own again. And you'd choose that over your family? Maybe I should request a psychiatric assessment as part of our divorce.'

'There's nothing wrong with me,' she said. 'My brain's clearer than it's ever been.'

'The way I see it, you've gotta be messed in the head if you're sleeping with that asshole.' He jabbed his thumb towards Ryan. 'Or is he just one in a long line?'

From the corner of her eye she saw Ryan's hands clench into thick, round fists. 'Thomas, you really need to go now.' Her voice was urgent.

'Don't talk to her like that,' Ryan said slowly. 'She's a beautiful, funny, intelligent woman you let slip through your stupid goddamned fingers.' He took a step closer, until he was all up in Thomas's face. Juliet's heart rate went into a hundred metre dash.

Somehow she managed to get herself between the two of them. With her back to Thomas, she slid her hands onto Ryan's chest, trying to hold him back. 'Please don't make this worse.' She looked at him, willing for him to look back at her. Eventually, he dragged his angry stare to hers. 'Please,' she begged again. 'Just go home and let me cool the situation down. This isn't helping.'

He was silent for a moment. Behind her she could hear Thomas shuffling on the porch. Maybe he realised this confrontation wasn't such a good idea after all.

'I don't want to leave you alone with him,' Ryan told her.

'He's going,' she replied firmly. 'And anyway, I'm a kick-ass, remember? I don't need a rescuer, I've got my own back.'

Ryan was hesitating, she could see that much in the way he was looking at her. He needed confirmation she was okay, that she could handle things. She nodded slightly, as if to say she had this.

'Yeah, I'm leaving,' Thomas said. 'But this isn't over, not by a long shot. If you think you're welcome anywhere near my kid, you're crazy, Sutherland. You can have my wife, but as far as I'm concerned that's all you can have.'

Juliet turned to look at him, to make sure he was going.

'I'll be calling my lawyer as soon as I'm home,' Thomas told her. 'I'll be fighting for full custody of Poppy.' He stood there, looking at her for a moment. 'Unless you want to reconsider my offer, that is.'

'What offer?' Ryan asked, his voice strained. She could feel the tension in his body as he stood next to her. He was like a bow pulled back, just waiting to launch the arrow.

'It doesn't matter,' Juliet said.

'Of course it matters.' Thomas moved his gaze to Ryan. 'If you want to know I've asked Juliet to come home. To stop this nonsense and come back to where she and Poppy belong.'

'Is that true?' Ryan asked her. His voice was dangerously low.

'Yes he asked, but I didn't agree.' She shot a look at Thomas who was standing halfway down the steps, willing him to get the hell out of there.

'She will though,' Thomas said, sounding more confident than she'd heard him in a while. 'She'll realise that you're just a weak asshole who can't even stand up for himself.' His lips rolled up into a grimace. 'I hope you enjoyed having sex with my wife, Sutherland. But just remember who had her first.'

Ryan was down those steps before the words even sunk into her brain, his fist flying through the air in a blur of flesh. There was a crack as it made contact with Thomas's jaw, and she covered her mouth to stop herself from screaming out.

What the hell had Ryan done?

24

My heart is turned to
Stone; I strike it, and it hurts my hand

– Othello

Punching Thomas Marshall in the jaw was a mistake. Ryan knew it before his fist had even slammed into the smug asshole's face. He was playing right into his hands, making him a martyr in front of his wife. But damn, it had felt good for a minute.

Thomas backed away, his hand covering his jaw where Ryan had punched him. Juliet was standing next to him, her eyes wide, her gaze shooting from one man to the other. The look of horror on her face was a kick in the gut. She felt so removed from him, as though his lapse of judgement had built a wall up between them.

His hand was throbbing like a bitch, too. He cradled it as he backed away, his eyes seeking out Juliet's even though she was trying to avoid catching his gaze.

'You bastard.' Thomas rubbed his jaw. 'You're gonna pay for that. Did you see that, Juliet? You're a witness, right? He hit me. Jesus Christ.' He let go of his jaw, and scrambled for his phone. 'I'm calling the cops. Nobody move.' Blood was running from the corner of his mouth, where his teeth must have jolted into the soft skin inside his cheek.

'Please don't . . . ' Juliet reached for Thomas, but he stepped away. Ryan stood on the spot, watching the two of them, trying to work out what the hell he could say to put things right.

He'd promised her he wouldn't get involved. She always said she could stick up for herself. The last time he'd tried to stand up for a woman – his mother – she'd turned on him. The thought of Juliet doing the same made him feel sick.

'Send them over to my place when they get here,' Ryan said. 'They've probably got a whole list of real crimes to solve, I don't think they'll be blue lighting their way out here.'

'I've got friends on the force. I'm sure they'll make it here fast.'

Of course he did. Men like Thomas Marshall had friends everywhere. The sort you paid for with money or favours. The kind of friends Ryan had spent his life avoiding – though they'd have come in pretty handy right about now.

'Thomas, put the phone down. Surely we can sort this out.' Juliet reached for him.

He ignored her completely, turning until his back was towards them as he spoke rapidly down the phone. Ryan couldn't make out the words above the sound of blood rushing through his ears, but from Juliet's expression it wasn't good.

She caught his eye again, and it made him want to run over and take her in his arms. She looked shocked and angry. As if she couldn't quite believe what he'd done.

He couldn't quite believe it either.

'I'm sorry,' he mouthed at her.

She shook her head. When she looked away he could see the tears glinting in her eyes.

'You should go home, Ryan,' she said, still not meeting his gaze. 'I'll send the police over when they get here. Let's not make a show of this for the neighbours.'

'What about Marshall?' He inclined his head at Thomas's back.

'I think I'll be safe with him. He's hardly going to do anything if the police are coming, is he? I'll take him inside and clean him up.'

The thought of her doing anything with that asshole was enough to make his blood boil. He wanted her to tell Marshall to leave, for her to ask Ryan to protect her. He wanted her to look at him the way she had last night.

Not like this. Never like this.

'London I—'

'Just go, okay?' she interrupted him. 'Don't make this any worse than it already is.'

His chest was aching from all the emotions fighting inside him, ones he couldn't quite name but were making his heart pound like a marathon runner. He wasn't sure if he wanted to punch Marshall again, or just scream out in frustration.

'If he touches one hair of your head I'll be over here like a shot. Just call me.'

'I can look after myself,' she said again. 'I don't need your help.'

And wasn't that the truth? Any other time he'd be rooting for her, glad that she could stand up for herself. But right now, he wanted her to need him, the same way he needed her.

There wasn't anything else to say. He took one last look at Juliet. She was searching frantically through her bag for her keys. She didn't want him there, and he sure as hell wasn't going to stay and watch her let Marshall into her house.

So he turned around and started walking down the steps. He'd barely made it to the driveway before Thomas called out again.

'Better line up a babysitter, Sutherland. Your ass is gonna be in jail before the afternoon is out.'

'Shut up, Thomas. Get in the house.' Juliet's voice was as terse with Thomas as it had been with Ryan, but somehow that gave him no satisfaction. He squared his shoulders, covering the hundred yards between their houses with long, heavy strides. Though the air around him was chilled, it felt as oppressive as a hot, humid day. Heavy and pressured, just like his thoughts.

His truck door was still open, from when he'd run over to check if she was okay. He reached in and grabbed his keys and his wallet, and the papers strewn across the passenger seat.

The papers he'd just signed to sell his shares, along with the proposal to buy the wharf. He could just take the money and run. Grab Charlie and leave. He owed Shaw Haven nothing. He owed his family nothing. And as for Juliet, he had no god-damned idea who owed who.

The first thing he did when he walked into the house was call his lawyer. The second, once he'd splashed his face with cold water and slammed his palm against the cold wall tiles until it hurt, was an altogether different call. One he made from the living room, staring out of the window that overlooked Juliet's yard. He stared aimlessly as he waited for the call to connect, scratching his chin and wondering how the hell things had gone so crazy so fast.

'Hello?'

'Sheridan, it's Ryan. I need your help.'

25

Come, let's away to prison;
We two alone will sing like birds i' th' cage

– King Lear

'So you admit you hit him?' The cop leaned back, frowning.
'Why did you do it?'

'Don't answer that.' Frank was already pissed. Mostly
because Ryan freely admitted to punching Thomas Marshall.
What was he supposed to say? No doubt Thomas's face was
bruised, as was Ryan's hand. Plus there was at least one witness
that Ryan never intended to have up on the stand. He wasn't
planning on fighting this. He just wanted to get out of here.

The cops picked him up just after lunchtime. The cruiser
pulled up outside Juliet's house, and two uniformed guys
went in, spending around an hour doing who knew what
in there. After that, they followed the same path Ryan had
taken earlier, crossing the front yards of the two houses
until they came to his door. He opened it almost as soon as
they knocked.

They took him down to the station straight away, and put
him in a cell until Frank arrived later in the afternoon. And
for the past hour he'd been sitting in this small room, his large

body almost too big for the orange plastic chair they'd given him, answering the same questions over and over, until he was getting bored of his own voice.

'I hit him because he was rude to Juliet.'

'His wife?' The cop looked surprised. 'Mrs Marshall?'

'His soon to be ex-wife,' Ryan corrected. He wasn't sure why he wanted to make that clear.

'Okay . . .' The cop looked suddenly uncomfortable. 'And what is your relationship with Mrs Marshall?'

'I'm in love with her.'

And wasn't that the kicker? He'd let his guard down, again, and here he was. Sitting in a police station asking questions while cradling his aching hand. His chest was aching even more than his hand was. He couldn't stop thinking about her face when he'd hit her soon-to-be ex-husband. Did she hate him for it? He wasn't sure.

They shot another barrage of questions at him.

What was their relationship?

Why had he done it?

Did he realise it was assault in the second degree?

He never should have come back.

'Does she know that you're in love with her?'

Ryan laughed, though there was no humour in it. 'I'm not sure what you're asking. Have I told her I'm in love with her? No. Does she know it? Well, she should.'

'Are you in a relationship?'

'I guess.' He felt stupid, not being able to say more.

'Mr Sutherland, you're not making this easy. We're just trying to get the facts here. Please can you state your relation-ship with Mrs Marshall.'

Ryan felt cornered. 'Juliet and I are friends. Or we were.'

God only knew what they were to each other now. He'd managed to mess everything up.

'So you're a friend who's in love with her.'

'Can we move on?' Frank rolled his eyes. 'My client has an impeccable record. He's a single father with a son who relies on him. We'd like to get him home as soon as we can.'

'We're just trying to establish the facts. As soon as we do then we'll follow procedure. Mr Marshall has stated he's extremely afraid of any further attacks. At the moment we need to keep the victim's wishes in mind.'

'He thinks I'm gonna hit him again?' Ryan was incredulous. 'I wouldn't give him the satisfaction.'

The questioning went on for another hour. Through the small, frosted window near the roof, he could see the sun slowly closing shop for the day, replaced by the early evening gloom. Eventually they took him back to his cell, while Frank left to go home for the evening.

They had the right to hold him for twenty-four hours without charge, so Ryan knew he had a night in jail ahead of him. Frank had promised to check on Charlie, who was staying with a school friend for the night, far away from the house and any gossip that might hit him. Ryan wanted to be the one to tell his son about the confrontation.

A couple of hours later they gave him some food – a plastic-wrapped peanut butter and jelly sandwich, and a bottle of water. He opened the bottle, guzzling the liquid down, then placed the sandwich on the concrete bench he was sitting on, and curled up, using the bread as a pillow.

Funny, the tricks you learned as a traveller.

He had no clue what time it was. They'd taken his watch, along with his phone and wallet, plus the laces from his shoes.

It could have been seven or eleven for all he knew. This grey square of a room had a time zone different to any other. Minutes felt like hours, and the only thing to fill the empty space were his thoughts. He couldn't escape them no matter how much he wanted to.

Couldn't escape the memory of Juliet's expression, either. The way she'd looked at him when she told him to go home. There was shock behind her eyes, but something else, too. Contempt, maybe, even disgust. All melded together with an anger that made his heart hurt.

This town was no good for him. It was making him crazy. It was breaking his goddamned heart.

He needed to know where they stood. Whether she felt the same way as he did. Whether getting thrown in jail had been another fool's errand or a noble gesture for the woman who loved him back.

He needed her to love him. Otherwise . . .

What else was keeping him and Charlie here?

The banging of the metal door woke him. Ryan rubbed his eyes, seeking out the figure standing in the backlit doorway.

'Come with me.'

Still half-asleep, Ryan followed the cop through the quiet corridor, his sneakers half-slipping off his feet as he walked. The cop pressed a code into the keypad next to the door, then led him into the foyer, and over to the desk. Laid out on the counter were his wallet and cell, shoelaces and watch. The desk sergeant gave him some forms to sign.

'Am I being released?' he asked.

'On bail. Somebody got up nice and early and spoke to the judge. He's set bail and you're free to go for now.'

'It's been paid?' Ryan frowned.

'Yes, by that lady over there.' The desk sergeant inclined his head at a space behind Ryan's shoulder.

A lady? His heart started to hammer against his chest. Slowly he turned, each movement of his body stiff and full of effort. He'd spent the night thinking about her, wondering if she was thinking of him. And here she was, waiting for him, bailing him out, letting him know exactly whose side she was on.

A second later, his hopes went tumbling down to the ground. The lady in question stood up, lifting a hand in a half-wave. Her face was serious, but kind.

'Ryan.' That old familiar voice. It wrapped him like a blanket and it pierced him like a knife. He wasn't sure which hurt the most.

'Mom? You bailed me out?'

'I got a phone call last night to tell me you were in jail. I called Frank to find out how I could help. Seems he needed the judge to set bail, so I dialled in a few favours.'

It was amazing how the world turned around money. Though it was benefiting him right then, he couldn't help but think how unfair it was.

'Thank you.'

She shook her head. 'Don't thank me. It's what a mother should do for her child. I should have stood up for you when you were younger, and I regret that I didn't. I'm just trying to make amends.'

He wasn't sure what to say right then. A lifetime of thoughts swirled around his head, but not one of them translated into words. A mixture of being woken up in the middle of the night, and not having to deal with his mother for all these years.

What time was it anyway? He glanced at his watch; it was almost seven-thirty in the morning. He grabbed his phone – there was enough battery for him to check his messages.

One from Charlie, who was having a good time.

Nothing from Juliet.

He held the door open for his mother, then followed her outside. The early morning air held a hint of frozen fog. He could see his breath clouding out every time he exhaled. 'Does my father know you're here?' he asked her.

She shook her head. 'I figured it's none of his business. I paid your bail with my own money.' She licked her lips. In spite of the early hour, she was still wearing a full face of make-up. Appearances still came first. 'I wanted you to know . . . ' For the first time her voice faltered. 'I wanted you to know I'm sorry.'

Ryan stared at her, frowning. 'For what?'

'For everything that happened. The way I treated you.' She shook her head. 'I'm old, Ryan, and I'm not going to change things now. Your father and I, we have an understanding. Things aren't like they used to be. He leaves me alone.'

Ryan had no idea why she was telling him this.

'Your son is beautiful,' she continued, her voice still thin. 'And one of the consequences of the choices I made is that I'll never be a grandmother to him.' The faintest of smiles crossed her lips. 'But at least I can bring his father back home to him. That's one thing I can do.'

Ryan stared at her for a moment. She really did look old. What had happened to that beautiful woman he'd tried – and failed – to protect?

She'd scorned his help. And she'd ended up this way.

Christ, he needed to speak to Juliet. She was the only thing that could make him feel better right then. He lifted his phone again, glancing at the screen. 'Do you mind if I make a quick call?'

'Go ahead. And after that we'll get some breakfast and I'll take you home. I imagine you're desperate for some sleep.'

'A shower would be good at least.' Ryan nodded.

He left his mom by the entrance, heading for the brick wall, past a metal bin and discarded cigarette butts. Unlocking his phone, he pulled up her number, and hit the call button.

But the last person he expected answered the line.

'Sutherland? What do you want?'

'Marshall? Where's Juliet?'

'She's here, of course.' There was some mumbling, then the sound of Thomas's breathing disappeared.

'Ryan? Are you okay? Are you still at the police station?' Juliet was breathless.

'You're with him?' Ryan asked, his voice low.

'Ryan, I . . . '

'Daddy says it's breakfast time.' Poppy's voice cut through the line. 'We've got waffles and real orange juice.'

'Are you at home?'

'No, I'm at Thomas's house.'

It felt as though somebody was pulling his guts out of his stomach, inch by inch. 'Did you spend the night with him?' He didn't want to know. Except he did. His head was in a mess. All he could see was red mist, pulling down inside his mind and making him crazy.

'I did. But it's not what you think. Have the police let you go yet?'

He didn't want to answer her questions. Not when his own were pounding at his skull. 'I'm on bail,' he said, his voice a monotone. 'Can I come and see you?'

There was a brief pause. Long enough for him to look up and see a red cardinal flying down from one of the leafless trees. 'It's really not a good time.'

That was all he needed to hear. He should have known it all along. The clues were there from the start after all. It didn't matter how good they were together. It didn't matter how he felt about her. Thomas had asked her to come home, and she'd gone running. She'd chosen him.

While he spent the night in a jail cell, imprisoned for trying to save the girl he'd fallen for, she'd spent the night in the arms of the man who'd treated her like crap. He wanted to punch something all over again. Wanted to make somebody else hurt the way he did.

What a goddamned fool he'd been.

26

O, teach me how I should forget to think

– Romeo and Juliet

'What did Sutherland want?' Thomas placed his coffee cup carefully on the table, his eyes never leaving her face. 'Have they let him out?'

Juliet stared at the waffles in front of her. Poppy had poured half a bottle of maple syrup over them. The congealing mess was making her stomach turn. She took a deep breath, choosing to ignore his question. 'Poppy and I need to get home. I have to go to the shop, and she's missing school.'

'Not until I know you're safe.'

He sounded so reasonable, so rational, And yet the thought of having to stay here in his house made her feel like a prisoner.

'Of course we're safe. Ryan isn't violent, you just riled him up.' She glanced at Poppy, not wanting to say any more. The poor kid had heard enough already.

'The man's a threat to all of us. He hit me, Juliet, he's an animal. I'm not willing to take a chance with my family. You need to stay here until I get a restraining order.'

She pushed her plate away, unable to look at it any more. For some reason Thomas's calm tone felt more threatening than any shouting he might have done. 'I've done everything I can. You asked me to stay here last night, and I did. You asked me to keep Poppy off school and I have. But we have lives to live. Ryan isn't going to hurt anybody, you know it and I know it. And no judge is going to put out a restraining order after he hears what actually happened.'

She took another glance at Poppy, who was making patterns in her own maple syrup. 'Honey, why don't you go and clean your teeth. After that we'll head home.'

'No.' Thomas's expression was implacable. 'You're not going anywhere.'

She brought her eyes up to his. 'Yes I am. I'm going home.'

Sensing the tense atmosphere, Poppy didn't say a word. Instead she ran for the stairs, leaving her breakfast behind. Juliet couldn't blame her for wanting to escape from the arguments. She'd heard enough to last a lifetime.

'Don't leave like this. Think about what I said. I know you have a thing for Sutherland, but you said yourself he's leaving soon. Don't turn your back on me for something that can't last.' He winced. 'I made that mistake, and I've regretted it ever since.'

Everything about his voice told her he was sincere. Her chest tightened at his words. And for a moment she considered his offer, considered staying here with Poppy, who was clearly delighted about spending the night with both her parents here.

But then the thought of Ryan came back into her mind, and she knew it would never work. 'I'm not in love with you any more, Thomas,' she told him, though it hurt to say it. 'I can't be with you, not after everything we've been through.'

His expression hardened. 'So you're taking my daughter home to be near him, even though he's violent?'

Juliet rolled her eyes. 'Oh for goodness sake, since when did she become *your* daughter? She's ours Thomas, and we'll decide together what's best for her. I know you're angry with Ryan, and I agree he should never have hit you. But maybe you shouldn't have said what you did either. You should apologise for that.'

Thomas snapped. 'What the hell should I apologise for? I asked you to come home, I asked you to be a family and you just threw it in my face. You've said a lot of things I've had to overlook, Juliet, and you've done a lot of terrible things, too. I even managed to persuade Nicole not to press charges when you hit her. And after all of this, you still won't do as I ask you.'

Juliet pushed her chair out, and stood resting her hands on the table. 'I hit Nicole because I found her in our bed, if you don't remember. You're the one who cheated, you're the one who brought another woman into our relationship, and you're the one who broke our marriage up. I've offered you a fair settlement, and you've rejected it.' She slapped her palms on the wooden surface as if to emphasise her words. 'And now I'm going to get our daughter and take her home. We'll see you when you come to pick her up this weekend.'

'So that's it? You're going to ignore my wishes?'

She shook her head. 'No, Thomas, I hear your wishes loud and clear. But I've decided that my needs – and our daughter's – trump them every time.'

He pulled himself up to standing, his face flushed red. 'You keep that bastard away from my daughter or I'll . . . '

'Or what?' she interrupted. She didn't need to hear the answer. She didn't care what it was. Thomas couldn't hurt her any more, not unless she let him.

He wanted to bribe her by withholding money? Well she could stand on her own two feet.

He wanted to threaten her with taking Poppy away? Well he'd been threatening that for months, and nothing had happened. He was all words and no action, he always had been.

How had she not seen that before?

The knowledge of it felt like a weight lifting off her shoulders. For all this time she'd been walking to his beat, when all she had to do was refuse. She felt like Dorothy, clicking her heels together, and realising she had the power all along. She just didn't know it.

But she did now. She saw it all too clearly. He'd been trying to control her, even after he'd been the one to mess everything up. Accusing her of not living up to his expectations, blaming her for his cheating, telling her she was a bad mother, when she put Poppy first in everything she did.

'If you leave, don't ever expect to come back.' His voice was low. Threatening. 'And don't expect me to make it easy on you.'

She shook her head. 'I've learned to have zero expectations when it comes to you. That way I'm never disappointed when you don't meet them. Now excuse me, I have a life to go and live. We'll see you at the weekend.'

By the time they got back home, it was almost lunchtime. Rather than take Poppy to school, she decided the excitement of the past twenty-four hours was enough for them both to have a day off. So with Lily agreeing to run the shop, mother and daughter pulled on their pyjamas and found an old movie on TV, snuggling under the checked blanket as they shared a bowl of popcorn.

The movie had barely been on for twenty minutes before Poppy had fallen asleep. Her hair fell over her rosy cheeks as her breaths became shallow and regular. Carefully sliding her phone from her pocket, Juliet tapped out a message to Ryan.

Are you okay? I'm so sorry I couldn't talk earlier.
I'll explain everything later if you can come over?

She couldn't wait to tell him about finally standing up to Thomas. About her revelation that she held all the cards. And even though she was still angry at Ryan's hitting her husband, she knew they could work it all out.

I'm fine. Can't come over. Too much to do.

His words felt like a slap across her face. She blinked a couple of times, reading them over again. Was he angry with her too?

Poppy was snoring softly, her legs curled up against her stomach. Lifting the blanket from her own legs, Juliet tucked it around her daughter and walked out into the kitchen. Looking out of the window, across to Ryan's house, she scanned the porch and windows to see if she could see him.

There was no sign.

She wrote out another message.

I'm free now if that works any better?
I'd really like to see you.

She pressed send before she could talk herself out of it. Writing those words made her feel uncomfortable, as if she was laying herself on the line.

Sorry, I've got too much packing to do.
I'm leaving tomorrow.

Her legs felt weak. She leaned on the worktop, trying to let his reply sink in. He was leaving? He hadn't mentioned anything before. She blinked, trying to recall the last time it was the two of them, lying tangled in his bed. Not once had he talked about going anywhere. Not until the school year was out and summer had come. Surely he wasn't going for long?

Rolling her lip between her teeth, she pressed the call icon next to his name. He answered almost immediately.

'Hi.'

'Where are you going?' she blurted out.

Ryan cleared his throat. She could hear music playing faintly in the background. Some kind of slow, country song. 'To New York. Something came up.'

'What kind of something?' Juliet felt almost embarrassed to ask. As though she was taking liberties that weren't hers to have.

'Something to do with my contract.' His voice was as short as his reply.

'How long will you be gone? Are you taking Charlie with you?' It felt as though a band of iron was wrapped around her chest. Getting tighter, more painful by the second.

'No. Sheridan's going to look after Charlie while I'm gone.'

Charlie's mom was there? Juliet sucked in some air, but it wouldn't go down to her lungs. 'Don't you have a bit of time now?' She rolled her bottom lip between her teeth. 'We need to talk.'

She could hear rhythmic taps, as though he was pacing the floor. She pictured him in his hallway, bare feet slapping against the warm, wooden boards. So close, only a few hundred feet away.

And yet so far.

'Lond—' He coughed. 'Juliet. look, we both knew this was a short-term thing, right? You've got shit to deal with, and I've got a job to do. We were never going to be compatible, and we were okay with that. I wish you all the best with things, I really do. But I can't be the one you lean on any more.'

The congestion in her chest worked its way up her throat, forming a solid lump that stopped her from inhaling. She could feel her eyes start to sting, and though she blinked the budding tears away, new ones replaced them straight away.

'I never asked you to do that,' she said quietly. 'I never asked you to do anything.'

Another silence. She could almost picture him staring down at the floor, shaking his head. Everything between them felt loaded, as though the air was thick between them, muffling their communication like a fog.

'I don't know what you want me to say.'

She closed her eyes, but the panic followed her in. 'Is that it?' she asked. 'No explanations, no promises, just a quick goodbye over the telephone? You couldn't even come and tell me face to face?'

'Tell you what? That I'm going to New York?' Ryan sounded confused. 'I didn't know until this morning.'

That wasn't what she meant at all. But what she wanted to say – what she wanted him to hear – was impossible to put into words. He wasn't just going to New York, it felt like he was leaving her behind. In every sense possible.

How could she tell him that?

'I guess I'll see you when I get back,' he added, when she failed to respond.

'I guess you will.'

'Lo . . . Juliet?'

She swallowed though her mouth was dry as dust. 'Yes?'

'It's for the best, right?' Was he really asking her that? 'It's not as if we were serious or anything. And you've got so much to deal with, the last thing you need is me hanging around. You were there when I needed you, and I hope I was there for you too. We're still friends, aren't we?'

A sheen of saltwater was forming behind her eyelids. She blinked to let the tears escape. Then she closed her eyes again, feeling the hot drops running down her cheeks, until they fell from her chin.

Still friends? She didn't even know what that meant any more. Didn't know if it was possible to hurt like this over a friendship.

Glancing across the kitchen, she caught sight of herself in the glass door of the microwave. She was hunched over, one hand grasping the phone to her ear, the other splayed on the countertop, her arm tense as it held her body up. In the shimmer of her vision she looked like a broken woman.

And she hated it.

'No, I don't think we can be friends,' she told him, trying to hide the pain in her voice. The need to run and bury her head somewhere warm and dark was almost overwhelming. 'Goodbye, Ryan.'

'Wait. London, I . . . '

But she couldn't wait. Not if it meant letting this pressure in her chest increase until it felt as though she was going to explode. Instead she ended the call, throwing her cell phone onto the counter top before she ran to the bathroom, where she locked the door and fell to the tiled floor, the tears flowing down her cheeks as though they were never going to stop.

*

Ryan threw his phone on the mattress and hit the cotton bed-cover with his still-bruised fist. A dull pain shot up his arm, but he ignored it, frowning as he stared at the open suitcase on his bed. It was half-filled with lightweight clothes, ready for his flight tomorrow.

'Ry, what time do we pick Charlie up from school?' Sheridan popped her head around the doorway to his bedroom. Her hair was pulled back, revealing her tan, youthful skin. Since she arrived that morning, she'd been sleeping in the spare room, and she was still wearing a pair of drawstring pants and a waffle-knit white sweater. If you were looking closely enough you could see the merest hint of a swell across the normal flatness of her belly. Three months pregnant, or so she'd told Ryan. The father – Carl – was a member of the band she'd been working with. The two of them were planning to find a place to rent near Ryan and Charlie, just as soon as his tour finished. She didn't want Charlie to feel pushed out by the new baby, she loved him way too much for that.

She was so excited about bringing her family together, and all the while Ryan was falling apart.

'Three,' he told her, not looking up from his suitcase. 'I'm going to take him to the ice cream parlour, and then explain I'm going away for a few days. I don't want to overwhelm him all at once.' He sighed. 'Maybe I should just take him with me. He won't miss much school.'

When he looked up, she was looking at him, a sympathetic expression on her face. 'You said yourself it's only for a few days. And you know he won't want to miss school. They've just started practising for their Christmas show, he was so excited about it when we talked on the phone.'

Ryan nodded. 'You're right. I don't want him to miss out on that.'

'And from the look of you, it might do you good to be alone for a few days. You've had a face like thunder ever since I arrived.'

Everything around him felt flat. Had done since he'd walked into the house after his mom had dropped him off. His whole life felt like a series of fraying strings. Nothing led anywhere, nothing knitted together. He was full of holes.

Finally he brought his gaze up to meet Sheridan's. She was still looking concerned, her brow furrowed with lines. He felt grateful to her for flying in so fast, catching the next plane into Baltimore after his urgent request. So maybe she was planning on coming here anyway, what with her pregnancy and all, but it had worked out well for them both.

'Are you sure you want to do this?' she asked him, tipping her head to the side.

'Do what?'

'Leave so suddenly. How important is this contract glitch anyway?'

He shrugged. 'It's just something I need to smooth out. And I should probably do it now, I could be in jail by the time January gets here.'

Sheridan grinned. 'I think we both know that's not going to happen. Didn't your lawyer say that at the very worst you'd get a fine? If they thought you were some kind of violent maniac, they wouldn't let you leave the state.'

That was true. The first thing he'd done was check with his lawyer if he was okay to leave the state, even if he was on bail. According to Frank it was no problem, as long as he turned up for his court date.

If there was a court date.

He looked up. 'I really appreciate you coming here at short notice, I know it wasn't easy. I hope you didn't get into too much trouble with the band.'

'It helps that I'm sleeping with the lead singer,' she said, rubbing her stomach. 'And touring isn't as much fun as it used to be. I don't know if I'm getting old, but I started longing to come here to spend some time with Charlie. Would you believe I'm actually looking forward to being able to take him and pick him up from school?'

Her wide-eyed astonishment made Ryan laugh. 'What happened to that cool girl who couldn't stay in one place for more than a week?'

She lowered her voice, as though she was talking in confidence. 'I think she grew up. But don't tell anybody.'

He shook his head. 'You're growing up, and I'm regressing. I feel like a kid right now.'

She tipped her own head to the side. 'She really did a number on you, huh?'

He closed his eyes for a second, but all he could see was Juliet. Opening them again, he looked at Sheridan. 'It's not her fault.' And in the end it didn't really matter. He was bleeding out regardless of who'd held the knife.

'I knew it. I knew there was a woman involved.' She clapped her hands together. 'Come on, who is she? She must be somebody special to make you run like a demon.'

'There's nobody.'

'Bullshit.' She folded her arms across her chest. 'You're running scared, Ryan. It's obvious. Is it that woman Charlie keeps telling me about, the one who lives across the way from here?'

'I don't want to talk about it.'

Her face softened. 'You never do. And though it drives me crazy, it's one of the things I like about you, too. You're a strong man, Ry, and I'm glad our son has you for a father.'

Her simple words touched him deep in his soul. His voice was gruff when he replied. 'Not as glad as I am to have him for a son.'

The corner of her lip quirked up. 'Then go and do what you need to do. As long as you're leaving for the right reasons. Because there's nothing worse than running away, only to find your troubles bought a ticket and decided to travel right along with you.'

27

The course of true love never did run smooth

– A Midsummer Night's Dream

Juliet tucked her knees beneath her chin, wrapping her arms around her legs as she sat on the window seat in her bedroom, looking out across the wintry yard to the white stucco building opposite. He was in there somewhere, packing a bag or printing out his tickets. Maybe he was laying his photographic equipment gently in their boxes, packing his camera and lenses carefully to transport them to who knew where.

The band around her chest hadn't loosened any in the hours since he'd told her he was leaving. If anything it had become tighter, as she stared aimlessly at her phone, wondering if he was going to call her back and promise he'd be home soon. If he was going to text her and tell her he missed her as much as she missed him.

She only had to close her eyes to picture him the way he was the last time they'd been together. When he'd slowly slid himself inside her, his eyes capturing hers with their intensity, his breath soft, his kisses gentle. She'd felt so safe in the circle of his arms. There'd been a moment – just after they'd both reached their peak – when they hadn't been able to take their eyes from each other. It had felt as though she'd discovered everything she'd always been looking for, right there above her.

Now it was gone and it hurt like hell.

Poppy had climbed into bed without as much as a complaint, falling straight to sleep in spite of her earlier nap. The house was quiet and dark. The silence bounced off the walls, reminding her how alone she was. That she wasn't even worth fighting for.

Juliet followed her bedtime routine on autopilot. Washing her face, cleaning her teeth, climbing into her fleecy pyjamas. Though the heating was cranked up to high, she still felt bone-cold. She climbed into bed, pulling the quilt tightly around her, but her body was still shivering beneath the blankets. A few moments later, she heard the padding of bare feet on the floorboards outside the room. Poppy pushed the door open and closed the short distance to the bed, wordlessly climbing in and hugging Juliet close.

When was the last time Poppy had slept in her bed? Juliet couldn't even remember. Maybe when she was a toddler, afraid of the dark, searching for comfort wherever she could find it.

Juliet hugged her daughter back, stroking her hair as Poppy nestled into her, closing her eyes tightly. Maybe another day she would have carried her back to bed, and stayed there until Poppy fell asleep. But not tonight.

Because tonight she needed the comfort as much as her daughter did.

Poppy woke before Juliet the next morning. The first thing she knew was the sound of the bathroom floorboards creaking as Poppy made her way to the bathroom. A minute later the sound of the flush followed by running water was enough to tell Juliet her day had started. She glanced in the mirrored door of her closet, seeing the telltale red rings around her eyes. Her skin was sallow, her cheeks thin, and her red hair – usually so wavy – hung limply below her shoulders.

She was a mess.

Somehow she managed to get Poppy ready for school. Hair was brushed, lunch was packed, and as usual she had to remind her three times to brush her teeth before Poppy finally relented, managing to walk to the bathroom while rolling her eyes at the same time. Her neediness of the previous night had disappeared, replaced by her usual Poppy-like strength. Even though it meant more work for Juliet, she was glad to see her daughter's fighting spirit was back.

They were only a couple of minutes late arriving at school. Juliet pulled into a tiny space at the far end of the parking lot, wincing at the expensive models she was sandwiched between.

'Open the door carefully,' she reminded Poppy.

'I know.' Another eye roll. Goodness only knew what she'd be like when she was a teenager. Juliet squeezed out of the narrow opening of her door, watching Poppy carefully doing the same. They followed the painted walkway around the edge of the parking lot, walking to the tall, brownstone buildings set in wooded parkland. This was what $8000 a term got you; the best education in the best surroundings.

Seeing her friends filing into the classroom, Poppy gave Juliet a quick hug then ran towards them, her braid flying out behind her. This time Juliet let her smile shine through – she was so happy to see her daughter's high spirits.

'Oh Juliet, I was going to call you. We're looking for volunteers to help decorate the classroom next weekend,' Susan Stanhope called out. She was standing in a circle with three other class moms. Juliet recognised Emily and Marsha – she'd known them for three years after all – but the third woman was new to her. Beautiful, too, even with her hair pulled back into a messy bun and no make-up on. The woman turned to look at her, a curious expression on her face.

'I have to work on Saturday,' Juliet said, standing five feet away from the women. 'What time were you planning on getting here?'

'Oh, I forgot.' Susan wrinkled her nose. 'That must be such a pain, having to give up your weekends.'

'It keeps a roof over our heads.' Juliet tried to keep her voice even. 'Anyway, I can donate some floral arrangements if that helps? I'll get my assistant to deliver them.'

'You work in a flower shop?' the woman beside Susan asked. 'That's cool.'

'I own it,' Juliet said. 'It's only small, but it's mine.'

Unlike the others, the brunette didn't seem at all fazed by Juliet's admission that she actually had to earn her own living. 'I'm Sheridan, by the way. Charlie Sutherland's mom.' She offered a slim hand to Juliet. Stepping forward, Juliet took it, shaking briefly, trying not to look too curious.

'I'm Juliet Marshall. Poppy's mom.'

Sheridan's eyebrows shot up. 'Poppy from next door?'

She nodded. 'That's us. If we make too much noise feel free to yell across.'

'I love your place, the garden is so pretty. You guys must have so much fun there.'

Sheridan clearly hadn't received the mean girls' memo of being rude to Juliet. And as much as she'd wanted to resent this woman, the one who had an unbreakable connection with Ryan, Juliet found herself warming to her.

'Isn't Sheridan lovely?' Susan interjected in her high voice. 'Ryan's a lucky man, right? I told her how so many moms have been hanging on his every word. But she's the one who gets to live with him.' She gave Juliet a knowing look.

'Oh, we don't live together,' Sheridan replied. 'We're not together at all. The two of us are co-parents, though Ryan has primary custody.'

Susan couldn't have looked any more appalled if Sheridan had just told her she practised satanic worship. She wrinkled her nose, looking the new arrival up and down, her eyes shifting from left to right as she tried to think up something to say.

'Anyway, I don't think Ryan's on the market right now. From what I can tell he's fallen for somebody.' Sheridan grinned, catching Juliet's eye. 'But he's like all men, kind of stubborn, if you see what I mean.'

'Well, I should get going. I have a pedicure booked in for nine-thirty.' Susan turned to look at Marsha and Emily. 'Coffee at my place later, ladies?'

'Sure thing. See you there.'

The three of them walked away without bothering to say goodbye, leaving Juliet and Sheridan standing there. 'I guess I should go, too. I need to open the shop,' Juliet said.

'That's a shame, I was going to ask you over for coffee,' Sheridan said. 'I don't know anybody here, and I was hoping you could give me the inside track.'

'Didn't Ryan give it to you?'

Sheridan laughed. 'You know Ryan, he wouldn't see the inside track if you waved it right in front of his eyes. Take those women, he'd think they were just being friendly. But you know and I know they're bitches, and they were trying to put you down. He's so blind to that kind of thing.'

'Aren't all men?'

'Damn right they are!' Sheridan nodded. 'Are you sure you can't come over for a coffee?'

Juliet glanced at her watch. 'I guess I could come over at lunchtime. My assistant gets in at eleven, she can watch the shop for a couple of hours.' Juliet reminded herself to give Lily a huge Christmas bonus. She'd earned it this year.

Sheridan's face lit up. 'That would be great.'

'Are you sure Ryan won't mind?' Juliet rolled her lip between her teeth. 'You could always come to mine if he does.'

'He'll be at the airport by then, his plane leaves this afternoon. So it'll be just us girls.'

Juliet nodded, trying to ignore the ache in her heart. He was going through with it, then. Maybe that was a good thing. Once he was gone, she might be able to breathe again, because right now, just remembering to inhale was taking every ounce of energy she had.

'Sorry about the cases, I haven't managed to unpack yet.' Sheridan led the way, weaving through the red leather luggage stacked in the hallway. 'I'm only supposed to be here for a few days. I definitely over-packed.' They reached the kitchen, where Sheridan grabbed the coffee pot, filling it with water. 'Decaff okay with you?'

'That would be great.'

'Take a seat,' Sheridan said, gesturing at the breakfast bar. 'I've got some bread if you want a sandwich. I bet you haven't had a chance to eat any lunch.'

Juliet slid onto the white plastic stool. 'I'm not hungry.'

'Ah I wish I wasn't. I've been eating like a horse. I swear this thing inside me is a goddamn cannibal.' She rubbed her

278

stomach. 'It's weird isn't it, you spend the first three months throwing everything up, and then the next three eating everything in sight. I'm a slave to my hormones.'

'You're pregnant?' Juliet asked, hypnotised by the slow circular movements Sheridan's hand was making on her stomach.

'Yeah, nearly four months. I'm as big as a house already.'

Juliet laughed. There was nothing to her. 'You look tiny.'

'I'm wearing baggy pants.' She pointed at her drawstring black trousers. 'Mostly because I can't fit into any of my jeans. I keep growing out of my clothes, hence all the suitcases.'

The coffee machine started to splutter and steam. Sheridan opened a cupboard door, then closed it right away, opening the next one before scratching her head.

'The mugs are in the one in the corner,' Juliet told her.

Sheridan turned around to look at her, putting her hands on her hips. 'And how would you know that?' she asked in an amused voice.

Juliet feigned an easy shrug. 'I'm a neighbour. I've had coffee here before.'

Sitting on the opposite stool, Sheridan slid a mug of steaming decaff over to Juliet. 'Just coffee?' she asked lightly.

Juliet leaned forward. 'Sometimes he gives me a cookie, too,' she whispered.

Sheridan coughed out a laugh. 'You're full of shit. I know that something's going on between the two of you. I'm not stupid, I can put two and two together. First of all you and Poppy are all Charlie talks about, and then I get a phone call telling me that Ryan's hit your husband on the jaw and is going to jail. And then there's the way he sulked around the house ever since I arrived, with a face like a stormy night in November.'

Juliet felt strangely cheered by Sheridan's description of Ryan. At least she wasn't the only one feeling low. 'There's nothing going on between us. Not any more.'

'Bull.' Sheridan stared at her over the rim of her coffee cup. 'I know there's something going on. What I don't know is why he's running away from it.'

'He isn't running away. He has to sort out his new job. It's important to him.' Juliet put her mug down, rubbing her bottom lip to capture a bead of coffee there. 'He never promised me anything.'

'So there *was* something going on?'

Juliet traced her finger around the rim of her cup, the tip squeaking as it completed the circle. How on earth did she end up here, sitting opposite the ex of her ex – and wasn't that a mess in itself – trying to explain what on earth happened between her and Ryan? He and Sheridan had an unconventional relationship at best. After all, she seemed completely comfortable grilling her about the two of them, while sitting in his house. But did she really want to hear the details of what happened between them?

More importantly, was Juliet comfortable talking about it?

She shifted uncomfortably in her seat. 'I don't even know where to start. I don't know how to explain whatever it was that was going on between us. All I know is it's over. He made no bones about that.'

'What makes you think it's over?'

An almost laugh rumbled from her chest. 'Oh I don't know, the fact he said it was. Not to mention the small detail of him leaving town like his ass is on fire.'

'Ah, but he's a man. They're stupid, remember?'

She met Sheridan's amused stare. 'Yeah, you've got that

right.' She couldn't believe how easy it was to talk to this woman. It reminded her of Saturday nights in the kitchen surrounded by her sisters, as they giggled about boys. 'Can I ask you a question?'

'Sure.' Sheridan gave a shrug. 'It's not as if I can refuse is it? I've been grilling you for the last ten minutes.'

'Why did you and Ryan split?'

'You think we were a couple?' Sheridan raised her eyebrows. 'Did he tell you that?'

Juliet blinked rapidly, trying to remember exactly what Ryan *had* told her about Charlie's mom. They'd barely spoken about her, beyond the fact she was touring with a band while Ryan looked after Charlie. 'Not really. He said you met while travelling in Asia. I guess I filled in the blanks myself.'

'Wrongly, by the sound of it.' Sheridan grinned to take the sting from her words. 'We were never a couple. Don't get me wrong, I love Ry, but he drives me crazy, too. Even if he didn't, he's totally not my type. So un-rock 'n' roll.' She shuddered. 'Whereas Carl is totally my type.'

'Carl's your boyfriend?' Juliet asked, confused.

'My fiancé,' Sheridan said, lifting her hand and waving it until the diamond on her finger caught the light. 'And this little monster's father.'

'I'm going to look really stupid here,' Juliet said, trying to work out what she was missing, because it didn't make sense at all. 'But if you and Ryan were just friends, then how did Charlie happen?'

'Tequila,' Sheridan replied, her eyes widening as if to emphasise her words. 'And pure idiocy. We were good friends, and we decided to travel to Koh Samui together. Even acted as each other's wingmen on the way. But one night we drank

281

too much and everything else is a blackout. When we woke up in the morning we took one look at each other and promised we'd never mention it again.

'But then I missed a period, and another, and before I knew it I was at the doc's having my pee tested. And once Charlie arrived we had him DNA-tested, too, just to make sure he was Ry's.'

'He told me he doesn't like being called Ry,' Juliet said, trying to take everything in. She'd always thought Sheridan was a lost love, but the fact she wasn't a rival – past or present – made Juliet happier than she could say. Because she really liked the woman.

'I know.' Sheridan nodded happily. 'That's why I call him it. Drives him crazy.'

Juliet couldn't help but laugh. 'What do you call Carl?'

'Asshole, mostly. Honey if I'm in a good mood. Which hasn't been often in the past three months.'

Juliet tipped her head to the side. 'Will you go back on tour when Ryan gets home?' If he gets home. Juliet still couldn't help feeling that he was leaving for good, in spite of what he and Sheridan said.

And in the end it didn't matter. Either way he didn't want her.

'I don't know,' Sheridan admitted. 'We're looking for a rental in New York right now. Carl's planning to fly in for Christmas so I'm hoping to have something by then. It would be nice to be near Charlie, I miss him, you know? Even if his dad does drive me crazy. No offence meant.'

'Do you really think Ryan's coming back?' Juliet asked her, unable to swallow the question down any more.

'He'll be back. I've no doubt about that.'

'Because he's got a court case?' Juliet asked. 'Or because he's buying the wharf?'

'He is? I had no idea.' Sheridan shrugged. 'And anyway, of course he's coming back. I've never seen him in such a mess. The cool, calm, irascible Ryan Shaw Sutherland is all crazy and het up. And if he thinks he can run away from all those feelings, he's gonna have a big surprise.'

'Maybe he's not as messed up as you think.'

'Oh, he's definitely messed up over you.' Sheridan nodded her head. 'You wanna see how I know?'

Juliet gave a half-smile. 'You're not going to go through his underpant drawer are you?'

'Hell no. Even I draw the line at some things.' Sheridan hopped off her stool. 'Come with me, I want to show you something.'

Intrigued, Juliet followed her out of the kitchen and into the hallway, where Sheridan came to a stop at the door to the basement. She unlocked it and pushed it open, flicking on the light to illuminate the stairwell. Sheridan ran lightly down the steps, with Juliet behind her, until they reached Ryan's dark-room at the bottom.

'Should we be coming in here?' Juliet asked. A sudden image grabbed her mind. 'We're not going to find dead bodies or something are we?'

'He's not Bluebeard,' Sheridan said. 'He's not scary enough for that.' Pushing open the door, she turned to look at Juliet. 'But you should probably prepare yourself. Because there are definite signs of an obsession here.'

They walked into the small room, the light from the stair-well spilling in behind them. Juliet looked around, her eyes becoming accustomed to the dim light, taking in the photos fixed onto the walls, hanging from the drying lines, piled on the countertops.

A few of them were of Charlie. Another couple of the boat. But the vast majority – at least twenty of them – had a single subject.

Juliet.

She swallowed hard as she circled around, looking this way and that. Images of her kneeling down and weeding her flower-beds, pictures of her standing on the deck of his boat, her hair flying behind her as they sailed through the bay. Still more showed her staring into the distance, a small smile playing at her lips, or kneeling down talking to Charlie and Poppy, as she pointed something out.

It felt strange to be surrounded by so many photographs of herself. And yet they were beautiful. Somehow he had taken something mundane and made it extraordinary. The curve of her arm, the shine of her hair, the smoothness of her skin were all explored in extraordinary detail.

'Tell me these weren't taken by a man obsessed.'

Julie turned to look at Sheridan. For a moment she'd forgotten she was there. 'I never knew he was taking these.'

'Of course you didn't. But they're beautiful, aren't they?'

She nodded. 'They really are.' Where she'd felt so empty before, Juliet could feel a pressure building inside her, a well of emotions mixing and bubbling. 'Why did he take so many?' she wondered.

'Because he's in love with you.'

She wanted to believe it, she really did. 'But he told me it was over. He wouldn't have said that if he loved me.'

'I told you he's stupid. He is a man, after all.'

Juliet looked at the black and white photographs again,

trying to work out what it all meant. Sheridan could be right, or she could be wrong, but right then it didn't make an ounce of difference. Because Ryan was in New York and she was right here.

She was going to have to wait to see what happened, even if the suspense killed her.

28

Under love's heavy burden do I sink

– Romeo and Juliet

Ryan pulled his shoes back on and swung his bag over his shoulder, glancing up at the flight information as he left the security hall. The departure gates were thronging as usual, and he pushed his way through the familiar families and business-men, heading for the business lounge.

He showed his ticket to the attendant at the desk, then made his way to the bar. After the anxiety of the past two days there was nothing he wanted more than a cool bottle of lager before his flight.

'What can I get you?' The barman greeted him before he'd even made it to the counter.

Ryan let his bag slide from his shoulder, putting it on the stool next to him. 'A Yuengling, please.'

'Coming right up.'

A moment later he had the bottle in his hand, the cool mist on the brown glass turning to ice-cold water, the beads pool-ing against his palm. Looking around he took in the people sitting around the lounge. A couple of businessmen in the corner were knocking back tumblers of spirits and laughing uproariously. On the other side a genteel old woman was knitting and sipping at a mug of something steaming hot. Coffee, Ryan assumed. But most of the passengers were in the office area, typing furiously at their laptops, printing out details and scrolling on their phones. Some of them all at the same time.

But Ryan didn't want to look at his phone. Didn't want to scroll through his laptop either, even though it was safely stowed away in his hand luggage. Instead he leaned on the bar and scowled at his own reflection in the mirror on the wall, not liking what he saw looking back at him.

Sighing, he took a big mouthful of beer. Then another. Within minutes the bottle was empty. He put it back down on the counter, using his finger to slide it over to the bartender, who picked it up and put it in the trashcan beneath the bar.

'You want another?' the bartender asked.

Ryan glanced at his watch. Another hour before boarding. He could remember a time – not so many years ago – when he would get to the check-in thirty minutes before the flight was due to take off. Not possible now, in these days of strict security.

'Yeah, sure. Hit me up.'

The bartender grabbed a bottle from the cooler and popped the cap. 'Can I get you anything else?'

'No thank you, I'm good.' The thought of trying to eat something made his throat want to close up. He hadn't managed more than a bowl of cereal all day. Messing everything up was ruining his appetite.

'You travelling on business?' The bartender was cleaning the counter with a soft yellow cloth. Ryan wasn't sure why, it was already gleaming.

'Yeah, something like that.' He raised his eyebrows at the man.

'You don't need to sound so happy about it.' The bartender smiled at him. Ryan leaned forward to check out his name.

'Sorry, Mike, I've just got a lot on my mind.'

'I can tell.' Mike folded the cloth up and stashed it beneath the counter. 'You have that look on your face.'

'What look?' Ryan frowned, and took another glance at himself in the mirror behind the bar.

'That one.' The bartender nodded at him. 'Don't worry, I see it a lot.'

'You do?' Ryan's frown deepened. What did that mean?

A couple sat down on two stools at the far end of the bar. Mike walked over to them to take their order, then poured out two glasses of red wine. By the time he came back, Ryan had finished his second beer. He turned down the offer of a third.

'You must see a lot of people come through this place,' Ryan said. 'It has to be great for people watching.' He wasn't sure why he was still talking to the guy. All he knew was it beat having to listen to his own thoughts.

'Sure do. A whole host of them.' He shrugged. 'But when it comes down to it, there are only two kinds of people.'

'There are?' Ryan leaned forward, his elbows on the bar. He couldn't help but be intrigued. 'What are they?'

The bartender leaned on the counter in front of him, mirroring Ryan's stance. 'There are the people heading towards a better place, and there are the people running away from it.'

Ryan laughed. 'And that's it. What about the people who are just going on vacation? Aren't they doing a little bit of both?'

'Not in my experience.' Mike shrugged. 'Working in this job, I overhear a lot of conversations, whether I want to or not, and I've not heard one yet that doesn't fit into one category or the other. That guy over there, for instance.' He nodded at a man sitting in the corner of the lounge, his phone to his ear as he typed on his keyboard. 'I see him every week. Sometimes he brings his wife with him, and sometimes he travels alone. When he travels on his own, he arranges for a little bit of company to take care of him at night.'

'How do you know that?'

'He told me. You'd be surprised how many people let things slip to me. It's not like I'm going to tell anybody, is it?' The man gave him a wry grin. 'Apart from you, that is. Anyway, he's constantly on the lookout for something better, but the fact is, his something better has been at home all the time. What he doesn't realise is the only person he's trying to run away from is himself.'

'What about me? Which camp am I in?' Ryan looked at him with interest.

The bartender looked him up and down, his eyes narrowed as though he was taking everything in. 'You haven't said a lot, which makes you harder to read. But judging from the red veins in your eyes and your hangdog expression, I'd say you're a runner, too.'

'That's where you're wrong. I'm flying to New York on business.'

'Sure you are.'

'I've got a whole new life ahead of me.' Ryan had no idea why he was trying to justify himself. 'And it's going to be great. What's better than living it up in the Big Apple?'

Grabbing a glass from the sink, the bartender picked up a towel and began to dry it. 'If that's really the case, then tell me what are you doing hanging around here with a face like thunder? If you were really excited about your future, then you wouldn't feel the need to justify yourself.' He shrugged. 'Sorry, man, but when I look at you I see a runner.'

Ryan looked at himself in the mirror again, not liking what he saw staring back at him. For the first time, he could see himself the way the bartender described.

He was a runner.

A runner.

And he was running away from the best thing that ever happened to him.

Twenty minutes later he was on the sidewalk outside of the airport, tapping his foot on the paving slabs as he waited in line for a cab. He jabbed his fingers on his cell phone to pull up her number. As soon as the call connected it went straight to voicemail. He held the phone to his ear as her sweet voice echoed through him. She wasn't available to answer his call. Please could he leave a message?

He swallowed hard. What message could he leave? It wasn't possible to fit into a few sentences the way he was feeling right then. He was an idiot, maybe he should tell her that. But she probably knew that already.

'London, can you call me back when you get this?' He winced at his words, before he pressed his screen to disconnect. Of course she wasn't going to return his call. The last time they spoke he'd told her she meant nothing to him.

He'd lied, and no doubt she'd believed him. After all, he'd almost believed himself.

When he closed his eyes, he could picture her, the way she'd looked after he'd punched Thomas in the face. The shock in her eyes, the panic, her trembling lip, all of them he'd taken as rejection. He'd been furious at her, for throwing his support back in his face, when all she'd tried to do was calm the situation down.

What a macho idiot he'd been.

His fingers were aching with the need to touch her, to hold her. He wanted to feel her silky hair between them, tangle himself inside. He'd known no tranquillity since he'd last been with her. Without her everything seemed muted and low.

A cab pulled up, and as the first person got into it, the line shuffled up. He tapped his feet on the paving slabs again, unable to stand still, unable to wait. It was as if he was at the starting line, his body ready, muscles tense, but with nowhere to go. If he wasn't fifty miles from Shaw Haven, he might've considered running there.

He needed to make things right. Even if she never wanted to talk to him again. He needed to tell her that he was a fool, that he didn't mean a word he said, that he wanted her in his life.

That without her, a fresh start meant nothing.

Maybe, all along, he was the one who needed a knight in shining armour.

As far as he was concerned, the cab couldn't get him there fast enough.

'Momma, your phone is buzzing.'

'It's okay, whoever it is can leave a message. Come over here and hold this for me, I want to twist the ivy around the frame.'

Poppy skipped over to help, putting her small fingers on the end of the strand while Juliet threaded the leaves through the wire. It was the third Christmas wreath they'd made so far today. They couldn't go fast enough to keep up with orders, and if she was being honest it was a great excuse not to go home and think about things too much.

'Is this the one for my classroom?' Poppy asked, as Juliet tied the wire off and clipped the ends with her scissors.

'That's right. I'll make a garland, too. We can deliver them on Friday, all ready to put up at the weekend.'

'Mrs Mason is going to love it.' Poppy's face shone with pride. 'I bet she'll tell everybody my momma made them.'

Juliet smiled at her daughter. The guilt she'd been feeling for not helping decorate the classroom on Saturday disappeared. She was never going to win class mom of the year, but the fact she was still making her kid happy felt like enough.

'I'm gonna head on home if that's okay?' Lily walked out of the back office, pulling a red woollen hat over her blonde bob. 'I'll start on the Devereaux order first thing tomorrow.'

'Sounds perfect. Thanks for all your help today. I really appreciate you standing in for me.'

'Any time. I was happy to help.' Lily grabbed her purse from beneath the counter. 'Those look great, by the way.' She inclined her head at the wreaths. 'I took orders for another ten this afternoon.'

'Looks like it's going to be a busy few weeks.' Juliet couldn't help but feel relieved. Her business was blooming, both literally and figuratively. It was a weight off her mind.

'Well, don't work too late. See ya later, Poppy.'

'Bye, Lily.' Poppy waved at her as Lily turned the sign on the door and then let herself out, flipping the lock behind her.

Juliet glanced at her watch. It was just gone five o'clock. Outside, darkness had already descended, lit only by the orange glow of the street lamps, and the strings of festive lights the bookshop across from hers had affixed to its windows. 'Let's finish this one up and then we'll head out,' she told

Poppy. 'Maybe we should stop at the diner for tea?' She was still avoiding going home.

'Can I have a hot dog?' Poppy clapped her hands together. 'And a chocolate sundae?'

'Why not?' Juliet ruffled her hair. 'As long as you promise to clean your teeth really well tonight.'

Poppy nodded, her expression serious. 'Of course I will. Teeth are very important. I'd look stupid without them.'

It was hard not to laugh. Juliet bit her lip to stop her chuckle from coming out. 'That's very true, sweetheart.'

It took them another half hour to finish up, and clear all the clippings away. Juliet checked the water levels in the pots of flowers before switching the main lights off and heading toward the alarm controls. 'Have you got everything, honey?' she asked her daughter. 'Your bag and your colouring pencils?'

'Yup.'

'Okay, let's go.' She lifted her hand to key in the alarm when her phone buzzed again. She'd forgotten all about checking it for messages. Sighing, she pressed her thumb against the button to unlock it, and it sprang to life. As soon as the photograph of Poppy sticking her tongue out appeared on the screen the notifications started to flash across it. Texts and WhatsApps, emails and voicemails.

Her mouth went dry. Thomas had been bombarding her with messages ever since she left his estate, and she'd managed to ignore every one of them. If he wanted to talk to her, he could do it through their lawyers.

But this time the voicemail wasn't from Thomas. Her pulse leapt when she saw it was from Ryan. From the timestamp, he must have left it just before he got on the plane to New York.

'Momma, can we go now?'

'Sure.' She slid her phone back into her pocket. She'd save that particular piece of masochism for later. Her heart was already in pieces, no need to shatter it even more.

The diner was half-empty when they arrived, and they slid into a booth and gave the waitress their order. A hot dog and fries for Poppy, and a coffee and a salad for Juliet. She didn't bother to order anything else, she'd only push it around the plate anyway. By the time they'd finished, and Juliet had laid down twenty dollars under the check, snow had begun to fall softly outside. Poppy ran out onto the deserted sidewalk, sliding on the wet concrete, and lifted her hand up to catch a flake.

'Look at this!' she squeaked with excitement. 'I caught one, I caught one. Did you know they're all different? Every single one of 'em. Mrs Mason told us.' She held her hand out, and her face fell with disappointment. The flake had melted on impact with her warm palm. 'Where'd it go?'

'There's plenty more to catch,' Juliet pointed out. 'Look, it's still falling.'

'But not that one. That one's gone forever. I can't ever get it back.'

Juliet searched her brain to find the right words to comfort her daughter. To explain that though each snowflake was special, they were just fleeting moments, frozen in time, impossible to capture. Things to be admired, not held.

Of course, that made her think of Ryan. He was so much more than a snowflake, and yet he was impossible to hold, too. A snapshot in time she could never recreate.

It made her shattered heart ache.

By the time they made it home, the merest dusting of white had settled on the driveway, crunching along with the gravel as they pulled up in front of the house. Juliet grabbed their bags, hurrying Poppy onto the steps. The air had taken on a distinct chill outside.

They were about to walk inside when she saw it. She leaned down to look closer, frowning as she picked it up from the doormat.

A yellow flower.

'That's pretty.' Poppy reached out to touch the orange flared trumpet. 'What is it?'

'A daffodil.' Juliet held it carefully by the long stem.

'What's it mean?' Poppy was used to her telling the meaning of flowers. Red roses for passion, a white daisy for innocence.

'It means rebirth and chivalry.'

'What does *that* mean?' Poppy's teeth chattered as she asked. Realising how cold it was outside, Juliet quickly opened the door and ushered her inside.

She placed the flower gently on the hall table, careful not to bruise the petals. 'It's kind of old-fashioned. It's the code people used to live by in the olden days. When beautiful maidens were wooed by white knights.'

Oh.

Oh.

She looked at the flower again. Her hand shook as she reached out to touch it.

'Why was it on our porch?'

'I don't know. Maybe somebody left it there.'

'But why?' Poppy demanded.

Juliet said nothing, still staring at the daffodil. She was wondering exactly the same thing herself.

29

Sweet flowers are slow and weeds make haste

– Richard III

'So what do you think it means?' Juliet held her phone in her hand. Lucy's face filled the screen. She was eating an early breakfast in her Edinburgh apartment. In Maryland it was the middle of the night, but Juliet hadn't been able to sleep a wink.

'I've no idea.' Her sister laughed. 'I'm a lawyer not a mind reader. What do you think it means?'

'I don't know,' Juliet admitted. 'I don't even know if it's Ryan who left the flower. All I know is he tried to call me this afternoon, and then when we got home this evening, I found the daffodil on the front step. Come on, Lucy, you're good with this stuff. Tell me what to do.'

'You're asking me for advice about men?' Lucy grinned. 'After I did almost everything wrong in the early days with Lachlan? You're asking the wrong person.'

'But you're the wisest woman I know.'

Lucy brushed her hair from her eyes, and took a sip of her coffee. 'What did he say when you called him back?'

'I haven't called him back,' Juliet admitted.

Lucy almost spat her coffee out. 'Jeez, you're right, you *do* need my advice. Rather than sit here all night speculating, why don't you just call the man?'

'What if it's not him?' Juliet asked. 'What if he wants to say goodbye again and rub it in?'

'Then you'll know he isn't the man for you.'

But he was. He was the man for her. He was the only man. The one she saw when she turned out the lights. The one who flickered through her thoughts in the morning before she even managed to untangle them.

'Jules?' Lucy prompted.

'Yeah?' She shook her head, trying – and failing – to get him out of her mind.

'Go to sleep. You look exhausted.'

'So do you.'

Lucy grinned. 'Thank you kindly for the compliment.'

'Goodnight, Luce.'

'Night, sweetie. Oh, and Jules?'

'Yes?'

'*Call him.*'

'Momma, there's another one!' Poppy called out from the kitchen. Juliet pulled her hair back into a ponytail, snapping it tightly in place with a band, and ran down the hallway, muttering to herself as her feet slapped against the floor. They were running late. *Again*. Thanks to her phone battery dying a slow death as she listened to his message over and over, and the alarm failing to go off.

By the time she reached the kitchen, Poppy was trying to fit the key into the back door, the metal scraping against the door as she failed to push it into the slot.

'You know better than to open the door without me here,'

Juliet scolded. 'What are you doing, anyway? It's freezing out there.'

Though the snow hadn't lasted long after they arrived home last night, the temperature was still frigid. She could hear the boiler working overtime in an attempt to counteract the cold.

'I wanted to see the flower.'

'What flower?' Juliet asked. She walked over to where Poppy was standing, staring out of the kitchen window.

There was a single red rose on the doormat, just where the daffodil had been the previous night. The bud had only just come into bloom, the petals nestling tightly together as if to keep warm.

'Another one,' Juliet murmured, pressing her forehead to the glass.

'It's pretty,' Poppy said. 'Where do you think it came from?'

'I don't know.' It was only a white lie. Designed to buy some time. Her phone felt heavy in her jeans pocket, a reminder of his message. Juliet tapped it, but didn't pull it out. She should call him, she knew it. But what if the flowers weren't from him?

That thought made her want to giggle. It wasn't as if she had a string of admirers lining up at her door. It was either Ryan or Thomas, and since she knew Thomas didn't have a romantic bone in his body, there really was only one answer.

Was he doing all this from New York?

Glancing at her watch, she let out a sigh. She didn't have time to be thinking about this now.

'Right, we need to go. You're going to be late again.'

'Can't I stay home and see if any more flowers come?' Poppy wrinkled up her nose. 'I want to make them look pretty like you do.'

'No can do. You need to go to school and I need to get to work.'

Half an hour later, Juliet pulled her car into the parking lot in front of the shop. As usual, Lily had opened it for business, and Juliet rushed in, giving her a quick wave before shrugging her coat from her shoulders.

'Everything okay?'

'All good. We've had a few orders this morning. Can you make them up while I work on the Devereaux table pieces?'

Juliet nodded, grabbing her apron and wrapping the ties around her waist. 'Hey Lily, has anybody bought any roses or daffodils lately?'

Lily frowned, looking up from the arrangement she was working on. 'I've no idea. Probably?' She shrugged. 'I can go through yesterday's inventory and see what was in it if you like.'

'No, it's fine,' Juliet said, ignoring the way Lily was looking at her, as if she'd gone slightly crazy. 'I was just wondering.'

The old brass bell hanging over the shop door rang out, as somebody pushed it open. A young man, twenty at the most, stepped inside. He was holding a huge bouquet of gladioli, with large purple florets blooming from the long, green stems. Looking around the shop, he began to frown, reaching up to scratch his head.

'Can we help you?' Juliet asked.

'Is this a flower shop?' He shook his head as if to try to get some sense in there.

She bit down a laugh. 'Yep, that's right. Are you looking for something in particular?'

'I'm looking for someone called . . .' He trailed off, then looked at the card nestled in among the plastic wrapped flowers. 'Juliet.'

'That's me.'

'I've got a delivery for you.' He held the flowers out. 'Though why somebody would send flowers to a flower shop I have no idea. It's crazy.' His shocked look was a picture. She almost wanted to snap it with her phone for posterity.

'They're for me?'

'Yeah, really. This is 1981 Lower Street, right?'

'Yep, that's us.'

'And you're definitely Juliet?'

She grinned. 'The last time I looked.'

'Okay then. I'll leave these with you.' He held the flowers at arm's length, as if he was afraid to get any closer. Maybe he thought the crazy was catching. From the corner of her eye she could see Lily watching with interest.

As soon as she took the proffered bouquet, the boy turned around and headed for the door. She could hear him muttering under his breath. 'Who the hell sends flowers to a flower shop?' By the time he opened the door, the amusement was almost bursting out of her.

'What was that about?' Lily asked, coming out from behind the table where she was laying out an arrangement.

'I've no idea. But you should have seen his face.' Juliet was still smiling. 'He looked as though I'd just run over his favourite dog.'

'Who are those from, anyway?' Lily asked, gesturing at the gladioli. 'Why wouldn't they just phone here and order flowers?'

Juliet shrugged. 'I've no idea.'

'Open the card.'

Plucking the small white envelope from inside the bouquet, Juliet ran her finger along the paper, opening the flap. Inside was a florist's card – from Simeon's Flower Shop – with four simple words written in blue ink.

Because you are strong.

'No name,' Lily murmured, reading it over Juliet's shoulder. 'Still, I bet if I call them they'll tell me who sent them.'

'No, don't,' Juliet said hurriedly. 'I don't want to know.'

'Why not?' Lily's question reminded her of Poppy. They were simple words and yet the answer was much too complicated to form. But there was something wonderful about everything that had happened since they'd arrived home last night. Something miraculous in the flowers and the meanings behind them. She didn't want to spoil it by confirming her suspicions.

She was going to do this his way.

'Because I don't want to know.'

'If you say so.' Lily shrugged, her eyes still narrowed with suspicion. 'I want to know, though.'

Juliet smiled, looking down at the flowers. They really were beautiful. Strong, vibrant, the kind of structural flowers she'd use to build up a bouquet. On their own, though, they were magnificent.

She grabbed a tall glass vase and filled it with water and sugar solution, clipping the bottom of the gladioli to make them fresh. Then she arranged them in the vase, putting it on the counter in front of her, happy to have something lovely to look at as they worked on their orders.

As it turned out, the gladioli weren't the only delivery she had that day. They came in fast and steady – one every hour – from seven different florists in Shaw Haven and the surrounding towns. And with each delivery she made up another vase, until all eight were standing in front of her, covering the counter completely.

Purple gladioli for strength. Pink and white hibiscus for

beauty. Red poppies for pleasure. White orange blossoms for fertility. Pink carnations for gratitude. Sky blue forget-me-nots for memories, pink camellias for admiration. The final two, brought in just before they were due to close, were full of red tulips and even more red roses – meaning true and undying love. She stared at them, these flowers that must have cost him a small fortune, so many of them out of season, and her heart felt full with the message he was trying to convey.

'You must know who it is by now,' Lily said. 'It's not Thomas, is it? Are you two getting back together?'

'Oh, they're definitely not from Thomas. He wouldn't know an orange blossom if it hit him in the eye.'

'But you do know who it is?' Lily prompted.

'I've got my suspicions.'

Her assistant perked up. 'Come on, you have to put me out of my misery. I've been trying to work it out all day. Hey, it's not Fred Simpson from the florist's in Mayweather is it? He's always had a thing for you.'

'No, definitely not Fred,' Juliet said. 'He's way too tight to order from any other store. If it was him, they'd have all come from Simpson's.'

'True story,' Lily agreed. 'So you're really not going to tell me who you think it is?'

Juliet took pity on her assistant. 'Look, once I've confirmed my suspicions, you'll be the first to know, I promise.'

'Okay. But you better tell me fast, because I can tell I'm going to be losing sleep over this.'

'Me too, Lily. Me, too.'

Juliet turned the ignition off and unclasped her seatbelt, leaning back against the car seat while she stared out of the window. The house was empty – Thomas had wisely agreed to pick Poppy up for the weekend straight from school, avoiding an encounter between him and Juliet. And thank God he was sensible enough to know she didn't want to see his face for a while.

Walking up the porch steps, her eyes were drawn to the mat, and she wasn't disappointed. Perched upon it was a small, china teapot with an image of London painted across it, depicting Big Ben and Tower Bridge along with red buses and telephone boxes. And planted in the top were delicate pink and purple flowers. Viscaria, or Sticky Catchfly.

An invitation to dance.

She picked the teapot up by its handle, lifting the flowers to look at their delicate blooms. They weren't expensive – she usually used them as fillers in the shop, but they were beautiful, nonetheless.

And they meant everything.

'They reminded me of you.'

She turned around. Ryan was standing on the porch behind her. He was wearing a thick blue sweater and jeans, his hair neat, his face freshly shaven. But it was his eyes that made her heart swell. Those deep blues, staring straight back at her, telling her everything she wanted to know.

'I thought you were in New York,' she said quietly. Her fingers tightened around the handle. There was no way she was going to drop the teapot, even if her whole body was shaking at his sudden arrival.

'I decided not to go.' He was still staring at her, his gaze soft as wool. She was staring back, too. Had it only been a few days since she last saw him? It felt so much longer. There was a hunger for him, rumbling deep inside her. Like a distant train that was speeding straight for the station. It made her blood run hot.

'Why not?' Her feet were glued to the floor. She didn't dare reduce the space between them, not when he was looking at her like that.

In the end it didn't matter, because he took a step towards her instead. Reaching out, he brushed a stray lock of red hair from her face, tucking it behind her ear. 'I was sitting at the airport bar,' he told her, 'surrounded by people travelling to one place or another. And I realised that I could be going anywhere in the world and it still wouldn't be enough. Not without you.'

'You can't say things like that.' Her voice was hoarse.

'Why not?' He dragged his fingers down her cheek, leaving a trail of fire and ice on her skin. 'Why can't I?'

'Because ...' She was lost for words. He brushed his thumb against her mouth, sending a shiver down her spine. 'Ryan, I ...'

He was beautiful. She stared at him, trying to take in every aspect of his face. His stare was heavy and deep. It drew her in without asking her permission. She could feel her whole body start to tremble at his touch.

'I've been to some amazing places,' he continued, sliding his hand to the back of her neck. 'I've seen so many beautiful things. But nothing compares to the way you look when you stare up at me like that.' He pressed his hand to the skin on the back of her neck, pulling her closer to him. She stepped forward without hesitation.

They were only inches away now. Close enough for her to breathe him in. She closed her eyes for a moment, feeling his warmth, his strength as their torsos brushed against each other. It was impossible not to be overwhelmed by him.

They were more than the sum of their parts. So much more.

'You left me,' she whispered. 'You walked away when things got tough.'

She opened her eyes to see him staring down at her, his gaze filled with an intensity that made her heart leap. 'I did, and I hate myself for it. Those were old behaviours, London. Old, ingrained reflex responses to feeling rejected. But I can promise you this, if you ever agree to take me back in your life, I won't be walking away again.'

Tentatively, she reached up to brush her fingers along his jawline. The heat behind his eyes deepened.

'But I didn't reject you,' she said. 'I asked to see you, remember?'

'By that point my mind was made up,' he admitted. 'I'd called you as soon as I got out of the police cell. All night I'd sat in there, staring at the bare brick walls, and you were the only thing on my mind. Then when I found out you were with Thomas, I lost it.'

She could feel the muscles beneath his jaw tighten. 'I was with him because I wanted to persuade him to drop the charges. I didn't trust him not to do something stupid, and I thought if I kept an eye on him I could stop him. Honestly, Ryan, the last thing I ever want to do is get back with Thomas.'

He breathed out a warm mouthful of air. It breezed against her fingers. 'I know you wouldn't. I think I even knew then. But it was like I was a kid again. Being rejected by my mom . . . ' His voice broke. He looked down, shaking his head. 'I'll tell you about it sometime.'

She knew better than to push. He'd already opened up more than she'd ever expected. Vulnerability was written on his face, making him look young, almost frightened.

'So about those flowers,' she said, trying to change the subject. 'They were beautiful. Thank you.'

A half-smile formed on his lips. 'I was afraid you'd think it was lame. Sending flowers to a florist.'

'I love flowers, that's why I do what I do. And nobody ever thinks to send them to me.'

'I'll send them to you every day of your life if that's what it takes for you to realise.'

'To realise what?'

'That you're worth it. That you're worth everything. More than the shit you've been dealing with for years. You're a prize, London, and I'm going to fight with everything I've got until I win you.'

Oh God, this man. *This man*. He knew how to seduce her with a few words and a look. Her body tingled at his proximity. 'What if you've already won me?' she whispered.

'Then I'll fight to keep you. I know this isn't a one-time deal. I'll do whatever it takes every morning to let you know how lucky I am to have you in my life.'

She blinked back the tears. 'That sounds like a pretty good way to wake up every day.'

He lowered his head until his lips were a breath away from hers. 'I can think of other good ways to wake you up, too.'

The corner of her lip quirked up. 'Oh yeah? Like what?'

His smile was more than skin deep. She could see it in his eyes, feel it in the way he was touching her. Hear it in the way his breathing sped up as he pressed his mouth against hers. His kiss was soft and slow, but she could already feel it shooting straight through her. He reached his hands up to cradle her face, angling her so he could deepen it, his tongue slowly sliding along the seam of her lips, until a small gasp from her parted them.

306

They were all lips and hands and heat. His fingers tangled into her hair, while she looped hers around his neck, pressing her body against his so she could feel his desire pulsing against her. Her own body was pulsing, too, her nipples hard, her thighs aching, and with every kiss he was making her need him more.

He turned around, pushing her until her back was against the front door, pressing himself ever closer into her until she didn't know where he ended and she began. Sliding his hands down her back, he cupped her behind, lifting her until her legs were wrapped around his hips, and his groin was pressed right into hers.

He flexed his hips and she moaned softly into his mouth. Flexed them again until she gasped. Still holding her tight, he slid his lips along her jaw, down her neck, finding that sensitive spot at the side of her throat.

'Ryan.'

'Mmm?' he mumbled against her neck.

'Do you want to come inside?'

He lifted his head, a deliciously wicked glint in his eyes. A slow, sexy smile formed on his lips, making her heart beat faster at the intent she could see there. 'Babe,' he said, still holding her up with his big, strong hands. 'You have no goddamned idea how much I want to come inside.'

30

Loving goes by haps;
Some Cupid kills with arrows, some with traps

– Much Ado About Nothing

Compared to Ryan's, Juliet's bedroom seemed as though it would be more at home in a doll's house than anywhere else. It was small and the floor space was filled with a small double bed and closet. Unlike his, though, she'd made it look like home. A pretty bedspread lay pooled at their feet, and the scatter cushions were now lying on the carpet where they'd thrown them in their need to get on the mattress as fast as they could. There were pictures on the wall – some snapshots of Poppy, and paintings of flowers and their meanings. He grinned again, still not able to believe his luck.

Because he *was* lucky. He had no doubt of that.

'Which flowers did you like the best?' he asked her, as she lay naked, nestled in the crook of his arm.

She rolled over, placing her hands on his chest, and leaning her chin against them. Looking up at him through thick lashes, a smile formed on her face. 'I loved them all. Every single one of them. But if I had to choose one, it would be the daffodil you left on my doorstep last night.'

'Why?' He wasn't surprised she'd chosen something so simple.

'Because it made me question everything I thought. Until I saw it lying there I thought we were over, and I meant nothing to you. But then when I saw the daffodil and I realised what it meant—'

'What did it mean?' he interrupted. Of all people, Juliet should have gotten the significance of the gesture. But he wanted to be sure.

'Daffodils have lots of different meanings,' she said, her eyes soft as she stared at him. 'But the most common is chivalry. So I guess I took it as a sign you wanted to be my white knight after all.'

His heart was hammering in his chest. He wondered if she could feel it beneath her palms. Having her so close – after all they'd been through – was overwhelming. But there was something else, too. An honesty, a vulnerability that he hadn't had before. If he wanted this woman he knew he had to fight for her, but the person he needed to defeat was himself.

His old self, anyway.

'You're close,' he whispered, his voice thick with emotion. 'But while I was at the airport I realised it isn't me who was the white knight. It's you. You've saved me, London, whether you know it or not. You've saved me from living a surface life, and from giving up the best thing that's ever happened to me.' He stroked his hand down the length of her fiery hair. 'You're the hero in this.'

She blinked a couple of times, rolling her lip between her teeth. Christ, she was sexy. He could feel himself stirring again, in spite of the short time since they'd come together, limbs entwined. Did she even know what she did to him?

'You saved me too,' she whispered. 'You made me realise that strength can only come from within. Without you I'd never have had the nerve to stand up to Thomas.'

'It was a matter of time. You would have gotten there without me.'

'I don't want to get anywhere without you.' Her expression was so earnest it hit him straight in the stomach. He pulled her closer, needing to feel her, to breathe her in. His lips found hers almost immediately, his kisses needy, demanding, as he slid his hands down her back.

'I'm so sorry,' he said against her lips. 'I'm sorry for walking away when you needed me. I'm sorry for believing you were capable of staying with that asshole.'

They broke the kiss and she tipped her head to the side, a concerned look on her face. 'What made you think I would?'

'Because my mom stayed with my dad even though he treated her like dirt.'

'Is that what you were trying to tell me earlier? That your reaction had something to do with your parents?'

A lump formed in his throat. 'Yeah.' He'd promised to tell her about it later, and he guessed now was as good a time as any. 'I told you about my folks, didn't I? The way they fought all the time. And my old man, how he used to run her down constantly, right in front of me.' He tried to push the memories out of his mind, but they were insistent. Fleeting images of his father's derision as he lashed out again and again. His accusations that his wife was flirting too much, that her dress was too short, that her smile was too wide. Anything she did was like throwing fuel onto an already burning fire, and it exploded inside his father like a nuclear bomb.

'How often did he treat her like that?' Juliet asked.

He shrugged. 'It felt constant. I can't remember a time when he didn't criticise her for something.'

'But she never tried to leave?'

Ryan squeezed his eyes shut for a moment, then opened them again. The brightness rushed in, displacing the unwanted memories. 'I think she was too scared. Or brainwashed, maybe. She'd tell me that it was okay, that it was her fault he got so angry. That it was just how marriages were. And I believed her. When you're a kid you don't know any better. You just want to be with your mom and dad, no matter how messed up they are.'

He was clutching the sheet with his fisted hands. His whole body felt tense and achy. 'And then when I was eighteen my grandfather died. By that point I'd been formulating an escape plan for years. I'd go to college, get a good job, and save up enough to buy somewhere that she could escape to. Anything so she didn't have to stay with my dad any more. When I got my inheritance, I didn't have to wait until I graduated.'

She was still lying on him, her face screwed up with concern. 'Oh Ryan . . .'

'The money was left in trust, but I could apply to have access to funds. I spoke to my lawyer, requested enough money to buy a small place in Annapolis. It was a new build, didn't need any work. Close enough to Shaw Haven, but still far enough to put some distance between them. What I didn't know was that my lawyer had decided my dad should be aware of what was happening. And as soon as I paid for that goddamned place, he called him up and spilled his guts.'

It was as though he was reliving that moment. The kid who thought he could save the world.

'By that point, I was at home, telling my mom that she

had the chance to be free at last. I told her to pack a couple of cases and we'd come back for the rest once she was settled in.' He looked at Juliet, and saw his pain reflected back at him. 'London, I really believed she'd come with me. I honestly thought it was that easy. All my life I'd waited for that moment, that time when I could save her from him. And when I asked her to come with me, she turned around and told me not to be so stupid. That she'd never leave my dad.'

Juliet blinked back her tears. 'So what happened next?'

He swallowed hard. 'I was still trying to reason with her when my dad came home. And as soon as Dad walked in, he wanted to know what the hell I was doing buying an apartment in Annapolis without running it by him first.' He licked his lips – dry from talking so much. 'I told him exactly why I bought the apartment, and that Mom would be moving in there to get away from him. I told him he'd lose everything he ever loved, that I'd make sure of it.'

'And then?' Her voice was filled with trepidation.

'Then he started laughing. As though I'd told some god-damned hilarious joke. He told me to go to my room, and to stop being such a little kid. And I looked at Mom, asked her to leave with me. But she wouldn't even look at me, London. She just turned away.'

She felt as if her heart was breaking for the young man he'd once been.

'And I realised something that night. That you can be surrounded by family and still be all alone. My parents used to go on about my heritage, about the Shaws and Sutherlands that built up this town, but every day they were tearing each other apart. It was killing me.' He rubbed the palms of his hand against his eyes. 'I couldn't save her. She wouldn't let me.'

A tear rolled down Juliet's face. 'It wasn't your job to save her, Ryan. It was her job to save you. She's your mom, she should never have let you go through that. You were just a kid.'

'The only time I heard from this place was when I got my dividends. All that time I was away and they didn't try to talk to me. It was like they were pleased I had gone.'

Gently, she stroked his cheek. 'They're bastards, all of them. They don't deserve you. No wonder you were so triggered after you hit Thomas. You must have thought I was the same as the rest of them.'

'But you weren't,' he said. 'Because you never rejected me. I just didn't wait around to hear how you felt.'

'That's understandable, too,' she told him. 'Why would you? You thought I'd gone back to Thomas just like your mom went back to your dad. It must have felt like a kick in the gut.'

'And yet I should have known you wouldn't do that. You're not her, you're nothing like her. You're good and you're strong and you always put your kid first. Always.'

'And so do you. That's one of the things I love about you.'

'One of the things?' he whispered. It felt as though his chest was cracked open, exposing his heart to her in a way it had never been before. She had the ability to save him or condemn him, and feeling this exposed hurt like hell. But he knew he had to do this, if he ever wanted to prove he was worthy of her.

'One of the many things,' she told him. 'You want to hear some more?'

'Yeah, I want to hear them.'

She cupped his jaw with her hands, pressing her lips to the corner of his mouth. 'I love the way you're so good with your hands. Watching you build that tree house was like having my very own lumberjack fantasy.'

He laughed. It felt as though his troubles were dissolving into thin air.

'And I love the way you see things differently. The way you can take a photograph that nobody else can. You see beauty in everything.'

'Keep going,' he whispered.

She smiled at him. 'And I love the way you want to save me, and yet you know the only way you can do it is by letting me save myself.' She kissed him again. 'And I love the way you dance, it's like having sex fully clothed.'

He felt the hope rushing through him, pulling her tightly against him until their bodies were aligned. Her skin was warm and enticing, firing up every nerve in his body.

'And I love the way you hold me, as though I'm delicate, and yet when you make love you're hard and you're fast and it's like I'm unbreakable.'

'I love that, too,' he said. 'Very much.'

'There's nothing I don't love about you, Ryan Sutherland. From the way you handle a boat to the way you handle a kid. Everything about you is sexy and strong and so perfect to me. I couldn't stop loving you if I tried.'

He didn't need to hear any more. Instead he took her face in his hands, kissing her with a desperate need, until any words she had were dissolved beneath his lips.

She loved him, and that meant everything. All the other shit could be dealt with another day.

Right now, they had things to do.

31

Some rise by sin, and some by virtue fall

– Measure for Measure

'Well that's it.' Gloria Erkhart – her lawyer – passed her the papers, a smile splitting her face. 'They agreed to everything. I have to admit I'm disappointed, I would have liked to hit them for more.'

Juliet glanced at the documents in her hand. *Verification of Divorce*. Beneath the confirmation that she and Thomas were no longer married, were the terms the judge ordered. 'This is all I need,' she told Gloria, her smile just as big. 'I can't tell you what a relief it is. Thank you for everything.'

'We could have gone for alimony, the judge would have agreed to it.'

She shook her head. 'I don't want his money. I don't need it. As long as he looks after Poppy, I can take care of myself.' She smiled. 'It was the custody I was worried about, and we nailed it.' She had seventy per cent, the way she'd wanted, and they'd be sharing Christmas and other holidays. It was fair, but more importantly it was written with Poppy in mind. She'd spend time with both her parents. 'And I have his agreement to take Poppy to my sister's wedding. That makes me very happy.'

'You should look on the second page, too,' Gloria told her. 'The judge confirmed your name change. You're no longer Mrs Marshall.'

She flipped over, reading the declaration on the other side. *Juliet Shakespeare.*

It was like seeing an old friend she hadn't spoken with in years. She blew out a mouthful of air, as the weight lifted off her. 'Isn't that pretty?' she said.

'A pretty name for a lovely woman.'

She laughed. 'Do I have to pay you extra for that?'

They'd made it to the courthouse steps. A couple brushed past them, the woman wearing a white dress and a veil. One couple's beginning to match Juliet's ending. It seemed fitting.

Somehow the world kept turning.

'So what else do I need to do? Is there anything else to sign?' she asked her lawyer. She felt suddenly anxious to cross all the t's. This divorce was hard fought for, she didn't want to do anything to sabotage it.

'There's nothing else at all for you to do,' Gloria told her. 'Apart from to go down those steps and start living your life.'

'I think I can do that.' She hugged the papers to her chest as a breeze shot up the steps. She opened her mouth to say more, when she felt a shadow loom over her.

'Are you satisfied?' Thomas's face bore no signs of a smile. His dark hair was messy, as though he'd been raking his hands through it. 'Did you get what you wanted?'

'Perhaps you could leave my client alone,' Gloria said.

Juliet placed her hand on her lawyer's arm, calming her. 'It's okay, Gloria. I'm happy to answer him.' Then, turning to Thomas she looked him straight in the eye. 'Since you asked, Thomas, then yes, I'm satisfied with our terms. I'm pleased our daughter will get the support she deserves. And I'm delighted not to get any alimony, because I can look after myself.'

His laugh was short. 'I know you can.'

'And we might not be together any more, but we still have a child. And for the next twelve years it's our job to make sure she thrives.' She looked him straight in the eye. 'And I'll do my best to make sure she does. Nothing else matters. Not you and not me.'

'Damn right,' Gloria murmured.

'But you also asked if I've got what I wanted, and the answer to that is no. I didn't want to be cheated on, and I sure as hell didn't want to be treated like crap by you and your family. I didn't want to miss my daughter every other weekend, but since you made all these decisions without me, then I'll do it anyway. And I'll do it well, because I'm a Shakespeare, and you can't keep a Shakespeare girl down forever. No matter how hard you try.'

Thomas narrowed his eyes as he stared at her, the cool breeze lifting the ends of his hair. 'Whatever,' he huffed. 'I'll pick Poppy up on Saturday morning. Make sure she's ready.'

'Of course.' Juliet gave him a patient smile. 'Whatever you want, Thomas.'

She wasn't going to let him get to her. Not today, and not ever again. Sure, she knew there would be hard times ahead. He wouldn't give up trying to bait her, and no doubt he'd do his hardest to mess her around whenever he could. But he had no hold on her any more, legally or emotionally.

She was free, and it felt wonderful.

As her ex-husband hurried down the courthouse steps, she turned to give Gloria a final smile. 'I guess I'd better go and share the good news, before my phone starts blowing up.'

'I don't need to ask who you'll be telling first,' Gloria said.

'No you don't.' They shared a knowing look. Ryan had wanted to come to court with her. It had taken a lot of persuasion to keep him away. Thank goodness Gloria had backed her up. As far as Juliet was concerned, the more distance Ryan could keep between himself and the courthouse the better. All charges of assault against him had been dropped – but Thomas was still a liability. There was no way she wanted Ryan to poke the beast.

Juliet's phone vibrated in her pocket again. She knew exactly who it was. 'I'd better go,' she said, smiling up at her lawyer. 'Thank you again for everything.'

'You're welcome, *Ms Shakespeare*.' Gloria gave her a huge grin.

She was going to have to get used to that.

Ryan lifted his gaze from the beam he'd been sawing, and saw the man stalking his way up the boardwalk. He recognised that walk – he'd seen it since he was little more than a child in the crib. Carefully he placed the circular saw back in its cradle, taking care to switch it off at the plug. Lifting the safety goggles from his eyes, he stood up, brushing the sawdust from his hair with a sweep of his palm.

'Dad.'

The old man stared at him through narrowed eyes. 'I've been calling you for days.'

Ryan touched the pocket of his jeans automatically. 'And I've been avoiding you for days.'

His father blinked. The dust in the air was settling on him, a fine layer of brown on his expensively tailored suit. 'You need to explain yourself.'

'I don't think so.'

'You sold your goddamned shares to a third party.' His dad's face turned puce. 'Why the hell did you do that? Do you understand what you've done?'

'It's obvious isn't it?' It was taking a lot of strength for Ryan to subdue his shit-eating grin. 'I needed the money to buy the wharf. In fact it was you who gave me the idea, after you suggested I sell the shares to you.'

His father shook his head. 'Do you know how long the business has been in our family? And now you've invited the sharks in. They're already demanding an audit, and talking about bringing consultants in.' He was rocking back and forth on his feet, his shiny leather brogues covered in the same dust as his shoulders. 'They even asked me if I'd consider retirement.'

Ryan would have liked to have seen that. The image of his father being told he was surplus to requirements made him want to laugh out loud. 'You're not getting any younger. Maybe you should think about it.'

'You don't know the meaning of family, do you? You never did. You tried to betray me once, and now you've done it again. You're scum, Ryan. You don't deserve to bear my name.'

Ryan shook his head. It was amazing how easily things could be turned around to suit your own point of view. 'I was a kid,' he said, trying to keep his voice even. 'You let me leave with nothing and didn't give a shit where I ended up. That's not the kind of family I want to be part of.'

And that was the truth, wasn't it? As a child he'd longed to fit in. Longed to be part of some mythical happy family with a dad who loved him and a mom who protected him. Then when it hadn't worked out that way, he'd spent half his life running away. Trying to persuade himself he didn't need anybody else. That he was fine all on his own.

But now? Well, things had spun on a dime.

He had his own family now.

Maybe they weren't traditional. But he and Juliet and their kids, along with Sheridan, Carl and their impending arrival, heck somehow they worked. And it felt so damned good.

Over his father's shoulder, he saw her walking up the boardwalk, her red hair streaming behind her, not even hesitating when she saw them standing halfway down. She was wearing one of those sexy dresses again, the ones she wore to meetings at the bank and sessions at the court. Grey wool, tailored, clinging to her curves in a way that made his thoughts turn sinful.

'You should probably go now,' he said, unable to take his eyes off her. 'My girlfriend's here, and we have things to talk about.'

His father turned, following Ryan's gaze. 'You mean Thomas Marshall's wife.'

This time Ryan couldn't stop the grin from breaking out. 'No I don't. I mean my girlfriend. So please get off my wharf, you're not welcome here.'

His father stared at him, his eyes tight. 'You betrayed me. I won't forget that.'

'I don't care whether you forget it or not. What you think is of zero importance to me. I have so many better things to occupy my mind.'

She was getting closer. Enough for Ryan to see the smile on her face as she met his impatient gaze. Enough for his hands to start clasping and unclasping with the need to touch her.

Every time he saw her, she was like a bright burst of sun on a crisp fall day. Welcome, warming, all-consuming.

'London,' he called out, ignoring his father still huffing next to him. 'What are you trying to do to me in that dress?'

As she came within a few feet of them, her face fell for a moment as she recognised his dad. Ryan watched her as she took in a breath before squaring her shoulders.

'Hey.' She smiled at him. The smile fell off her face as she addressed his father. 'Hello, Mr Sutherland.'

'Ah, no need for the pleasantries,' Ryan told her. 'He's just leaving.'

She raised an eyebrow. 'He is? I hope it wasn't something I said.'

Ryan laughed. 'You didn't say anything, babe.' He reached for her, pulling her close against his side. The contact made his body relax almost instantly. 'It's more that he has nothing else to say.'

'You're right. I've got nothing to say to you,' his father spat out. 'I'm ashamed of you, messing around with a married woman. No wonder you broke your mother's heart.'

Ryan couldn't help it. 'Hey, London, are you a married woman?' he asked her.

She shook her head, beaming. 'Nope.'

'Didn't think so.' Though his words were calm, his heart was racing. He turned to his father. 'Now get out of here. I want to talk to this beautiful woman.'

Stepping back, his father looked them up and down, a sneer pulling at the corner of his mouth. 'This isn't over,' he warned. 'Not by a long shot.'

'It is for me,' Ryan said. His tone left no room for argument. For a moment his father remained, his mouth opening and closing as if he was trying to find something to say. But then he turned on his heel and stomped back up the boardwalk, leaving a trail of sawdust behind him.

He was going to have a hell of a job trying to get it out of all his clothes.

Juliet reached up to stroke his cheek, her hand grazing the bristles there. 'What was that all about?'

'Ah, just my father being himself.'

'Sounds as delightful as Thomas being Thomas.'

'Those two are like peas in a pod,' Ryan agreed. 'So tell me, is it true? Is it really over?' He turned until he was facing her.

She nodded slowly. 'I'm no longer Mrs Juliet Marshall.'

He sighed, feeling any tension seeping out of his muscles. 'Thank God for that. Did you get what you asked for?'

'Everything. Gloria was like a hungry shark.' She smiled. 'Not that I came out of it with a lot. What do you think about having a broke woman for a girlfriend?'

'What's mine is yours.' He laughed. 'Not that I've got a whole lot either.'

She jabbed him in the side. 'Liar. You've got a son, a house, a wharf. An ex-girlfriend living around the corner and a new girlfriend living next door. Whether you like it or not, your life is full of things.'

'It sounds complicated,' he said.

'It does,' she agreed. 'How do you feel about that?'

A smile tugged the corner of his lips. 'I feel pretty damned good,' he told her. 'Sticking around is only scary when there's somewhere else you'd rather be.'

'And there's really nowhere you'd rather be than Shaw Haven?' she questioned.

He leaned down, pressing his lips against the tip of her pretty nose. Almost immediately the dust did its magic, making her face wrinkle before she sneezed loudly.

'There's nowhere else I'd rather be in the world than right here with you,' he whispered, trying to stifle his laugh as she started sneezing again. 'You're my family. You, Charlie and Poppy. Home is wherever you are. I'm a photographer, all I need is a camera and I can earn a living. I figure Shaw Haven's as good a place as any to do that.'

It had warmed her heart when he'd decided not to move to New York. Though she'd promised him they'd make it work, even if they were long distance, he hadn't wanted that. He wanted to stay with her. And now he was working on the wharf and taking freelance photography commissions when they came. Between the two things he was crazily busy.

They both were, but that was the way they liked it.

'I like the sound of that.' She wrapped her arms around him, trying to pull him close.

'You're going to get that sexy dress all messed up,' he warned her. 'There's dust everywhere.'

She moved her hands up, hooking them around his neck. Without needing to be asked twice, he grabbed her by the waist, leaning down so his face was only a few inches from hers.

'I don't care about the dress,' she whispered. 'If I had my way it'd be crumpled on your floor by this evening anyway.'

'Oh yeah?' He brushed his lips against hers. Her gasp warmed his skin. 'I look forward to it.'

'Me, too,' she whispered, the words vibrating against his mouth. 'But first we have to pick up the kids and explain what the hell's been going on.'

'Do we have to? Can't we just go home and jump on each other?' His tone was enough to let her know he was teasing.

'You're as rampant as a teenager.'

'I feel like a teenager,' he told her. 'It's like we've got to explain to our parents that we've somehow fallen in love. What if they don't like the idea? What if they're unhappy?'

'What if they forbid us to see each other again?' She smiled against him. 'Relax, they're going to be delighted. We're not Romeo and Juliet. The stars aren't crossed against us.'

'That's good, because I'd defy them anyway.'

She looked up at him, her brows raised. 'Are you misquoting Shakespeare to me?'

'You know it, babe.'

She laughed loudly. 'Come on, Romeo, let's go and pick up the children. We've got some explaining to do.'

'Does that mean we're going to live in Ryan's house?' Poppy asked, her brows knitted together. 'Will I have to share Charlie's room? Will he get angry if I put my stuff in there? Remember what he was like when I tried to put flowers in the tree house?'

'You won't make her sleep in my room, will you, Dad?' Charlie asked. 'She can have one of the other bedrooms can't she?'

'Can I paint it pink?' Poppy clapped her hands together. 'I want it pink with white clouds, and a princess bed. Please can I?'

Juliet looked over at Ryan. A mixture of amusement and surprise had made his eyes wide and his mouth drop open. For the past five minutes, ever since they'd sat Poppy and Charlie down in Ryan's kitchen and explained things, the two children had been shooting questions at them like snipers at a range.

'Slow down,' Juliet said, laughing. 'We're not moving in here.' Ryan tipped his head to the side, looking questioningly at her. 'Not yet, anyway. We need to take this slowly.'

'But I like this house better. Ryan, you want us to move in, don't you?' Poppy asked him.

He put his hands up. 'Your mom's right, we can take this slowly. But Charlie and I love having you around, and you know you're always welcome here.'

'Should I call you Daddy?'

Juliet covered her mouth to stifle the laughter. Ryan rolled his lips between his teeth, looking at her for help.

'You already have a daddy,' Juliet reminded her daughter. 'Ryan's your friend, not your daddy.'

'He's my daddy though,' Charlie said, proudly.

'Yes I am.' Ryan pursed his lips and blew some air out. 'And it would give me the greatest pleasure to be your friend, Poppy.' He offered her his hand, and she shook it firmly, her face lighting up.

'It gives me the greatest pleasure, too, Ryan.' Her voice had a serious tone. Juliet bit down another smile.

'Wait, does that mean Poppy's going to be my sister?' Charlie asked, still looking confused. 'And what about the baby in my mom's tummy, will Poppy be her sister, too?'

'Oh yeah, will I be their sister?' Poppy echoed.

Taking a deep breath, Juliet reached for each of their hands. 'Try to take it easy, guys. I know there's a lot to take in at the moment, and you have so many questions. And we'll both try to answer them as honestly as we can. But we don't have all the answers either. This is new to all of us. We'll work through it all together.'

She felt Ryan wrap his arms around her. 'She's right,' he said, his voice low. 'We haven't got it all figured out yet, but we know the important stuff. We love you both, and you love us.'

'And you love each other, right?' Poppy prompted.

He laughed. 'Right. We love each other, too. We're a family, and we want to be together. The rest we can figure out over time.'

'We're family,' Charlie echoed, his eyes wide with wonder. 'Poppy, me, you and Juliet, Mom and Carl . . . '

'And the new baby,' Poppy added.

'Yeah, when she gets here,' Charlie said. 'But I'm not cleaning any poopy diapers.'

'Me either,' Poppy agreed, wrinkling her nose up. 'Mommy, how did the baby get in Sheridan's tummy?'

Juliet's mouth dropped open. Where the hell did that come from? Ryan winked at her, biting down a grin, as he waited for her response.

'Um, who wants a drink?' Juliet asked. 'I could really do with a glass of water right now.'

A moment later she was headed into the kitchen, thankful for a moment's respite from the constant questions. Taking four glasses from the cupboard, she placed them carefully on the granite work surface as she felt two arms wrap around her waist from behind.

'You okay, London?' Ryan said, nuzzling his face against hers. 'I thought you were going to have some kind of heart attack in there.'

She turned her head to look at him. 'I'm sorry about all the questions.'

'I think they let us off lightly. Just wait until tomorrow, they'll have even more to throw at us.'

She laughed. 'You're right. And you know them too well.'

'They're arguing about whose house is best, yours or mine. If they're not careful, they'll both be living in the tree house.'

Her eyes widened. 'Don't suggest that, they'll jump at it. And then they'll start arguing about whose house it is.'

He put his arms around her waist, pulling her against him. His eyes softened as he smiled at her. 'Do you get the impression that they're the ones who really rule the roost?' he asked her. 'Imagine what they'll be like when they're teenagers.'

She shuddered. 'I don't want to think about that at all.' Tipping her head up, she smiled at him. 'At least we'll have each other. Maybe we can hide out in the tree house instead.'

He pressed his forehead against hers. 'I'd like that.'

'You would?'

'Yeah. Wouldn't you?'

She opened her mouth to tell him she'd be happy wherever they were, as long as they were together. But then she closed it again, silenced by the intensity of his stare. There was no need for words when actions said it all.

Ryan was too busy kissing her for that.

Epilogue

Doubt thou the stars are fire,
Doubt that the sun doth move,
Doubt truth to be a liar,
But never doubt I love

– Hamlet

Cesca walked into the small room where her sisters were waiting, her hands lifting her dress at the hips so the hem wouldn't get caught in the doorway. Juliet gasped, covering her mouth with her hands, feeling tears stinging at her eyes.

Her sister looked beautiful. The way every bride should on her wedding day.

The tears spilled over, hot saltwater cutting through Juliet's make-up – expertly applied that morning by the artist Cesca had flown in. Silently, Lucy handed Juliet a small white handkerchief, and Juliet lifted it to her cheeks, surreptitiously dabbing the tears away.

'You look amazing,' Kitty said, stepping forward with a big smile on her face. 'Sam's going to freak when he sees you.'

'You're gorgeous,' Lucy agreed, beaming at her younger sibling. 'That dress is just as lovely as I remember it.'

She was wearing the white gown she'd modelled for them

all those months ago, when they'd Skyped into her dress-fitting session at a Beverly Hills boutique. The white fabric flowers appliqued to the sheer material of the bodice matched the flowers Cesca's hairdresser had artfully woven into her hair. Cesca had wanted to keep things simple – white dress, white flowers, white ties worn by the groomsmen. The only colour was on her sisters' and niece's dresses. Lucy, Juliet and Kitty were sheathed in the palest of pink, while Poppy's dress was a little darker, and unlike their body-skimming fabric, hers was voluminous, her underskirts pushing her dress out until she looked like she belonged on the set of *Gone with the Wind*.

Of course, she was in heaven.

'Where's Poppy?' Cesca asked, looking around. It was as if she could read Juliet's mind.

'She went to the bathroom.' Juliet wrinkled her nose. 'I had to help her, of course, but then she shooed me away and said she wanted to primp and preen – her words – in front of the mirror for a while.'

Cesca bit down a smile. 'Well, she did look gorgeous. She's the perfect flower girl.'

Juliet raised her eyebrows. 'Let's hope so.' She looked back at the table full of flowers, the bouquets she'd made up first thing that morning before her sisters had even got out of bed. 'Are you ready for your flowers?' she asked Cesca.

Cesca nodded.

Carefully, Juliet lifted the bouquet, feeling her throat tighten. Surely she wasn't going to burst into tears all over again? Since they'd arrived in the UK two days before, she must have cried a river. First at being reunited with her father – in spite of his frailty – and then at showing Poppy her childhood city. And now they were all in the Highlands of Scotland, spending time in the place Lucy called home, and she was as emotional as hell.

Cry me a loch.

'These are amazing,' Cesca said softly, as Juliet placed the flowers carefully into her grip. White roses were mixed with white poppies – their black centres adding a depth to the arrangement. In between, Juliet had laced them with baby's breath – symbolising everlasting and undying love. 'I can't believe how clever you are.'

Juliet gave her sister a watery smile, determined not to steal the limelight with her emotions. Somehow she needed to get them under control, otherwise she'd end up sobbing during the ceremony, and that really wouldn't do.

There was a knock on the door, then the vicar popped his head around, the sun through the window behind them glinting off his shiny domed head. He was dressed in a black robe, with a white surplice over the top, and a long scarf lying down the front of his tunic. There was a big smile on his face – from the start he'd been enthusiastic about this wedding, promising he'd do his best to keep it as private as possible – and he held his hand out to Cesca, telling her how lovely she looked.

'Are you okay?' Lucy whispered, as Juliet bit her bottom lip, feeling those emotions swirling up all over again. 'I haven't seen you like this for years. Not since that time we went to see *Mary Poppins* at the theatre, and you were wailing like a banshee.' Lucy grinned. 'Of course that time you were pregnant, so you had an excuse . . . ' Her voice trailed off.

Their eyes met, both wide and shocked. Juliet found herself touching her stomach with her hand. It was as flat as ever – or as flat as it could be after having a child. No, she couldn't be, could she?

They'd been careful. They really had.

The door behind them opened – the one that led to the bathrooms – and Poppy ran in, sounding out of breath. 'You're not leaving without me are you?' she asked, having to force her way past a chair and a table, her pink dress knocking everything out of her way.

She was a tour-de-force. One of a kind. Surely there couldn't be one more of her?

And really, Juliet meant that in the nicest way.

The vicar looked completely unperturbed by Poppy's entrance. The smile was still plastered to his face. 'So we'll do it just as we rehearsed. I'll walk in first, then Poppy will come in and lay the petals down as she walks. Then Cesca will follow, and her bridesmaids will be at the back.' He looked at them, nodding. 'In age order.'

Okay, so they might have squabbled a bit over who was walking at the front. Old habits died hard.

'Are you ready?' he asked Cesca again.

She nodded, her face resolute. 'I'm ready.'

Lucy took one last glance at Juliet, concern on her face. 'We'll talk later,' she mouthed. Juliet wasn't sure if that was a threat or not. She was sure that she wasn't ready to talk, even if there was anything to talk about.

Which there wasn't. Because there couldn't be.

They followed the vicar out of the small dressing room and into the main lobby of the chapel. Even though they'd tried to keep the wedding under wraps, there was still a sizeable crowed outside, Sam's fans mostly, desperate for a glimpse of the famous actor, and Cesca's soon-to-be-husband. The low murmur of conversation from outside the chapel was matched with the noises coming from inside the double doors. The chapel only seated eighty, the guests had been hand-picked by Cesca and Sam. Juliet felt like she was at a royal wedding.

And then the vicar was pushing open the doors, and the big church organ burst into life, piping out the wedding march as they made their way down the aisle, Poppy clearly in her element as she sprinkled rose petals ahead of Cesca and her sisters.

Just as Juliet had imagined, the pews were almost bursting with people. Famous actors and directors sat amongst Cesca and Sam's family and friends, all turning to look at the radiant bride. At the front, on two reserved seats, sat her father and Cesca's godfather, their weathered faces beaming back at them. Not having her father walk her up the aisle had been a source of disappointment to Cesca, but at least he was here, and well enough to watch her get married.

In the row behind them were more familiar faces. Lachlan, Lucy's boyfriend, sat next to Adam, Kitty's fiancé. And then there was the man that set Juliet's world on fire. The man that stole her breath away and gave her life at the same time.

Ryan was looking straight at her, his hand resting lightly on Charlie's shoulder as they watched her approach. His eyes were soft, appraising, and there was a smile on his face. Juliet licked her dry lips, trying to keep her face straight, and not crumple all over again into the mess of emotion she'd been all day.

Could she really be pregnant? She thought back over the past few months. Yes, they'd been having a crazy amount of sex, but they'd taken precautions. They'd been careful.

The same way she'd been careful before she had Poppy. The same way Ryan had been careful before Charlie.

Oh God, they were clearly crazily fertile. Together they were like a time bomb waiting to happen.

She really needed to take a pregnancy test.

They'd come to the front of the church, and Sam stepped forward to take Cesca's hands in his, grinning from ear to ear. He looked like a man who'd just won the lottery, and wanted everybody to know it. And as he reached out to cup Cesca's face, love shining from his face as he whispered something in her sister's ear, Juliet couldn't help but feel the emotions welling up inside her all over again.

And yes, of course she started to cry.

There was something wrong with Juliet. Ryan had sensed it as soon as the doors had opened and the vicar had walked into the chapel, followed by Poppy, her aunts, and of course Juliet. He didn't think it had anything to do with Poppy – she was as ebullient as ever, twirling around and showing off to Charlie, before dragging him onto the dance floor whether he wanted to dance or not.

Juliet, however, was quiet. Deadly quiet. She'd barely said anything during the sit-down meal in the main hall at Glencarraig lodge, and then after the speeches were over she'd practically run to the bathroom, her sister Lucy following close behind, leaving Lachlan and Ryan to prop themselves up at the bar.

'I like your place,' Ryan said, lifting the pint of beer to his lips. He raised his eyebrows as he looked around the room. This place was more of a castle than a lodge, the expansive hall decorated with huge tapestries depicting scenes from Scottish history, the space easily accommodating the hundreds of guests Cesca and Sam had invited to their reception.

'Thanks.' Lachlan lifted his glass up to Ryan. 'But it's not really mine. I own less than half of it.' He took a mouthful of warm beer. 'Jesus, I still can't get used to the taste of this stuff.'

From the moment they'd been introduced, Ryan had liked Lachlan. They were of a similar age, both Americans, both successful. And of course, they had the Shakespeare sisters in common.

Which made them the luckiest men he knew.

'I was half expecting us to have haggis for dinner,' Ryan said, drinking his beer in spite of the taste. 'Not that I was disappointed, the steak was amazing.'

'They know how to cater for a crowd up here,' Lachlan agreed. 'They've been doing it for about five hundred years.'

Ryan laughed. 'Practice makes perfect.'

'Daddy, please can you tell Poppy I don't want to dance any more?' Charlie threw himself at Ryan, his eyes wide. 'She keeps knocking me over with her dress. It's stupid.'

'It's not stupid,' Poppy said, running up to them. Her skirt caught on the edge of a bar stool, knocking against it and making it wobble. 'It's beautiful. Isn't it, Ryan?'

He still hadn't gotten the hang of intervening with their squabbles yet. 'Yes it is,' he agreed, nodding at her. 'But maybe Charlie needs a break. Why don't I get you both a drink?'

Where was Juliet anyway? He looked around in the direction she'd left. The door pushed open and she walked in, her face paler than he remembered. Lucy was walking next to her, and she patted her sister on the arm, then whispered something in her ear.

Lucy was the first to reach them. She smiled at Lachlan and took his hand. 'Why don't we go and check on the evening buffet,' she suggested. 'Poppy and Charlie, you can come with us. We might need your help.'

Juliet had reached them, and yes, she definitely looked pale. Ryan stared at her, willing her to look at him, too. And when she did, he felt his heart skip a beat. Jesus, she really was beautiful. But that beauty was more than skin deep. She was funny and kind, a great mother and businesswoman, but more than anything else she was his.

And he intended to keep it that way.

'Are you okay?' he murmured, reaching out for her hand. It was cold to the bone. He folded it in his, trying to warm her up.

'Can we talk?' she said, her voice quiet. 'Somewhere private?'

He nodded, feeling perplexed. 'Sure.'

They found a small room at the front of the lodge. It was filled with boxes, the cardboard covered with a layer of thick dust. As soon as Juliet walked in she sneezed. Then she wrinkled her nose in that adorable way, and Ryan couldn't help but reach out for her. The need to touch her, to feel her against him, was so strong.

'Are you okay?' he murmured, pulling her close, feeling her body melt against his. 'You've been acting strangely all day.'

'I know.' She shook her head against his shoulder. 'I've been a mess.'

'Is it the wedding?' he asked her. 'It must be hard, seeing your little sister getting married.'

'No, it's not that. I'm so happy for Cesca.' Her face crumpled again. 'I really am,' she sobbed.

'Baby, what's wrong?' He smoothed her tears away with the pad of his thumb. 'Is it me? Are you upset that it's not us getting married? Because we can, you know, and we will. When the time's right.'

That only made her cry more. Shit, he was as bad at handling her emotions as he was with Charlie and Poppy's arguments. Ryan licked his lips, pulling her against him tightly. She was so soft and supple against him.

'I've messed up,' she whispered against his shoulder. He could feel the fabric of his dress shirt moisten with her tears. 'Please don't be angry with me.'

'Why would I be angry? I love you, remember?' He tucked his finger beneath her chin, lifting her head until she was looking straight into his eyes. And he saw it there, the love, the passion and, hiding behind it, the fear. He brushed his lips against hers, feeling her exhale against his mouth. Damn if it didn't make him want her all over again. 'You can tell me anything, you know that.'

She closed her eyes for a moment, and he immediately missed her gaze. 'It's such a mad thing to happen,' she whispered. 'I'm not trying to tie you down or anything.'

'You don't tie me down. You set me free.' He kissed her again, this time cupping her face with his palm. 'We fit together perfectly.'

'A little too perfectly.'

'What?'

She opened her eyelids. 'I ... ' she sighed. 'I mean we ... we're having a baby.'

'*What?*' It came out a little too loudly, but it was the last thing he'd expected to hear. 'How did that happen?'

'You want me to draw you a diagram?'

He couldn't help but laugh. Juliet was looking so scared, her eyes wide, her expression tight. 'Wow,' he said quietly. 'Another baby.'

'Are you upset?'

'Why would I be upset?' He couldn't help but reach down and stroke his fingers gently against her belly. 'It takes two to tango, after all. We're having a baby, that's something to celebrate.'

She relaxed against him, the stiffness in her body melting away. 'It is?' Her voice was full of hope.

'Of course it is. It's amazing.' He was getting used to the thought. Loving it. There was a new life growing inside her – something they'd made together. He could picture her now, belly rounded, face glowing. He couldn't wait to see it. 'I guess that explains the emotions.'

She nodded. 'I guess so. Will you still love me though I'm a hormonal mess?'

'London, I'll love you even more.' He was grinning now. Couldn't get the smile off his face if he tried. 'You're carrying our baby. What's not to love?'

For the first time her lips curled up. 'I am, aren't I?'

He reached out, tracing his fingers around her stomach again. 'It's the best surprise I've ever had.'

'I was so afraid you'd be upset,' she confessed. 'That you'd think I was trying to tie you down.'

He looked at her, confused. 'Babies don't tie you down. Not if you don't let them. Look at you, you moved continents when you were pregnant. And Charlie was born in the middle of nowhere in a goddamned hospital tent. Babies are the most portable humans you want to come across.' He took her hand and pressed his lips against her palm. 'I'm delighted I'm going to be a dad again. And when the time is right, Poppy and Charlie are going to be delighted, too.'

She groaned. 'They're going to be a nightmare. Imagine how often they'll bicker over the baby.'

'Ah, let them fuss. We could even turn it to our advantage. Who knows, we may never have to change a dirty diaper again.'

338

His grin widened. 'This baby will be loved, Juliet. And it's already so wanted.' Kissing her palm one last time, he folded his hand around hers. 'Now let's go and dance and celebrate your sister's marriage.'

'Yes, let's do that.' Her eyes glinted, and this time it had nothing to do with tears. 'Just remember what you do to me when you get me out on that dance floor.'

'Oh I remember.' They walked into the hallway and he slid his arm around her waist, pulling her in to his side. It felt so good to hold her, to have her close. Everything he wanted was here in this castle. Juliet, Charlie, Poppy and now the baby growing inside Juliet.

Home wasn't a building. It wasn't even a country. Home was where your family was, and that was exactly where Ryan wanted to be, too.

Acknowledgements

To Eleanor Russell, Anna Boatman and all at Piatkus, thank you for your hard work, enthusiasm and guidance in making this book the best it can be.

My thanks as always to my agent Meire Dias, and all at the Bookcase Agency for your continued kindness and support.

Ash, Ella and Oliver – I love you all to bits, and am always grateful for everything you do when I'm deep in my writing zone. You'll be pleased to hear I'm no longer 'buffering' and may even answer your questions as soon as you ask them!

So many people have supported me in my writing journey, I want you all to know how much I appreciate your support. Whether you're an author, blogger, reader or friend – you mean a lot to me. Special mentions to Claire Robinson and Melanie Moreland for pre-reading, and for being such great Shakespeare Sisters cheerleaders. Thanks also to all who follow my Facebook page – we have so much fun there, and you always inspire me to write more words. It truly is a happy place.

Finally thank YOU for reading this book, I truly appreciate it. I hope you've enjoyed spending time with the Shakespeare Sisters as much as I've enjoyed writing about them.